D0890440

Sehkmet

Robin
H

Sehkmet

Robin K. Springer

Northwest Publishing, Inc.
Salt Lake City, Utah

Sehkmet

All rights reserved.
Copyright © 1995 Northwest Publishing, Inc.

Reproductions in any manner, in whole or in part,
in English or in other languages, or otherwise
without written permission of the publisher is prohibited.

This is a work of fiction.
All characters and events portrayed in this book are fictional,
and any resemblance to real people or incidents is purely coincidental.

For information address: Northwest Publishing, Inc.
6906 South 300 West, Salt Lake City, Utah 84047
ESH 01 09 95
Edited by B. Jorgensen

PRINTING HISTORY
First Printing 1995

ISBN: 1-56901-372-1

NPI books are published by Northwest Publishing, Incorporated,
6906 South 300 West, Salt Lake City, Utah 84047.
The name "NPI" and the "NPI" logo are trademarks belonging to
Northwest Publishing, Incorporated.

PRINTED IN THE UNITED STATES OF AMERICA.
10 9 8 7 6 5 4 3 2 1

Foreword

4500 B.C.

The ancient Egyptians were a reverent people, their lives spent in service to God. They called him Ra, and His first known act was the command to bring light out of darkness. With a single word He made the world, then willed the land to rise up from the sea. Man He fashioned from the clay of the Nile, on a potter's wheel.

Man was not created free, however. In return for the gift of Life he was made keeper of the Divine Order on earth, called Maat. Each day thereafter the Eye of Ra looked down from Heaven to see that Maat was fulfilled. Each day it came—a stunning gold, a blinding light—and its dazzling shimmer filled every corner of the land. All men feared to look on it and raised their hands to shield their eyes, hoping that their sins would pass unnoticed.

How they envied the other creatures of the world, godly in all their actions, free from judgment. Yet that divinity did not shine like the mighty Eye of Ra, so they called this divinity in all things Amon, meaning "The Hidden." Man, too, possessed this spark of Amon, but only if he cared for his family and Pharaoh and the bounty Ra had bestowed.

If he cheated in any way then his heart was bad, an evil which must be removed to keep the Divine Order intact. Certainly he would be found out, if not in life then after death when his heart was weighed on the perfect scale of Truth against the feather of Maat. A lighthearted man would find a happy eternity, laughing with his friends and family in a golden boat pushed by gentle breezes. But a man whose heart was heavy with sin, that heart would tip the scale and roll down into the crocodile of darkness. No eternity for sinners: it ended there, in Sobek's jaws.

Women were equal partners in this divine plan, judged every bit as sternly. Yet their differences were celebrated each month by the arrival of that bright sphere in the night sky they called Hathor—which means, not surprisingly, "Where The Face dwells." It was welcomed with singing and dancing, for this shining face of love dispelled the blackness of night— even Ra couldn't do that. On some nights, though, only a horn was visible, so Hathor was also called The Great White Cow, and was thought to suckle talents into every baby at birth.

Hathor had another side, however, another office. She never knew it, and the Egyptians prayed she would never know, for it involved a trick they had played on her when Egypt was very young.

One morning in his travels Ra noticed a change in the land: evil was afoot and Maat was in danger. It was late summer, a time the Romans would call the month of Augustus, and vats of wineberries were brim full to celebrate the bounty of Ra. But Ra's anger was kindled: by the end of that day His golden Eye had turned blood red with fury.

He would not wait till morning: He called to Hathor, quietly grazing in a field of stars, and his molten rage shot through her eyes and dried her udder. She fell from Heaven, tumbling down through the sky to earth, and as she fell she changed, became a lioness made of moonglow, racing through the black night, ripping out and feasting on the hearts of the wicked.

Alas, to her all humans were wicked, and as the night wore on the screams of the innocent soon mingled with the shrieks of the guilty. Ra was appalled. He called out to Hathor but she had absorbed all his vengeful spirit and was Hathor no longer: blood was her soul and substance and only want. If Hathor could not be coaxed out of the body of that crazed lion, all Egypt would perish.

Ra called on the remaining Egyptians to help him, and they readily complied. He told them to take the wineberry vats and dump them over the fields, crushing the berries.

Then, when the light of Ra rose over the land, what did the furious lion behold but field after field of glistening blood. Eagerly she lapped it up. After many, many fields (how many nobody knows) the lion yawned, closed her great green eyes, and stretched out on a dune, fast asleep.

As she slept Ra breathed his love and pity back into her heart. It worked: the milk-white shape of Hathor floated up to her celestial station, and the body of the sleeping lion turned instantly to stone. It was left as a lesson to the wayward, never to break their covenant with Ra.

The Egyptians gathered around the great stone lion and marvelled, and glorified Ra for saving them. But as the shadows of midday began to lengthen, their thoughts turned once again to Hathor. What if the sky was clear, and her dark eyes found the great lion of the dune. Would she remember? And, if she remembered, would she forgive? The wineberries were gone, soaked out, covered by shifting sand. How would they stop the lioness this time?

On a desperate impulse they gathered all the chisels of the land and hacked away at the head of the stone lion. They knocked off the huge crescent ears, smoothed out the left-over knots, and dug lines to look like hair. They rounded out the square heavy jaw and etched in a brow line. They carved open the sleeping lids and dug away the lower half of the nostrils, replacing the lipless mouth with a slight, human smile. They had no time to refashion the body, for twilight showed the faint face of Hathor in the darkening sky. They dropped their chisels and fled.

Generations to come would call the strange colossus they left The Sphinx, and forget or refuse to believe how it got there. When the face of the Pharaoh Khephren was later chiselled on the Sphinx's head they called it "The Father of Terror." Indeed they were right, for Pharaoh was Ra come to Earth, and Ra was the Father of Terror.

They never forgot the dreadful penalties awaiting those who did not lead good lives, so many more sphinxes and statues and paintings were made to direct them on the rightful path. The long, ugly snout of Sobek the crocodile reminded them of the deathbed judgment.

Other walls showed the face of the lioness on a woman's body. Her mouth was closed, her eyes implacable and all-seeing. In her hands was the fate of man, according to his choice—either the ankh of happiness or the axe of justice. The Egyptians shuddered when they passed by her and prayed she would not spring to life, for she knew all their secrets, all of mankind's evil ways, and she was waiting for the call from Ra. They threw wineberries at her feet and begged her to be still. "Oh, Sehkmet," they chanted, "Daughter of Ra, have pity on us, for we are weak and confused and want to be good."

And Sehkmet sat, and Sehkmet listened; but she did not believe. She waited in the baking heat of the day while her brother, Horus, bore her father, Ra, across the sky on wings of fire. She waited in the night when the Nile breezes blew cold across her feet. Sometimes there was no breeze, and her mother's sweet face was covered in lazy clouds.

Centuries passed, and the power of ancient Egypt and its gods waned. Unspeakable evil was loosed upon the world, and the voice of Ra was sadly silent. Locked away in her stone prison Sehkmet waited, confident of the terrible summons that was to come.

Then one evening mysterious red clouds appeared above the temple, red with the anger of Ra. Then there was nothing, or so it seemed: no lightning, no thunder, no fire and brimstone, just a voice in the night air. It was not a voice in human terms, not words as we know them; rather it was a sound, a sound of such force and resonance it could crush mountains and incinerate stars. It was for Sehkmet alone. It nestled in her ears, and something suddenly changed. A green fire sprang to life behind those sightless stone eyes, and a roar that shook the temple bricks went out to warn the world: the long wait was over. The time had come.

Hellweek

The summer rains didn't come that year, and by August the city of Jacksonville was in a rosy haze of dust and smog. Cars and motorists steamed along the roads, dodging sniper fire on the beltway.

By the second Monday in August the city's murder rate had tripled, a fact blamed on drugs, gangs, and the heat.

On Tuesday a man with a tire iron bludgeoned two old ladies to death in a shopping mall in broad daylight. Citizens who saw it chased the man and caught him, and were commended by the sheriff for their bravery.

Two days later a cadre of lawyers presented Robert Gadsen the remorseless killer as a drivelling idiot, eating cigarettes out of ashtrays, obviously too crazy to stand trial for murder.

By Friday people all over the city were screaming at a system that was doing all it could to insure the safety of this "alleged" killer.

By Saturday, August 11th, anyone connected to the tragedy (and many who weren't) had been interviewed, and interviewed again—all but one, who surfaced on the six o'clock news. He was one of the men who'd caught the killer, and he jabbed his finger at the camera as his anger spilled out: "I tell you what, I hope they fry his sorry ass, him an' his lawyers both. They all say he's crazy, well a course he's crazy, so what? Lemme tell you, we chased his butt through forty blocks a' traffic, an' I never see a man drive like that what didn't know what he's doin'. An' if he's so crazy how'd he know enough t' run away? I mean he kill't those li'l ol' ladies, and I saw it!

"Now look what's happened! He's gettin' three squares a day on our money till some stupid shrink gives him a (bleep) visiter's pass so's he can go kill some'n else's granny. I mean why'd we catch the sonofa(bleep)? You think those li'l ol' ladies are thankin' us up there? Why, I bet that sorry Gadsen's watchin' us right now, laughin' his ass off at how stupid we all are.

"Well, Gadsen," he jabbed his finger at the lens again, "jest you remember: when ya get out, the party's over. Some of us know who ya are, an' we'll be lookin' fer yer ass."

His directness wiped the smile off the anchorwoman, but she recovered it to introduce the weatherman. His news was uplifting only in degrees: temperature still climbing (106 in the shade with ozone the main pollutant) old people and those with respiratory ailments advised to stay indoors; try not to use your air conditioning; and don't water your lawn or wash your car.

A great cloud had settled over the city, its orange glow causing thunderstorm and tornado watches. Nobody believed it, of course: black clouds had been threatening rain for months, only to roll away.

Then, just before midnight, rain began lashing a strip of beach and the woods up on Merrill Road.

The following Monday policemen found two bodies in the ditch by Merrill Road. One was a young woman with multiple stab wounds. The other was a man covered in gashes so deep his body hung in threads. When the police linked that body to a car carrying stolen jewelry and partial scalps, they knew that the infamous Seaboard Slasher was dead.

So where was the man who called 911 on Sunday night to tell them what he'd seen on Merrill Road? They had shaken their heads at the ravings of a drunk, and ended up with bodies in a ditch.

In Atlantic Beach the police were more than mystified, they were frightened. Something huge and dangerous had arrived in the community, and they felt its presence the moment they arrived at the big white house on Ocean Drive. The call came in at 11:47 P.M. Neighbors reported gunfire, screaming, and other horrible noises coming from the daycare center on the corner.

When the police arrived they thought they heard a dog inside the house, but it was hard to tell because of all the barking outside. The front door was locked, so they crept around to the back and found the bedroom light streaming through the smashed window. The window was down, glass shards and blood everywhere. On the bed was a gutted body, its head torn off. The crushed head was found under an end table, its face raked away.

Across the bedroom doorway was another body: female, nude, tan, early twenties—face down but no face. Her head, back, and chest were pulpy craters. Her hands held strips of flesh, hair and fingers.

Down the hall, next to a shotgun, lay an old woman staring up at the ceiling.

The small dog whose voice they heard was beside her, snapping at anyone who came near. An officer picked him up and carried him, yelping and struggling, to the waiting arms of a neighbor.

Outside his frightened barks joined the howls and yelps that didn't stop all night long.

In one yard, though, the dog was quiet. The brindle mastiff lay across the deck like a disembowled zebra, his eyes two orange dots in the porchlight's amber glare.

Carla

Carla couldn't get comfortable. The box kept teetering under her, the braids wouldn't braid, and Jessie would not hold still.

"How much longer, Mommy?"

"Just a few minutes," Carla lied.

So far these two wispy braids had cost her half the morning. They'd gone to K-Mart to buy strapping tape for the boxes, and Jessie immediately vanished among the toy racks. When Carla caught her she was ooing at two small packs of clear plastic.

"Look, Mommy, aren't they cute?" Daisies, plastic daisies in one. Fuzzy fluorescent ladybugs with rolly eyes in the other. Both attached to elastics so thick they would fall from that web-fine hair in a minute. Then they'd be lost and oh, the tears. Well so what, that would be later. Meanwhile she was grateful that little things wrapped in plastic kept her daughter happy. Carla bought the elastics and mentally subtracted a dollar thirty-two from her budget.

Times are tough when a dollar thirty-two makes a difference, she thought, struggling with Jessie's slippery hair. Damn Kenny. Couldn't he have left his daughter a curl or two off that glistening mop?

Nope, not Kenny: took all his glistening goodies with him, plus of course the money. Even Jessie's silver dollar. Jesus Christ. Carla thought about it every time she went to the bank. As a joke she had put it in an envelope pencilled "Jessie's college fund" and plopped it in the safe deposit box.

It was even Kenny's suggestion. Unusually prudent for Kenny, Carla thought. Oh, he was sweet enough most of the time; but the details of daily life bored him silly, and he'd rather go surfing. He bored easily, and he surfed a lot. But he always seemed happy to come home, covered in sand and amorous and hungry.

"Mommy!" Jessie interrupted. "Are we almost done?"

"Yes, Punkin." Carla opened her eyes, looked down at the braids, and was amazed to discover they were finished. She pulled the plastic packets out of her pocket and held them up in front of Jessie. "Okay, pick."

"You pick, Mommy."

"What if I pick wrong?"

"Um, okay." Jessie scrunched up her face to signify concentration and pointed to the ladybugs. Carla then wrapped some more elastics under the thick bands of the fuzzy critters, pointing them head up to show the eyes.

"There we go. All done."

Jessie reached up to pat the "bugs" and laughed delightedly. "Thank you, Mommy." She turned to hug her mother and Carla popped her eyes.

"Ooh, wow! Super! Go check yourself out in the mirror." Jessie raced off to the bathroom and Carla yelled after her: "Hey, Jess. Try to tinkle while you're in there. I don't wanna hear 'Mommy, I hafta go' the minute we leave, okay?"

From the darkened hall: "Okay, Mommy."

Three minutes later: "Mommy, I can't! You'll hafta run the tap."

"Okay, Jess. Be right there." Carla stood up, pulling her jeans down from the knees and out of her crotch. Hmmm, she smiled. Designed by Paul...

She stretched and caught a whiff of the great magnolia in the next yard. Wheeyooh, what a smell! Already she could feel her sinuses closing ranks around the pollen. Her eyes teared up and she sneezed, three big ones. The last one popped the button off her jeans and made her pee.

"Mah-mee! Where are you?" Sing-song from the door-way.

"Cah-ming." Sing-song back, several octaves lower, hoarse with snot. Carla wiped her face on her sleeve and looked at the splops of mascara. Great. Now I look like a miner. She felt another sneeze coming on and prayed it wouldn't happen. Too late: one, two, three, and her face and her jeans were soaking. "Hey," she gasped, shaking her fist at the sky, "Ya wanna stop this before I drown?"

She ripped open the tape of the tallest box with her thumbnail, then dug down to the slick panties. She pulled up the terrycloth shorts and top, laid them on the box and tried to brush the wrinkles out by hand. No luck. Oh well, guess I go wrinkled. She stepped gingerly down the hall and said as she passed the bathroom, "Hang on, Jess. Mommy has to change. It's too hot for jeans."

Carla hopped on the orange bedroom carpet, peeling off her jeans. She walked to the kitchen, holding the shorts set over her torso so that Jessie wouldn't see her walking nude and troop her little buns down the street, saying, "Iss okay: Mommy does it alla time."

In the kitchen Carla rinsed off her face and lower half, grabbed the last square of paper towelling, and dried off. Then she shimmied on the shorts set and closed her eyes to imagine the room in Rachel's house where she and Paul would be living till the move to Orlando.

Damn nice of Rachel, but living with Rachel's paranoia, that was something else again.

Not that she didn't have her reasons, Carla was quick to remind herself. Hell, how could you recognize a masked rapist without his mask? So what if he was blond and tanned—who wasn't in this town of peroxide-pumping sun worshippers?

Paul's 'ooga' horn sounded in the driveway. She heard him yell: "Car, is this all of it?"

She yelled back, "Yep, just have to gather up The Twink."

She was about to call Jessie when she had a vision of her sister pacing in the kitchen, those short fingers tapping on the Formica. Jesus Christ, Rachel, we're only an hour late. Lighten up, dammit. Then she flushed and said aloud: "I'm sorry, Rachel."

Jessie

Rachel marched from the living room window back to the little Florida room that was to be Jessie's bedroom. Jessie went with her to pick wallpaper, and they found a remnant with seashells, daisies and puffy white clouds on a background of sky blue. Jessie was ecstatic. She told her mother how Jesus had left it for her.

Carla said: "Honey, wallpaper's just stuff, things people make, things that you buy. Jessie, you can't ask Jesus for things, not even if you think they're pretty. You ask Him to take care of the people you love."

Jessie knotted her brows: her mother seemed to have missed the point. "But why was it there if He didn't leave it there after I ast Him?"

Rachel broke in: "Jessie, do you remember what we did after we got the wallpaper?"

"Uh-huh. We took it to the man at the table, an' you gave him a money."

"That's right, Jessie. I gave him money. Anything you buy with money has nothing to do with Jesus: stuff like your jelly shoes, or that wallpaper. Honey, Jesus has to take care of all the little boys and girls and old people who don't have families to love them. He leaves stuff like wallpaper to your Mommy and me and other big people. Somewhere out there a big person painted up that wallpaper, hoping that a little girl like you would come into the store and buy it. So what say we get some chocolate milk and hold up our glass and say thanks to that nice big person."

"Yeah!" Jessie leaped off her mother's lap and raced for the kitchen. Then, over the plastic elephant cup, she said: "So how'd he hear me when I ast Jesus? The big person?"

Rachel arched her brow and said, "Over to you, Paul."

"Well, Jessie," Paul began, but couldn't improvise an answer.

Jessie said: "Iss okay, Uncle Paul, I'll ask Miz Emily. She knows everything about Jesus."

That night, after her mother had tucked her in, Jessie lay staring at her Care Bear night light.

She had her five fuzzy friends tucked around her, with her Jessie-sized purple rabbit, Andre, on the right. Andre's long furry ears had wires to bend them, and she pushed them into a curve so she could fit her face against the pink linings. Sometimes she'd lick the linings and rub them on her face. Then she'd wait for the breeze from the fan to cool her. That was fun, even if she did wake up sticky.

She liked sucking her thumb till it was sloppy wet, then holding it out to get cold. She was just about done "colding" her thumb when she decided that Jesus had so put it there. After all, Miz Emily said that Jesus could do anything. Ask for it, and it was yours. Satisfied, she rubbed her cheek against Andre's wet ear, and popped her thumb back in her mouth.

The sleep fairy was coming. Jessie could feel it in the darkness behind her eyes, making her eyelids droop.

She had one last thing to do in the wake world, one very important thing. She pulled her thumb out for him to hear her say: "Tank oo, Jesus."

Rachel

It was a glorious May Saturday, a weekender's dream. The sky was clear with nary a tuft of cloud. The sand was already too hot for feet, and all along the shoreline, half in and half out of the surf, the dedicated tanners lay on their fold-out chairs, basting each other in coconut oil. Families marched into the waves, holding hands and laughing as they rose above the white-topped pyramids.

Farther out the surfers were practicing Devocean, paddling toward the sun after partying the night away. They had their little portions of paradise all staked out by the time The Breakfasters arrived.

Breakfast was a weekend tradition at the beach, a social outing for all ages. By 9 A.M. the restaurants on Atlantic, Beach, and Third Streets overflowed with T-shirts and tank tops, ordering anything that came with grits or hash browns.

So it's 11 o'clock already and where the hell are they?

Rachel was in the front yard, thinking it should be fenced off for Jessie.

Rachel's house was two blocks off the ocean in Neptune Beach—not the rich oceanfront, she would quickly point out, because Rachel thought everything was too expensive. She was constantly fretting over money—except when she was emptying her bank account to save some creature in peril. No cause ever left her cold: somewhere out in the vast ocean a whale was singing "Send Money," and Rachel was writing a check.

"It's Dad's fault," she'd say, and shrug and smile wistfully.

"Yeah, him and his silly fish," laughed Carla, and instantly regretted it.

Pain overcame Rachel like a summer storm. Her face flushed, her eyes locked on something straight ahead—and then for a moment she was gone, snuffed out by this dark presence no one else could see.

It had been two years since the attack, but Rachel seemed unable to grow past it. The counselling sessions had brought back her funny, facile demeanor but it was a thin mask, easily torn. A phone call, a doorbell, a word, a noise, and Rachel would start.

Carla couldn't help worrying. Why wasn't Rachel getting better?

The week before she moved in with Rachel, Carla called Rachel's therapist, Dr. Phillips. A cheery voice raced through Martel, Rienhardt, and Phillips, and put Carla on hold.

The phone clicked. A throat cleared. "Hello? Miss Williams? Carla?" It was the doctor's voice.

"Yes. I, um, want to talk about Rachel."

"Yes." There was a pause. "Well, what do you want to know, or what is it you want to tell me?"

"I, uh, want to know why Rachel isn't getting any better, and if there's something I could be doing to help that I'm not doing and she's just too damn proud to ask for."

"Carla, let me tell you that Rachel is making definite progress, but you'll have to take that on faith. Don't be so hard on her, and don't be so hard on yourself. There's no magic in this: it's a slow, intolerably slow process, and I told you two years ago there was no calendar for recovery. You're doing exactly what you should be doing, you're loving her. You and Jessie are the most precious things in Rachel's life right now. In time, she may meet a man she trusts, but she's got a long way to go yet."

She rustled some papers on her desk, said, "Here they are," and was quiet while someone walked away from the desk. Carla heard a door shut, and Dr. Phillips resumed: "Be patient, Carla, that's all I can tell you to do." She hesitated, then said, "Hell, just feel lucky the son of a bitch didn't kill her."

"Whew," said Carla, "I'm glad you said that. Um, you always sound so formal I feel like I'm not doing something right."

"I'm sorry I made you feel that way," said Dr. Phillips, genuinely concerned. "Maybe I need a tonal adjustment. Thanks for letting me know. And, Carla, you feel free to call me any time you need to talk, all right? I may not be available, but I promise to get back with you as soon as I can."

"Thank you, Dr. Phillips." Carla sighed. "I feel better now. G'bye. And thanks again."

Carmine Phillips listened to the click on the receiver, pulled out her pocket mirror and retouched her lipstick. She shook her head, glad she could give Carla some solace, wondering what it was that Rachel refused to be hypnotized to find. Rachel said she couldn't go through the pain again but Carmine was sure it was something more. Alas, Rachel wouldn't let anyone help her, so what was there to do but watch and listen?

And Baby Makes Four

It was a Saturday when the years fell away, probably because Rachel was tired of knob flipping and left the radio on an oldies station. She was thinking about her dad, always in his study correcting papers around the time that Carla was born. And of course she could not help but see those fish in the wall-high tank by the window in her father's study.

They were oscars. Fat, brown, and bug eyed. There were no other fish in the aquarium, and Rachel wished that the fish fairy would come in the night and poof them into betas or clownfish, anything bright and darting.

One evening she carried in a large mirror and held it up to the tank. George pretended not to notice while Rachel struggled with the mirror. Finally he turned in his chair and said, "Yes. What is it this time?"

Rachel stared intently at the oscars and said, "I'm waiting for them to get a good look at themselves so they'll die of embarrassment and we can get some real fish."

"Not a bad idea," said her mother, in that husky French Canadian that sounded like plugged sinuses. She was leaning against the wall, filling up the doorway with her blue shift and pregnant belly. Her face and neck trickled sweat that she wiped with a bandanna.

George saw that she was tired, swivelled the chair to face her and stood up to let her sit down. She eyed the papers strewn across the floor and asked, "Where can I walk?"

George bent down and scooped the papers into three piles that left a path for her. She struggled over to the chair and sank into the vinyl cushion. "Dis is no fun: I can't cross my legs." They watched her squirming to get comfortable till she caught their eyes and stuck out her tongue.

Claire was a constant delight to George even after twelve years of marriage.

He hoped the new baby would have more of her coloring, maybe even that rapturous singing voice that held people spellbound.

Fortunately for George, fantasy and speculation were his favorite toys, which made him an excellent teacher and kept him happy in spite of his frugal lifestyle. Of course he wished there were more money, especially with the new baby coming. In the staff room at school they talked about chicken recipes and cheap mechanics when they weren't bemoaning their lack of raises.

George remembered how good it sounded when he arrived twelve years ago. Back then the newly erected Brayton High had gleaming green walls, a lighted stadium, and no air conditioning. The principal's office and adjoining foyer had cool air but the rest of the building from April through October was still and steamy. The school board bottom-liners argued that air conditioning was superfluous since the school was vacant in summer anyway.

George requested a meeting with some of the Board's

bigwigs and drove all the way to Tallahassee to plead the teachers' case. He asked, quite logically he thought, what about the final exams in June? Wasn't it hard enough for kids to concentrate on math and grammar without fighting to stay awake in stale air?

They were touched by his concern, thanked him for his lucid presentation, and sent him away thinking he had made an important contribution to all future students. It was a speech they had heard many times before, and their standard response was to blame the lack of student involvement on the moral disintegration of the country. And whose fault was that but lecherous men like George, who leered at those sweet young things over charts about reproduction, and probably espoused the pernicious doctrine that all of God's lambs came from dinosaurs.

George came very close to being fired that day. He had unknowingly squared off against the literalists in a section of the country where the question, "Did the earth move for you, too?" meant: "Is your hoe working?"

It was often said of Jacksonville that the Florida border had been set too high, that Jacksonville more properly belonged in south Georgia. It had a very rural feel. In fact, when George brought his new wife to Jacksonville to start his career at Brayton High, University Boulevard was a two-lane road that barely saw five cars an hour. Scotch pines and scrub oak stood side by side for miles and miles. Curls of Spanish moss hung from countless trees: the acid rain as yet was years away.

Claire's excitement at living in a land of perpetual sunshine quickly evaporated when she saw how isolated she was from the things she really loved, that she took for granted as part of her identity. Where was all the good cheap wine? Why did the bacon taste like chunks of Lot's wife? And why were all the stylish clothes designed for someone five-foot-seven?

Insulted by what she took to be a slur on her height, Claire began to design her own clothes. George would come home, and there she would be in something he had never seen before. She had drawn the pattern on his desk after breakfast and sewn it up that very afternoon. She wore a lot of greens—jade, emerald, teal, mint—and her large hazel eyes took on all those colors, and dazzled anyone who saw them.

Not now, of course. Now she had purple bags under her eyes and was tired and irritable, counting the days to delivery. "Dat silly girl's going to be born in July, George," she sighed, wiping her neck at the rim of her collar.

"Oh, so now it's a girl. May I ask how you know that?"

"I just feel it. It's a girl, dat's all." She looked over at Rachel, who was gingerly trying to place the mirror on the floor by the aquarium, and said, "Rachel, take dat t'ing back where you found it before you break it."

"Aye, aye, Mon Capitaine." With a loud groan, she lifted the mirror and slowly picked her way back toward the door. They heard her clumping down the hallway toward her bedroom. Halfway down the hall her step changed; obviously the mirror was no burden.

George grinned at Claire and said, "Our daughter, the comedienne."

Claire, who usually laughed at Rachel's antics, said: "Shut da door, George. We 'ave to talk."

George obliged her, then planted himself on the pile of papers beside her feet. "Now then, ma belle, what's the problem?"

"It's Rachel, George. She t'inks dat fun is just showing off for you. She doesn't 'ave any friends her own age. She's always reading. Dis is Florida, George, an' she's white as a sheet. She takes walks by herself, I ask her where she goes, she says it helps her to t'ink. George, dis isn't normal. She's a li'l girl, eleven years old. I know she does it to please you, George, so you won't t'ink she's stupid. But she's gonna 'ave a sister soon, an' responsibilities. I don't want her t'inking dat taking care of a bébé is not a gift. I don't want her growing up like dese spoil English girls who can't press a shirt or pass da vacuum. You 'ave to tell her she's doing enough, George, dat caring for udders takes anudder kind of smart, so she'll know you won't t'ink she's stupid if she's not acting all da time like a—a—"

She fought for the word in English. She could see it clearly, but it wouldn't—

"Dat's it!" she exclaimed. "A train seal! Dat's exactly what she remines me of: every night she runs to show you her tricks. Oh, George, she's so much more dan dat. Let her explore dose parts, too. Don't let her grow up t'inking dey don't matter. You always say, George, dat books are your best friends. But you 'ave many udder t'ings besides dose, an' you 'ave me. Promise me when Rachel's ready for college you'll send her to McGill so she can be wit' women who are chic but not empty, wit' men who expect her to be pretty an' smart. She needs to go where people will listen to her, George." She grinned at him, and lightly pulled his hair. "She's like you, George—she 'ave a lot to say. Perhaps one day she'll be a teacher, like you.

"Now, about my udder girl…Yes, don't you look at me like dat, she's gonna be a girl. I want to name dis one, George. You got to name Rachel after dat carport woman wit' da dead robins. Dis one's for me, George, an' for my mudder."

"If it turns out to be a boy—"

"It's gonna be a girl."

"You were wrong the last time, you know."

"Yes, but dat was eleven years ago, an' I'm much smarter now."

Rachel heard them laughing from her bedroom. She smiled, an upside-down smile because she was trying to stand on her head, using the wall to "walk" her legs up into position. She pulled her legs away, pointed her toes, tottered from side to side, and came crashing to the floor.

"What the hell was that?" George's voice. Footsteps running down the hallway. "Rachel, are you all right?"

"Fine, Daddy. I just tried to stand on my head."

"It looks like you tried to stand on the wall."

"Yeah, well, I took a shortcut and it didn't work."

"Yeah, and if you don't get those marks removed before your mother sees them, your whole life will be cut short."

Rachel saluted. "Aye, aye, Mon Capitaine." She picked

herself up and slumped against her father.

He held her shoulders, pointed her toward the kitchen and said: "Playtime's over, Sport. Time to pay the piper."

"Oh, boo," said Rachel. "What does that mean anyway, pay the piper?" She was counting on George's tendency to provide complete and endless answers to any question.

George, however, was onto her. He pointed toward the kitchen and said: "Now, young lady."

Rachel winced and dragged her feet in widening swirls toward the kitchen.

George turned toward the study and yelled: "Hey, Claire. You're not the only one who's learned something in eleven years!"

L'Aventure

George met Claire while he was in Montreal on vacation. Actually he had arrived there looking for some "rejuvenating experiences" with some fellow escapees from a high school reunion in Vermont. There were four of them, friends through school who'd enlisted after graduation to fight whoever was menacing democracy and save the world. There was Gates "The Ace," so called because he always knew the best deals on anything legit or shady and played a mean hand of poker, now making a killing in real estate in Florida; Barry Stryker, the football hero and local Lothario, now selling used cars in Maine; George Williams, known alternately with awe or derision as "The Brain"—but also as "Stryker's friend," which gave him a little respect; and Angus Campbell, nicknamed "The Goose" because he could do accurate, astonish-

ing bird calls, and was now head of the local chapter of the
N.R.A.

Twenty years, they ragged each other. What had they done
in twenty years, besides keep the world safe for Uncle Sam,
get married, raise bambinos and pay taxes. Well, Stryker,
good to see you've put on a few pounds, haw haw. Ace, what
happened to your hair? God, George, you look good. I hate to
say it, I really mean it. Whaddaya mean, you never married?
Well, maybe that explains it, haw haw. You like women,
though, huh George?

It was a question that took a great deal of courage to ask,
because once in tenth grade Gary Murphy had made the
sniggering suggestion that "Ol' Wimpo" was probably a fairy,
and that's why he was hanging around Stryker. The word got
back to Stryker, who chased Murphy all the way to Barnaby's
car lot and pounded him into the ground. Gary wasn't seen at
school for days and the only person who didn't know the story
was George, and nobody was going to tell him.

"Hey," said Stryker, now that the conversation had made
the inevitable shift from cars and sports and who fought who
to who married who and let's get laid, "I know where the
women are really wild, and they don't charge for it either, haw
haw. Whaddaya say we drive over the border and get us a little,
uh, change of oil. Ace, Goose, your wives aren't there, whaddaya
say we trip the light fantastic for old times' sake."

Angus was a little bleary-eyed. "Isn't Mexico a little far to
go for pussy? Don't those greasy senoritas all have syph or
something?"

The other three looked at him and laughed. We're talking
about Canada, Goose. Hey, Canada goose. Haw haw haw.
Never mind, let him think he's in Mexico. So who's gonna
drive? Who's sober enough to steer?

"I'm gonna drive," said Stryker. "I'm the only one with
enough insurance. Now everybody pile in."

George wondered why Stryker mentioned insurance, until
he looked at the speedometer and saw it climbing past ninety.
Common everyday stuff for Stryker. The two hell-raisers in

the back seat were slumped over each other and Ace was snoring.

"Goddamnit that's a terrible sound!" yelled Stryker, banging on the horn and whipping the wheel back and forth to wake them up. "No wonder your old lady wants to get poked all the time, she's afraid you'll go to sleep!"

George stiffened as the car careened from one side of the road to the other. With any luck they'd be crossing the Champlain Bridge in twenty minutes, either that or fording the St. Lawrence in a Rambler.

By his watch it was nine-fifteen when he and Stryker left the sleeping Goose and Ace locked in the car and walked under the glittering marquee "L'Aventure." Immediately they were immersed in reddish smoke. People were dancing and laughing. George wondered if there wasn't some kind of celebration going on that made everyone look so exultant.

"No," said Stryker, "it's this way all the time. These people just know how to live, George. I come up here a lot. And wait'll you taste the food! The streets are clean, the city is beautiful. I'm surprised you've never been here, big time educator like yourself. Why not take a couple of days and look around? If you're low on cash, I'll spot ya for it. Whaddaya say?"

"I say it's a great idea," said George, looking at his watch and concluding it was dead; it had said nine-fifteen for the past three hours. He was about to ask the bartender for another scotch when he saw two good-looking unaccompanied girls walking toward the piano bar.

He tapped Stryker and said, "Barry, you're making this weekend possible for me," He crooked his head to indicate the women who'd come in. "You pick whichever one you want, as long as it isn't the one in the red."

Stryker laughed. "Get your clammy paw off me, you drunken sonofabitch. And let's hurry over there before those Frenchies abscond with the bullion."

George finally found himself at the piano bar behind the magnificent lady in red. Her friend seemed to have disappeared but she was so tiny that she might be close by and he couldn't see her. He looked over at Barry and shrugged. "Sorry, Buddy."

Barry, however, waved him off. He had already spotted an astonishing beauty in a tiny purple hat with iridescent feathers. She had very red lips, and she was smiling at Barry. Damn, these women were friendly.

But then, when it came to Stryker, all women were friendly. Every couple in school had fought over him. The relationship usually ended with the tremulous question: have you or have you not gone all the way with Barry Stryker? This usually followed on the heels of the girl being seen talking to Stryker, which would shit-can her reputation on the spot. It was said that Stryker had had every girl north of the Mason-Dixon line, and possibly every girl in the Northern Hemisphere, including the ones who were just visiting. No matter what place you mentioned, what city, what country, Stryker would say yeah, the girls are nice there.

George wondered what it would be like to have such raw magnetism that any effort you made was a guaranteed success. Living in Stryker's shadow for so many years gave him time to wonder about a lot of things. On his own, looking in the mirror, he thought he was attractive: square jaw, nice eyes, not a big nose, lots of sandy hair, even now—but it didn't matter, it wasn't that Rock Hudson knock 'em dead in their tracks look like Stryker had, it was... What the hell was it anyway?

Damn, thought George, I can't even think anymore, let alone talk. There was a train running backwards through his head. He'd had this sensation on gin, but never on scotch—at least not while he was standing, and he'd gone from standing to leaning on the bar, propping his chin on his hand.

He noticed the pianist talking to the friend of the woman in red. They were laughing, and the man slid off the piano bench, and walked to the other side of the bar. Now what? This pissant little broad prob'ly thinks she's Ethel Merman. Nah, she's French. Prob'ly Maurice Chevalier. Haw haw, I'm so funny.

What happened next George couldn't quite remember. The little woman—really she was a girl, she couldn't have been a day over twenty—began to sing in a heart stopping soprano. Everyone stared at this tiny girl in green taffeta, her dark hair waving down her collarbone, her crucifix gleaming in the spotlight above the piano keys. The song ended to wild applause and money flew over the bar as people screamed to buy her a drink.

George, in what turned out to be a rare inspiration, had already ordered a glass of beaujolais for her, and waved at her when the bartender placed it on the piano top. She saw him, waved, and raised the glass of wine to thank him. He watched her giggle, showing deep dimples and slightly uneven teeth. She got up from the bench to much applause, and pushed her way through the crowd till she was standing in front of him.

He was smiling, he hadn't stopped smiling. Whatever happened, he mustn't leave this bar, it was the only thing keeping his face from falling through the floor.

He said: "Look, Mademoiselle, I'm very sorry, but I'm a little… drunk. Could we continue this conversation… tomorrow? Wou… would you have lunch with me?"

She stared up at him, one eyebrow cocked. Was she studying his face or considering his offer? He found it difficult to focus on her because he had to look down and her face tilted along with the floor.

"Geez, you're short!" He blurted, and immediately apologized.

She raised both eyebrows and laughed. "Well, at least dere's notting wrong wit' your eyes. Dere's notting wrong wit' being short, eider. If you mean it, de lunch, I meet you tomorrow *a midi* on top of Mount Royal, hokay? If not," she paused, the dimples deepening, "If not, your loss. I must leave now."

George saw Stryker passing on his right and lurched out to grab him. "Barry, ol' pal, call me a cab. Where is it we're staying again?"

"Jesus, George, you're a mess!" Stryker found it hard to

believe that anyone could be so blitzed on only five drinks, but the proof was right in front of him. He carted George out of the club and loaded him into the car, hoping George wouldn't barf before they got to a hotel.

They ended up in the elegant Mount Royal Hotel in the English part of town, Ace and Angus carrying George litter fashion into the suite.

George spent the remainder of the night on the tiles of the elegant bathroom floor, with his head over the elegant commode. His last memory of that night was very pleasant as he called out to Stryker, "Hey Barry, ol' buddy, ol' pal, ol' sock, ol' thing, guess what, guess what? You'll never believe this, but I got a date!"

Good Things Come...

George somehow remembered "a midi" and Mount Royal from the previous night and was able to get his suit clean, shower and shave by 11 A.M. Ace and Angus had already taken the bus back to Vermont.

George was miserable. His stomach gurgled, his mouth was cottony. He downed two orange juices and three aspirins and still felt like shit. All he remembered of the girl was her song and that rustly green taffeta. Stryker said he was doing great to remember that much. "Oh, yeah," said George, "and she's short."

Stryker nodded and grinned. "That's really gonna help you, George. Most of the women here are short."

George suggested that Barry come along to identify her, then take off so she wouldn't fall in love with him. Stryker laughed: did George really believe all that ladykiller bullshit? George avowed that yes, he did, and why take chances? Besides, Barry, you got me into this…

Twenty minutes later they were climbing the steep sidewalk of Peel Street, heading for the top of the city, the famous Mount Royal. Here no cars were allowed to travel, and horse drawn carriages and couples of all ages could be seen ambling slowly through the greenery. Families spread blankets on the sloping green fields, and baskets of bread and wine and cheese were opened: it was 12 o'clock.

"High noon," said George, standing on the steps of the chalet at the top of the mountain. Around the concrete plateau in front of the chalet small horse-drawn carriages called caleches stopped to unload tourists. People lined up to look through turretted binoculars at the city's famous landmarks.

Someone walked by with ice cream from the chalet. Good idea. George was getting hungry. His mouth was dry. So were his eyes. "High noon," he said again, and Stryker laughed.

"Don't worry, George, you packed your gun. She'll be here."

George saw a small brunette with shoulder-length hair standing by the railing and pointed her out. "Do you think that's her?"

"Only one way to find out. Want me to walk over there with you?"

"Nope," said George, "Your job is to find her, not steal her." George walked down the stairs and over to the railing. The girl was looking at him but didn't smile until he was about twelve feet away. Then those dimples popped and George knew he'd found the right girl.

"'Allo," she said, and laughed. "I see you brought your chaperone. Is he coming too or do you t'ink I can be trusted alone?"

George grinned, and said he would be right back. "All right, Barry, where do I take her for lunch? And when should I come back to the hotel?"

"George, look, we'll just reconvene at, what, 1600 hours

a demain? That's tomorrow, George. Hell, you may not want to leave after tonight. You've got two free months ahead of you, you lucky stiff. Better get back now, before she gets antsy." He smiled at the girl and waved and held up his index finger.

"She's cute, George, and she was smart enough to pick you out of a crowd, drunk as you were, and you were plastered. She came here all by herself. Now all that, for a little Catholic girl who certainly is no harlot—I mean, you can pretty much tell that by looking at her—I think that's pretty amazing. Either that or it's I hate to say fate that brought you two together. Now get the hell over there and at least invite her to lunch so I can get out of here because this fucking fate stuff gives me the willies." He rubbed his thumb and fingers together, then said, "Last chance. Need some more?"

George said no, he was fine, and waved good-bye.

Stryker walked down the hillside whistling, watching his shy friend hurry over to the little French girl. He tried to picture them in bed together but it was easier to picture himself. By the time the fantasy had passed George and the girl were gone.

Stryker briefly considered their conversation before George got smashed. Of all the men he knew, he was sure that George Williams would make the perfect married man, sensitive, caring, and responsible. How could all these women weeping and wailing for want of a good man have missed a prize catch like George Williams?

It turned out that Stryker was on the wrong track: he almost fell over when George told him "he couldn't find the right girl." He was looking for someone unique, he said.

"Hell," said Barry, "they all start out that way. It's just hard to put somebody in a static situation and expect them to stay interesting. The sameness kills it, everything gets old."

"Then what I need," said George, "is someone strong enough to beat the rap. She's out there, Barry. If I have to look for the rest of my life, I'm gonna find her."

That afternoon Claire, for that was her name, Marie Claire

Louise Guenette, took George to a small Argentinian restaurant. A huge rack of lamb rotated in the window by the door. The waiters were dressed as gauchos, all in black, with broad belts covered in silver conchos. A bland vegetable broth in a shallow gilt-edged bowl was followed by slabs of lamb, hot off the rack by the door. The lamb was basted with cinnamon, garlic, and some kind of fruit that he could not place and they refused to divulge.

The wine, which she ordered and he was afraid to drink, but she encouraged him "just to try," was light red and had barely any flavor. It slid down his throat like oil. She told him it was made by monks in a Quebec monastery, then she laughed and said that God's special servants needed to have some fun too. Dinner was followed by thin slices of pie with frothy cream filling topped by a glaze made of apples and peaches.

He noticed people lighting cigarettes and asked if she would like to smoke. No, she said, she liked to taste her food. That made him happy, because he didn't smoke. He thought it a crass and smelly habit. He swore he would never kiss a woman who smoked, and he never had. This woman, he thought, doesn't smoke, and he began to study her mouth. She had soft full lips, a fine nose pointed slightly starboard, and eyes of emerald green.

George was enjoying the conversation so much, her husky laugh and unexpected wit, that he found himself thinking: Would she look this good when she first wakes up? She excused herself to go to the washroom and when she came back George was enchanted again by her tiny stature. He grinned as she sat down, and asked, "Just how tall are you, anyway?"

Immediately her face changed. She frowned, rolled her eyes, and stood up so that she was staring down at him. She snapped: "How tall was Napoleon! How tall was your wunnerful president Lincoln! How tall was Jesus!"

When he had no rebuttal, she continued: "You see, it doesn't really matter de height of people. Only to stupid people it matters. It took me many years of hearing dat question before I figured dat out. Tank you for dinner. Ave a wunnerful time in my city. Your hotel is dat way." She pointed to the far wall and walked out the door.

George glanced at the bill, dropped twelve dollars on the tray, cursed himself for leaving so much, and charged after her.

"Wait! Claire, please, wait! I wasn't insulting you! That stuff doesn't matter to me, God help me it doesn't!" He ran down the street after her, and it was, literally, down the street, for the restaurant was on the mountainside, like everything else downtown.

He raced across the street on a red light and braved the honks and obscenities to catch her half a block away. He hated making an ass of himself but hell, more than his pride was at stake here, international relations were going down the tubes.

When he finally got her to speak to him she said: "I don't know about you, George. I don't like stupid people, an' wat you said was really stupid. De problem wit' stupid people, George, is dat smart people pay for all dere mistakes. But…I like dat you run across dat road for me. Dat was very stupid. Dese people drive worse dan my temper." She braced her back against a store front and grinned up at him.

George laughed. "Soooh, it's okay to do something stupid that almost gets me killed as long as it doesn't insult you, right?"

She paused before she answered, looking at his shirt rather than his eyes. George realized that she was composing her answer in French before she ventured it in English, and that she had been doing this every time she looked off somewhere. Here he had been wondering if he wasn't boring her when in fact she was paying him a wonderful compliment, giving him the best she had to offer not once, but twice. He resolved to return the compliment by treating anyone trying to speak English with the utmost courtesy.

On the heels of this noble resolution he found her staring into his eyes. Had she said something? She looked expectant.

What should he say? He cleared his throat and thought of a believable out: "I was trying to think of something to say in French."

Then suddenly it wasn't a lie, it didn't have to be. "How do I say you're pretty?" He was almost afraid to say it, afraid he would be branded superficial again. He had never known any woman who treated physical endearments as patronizing statements. What could he say that wouldn't offend her?

"Look," he said, "I'd like to stay up here for a couple of weeks, and if you could show me around I'd like that very much. If I say something that hurts you, believe me it isn't meant to hurt you, but I won't know till it happens. Promise me you won't get upset if I make a mistake? I mean, it's a beautiful day, I'm with a beautiful girl, and I want to be happy. So, do you have any questions for me?"

"Yes." She scanned his face. "How old are you, George?"

"I'll tell you, if you promise to tell me how old you are."

"Bouf," she said, "Dat's easy. I'm twenny, almost. Next week."

"Great, I'll be here for your birthday. I love birthdays. We can celebrate."

"Don't change de subjeck. You are how old, George?"

"Thirty-six."

Her eyes widened and her jaw dropped. "No! You're joking, no?"

"No. Now you're hurting me."

"I'm sorry, I just t'ought you were younger. You look, mebbe, twenny six..." She was quiet for a moment, then said softly, "Are you married, George?"

"No! Why do you ask?"

"You're too old not to be married, George. My fadder's six years past you an' he 'ave seven children. You will see when you come to my party."

Three weeks later Claire and George had walked all over the city, seen all the sights, and talked about everything in the world. George was constantly startled by her observations, enchanted by her humor and high spirits.

Every night he walked her to the door of her noisy little home on the Rue de Rachel.

Five or six sets of eyes would be hovering at the windows, and always the voice of Claire's little brother Michel would be yelling the French equivalent of "Papa! Mama! That old American guy is back!"

Old? George had never thought of himself as old—old was brown pictures in a photo album. He thought of the difference in their ages as negligible because Claire was so quick, so savvy, so understanding.

In fact his determination to keep this trip a simple fling had fallen away: he had fallen in love. He told himself that it would never work, that it was just the romantic mood of the city. How could he ask her to leave her hundred relatives and friends and a city that hummed with love and energy for some dinky apartment and just him? He told her that tomorrow would be their last night, that he had to leave because he was out of money.

Tears rolled down her face and she asked if he would write to her, or was this the end as her father had said it would be, that he would go home to the wife he said he didn't have.

"Claire!" He held her arms and yelled, "Stop it, Claire! I told you I wasn't married. I didn't lie. Have I lied to you at any point?"

"How do I know? I only know wat you say. You see everyt'ing I say, you know it's de trut.' I know notting, George, only wat I feel. Dat's all I 'ave. Wat, we laugh an' joke so you t'ink we're just toys for your convenience? My fadder was right, an' I have been a stupid—" Her voice broke in sobs.

For a split second George thought he was being tricked into marriage, then realized she'd said yes to the question he wanted to ask anyway. He held her arms while she struggled to get away. "Oh, no, young lady," he laughed, "You're not going to endanger my life a second time. I've run my last red light for you!"

Then he said, "Look at me, Claire."

She turned her chin up defiantly, mouth trembling and nose streaming.

He took the handkerchief out of his shirt pocket, wiped her face and said, "If I ask you to marry me, will you go to bed with me after we're married? I mean, I don't know all the customs up here, but I hope that's one of them."

Claire's eyes became wet green spheres, and she gasped, "Why George, you're a teacher an' you don't know where de *bébés* come from? How you t'ink I got all my family, from de big bird wit da long nose? I'm tol' dat da first time it hurts, dat it hurts to make dem an' it hurts to 'ave dem. But I don't believe you would ever hurt me, George. I depend on you for dat. Now give me back dat *mouchoir*, I'm going to cry, I can't help it."

George sat on the steps of the bandstand, watching her cry, laugh, and cry again. It was one soggy hanky she handed him afterwards.

Then she leaped on his lap and covered his face in kisses— big ringing smacks, tiny pecks, light lingering brushes like the feathers of birds. Gently, she ran her tongue under the edge of his top lip, and he eased his tongue between her bottom lip and her teeth. She had never kissed him like this before. The word marriage had unlocked a whole other Claire: George couldn't wait to meet the rest of her.

He asked Claire's father, Roland, for his blessing, explaining very shamefacedly about his financial circumstances.

Roland listened with one raised eyebrow, rubbing the back of his neck. He waited for George to finish and said, "Is dere some problem about money?"

George looked down, his face reddening. "I just want you to know that I'm not offering Claire a palace to live in. I'll love her, and I'll give her everything I can, but there probably won't ever be a lot of money."

"So," said Roland, "You can't offer her diamonds an da streets aren't paved wit gold. Wat does dis look like to you, Fort Knox? If you're offering her love an' children an' a home where she won't starve, wat's to be ashame of in dat? So, wen you want to do dis? We 'ave a lot to do. *Sacre bleu*. Dere's de church, an' da reception, an' da gowns. Merde, I'm glad I got only t'ree daughters." He grinned and said, "Wait until iss your turn!" Then he brought his hand down from his neck, wiped it on his overalls, and offered it to George.

The wedding was held one month later in the Church of The Assumption in the town of Sherbrooke, a hundred miles north of Maine. The service was held in French, except for the vows, which were spoken in two languages. The priest did his best to sound majestic in English, and when Claire lifted her veil George stared as though he had never seen her before.

She was wearing eyeliner, mascara, blue-green eyeshadow, and rouge. Her lips, which were never painted, were a startling red. Her hair, which she always wore loose, was pulled back and flowered out in soft curls around a glistening mother-of-pearl comb. Their lips met and she smelled of lilacs and roses and George didn't want to open his eyes and look anywhere else.

At the reception the champagne flowed and everybody danced. The men walked over in their correct blue suits and slapped him on the back, then handed him envelopes stuffed with Canadian dollars. Dinner was served and George was treated to all the favorites, tortiere topping the list. Toasts were made and everybody cheered and finally it was George's turn to say something. He whispered to Claire to translate for him, and she rose to a round of applause.

He thanked Roland and Lisette for their preparations and their beautiful daughter. He told them it was the most wonderful wedding he had ever been to and he was glad that it was his. He apologized for not drinking more of their fine champagne but since this was going to be the greatest night of his life he didn't want to miss it. Claire blushed as she translated for him, and everybody laughed and banged spoons on their glasses to watch the couple kiss.

When George and Claire were ready to leave, they ran through a shower of rice and confetti to a Cadillac covered in shaving cream and streamers, trailing an army of tin cans. The back seat was brimming with mauve and white lilacs, Claire's favorite flower. Nestled among the lilacs was a huge jar of honey, filled to the top with Canadian and American silver dollars. Claire squealed and pulled out the jar to show everyone. Then she threw a kiss to the assembled multitude and climbed in the car. The camera bugs had stationed themselves around the windshield to record the last wave, and Claire's family stuck their heads through the window to give her a last kiss. The men all shook George's hand again, admonishing him to "take good care of our girl."

Stryker, who had been George's best man and had loaned him the Cadillac, leaned down and said to George: "Just bring that baby back in one piece by the end of next week or Old Man Richards'll have a cow. Better yet, leave on the cans and the shaving cream, fill it with used rubbers, and I can watch him have a stroke right there in the yard." He was talking low and smiling so Claire wouldn't understand him.

George laughed and they grasped each other's hands Roman style.

"Barry," George grinned, "you're one of a kind. Thanks for everything: for coming here, for the car, and," he held Claire's hand up and kissed it, then looked back at his friend, "and especially, thanks for us. If you hadn't gotten me up the mountain that day. Well, what can I say?"

"Shucks, twarn't nothin'." Stryker stepped back from the car and yelled, "So whaddaya hangin' around here for, Mr. and Mrs. Williams, get going!" Then he winked at George and said, "Oh yeah, George, and drive careful!"

George wiggled his eyebrows at him and said, "Hey, no problem. I understand this car's pretty heavily insured," and the two of them burst out laughing. George turned the key, pumped the gas, and the motor hummed as only a Cadillac can. They drove off down the road to waves and whistles and shouts of "Bon Voyage!"

It was a long drive to the fortress city of Quebec. They had reservations for a suite in the magnificent Chateau, a towering castle on the rock cliffs overlooking the St. Lawrence Seaway. From their window they could see great ships float below like toys.

Claire framed the image of a ship with her arms and laughed, "Look, George, I caught one!"

Then she turned to look at George sitting on the massive cheneille bedspread, trying to remove his shoes.

He yawned and tried to cover his mouth, then said, "Claire, I'm sorry. I'm just so tired, I can't keep my eyes open."

She walked over and sat cross-legged on the floor in front of him, twisting his shoes lightly from side to side until his feet were free. "No problem, George. You're just tire from all dat driving. Tomorrow you teach me an' it will be easier for you dat way."

What would be easier? George's eyes flew open, and he said, "We'll talk about it tomorrow." What could he do to dissuade her? The last thing he wanted to do was teach any woman how to drive. It was his personal conviction that America's involvement in World War II was only incidentally triggered by Pearl Harbor, that men of all ages began showing up at induction centers begging to be shipped overseas rather than face the harrowing hours that followed: "Now, Dear, this is the gas pedal and this is the brake; that's the important one…"

But he knew, even as he promised himself never, never, that tomorrow would find Claire at the wheel of Stryker's car, and he made a mental note to buy her a Saint Christopher medal. Better make that two.

He drifted off to sleep with the sound of the fan overhead, and Claire chattering happily about all the things he was going to teach her. Tomorrow, George. His eyes closed. You earn your stripes tomorrow.

Sweet Surprises

The week flew by. George and Claire tramped around the tiered cobblestone streets, rather than attempt the connecting cliffside stairways with their tiny, almost perpendicular steps. They watched artisans ply their trades in "authentic" settler's garb, and bought little trinkets, including a sidewalk artist's rendition of the Chateau. They ate hot croissants in the morning and at night devoured the gourmet fare of the Chateau's famous salon. George had never eaten so many pastries or drunk so much wine, but being with Claire brought all his appetites boiling to the surface. He wanted to go everywhere, see everything, and show his laughing little pixie all of it.

On their third day in the Chateau George said he didn't feel like sightseeing, that there was only one sight he cared to see, and Claire understood him and blushed. They climbed the stairs from the sumptuous foyer and walked to their room. Hand in hand they stood at the doorway, then George scooped her up and carried her across the threshhold, for Claire had said: "You gotta pass me over da mat for it to be real."

George was thrilled at Claire's ease in her nakedness. She loved the feel of the sun on her body, and she didn't cringe when he looked at her. She said it was fine, that God made them without clothes. One thing she never took off was her crucifix. It was not a piece of jewelry, she said, it was a piece of God. The cross glowed above her breasts in the afternoon light and she shaded her eyes to look at him as George came out of the bathroom carrying two large white towels.

He laid them out in the middle of the bed, one on top of the other, and Claire on top of them. He told her it would probably hurt, but only for a minute, and never again if he could help it. He said she might bleed, but not to worry if she didn't, that bleeding wasn't the only sign of a virgin, and that he would have loved her even if she wasn't.

Claire believed him. Her hands locked behind his neck. "Kiss me, George, an' hold me tight tight, like dey do at da doctor's, an' I won't be afraid."

He fastened his mouth on hers, and pushed himself inside her, moving up as slowly as possible. He wrapped his arms around her back, feeling her heart pound against his chest.

He pushed again and she stiffened and whimpered. Tears rolled down into her ears.

Then she kissed him fiercely, digging her hands in his hair and pulling the strands on the sides. Her intensity brought back that first kiss on the hillside, her tongue sliding over his as her thighs stroked the top of his penis through their clothes. That vision, along with the sensation of being inside her while he held her body, soft and sweating, triggered his ejaculation. He pulled his mouth away and was drawn into a tunnel of pure sensation. For a flash of a second he left the world.

Claire stared up at his red face in shock. The veins on his neck and forehead pulsed like moving snakes. Then his jaw relaxed, his smile returned, and the redness in his face and chest began to fade. "Are you all right, George?"

He grinned, kissed her softly, and said that everything was fine, terrific, and how was she?

"I'm fine," she said, "but you looked so strange, George, like you were hurt an' happy, bot' togeder. Is dat how it is for men?"

George was sitting on his heels at the end of the bed, watching the red liquid drain from the lips of her crotch onto the towel. He could use a towel himself, he was covered in blood. "Claire," he said, "I felt wonderful, whatever I looked like. And yes, I think most men look like that. But then, you're not gonna see any other men looking like this, so you don't have to ask about them."

He raised his eyebrows at her and she laughed, saying she was starting to stick to the towel.

He walked into the bathroom, ran cold water over two washcloths, and brought them into the bedroom. Dots of blood trailed behind him, soaking into the carpet. Claire saw them and insisted on cleaning them.

He flipped the washcloths over his hands and held a dialogue between them. Should they clean the floor? No, they should clean George and Claire first, who were in sorry need of a shower, not to mention deodorant. Claire laughed and pulled one of the cloths away from him, then reached out to wipe his genitals.

Suddenly her face clouded, and she drew back: would he think her a *putain* for touching him in "dat place"?

George was astounded. He raised her chin and looked in her eyes and said: "You're my wife, Claire. I want you to touch me. Anywhere you touch will bring me pleasure. And I want to learn the places to touch you that will make you happy. I want to make you come, Claire, like I did, like you saw me."

"Will I look like you do, George?" It was a sly question.

"Everybody's different, Claire. We all do things different ways. Anyhow, it doesn't matter what anybody looks like, except us. We're all that matters now."

"So dat means when we go to America you won't leave me

for dose big-leg blonde wit' da high hairs an' grand patates ?"

"Big potatoes? Oh, you mean…" He cupped his hands in front of his chest and they both grinned. Then he waved his hands and shook his head. "Not a chance, Mrs. Williams. Why, if Elizabeth Taylor and Brigitte Bardot were both to walk in here naked, I'd still choose you."

"An' if I wasn't here?"

"Then they'd just have to put their expensive sweaters back on and vamoose."

"Bouf, I believe you 'bout Lizbet' Taylor. I don't know 'bout Brigitte Bardot."

George's grin widened. "Ya wanna bring 'em in for a test?"

"No, I don't worry 'bout dem no more, dey're no good wit puppets." She curled her fingers under the pink spot on the washcloth till it smiled. Then she climbed off the bed, gathered up the towels, and plunked them in the sink.

She was about to march back and attack the spots on the carpet when he grabbed her hand and yanked her into the shower, turning the taps on full force. After she was thoroughly drenched and sputtering, he stood beneath the shower head and blocked the spray. She called him a *cochon* for hogging all the water. He maintained there was more of him than her, so he needed more water. They rubbed fragrant soap on each other, George bending down so she could reach his shoulders. They kissed with water streaming down their faces and soap burning their eyes. Claire asked for cold water, and they shivered as chill bumps rose against their hands. They laughed as the last of the soap swirled off their feet and gurgled down the drain.

George turned off the taps, pulled the curtain aside, and grinned at his dripping bride. Then he grabbed her buttocks and heaved her over his shoulder, carrying her to the window.

"Put me down, fou! " She yelled. "Put me down an' I tell you a story."

"A story, huh? Okay, Scheherazade, but it better be good." He bent down and deposited her on the rug, kissing her left buttock before it slid out of range.

She backed up and perched on the end of the bed, pulling the hair out of her eyes and tucking it behind her ears. She began: "Da man who built dis place, Frontenac, fought wit' his wife all da time, tried to trow her hout da window, he had such a bad temper—"

"Tempers are all bad here, huh?"

"Mon Dieu!" she screamed, covering her ears and shutting her eyes. "Mon Dieu, I can't say notting, you're always interrup' me!" She hopped off the bed and punched him in the stomach.

George let her have three swings, then grabbed her wrists. "Claire, whoa! Stop it, stop fighting. I won't interrupt you anymore, I promise. Cross my heart. Hey, if I do it again, just hit me." She probably will anyway, he thought. "Look," he said, "I just like to tease you, Claire. I'm not insulting you, honest. I think what you say is important. I just like to joke around. But I'll try to listen better, instead of trying to be funny all the time. That's something you can teach me. Okay? Am I forgiven? Can we kiss and make up?"

"Sure t'ing." She kissed his gurgling stomach and they laughed. "How many more days we got here, George?"

"Just two." He shrugged and pursed his lips. "Saturday morning we head for the States."

"Good. I gotta surprise for you, M'sieur Interrup.' Friday night." She dimpled up at him, then giggled, "Be dere or be square."

Friday found them dancing naked in their suite to the music that floated up from the Grand Salon. Actually only George was dancing, carrying Claire around like a doll. She snuggled her cheek against his as they whirled and dipped. Finally, he fell on the bed with her on top of him, and said: "Okay, where's my surprise?"

"Close your eyes," she said in that husky whisper, "I got it right here." She reached under the bed and dragged something out. "Don't peek," she commanded, and it killed him, but he didn't. He heard something squeaking. She told him to lie back. He pulled the large down pillow under his neck and crossed his hands behind his head. Then he felt a warm liquid on his chest that followed the line of his hair down the middle of his body onto his penis. He opened his eyes and found her slathering his cock with the honey from the coin jar. She smiled, bent her head, and dug a spiral groove in the honey with her tongue. She took the head of his penis in her small mouth, and drool and honey poured down his shaft like slow rolling candle wax. She licked off the honey, using her tongue like a paintbrush, daubing and stroking. She licked it off, kissed it off, sucked it off, and George put his middle finger between his teeth and his tongue on the side of his finger and went off like a rocket.

She laughed softly, triumphantly. He looked at her in the half darkness, crouched over like a cat, her eyes gleaming, her chin and her mouth glistening with semen and honey.

"Your turn," said George, and his voice seemed to come from a great distance. He made her lie back then poured the honey down her front exactly as she had done to him. He dug his fingers in the jar and swirled them in the honey, then gently stroked the small mound below her hair where the outer labia met, feeling it rise and swell, the little ridge underneath slowly hardening. Her breath came in sharp gasps and her legs quivered. Suddenly she shrieked and rolled sideways, jacking up her knees and burying her face in the pillow. A shudder passed through her and she went limp.

She pulled the pillow off her face, gasping and grasping his hand: "George! Feel my heart!"

He did and smiled. "How do you feel?"

"Good. Wunnerful. Scared. Da whole kit."

"That's just the beginning, Claire. One day we'll even come at the same time, with me inside you."

"Ooo, I can't imagine dat!"

"Hah. Imagining it's easy. Finding you, now, that was tough. The rest of it's gonna be a piece of cake, compared to that."

"Piece of cake? Oh no, you're not hungry again!"

"If I am, Mrs. Williams, it's your fault: that come stuff takes a lot of energy. I can see our food bill is gonna be tremendous. Actually, I'm kinda tired. How about you? Maybe we should take a nap, huh? All in favor, pass out..."

Two minutes later, two voices together: "I think we should shower now."

They laughed and slid off the bed, glazed hands interlaced. They walked into the bathroom and climbed in the shower.

Above the rushing water, Claire's voice: "We made a hawful mess of dat bed, George."

George, spewing water: "Well, what's a honeymoon without honey, honey? Sorry, Claire, I just can't help—"

"Shut up, George."

"Right, Claire."

Rushing water. Taps turned off. Flesh squeaking and sliding against the tiles. Gasping, faster gasping, more squeaking, more sliding. Mutual moans in different registers, one of them almost a whimper, the other almost a groan. The bodies stop moving, a series of gasps ensue. Quiet descends, and then:

"I love you, George."

"I love you, Claire."

Coming Home

They drove down to Maine as the trees were turning from green to gold, and thin lines of black smoke rose from piles of leaves. Roadside stands were heaped high with pumpkins, and all along the route people smiled and waved—horseback riders from the fencerows, farmers on their tractors, families picking berries in the bushes by the road.

When they arrived at Richards and Sons Used Cars, Barry was there with his big grin, holding a bunch of congratulatory cards.

One of them was from Ace, and in it was an ad for a biology teacher in a new Florida high school. Barry elbowed George and said it was probably a trick to sell him real estate. George agreed, but thought the tip merited further investigation. They had advertised in The Times, so clearly the local talent wasn't cutting it. He studied the ad while Barry took Claire across the lot "to poison her with our coffee."

Claire was holding onto him, looking up with that enchanting smile, and for a moment George was jealous. He shook off the feeling, concluding it was just a distraction ploy: the real business was the ad, which was making mincemeat of his sanity.

George had been cautious all his adult life, frugal beyond need. He had worked hard to be indispensable at Jefferson High—and now that he almost was, he wasn't happy. He was due to sign up for his sixth year but kept putting it off, trying to articulate the source of his reticence. There wasn't any pressure on him to sign, his return was taken as inevitable. Until a week ago he would have agreed, but along with his new wife he wanted a new life, and in that frame of mind he dialed the operator.

Ace was apparently on two lines at once: Barry said that was just one of his cons. The other caller vanished, and Ace began his spiel.

In a lot of ways, said Ace, Jacksonville was like Vermont—homey, family-oriented, lots of unspoiled country. Property values were next to nothing. Where else could a teacher be a homeowner?

"Okay, okay," said George, "You've done your job, now tell me about mine. Is it true they're still fighting the Civil War down there? Will I be lynched if I don't wear a white sheet and kiss the Confederate flag every morning?"

"Haw, haw, George, you're such a kidder. Just call 'em. I already gave you a ringing endorsement. I told them about your degrees, and that you just got married and were looking for a decent place to raise a family. They can't wait to talk to you. Stryker told me when you'd be back so I told them you'd call Tuesday. That's tomorrow, Mr. Honeymooner. Call me and let me know how it goes.

"By the way, there's a beautiful little two-bedroom ranch-style house on Azalea Circle in the Southside of Jacksonville, just perfect for you and the missus—speaking of whom, congratulations, George. Stryker says she's a real live Kewpie doll, and a sweetheart to boot. Y'know, we all kinda felt bad for you after Polly and Cecil died—you just sorta went limp and didn't recover. Stryker says the old George is back, and I'm glad. If it took a little French lass to do it, then more power to her. So, may I say hello to your little bit of heaven?"

"Sure, Ace. She's right here. Claire, a good friend of mine wants to talk to you."

George was thinking about Ace's legendary charm while Claire shyly giggled into the phone. He showed his true potential the day George and Barry walked through the Williams's kitchen door and found him polishing off a plate of cookies with the words: "Delicious, Polly! No wonder George won't share his lunches." After that George always had to bring an extra piece of dessert for poor deprived Herbert who didn't have a mother to cook for him. But the real corker was hearing Herbert call George's mother "Polly": let them try that on somebody's mother and get barred from every house in town.

Herbert, then, became their ticket to freedom, the name invoked before every enterprise, like grace before dinner. Just say Herbert would be there and normally strict, suspicious parents would wave good-bye, smiling because their sons were friends with "that nice Gates boy." Even after grade eleven, when Herbert spent the summer fleecing everybody at camp with a marked deck and came back with a car, a pack-a-day smoking habit, and a smashing girlfriend who called him "Ace," the folks never caught on: they just applauded his hard work and initiative and continued to hold him up as an example.

It was Ace's plan to party till they passed out or vomited, whichever came first, at George's house while his parents were vacationing in the mountains of Tennessee. Ace was in the driveway saying: "Don't worry, Polly. I'll keep an eye on things."

Polly, not a complete fool, told George to check in with Mrs. Stryker regularly, and to have fun but behave himself.

George's dad told them to leave the place standing and don't run over the cat.

It was a blue sky Wednesday afternoon when the car rolled out of the driveway, not to be seen for another two weeks.

Friday night the four friends were sitting in George's living room, thinking of all the mayhem they could commit that wouldn't be traceable, when the phone rang and George picked it up, figuring it was his mom. It wasn't.

George identified himself, then was quiet. He asked the caller if there couldn't be some mistake. Then he said yes, yes, and yes, then slowly sat down on the chair beside the blondwood taboret, staring at the receiver in his hand. He began to rub his face with the other hand, then banged the receiver on the tabletop.

"Barry," he said hoarsely, "Ace, Goose, somebody." He waved the receiver up and down, then put it up to his face and yelled: "Wait a minute! My friend…is gonna talk to you." Ace took the receiver out of George's hands as George said, "I can't talk. I can't…talk." A huge knot had formed in his throat, pushing the tears out of his eyes.

Ace took the details while Barry and Angus put their hands on George's shoulders and tried to help their friend through a crisis they couldn't relate to, that George himself couldn't comprehend. The car had skidded off the road trying to avoid something, probably a deer. They almost didn't go over the edge, but the car must have flipped over, then crashed down the embankment. There was nothing but smashed pieces at the bottom, and the bodies in the car were completely mangled. Their identities were traced from the crumpled license plate and from Cecil's wallet, which was found with the contents strewn across the roots of a spruce, about twenty feet from the embankment. Cecil was in the habit of throwing his wallet on the dashboard, and it could easily have ended up on the ground before the car went over the edge. That detail made the accident visible to George. How awful their last moments must have been!

"It's not true! It can't be true! They never did anything to anybody!" He was banging his fist on the wall, his face getting redder.

The boys were lost. What could they do? It was time to call somebody's parents.

Mr. and Mrs. Stryker came over and George and his friends left the house.

George stayed at Barry's that night, and many nights after. Many nights he couldn't sleep and had pains in his chest. Finally he decided it was heartache, when he correlated the pains to his mom and dad. Just say their names and his mind froze on that night, on the wallet and the tree, and his chest would start to hurt.

Why couldn't he see anything else? Why was this the image he was left with, after sixteen years of comfort and closeness. It'll pass, they told him, and you'll start to remember the good times. He'd try, but nothing would happen, even looking at their pictures didn't help.

Then sometimes, all unbidden, they'd come to him: he'd see one or the other of them in the kitchen or the garden, smiling, explaining, dad with the pruning shears, mom in a dress with a lacy collar, opening the screen door. It only happened when he was alone and he could concentrate on their images, not their legal identities, the names on the death certificates. Polly and Cecil were buried in Safe Haven Cemetery, but mom and dad were still out there, looking as they always had, in hazy moments just for him.

Everyone was full of good advice, the main directive being to "stop moping." George couldn't believe the nerve of people and their chirpy hogwash. At least he knew it for what it was, and didn't torment himself for not "bucking up" or "pulling himself together." He didn't question his sanity or his manliness, though he knew other people were speculating about it. He just wanted to stop hurting.

The one thing that made it bearable was the Strykers' kindness. Two months after the accident Barry's father put his arm around George and said: "Son, I know it's no help to hear this, but you are never gonna stop missing your folks. I mean,

I'm an old man to you, but I still miss my mother. She's been gone ten years now, God rest her, and I didn't lose her anywhere near as young as you. Not a day goes by, George, I don't think of her. I figure she's in Heaven, dusting clouds, and pressing the angels' uniforms.

"Now, we know you're slated to go live with your aunt in Connecticut. But if you want to, George, you can stay on with us. We're kinda used to havin' you here, and hell, we can always use that spanking intellect to mow the lawn or fix the shingles. Hell, there's never enough men in a house, and there's always too damn many chores. Whaddaya say?"

George called his aunt Marj, and asked if she would feel hurt if he stayed on with the Strykers? Mr. Stryker told her not to worry, that George was like a second son. She was relieved. She said she wanted to talk to George when the will was settled, so they could find out what George wanted to do about the house. She said that George was lucky his father was so careful, that he'd been saving for the boy's college since he was born—and, can you imagine, there are actually people with families who don't leave a will?

Ed's ears were burning as he hung up the phone. He would have to speak to Myrna about finalizing that will. She couldn't bear to talk about it, but both Barry and Linda were still under age, and could he imagine them with his ailing dad, or that bickering idiot who married his brother? Jeez, please, let's get those kids on paper, just in case.

He looked at George, who was waiting to thank him. "Shucks, twarn't nothin', son."

George shook his hand and held it. The boy's eyes were clouding up, and Ed saw a way to save his dignity: "Now scram, Sam. Barry's down at Grover Park throwing passes, and if you don't get down there he'll have to catch 'em, too!"

George watched Claire on the phone, racking up the dollars. Ace was flattering the hell out of her, loving her accent. George took the phone back and Ace was laughing.

"So, George, ya gonna call 'em?"

"I thought you said I had twenty-four hours."

"Just dial the number, George. It'll come to ya."

George did and was overwhelmed by their enthusiasm. Well, his cousin Herbert thought so highly of him, and Herbert was just the nicest man. Could Mr. Williams please send his resume, references, and other pertinent data posthaste? Apparently their first choice had backed out and run home to Long Island, proving himself to be the low Yankee dog they'd always figured him for. George, however, was no "cranky Yankee." They interviewed him on the phone, and one day later called him and asked him to come down: the job was his if he wanted it. He did.

He asked Claire how she would manage so far away from her family.

She shrugged and said, "Bouf, no problem. We don't like it we just come back, dat's all. Florida, Maine, Vermont, it doesn't madder, George. I'm wit' you. Da rest is notting."

"I hope you always feel that way, Claire."

They were holding hands, George on the end of the bed and Claire on the floor, glasses and plates and newspaper all around her.

"Dat's hup to you," she giggled, reaching up to kiss him. "I love you, George. Now help me wit' dese boxes. Take dat stuff from da drawers. Not now, George, we 'ave to pack! *Sacre bleu*, I knew we should 'ave left dis room for last!"

And Baby Makes Three

They bought the house on Azalea Circle, though it wasn't exactly "dirt cheap" as Ace had said. George became the arguable hit of Brayton High, and Claire began singing in the choir of Our Lady of The Palms. Her voice was so astounding it was described by one columnist as "a link between Heaven and earth" and she quickly escalated from featured soloist to featured attraction. She was in such demand at church functions and ritzy parties that the Williamses became minor celebrities. Everyone wanted to hear Claire sing, and they loved to hear her talk. George didn't need to worry about her adapting anymore, because nobody wanted her to adapt. She was like an exotic bird to them, and they wanted to keep her strange.

George clipped out the articles where her name appeared

and taped them in a scrapbook for her birthday. He took her to La Mirage that night, an elegant French restaurant on the ocean, and they barely got to their table before people began stopping them to congratulate her. Would she honor them with a song later in the lounge? Claire smiled and said she would try.

She smiled over the candlelight at her husband while they toasted each other with a bottle of Royal de Neuville.

"To you, Claire," said George, raising the glass of rosé. "My own personal link between heaven and earth."

Claire twisted her mouth and said: "George, dat silly man wrote dat in de ad. You're much smarter dan him. Say somet'ing else."

"How about to Claire, the woman I love?"

"Dat's better. How 'bout to Claire, da mudder of my child."

"What?"

"You heard me, George. Da doctor says he's gonna be here in June."

"He? Sooo. You're one of those people who can tell the future."

"Don't joke, sometimes I can. Anyway, I feel it, dat's all. My mudder knew which every one of her kids was, except Michel."

George would have liked to say that's because a zookeeper left him in a basket and threatened your folks with bodily injury if they didn't adopt him, but he didn't. Every family had its spoiled darling whose charms were a mystery to everyone else. George firmly hoped that on their next visit to Montreal, Michel would be either on his way to camp or reform school.

In any case, Claire was wrong. Rachel Marie Williams was born with all her working parts intact, especially her lungs, at 2:25 A.M. on June twenty-second.

Eleven years later Claire was right, and Carla Lizette Madeleine became their second summer baby.

Rachel studied the little red-faced prune in the crib and said: "When does it start to look human?"

George laughed and put his finger to his lips. "Don't let your mother hear that, by golly. She'll think I put you up to it."

"Well, gee, Daddy, with her eyes puffed up like that she looks worse than the fish!" Rachel shook her head and frowned. "Are you sure she's all right? Was I like that?"

"Yes, Hon, yes you were. That's the way we all get started. Pink and pruny, just like her."

"Then why am I always hearing how beautiful babies are? Who makes this stuff up? I mean, look at her, Daddy. Is Mommy gonna come in and say how beautiful she is?"

"Rachie, it's not how she looks, it's what she means to us. She's just a little prune right now, but you'll see. Every day she'll get prettier and prettier. I mean, how can she not be pretty? Look at your mother."

"But I don't look like Mommy. Everyone says I take after you. So am I pretty?"

"Yes, Rachie. You're pretty." He knew she wanted to hear that, but he really didn't know how to answer her. She had his square face, thin lips and sandy hair, her mother's fine nose and dark brows—but where those amber eyes came from he had no idea. Both he and Claire had hazel eyes—his browner, hers greener—but Rachel's eyes had little brown or green, they were almost yellow. The effect was startling when she squinted, like small suns. He reckoned that Rachel would be smashing one day because her mother, quite simply, wouldn't have it any other way.

George was right: Rachel's tomboy days were numbered—that Montreal flair was about to descend without mercy. On Rachel's thirteenth birthday Claire came home with a new kid, having dropped the old one off piece by piece at the mall. Gone were the pigtails and tennies and the plaid shirt with pockets that bounced lightly at every step. Her cinnamon hair was styled in a pageboy, her budding bosom was imprisoned in elastic, and she had on a yellow dress with a full skirt. Her lips looked wet, her lashes were dark, and she was smiling, pleased with herself and her mother's efforts.

Claire was absolutely beaming. "Look what we found at

da mall, a young mademoiselle. We traded her in for Rachel. We got a pretty good deal, dey only hask for our car an' t'ree years discount coupons."

George was dazzled. "Hey, let's get out the camera. Rachel," he grinned, spinning her around the floor, "I told you you were pretty, but you are smashing today! Here, now, Claire, grab the baby, and all three of you stand together, and I'll have a picture of the three prettiest girls in Jacksonville. Hold it now. Steady. Say 'cheese.' Voila!"

New Horizons

Rachel was nineteen when she left for McGill, and Carla sat in her lap in the airport lobby, the top of her head touching Rachel's chin, her freckled face pink from crying. Rachel had her arms around Carla, and their identical sun streaked curls made a wavy line around their faces.

Claire looked across at her daughters and whispered in George's ear: "Don't dey look like two heads in a hair poncho?"

George grinned and got up to get drinks and lozenges. It was a half hour to boarding and his throat was parched in the dry cold of the terminal.

Claire cursed these indoor "atmospheres." They made her nose drip. She had developed what they called "a summer cold." Against her will George had carted her off to a doctor who was one of her fans and loaded her up with prescriptions. Once Claire saw that the prescriptions weren't curing her, she threw them out. Her own remedies were simpler and a lot cheaper: homemade chicken soup, hot toddies, hot tea with lemon and honey; and honey-lemon lozenges. She became a honey-lemon lozenge junkie, carrying them in the pocket of her husband's old cardigan, along with a roll of toilet paper. She would sneeze on a few squares of paper, then stuff the wadded squares in the other pocket.

"*Merde!*" she cursed, having dug her hand in the wrong pocket. She started to shiver and draped the sweater around her, thankful it went over her knees. She smiled at her girls. How sweet they looked together.

It would be months before Carla saw her sister again, and they knew she would take it hard, but none of them knew how hard until that morning. Carla watched Rachel stuff all her closet things in a garment bag and the rest of her belongings in a suitcase. From the hallway Claire and George could hear Carla asking: "Are you taking that? Can I help? What can I do, Rachel? When will you be back? Will you come on Halloween to make our costumes? Are you taking that? Rachel, why are we going to the airport? Daddy said you were going up on your scholar ship. Oh. Will you come home for Thanksgiving? Not till Christmas?" When the word Christmas sank in the crying started.

Carla had never been separated from her sister for more than a couple of weeks, and Rachel took Carla everywhere. She taught her how to read, to play checkers and "Fish," took her to movies, walked with her hand-in-hand through the local mall, instructed her on what to wear, and helped her find sharks' teeth in the sand.

Rachel even took to wearing straw hats when the sun was high to convince Carla to wear one. When other kids tried to make fun of them for wearing hats instead of getting properly burned and blistered, Rachel would say: "My Daddy says the sun is bad for you, and he teaches science, so he knows better than you do."

Carla could be heard saying roughly the same thing, except that it came out: "My sister Rachel says the sun is bad without a hat, an' she's way much smarter than you or anybody, so there too!"

George worried somewhat about how close Rachel and Carla were, although he had to admit they couldn't find a better babysitter. Claire, on the other hand, reveled in it. Her greatest fear had been that Rachel's bookish nature would recoil from the messy realities of a baby and the added demands on her time. On the contrary, Rachel's snobbery was of such egregious dimensions that nothing was good enough for her sister. The whole neighborhood gained the mixed blessing of Rachel's supervision, because Carla's playmates were taught right along with her, which meant that they all sang "Rudolph, The Red Nosed Reindeer" till they got it right.

The only time Rachel stopped playing Follow-the-Leader was at exam time, when she and her father would hibernate in their respective lairs, Rachel growling out facts in her bedroom, and George humming tunelessly, sometimes laughing (and sometimes cursing) behind his study door.

Carla would wander from door to door, not daring to knock. The last time she gained access to the bedroom when Rachel was studying caused such a violent argument between her mother and sister that Carla wouldn't chance it again.

It happened when Carla was four, and Rachel was studying for finals. Carla asked Rachel if she could come in the bedroom and color, as long as she promised to sit in a corner by the window and not talk. Rachel agreed, but said that if Carla made one peep she would be out.

Claire was dotting cloves on a pork roast when she heard Rachel yell: "No, Carla , you can't do that! That's a library book! Now give it to me!"

"No!" screamed Carla.

"Give it to me!" yelled Rachel.

There was the sound of something being dragged across the floor, then Carla's scream tore through every nerve in Claire's body. Claire swore, wiped her hands on the towel, and marched into the girls' bedroom just as Rachel hit Carla across the face. Carla had been bent double trying to hold onto the book. Her arms fell away, her head fell back, and then came that ear-splitting shriek.

"So!" snarled Claire, "Dis is how you treat your sister when I'm not around! You miserable *mechante*! You wanna fight wit' someone a liddle more your size, maybe? Well, try dis!"

She raised her small right hand and hit Rachel with incredible force across the face. "Dere!" she hissed. "How you like dat! Want some more?"

Claire bent down to pick up Carla, and gathered up the book along with her. "I'll deal wit' you lader, Rachel," she said over Carla's shoulder. Carla was sobbing with her thumb in her mouth.

"*Viens, ma petite,*" said Claire, kissing the little pink face. "We find somet'ing fun to do beside fight wit' dis ol' dragon." As she walked down the hall Rachel could hear her saying, "So you put lipstick on Presiden' Kennedy. Big improvement. He looks more like Jackie, now. Maybe we draw a liddle box on his head an' he'll look even more like her. But we don't do it in dis book, all right? We get anudder book, one special made to color, just for you. Dere now, stop crying. She didn't mean it, she's just forgot wat it's like to be a liddle girl who can't read. Hokay?

"Stop crying now. You're gonna help me make a roast, an' I'm gonna teach you all da t'ing to make it taste good. Here, we take da chair an' you watch me. We're doctors, now, an' we must operate to save da life of dis roast. Here is your mask, Docteur Carla."

Rachel sat on her bed, wiping her eyes as she listened to the giggling from the kitchen. There was no lonelier place to be than on the wrong side of her mother, who could shame the devil back to Heaven with one of those furious slaps.

Rachel was jealous of Carla's sweet hours with their mother, try as she might to purge the feeling. Here she was, struggling to coax reluctant facts off their comfortable white pages when she'd hear those two munchkins giggling away as they came home from the beach or the mall or from playing jacks in the driveway. She looked at the picture of them hugging each other after coming third in the sand sculpture contest, waving the yellow ribbon that was now pinned to Carla's headboard.

Next to it was the big red button that became Carla's first guardian: whenever she momentarily vanished and the quiet became too audible, George or Claire or Rachel would yell: "Who wants to play Button, Button?" and Carla would come racing around the corner, pigeon-toed and bound to trip, holding up the red button and yelling: "Me! Me!"

Rachel started calling her Button, and she accepted it from Rachel, but would make a face if either her mom or dad called her "that baby name."

Rachel heard footsteps in the hallway and tried to look absorbed in her book, but over the pages she could see her mother and sister standing in the doorway, hand in hand.

"Go on, now. You tell her," said Claire, pushing Carla into the room.

Carla walked across the rug and stopped halfway between the bed and the door. She never took her eyes off Rachel, and her face began to pinken and pucker. "I sorry, Rachel. I won't do it again." She stuck her thumb in her mouth and looked back at her mother.

Rachel spread her arms and said, "C'mere, Button. I'm sorry I hit you. Kiss 'n' make up?"

Carla ran to Rachel and jumped up on the bed, snuggling under Rachel's chin as Rachel wrapped her arms around her. The two shed tears of relief.

"Uv you, Rachel." Sniffle.

"Uv you, Button." Sniffle.

Now, three years later, they were sitting in almost the same position.

Final boarding call sounded as George handed out the lozenges, two packets for Claire and one for Rachel. He bought some Life Savers for Carla, who said "Goody!" and stuffed the whole roll in her mouth.

"Hey, Button, you're supposed to suck those," said Rachel, as she listened to the candy cracking under her chin.

"At's boring," said Carla, turning her head and opening her mouth to shock Rachel. A pile of colored crescents swam in bubbles on Carla's tongue.

"Ack, that's awful!" Rachel put on a face of disapproval. "You wouldn't dare do that to Mommy!"

"At's right!" laughed Carla. "An' you're not Mommy."

"Nope, you and Mommy will be here having fun like always while I slave away over the hard books. I'll be freezing in the snow while you're playing on the beach. Hey, why are you crying? I should be the one."

People were filing out the gate, and Rachel lifted Carla off her lap. George stood up and handed her the garment bag. Claire stuffed a wadded Kleenex into the cardigan, then held Rachel's face in her hands, kissing her on both cheeks.

Rachel was now six inches taller than her mother and looked down into her eyes, sensing her fear. "Mom, don't be scared," she smiled. "God didn't bring me this far to blow me out of the sky."

Claire hugged her fiercely and forced a smile.

George hugged them both, and kissed Rachel on the forehead. "You'll do fine, Rachie. You're gonna be our ambassador of goodwill. Just remember that men are men in any language. Got that?"

Rachel smiled and said, "Yes, Dad," and picked up the little case Carla was struggling to hold. She bent down to kiss Carla.

Carla wrapped her arms around Rachel's neck, said, "Uv you, Rachel," and planted a gooey kiss on Rachel's cheek.

"Uv you, Button," said Rachel, and pulled away. She walked through the doorway to the line of tans holding bags of souvenirs.

"Rachel!" yelled George. "We'll be watching you from the roof. Call us when you get there."

Rachel turned, grinned and waved, then walked down the ramp and was gone.

Happy Halloween

It was late October. Claire was sewing up Carla's witch costume while Carla walked around the house improvising cackles. Outside the temperature had taken a swan dive into the fifties, and the sky was beginning to show its gray winter face.

"Honey, you gotta stop dat hee hee hee. Witches must 'ave udder t'ings to say. What did Rachel say last year? It must 'ave been good, you got alotta stuff."

"You don't wanna know, Mommy."

Claire grinned. "Dat bad, eh?" She looked over at Carla and said: "So tell me. She can't get in trouble now."

Carla waved the foil-wrapped paint brush at her mother and said, "'Trick or treat, I'm a wizard. Make it good or poof you're a lizard.' Another one goes: 'Trick or treat, loop de loop, fill these bags or you're dog poop.'"

"Bouf, dat's not so bad."

"Well, I didn't tell you the bad ones."

"Hmmm. Mebbe I don't want to know. *Viens*, I 'ave to fit dis on you. Turn around, stand still, an' put your arms out to da sides. Dere, like dat. Now, keep verrry still, so I don't pick you."

Carla was staring into the full length mirror beside the sewing machine, looking at the little crescent moons Rachel had glued on the black cone hat. She remembered asking Rachel if lady witches got to wear moons, because she thought only the men witches, the wizards, had them. Rachel said there were good lady witches called white witches, and they could wear moons if they wanted. If Carla was going to be a witch, then she was going to be a good witch. There were only going to be good witches in the Williams family. Carla asked why they were witches if they were good.

"Oh," said Rachel, "that's sort of sad. Any old woman who lived alone and cured people with herbs instead of drugs was considered to have bad magic working for her, and was called a witch."

"But if she cured people why did they think she was bad?"

"I don't know. I guess the doctors wanted to sell drugs and didn't want to lose money to the old women who made medicine out of herbs, so they called the herbs 'old wives' tales' and everybody believed the doctors, and nobody believed in the old women's herbs anymore, even when they worked. That's not to say there aren't bad witches who do terrible things, like cut up little children and drink their blood."

"Not really, though, eh? That's just on TV, eh?"

"Well, not quite. There are bad people out there, Carla, and you gotta be careful."

"No sirree!" cried Carla. "They'll never catch me, I'll fly like the wind!" She flapped her arms and ran around Rachel, yelling: "Try to catch me!"

Rachel made a grab for her, let her hand fall short, and laughed. "No, Button, they'll never catch you."

Carla never mentioned it again, but after Rachel left for McGill, Carla would lock the window at night, then look under the bed and in the closet, then after her prayers add a special p.s. to keep her safe from child-eaters.

Now she was tired of standing with her arms out, and asked her mother how much longer it would be. Then, as casually as she could, she asked The Question: were there really were bad witches and bad people who carved up little children?

"But of course," said Claire. "Dey make pies out of dem. We had one last week."

She grinned at Carla, who stuck out her tongue and said, "Mommy, I'm serious! I want a real answer."

"Okay, here it is: yes, dere are bad people, and yes, dey hurt children, but if anyone hever tries to hurt you, my girl, you just tell me an' I'll break his face wit' my own two hands. Is dat good enough for you?"

Carla wrapped her arms around her mother, and Claire yelled as the pins connected: "Yie! Yie!"

Romeo and Juliet

It was the third week of November and Rachel was on a Mount Royal park bench, watching brown leaves swirl across the straw-colored grass. She pulled her father's letter out of the binder and smiled again at the pictures: Carla at the Halloween party, Carla holding a beige lop-eared puppy whose name they couldn't agree on and did Rachel have any suggestions? George's personal favorite was Arful, because he never shut up. Claire wanted to call him Sultan, as if that would make him majestic. Carla wanted to call him Murph, because that was one of his noises, and maybe he was trying to tell them his name. So how were her studies? How was her money holding out? He hadn't heard much so he was assuming no news was good news, just don't mail home the laundry.

Rachel felt a twinge of guilt, then shrugged it off. How

could anyone concentrate on paper in a city like Montreal, where everybody danced? Look at that, she thought, even the leaves dance here. Blown briefly upright, a pair of dry curled maples whirled tip to tip across the walkway.

She sighed, wondering if Hoffman's course would be her undoing. So far her 4-point average was drowning in paper-work, mostly for Hoffman's class. She pored over the volumes on Shakespeare, hoping to break new ground, but it was like looking for a needle in ten haystacks.

"Well, don't worry," said Aaron, "that's all these dust makers ever did."

"Dust makers?"

"Yeah, all these books are turning to dust. In another hundred years they'll just be circus flooring. Plus who's gonna get an A in Hoffman's class? He's already said he doesn't give 'em. Not to nobody, not ever."

"Oh, come on. Surely he just said that to get us riled. Didn't he?"

She looked over at Aaron, who was slowly shaking his head. "Read my lips, Yankee Doodle. Not to nobody, not ever. Wish you'd transferred out now, or are you gonna be the one to smite the tyrant and get an A?"

"Well, now, I just might surprise you."

"And what if I distract you from this outsize, incredibly boring venture?" He was holding Rachel's hand, batting his eyes at her.

She batted her eyes back and purred: "What did you have in mind? Casting a spell?"

"Why Rachel, how perceptive. Of course, that's assuming nobody else has dibs on the laundry room." He grinned, and she blushed.

Rachel was living in the laundry room of her cousins' apartment on Durocher Street, four blocks off McGill campus. The neighborhood was called the student ghetto, and much of it was being torn down. The apartment of Colette and Alain, Rachel's cousins, was nine months from the wrecking ball. Rachel was saddened at the deterioration: at the scuffed marble stairs, ill-fitting doors, and lengthy cracks in the walls and mahogany staircase. It reminded her of those soot-covered mosaics in the New York subway, where the pride in those old walls shone even through the grime.

Of course, Colette said, Montreal buildings needed neither vandals nor neglect to wear them down. Slight seismic tremors passed through the region every day, and no building stood for any time that had no cracks. Anyway, she said, Montreal isn't about buildings, it's about people. It's about style.

Colette and Alain were typical young Montrealers, bon vivants on the cheap. Living in a nearly condemned building left them free to paint outrageous murals, hold raucous parties, and grow cannibis in three of their closets. They apologized for sticking Rachel in the laundry room, but she simply didn't need to be in a room with one of the closets.

"Aren't you afraid of the police?" Rachel asked.

"For wat?" Alain grinned. "Da worse dey'll do is take away da plants, charge us fifty bucks an' say don't do dat no more."

"That's all?"

"Hey, dey got serious problems to deal wit', real pushers, big money. T'ree closets is hardly a dope ring, eh? Of course, it's hard to go to confession when I make love to a girl I won't marry, drink tequila all night an' miss work next day, but Rachel, you're only young once, eh? You don't sin now, you won't be able to when you're older, an' den you won't 'ave notting to regret an' notting to remember, eider. So when you gonna bring your boyfriend by?"

Rachel blushed. How did he know about Aaron?

"You're holding hands on Sherbrooke Street for two hours in front of a restaurant, you must be too broke to eat or too shy to come here. He looks good, dis guy, sort of like me."

Colette shook her head and laughed, and motioned for Rachel to follow her into the kitchen. She handed her a large knife and placed her in front of the counter which doubled as a cutting board and was covered in vegetables. She passed

Rachel a glass of Dubonnet on ice—"Fueling the machine," she said. Then she pulled out the empty bottle of Bordeaux that was soaking in the sink, peeled off the label and pinned it to the bulletin board by the phone. "Dat was da wine we had last night: I t'ought it was pretty good."

"*Oui. Tres bon*," said Rachel, and she and Colette exchanged smiles.

"Good show, Rachel," said Alain, behind her. "Before you leave here, you'll be speaking French an' singing Charlebois."

Robert Charlebois was the Quebec rock star, the voice of all French Canadians who wanted English and European influence off their backs and out of the province. Rachel felt the psychic gnashing of teeth whenever she announced she was American. Not from her cousins, who had known her since childhood, but from practically every person she met who was not a relative.

One night, more than somewhat tipsy, she faced a bunch of these disgruntled patriots at a party and screamed: "All right, that's it, I've had enough! I'm American, and I've as much right to be proud of my country as you are of yours. I came here to study, not fight some goddamn political battle every time I walk into a room. But if you want a fight, I'm ready. Words, fists, or pies, I don't care. C'mon, stop grumbling, let's settle it here and now!"

Unlikely enough, it resulted in a round of applause as Rachel, holding a pie and ready to hurl it, became the hit of the party. Feisty displays were very French, so suddenly everyone was very happy with her. She had, after all, a French mother.

Neither Colette nor Alain insisted that she speak French but she did try—when she could summon the courage to make mistakes and be teased. She was truly embarrassed at her difficulty in following their endless banter, and she hated being left out while they giggled at things she couldn't catch. She was just starting to imitate the speech patterns and engage in limited conversation, but jokes were hopeless: straightforward thoughts were hard enough to follow, let alone thoughts with a twist.

Thank goodness she had fallen in love with an English-
man. Well, actually Aaron was Jewish, but he looked Gallic.
He had saggy blue bedroom eyes and a nose that had been
reshaped twice, once in a fight and once by the surgeon's
knife. He had a lean face, a pointed chin, and black hair that
fell in shiny petals to his shoulders. He had a brass ring in his
left ear, and laughed that it might be the closest he came to the
real thing. He wore velvet jackets in different colors, with
faded jeans and snakeskin boots. He carried a guitar which
served a multitude of functions—intriguing guys, serenading
girls, and pissing off his father.

Aaron's father let Aaron's band, Carnivore, play in the
back of one of his carpet warehouses. He didn't for a moment
believe that his only son would be anything but a doctor. So
Aaron went to McGill and took all the courses leading to
medical glory: it was the only way to get the warehouse and
equipment.

He never thought about where his energy was going until
he took Advanced Shakespeare and met David Hoffman, the
dwarfish and cantankerous embodiment of true commitment.
Hoffman was a bona fide Shakespearian scholar and actor,
and his entire purpose in that class was to rebuild their
vocabulary to appreciate The Bard. "Did you know," he
roared, "that Elizabethans had a vocabulary of over thirty-five
thousand words, many of which Shakespeare invented? Did
you know that we use approximately nine thousand, including
all our jargon?"

Nobody knew anything, they just stared at him, mesmerized by his voice and great caterpillar eyebrows.

"Did you know," he roared, "that we have The King James
Bible to thank for that, because they stripped the language
down to 8,000 words, so that every grade school poppet could
read the word of God, but not the words of one of His finest
sons.

"You have no doubt heard how English is not romantic, as
is French or Russian: I defy you to read Shakespeare and not
feel the romance, the sensuality. Some of the men's lines in

Shakespeare are so hot that to deliver them properly you practically need a standing erection; the passion of those women could make you melt.

"What I'm saying here, folks, is that these aren't just words, they're flaming, dancing explosions of the finest mind, the greatest genius the language ever produced. If you want to look at beauty with your eyes closed, be a lover, a king, a clown, a soldier, a drunk, old, mad, rich, poor, saint or devil, man or woman—you can be all these things in Shakespeare, you can feel them all. Come with me, now, and we'll meet the greatest temptress of all time. Open your books to *Antony and Cleopatra*, Act 2, Scene 2, line 186…"

Rachel came out of Hoffman's classes completely drained. Aaron said it was because Hoffman sucked all the air out of the class with his grandiose monologues.

Rachel narrowed her eyes. "You're jealous, Aaron. Jealous that he cares so much, that he can make us care."

Aaron laughed. "Bullshit, Rachel. I'm there because I have to be, because the time's bought and paid for. You think I care if that dried-up old windbag gets erections off Shakespeare? Bullshit!"

"It's not bullshit, Aaron."

"And how do you know? Your old man get his rocks off reading Einstein or something?"

"You leave my father out of this!" Rachel snarled, then continued: "The reason I believe that erection stuff is that I came once reading Hamlet."

"Oh yeah?" He sneered. "Tell me what did it, his sword or his finger?"

"You're such a pig! Will you let me finish? I'm trying to tell you how it happened. It was the part where Hamlet tells Ophelia it would cost her a groaning to take off his edge, and I felt like I was making it with him right there in the classroom. Thank God I was sitting down. It was wild."

"Shit, Rachel, that's some story. Tell me, do real people do as much for you? Could I?" He couldn't link this story to the Rachel that got flustered at dirty jokes and was always toting an armload of books. He was sure she was one of those miserable creatures, a virgin waiting for Mr. Right.

He shook his head. "All right, Mary Poppins, you win. What say we go for a walk and talk to the trees. Relax, you know? Or don't they do that sort of thing in the U. S. of A.? C'mon, everything doesn't have to be fraught with tension and learning all the time, does it? Why don't we just dump the books off at your place and, oh, I dunno, go for a quick spin in the dryer, maybe?" She blushed and he laughed. "So, is the no-good sex fiend still invited for dinner?"

"Yep. Hope you like spaghetti. We eat a lot of it at Colette and Alain's."

The spaghetti was Colette's special recipe, liberally sprinkled with cannabis. There were smoked oysters, clams, Caesar salad, egg bread and unsalted butter. Two bottles of beaujolais and one of chianti were lined up on the coffee table in front of the green velvet couch. It was seven-thirty and the house was dark but for the candles around the livingroom. They sat on the floor with their backs to the couch, dipping their bread in the clam sauce while Alain quizzed Aaron on his political views. Fortunately Aaron didn't have any, but he had one golden opinion: he liked some Charlebois songs.

Colette raised her glass to welcome Aaron. "Here's to a night to remember, dat's if we remember anyt'ing," she laughed, thinking of the 'oregano' in the spaghetti. When she heard the phone ring she groaned, "*Merde!*" and got up to answer it. "If I walk slow," she giggled, "maybe it'll stop."

It didn't. Ten rings later she picked up the phone and said, "Allo?"

A little girl's voice asked to speak to Rachel. For a moment Colette was lost, then she said, "Carla? Is dat you, Princess? *Un instant, ma petite*, I go get Rachel." She poked her head around the livingroom door and said, "Rachel, it's your sister. Shall I tell her to call back later?"

"No, I'll take it," said Rachel, and pulled herself out from under the table, nibbling Aaron's ear on the way up. He drew her face down and kissed her. Their tongues met, they reeked of garlic, and they didn't care. Rachel pulled away, flushed and smiling as she stumbled toward the phone.

Alain watched her unsteady passage and said to Aaron, "We call her Grace," and they laughed.

But Aaron was past being witty or social: he wanted the damn dinner over with, he wanted Rachel. "Fuck you, Hamlet," he said to himself, downing his glass of chianti. "Fuck you, you sour old Danish wimp. I say fuck you, she's mine tonight."

He was dimly aware that something was wrong in the kitchen, dimly hoped it would pass and leave him free to fuck Rachel. Suddenly the conversation came in loud and clear, and he knew that the little girl in the picture, the one proudly holding the puppy, was crying.

The Call

The kitchen light was on and Rachel could be seen in the doorway, telling her sister not to worry and fighting to hold back the tears. "Button, it's gonna be okay. Hey, wouldn't Daddy have phoned me if something was really wrong? Listen, Honey, people get ulcers all the time and they spit blood and the doctor gives them this white icky stuff to drink and they're fine afterwards. Really. Cross my heart and point to Heaven. Listen, now. Stop crying and listen.

"I'm gonna come home tomorrow, Button. No, I don't think anything's really wrong, I just know Mommy won't be up to making Thanksgiving Dinner, so you and I are gonna surprise her and make it for her, okay? Then she won't have to worry about us and she'll get better a lot quicker, y'know? We'll just hafta plan to take care of her for a little while so

Daddy can go to work and not worry, okay?

"She what? Oh, hey, sometimes people lose their hair when they take antibiotics. It's just temporary, it grows back. Yeah, well, those drugs are pretty strong. They make you dream, too. Button, those drugs are so strong they're gonna knock those cold germs out of Mommy and she'll probably never have another sniffle again. Now, won't that be great? So, you plan to see me tomorrow, just don't tell Daddy. Let's make it a surprise for him, okay? A Thanksgiving surprise.

"No, I'm not crying," she lied, tapping the mouthpiece with her finger, "We just have a bad connection. Now Button, you just think about the dinner we're gonna make, and don't worry, Mommy's gonna be fine. Yeah, I promise." Oh please God, she prayed, the tears pouring down her face, please God let it be the truth. "Carla, you okay, Honey? You sure? Okay, then hang up the phone 'cause this call is costing Daddy a fortune. Now, listen, if you get scared before Daddy gets home you call me, okay? And I'll be on the fastest plane that flies tomorrow, the one that flies like the wind. Yes, Carla, uv you too. Bye now."

She made a kissing noise and hung up the phone, then sat down at the kitchen table, put her head on her arms, and sobbed.

Colette and Alain and Aaron gathered around her. Colette offered to make the travel arrangements, and Alain had a schedule of shuttle flights to La Guardia. Assuming no delays, Rachel would be in Jacksonville by noon.

Aaron felt extraneous, even intrusive. He heard Colette and Alain rifling through all their hidden reserves and counting and swearing in French. Between them all they could come up with was twenty dollars, not nearly enough, and the banks wouldn't be open till ten. Aaron dug under the lining of his jacket and pulled out fifty dollars in small bills. From the toe of his boot he pulled the plastic card that would get Rachel her ticket. It would be a month before his old man eyed the bill and threatened to rescind the card again.

"Listen," said Aaron, addressing his hosts, "If it's all right

with you, I'll crash here on the couch and take her to the airport
in the morning. I can spring for a cab so she can get some more
sleep: if she takes one of those hotel limos she'll have to get
up at four. Oh, and I've got the ticket." He dropped the money
and the card on the table in front of Rachel and smiled at
Colette.

Colette hugged him, and Alain shook his hand, grinning.
"I told Rachel you were a good-looking guy."

It was 4 A.M. when Aaron felt someone shaking his arm.
Streetlight streamed through the French doors, making white
rectangles on the rug. Rachel's silhouette blocked the light.
Aaron's eyes travelled up her flannel nightgown, and he heard
her whisper: "I won't be back, Aaron. Not this semester,
maybe not for the rest of the year. My mom won't be able to
get well without help, and we're not rich, so there's no choice.
Besides, I want to be there. I have to be there. So you'll just
have to get the A in Hoffman's class. Oh God, I'm gonna miss
you, Aaron… so much…"

She knelt down in front of him. Tears dribbled off her chin
onto the nightgown. Aaron reached for one of the napkins on
the coffee table and dabbed her face, then formed the words
she couldn't say. "Yes, Rachel, I want to."

"Do you have, uh—"

"Sure. We boy scouts don't worship Akela for nothing.
Lemme go dig in the old cornucopia." He zipped open his
guitar case and pulled out a small square packet. "I bought it
for the design," he said. "I figure if Ramses could make the
pyramids last all those years it was a good omen for whoever
borrowed his name—good for at least an hour, anyway. Hey,
Rachel." She was holding her arms, shaking. "Rachel, I'm
sorry. I don't mean to make light of this. I just, dammit, I wish
we had more time. I wish you weren't going. God how I wish
you weren't going."

He crossed the squares of light, tearing off his clothes
while she peeled off her nightgown. They rolled over and over
on the carpet, kissing every part of each other, spitting out
carpet fuzz. Rachel tore the sheet off her bed and Aaron spread

it on the carpet. Then he pressed himself inside her, pressed her buttocks together and groaned: the moment was too strong, he'd come too quick. He wanted to apologize, to bring her off orally, but she was shivering and crying, so he got the crocheted comforter and wrapped it around them. He held and rocked her till she stopped crying, then the alarm went off.

Rachel stepped into the old tub with its hose-attachment shower and sprayed away the sweat and carpet fuzz, then powdered herself with Colette's little dish of mixed scents.

With much hugging and hollow cheer Colette and Alain loaded Rachel into the cab, closing her fingers around the last of their cash.

It was 6:42 A.M. when she and Aaron shared their last kiss, and 7:14 when the plane left the ground. She could still taste his tongue, wished it was still inside her mouth. She had a window seat and pulled the shade to keep from being blinded every time the purple clouds dipped below the wings. She cupped her hands around her mouth and her breath smelled as bad as her mouth tasted.

The plane bounced and tilted, the seatbelt sign flashed and chimed, and suddenly her breath was the least of her problems. For all the nights she'd looked out those windows at lights below and thought Hell, if I died it wouldn't matter, there'd be millions to replace me, suddenly it mattered very much. Hang in there, Mom. I'm on my way.

Fair Mal

It was ten minutes past twelve when the plane taxied into Jacksonville International Airport. The sun was high and Rachel's eyes were aching. She got in the limo headed downtown and as they approached the St. John's River gag-inducing odors assaulted the car. "Ah," she winced, "home sweet home."

She got out at the Hilton, checked her bags in the cloak-room, and walked down the road to the hospital. It was a lovely tree-lined area on the river: it would be nice to forget why she was there.

She couldn't, though, and with mounting dread walked through the glass-walled entrance and asked if Marie Williams was registered. She most certainly was, she had just been moved from intensive care that morning, and her condition was listed as stable. She was on the fifth floor and—Miss, Miss, are you all right, Miss?

Rachel felt her temperature rising as she raced for the elevators. She debated about taking the stairs, then got on the elevator. That five-floor haul seemed to take forever, as one person after another got on or off and the doors rumbled slowly open and shut.

She followed the colored stripe down the hall to the next series of signs. She stared at them and blinked: nothing registered. Suddenly her father materialized with a doctor, walking toward her. My God, how bad he looks, how old. He can't have been getting any sleep. Oh, Daddy.

He saw her as a figure in the corridor, but wasn't looking for her so she didn't register. When she ran toward him he recognized her, and his face crumpled into lines. "Oh, Rachel," he whispered as she flew into his arms. She felt him shaking as he hugged her. "Oh, Rachel, thank God you're here, it's been a nightmare. You... you haven't seen her yet, have you?"

There were tears around his eyes as he said: "Rachel, before you go in there let me tell you what's happened. Remember she had chest X-rays in August for that lousy endless cold of hers and they didn't find anything? Remember how she said that by the time the damn machines found something it would be so big it would be in everything but her toes?

"Well, I took her to an allergist in September. He prescribed some medications, and I thought the drugs were making her drowsy. Six weeks ago I find out she wasn't even taking them! Carla told me!"

"That's not so strange, Daddy. Carla's a sharp little cookie. I'm here because she called me."

"Well, how 'bout that? Chalk two up for little old Button." A brief smile lit his face, and he hugged Rachel. "Damn, I have great kids." He stepped back and released her, then spread the fingers of his left hand over his heart. He winced.

"Rachel," he whispered, "I have to sit down while I tell you the rest. Every time I think about her pain I get this big hurt in my chest, you know, like men who experience their wives' pregnancy pains? It's just psychosomatic. There's no good scientific reason for it. I've had my heart checked, and there's nothing to worry about, believe me."

George walked her to the non-smoking lounge and sat down on one of the chairs. He pulled up a chair for her and she sat down, holding his hand.

He sucked in his breath and resumed his story. "The technical name for her condition is non-Hodgkins lymphoma, a very pernicious form of cancer. If they'd caught it in the initial stages they might have been able to burn and poison it out of her, but it got hold of her midway between her heart and her lungs, and grew like Georgia kudzu. Now part of it's crushing her left lung and part of it's in her right lung, cutting off her air. Oh, Rachel, she's gonna drown in the crap she brings up or choke to death fighting to get the air in. If they put her on a respirator she won't be able to make a sound, and we won't know if she has something to say to us, so I won't let them do that.

"She has lucid moments, very few: the morphine's got her so gaga that most of the time she just rambles off in French and I can barely understand it. I'm afraid if they cut it back and let her be more lucid she'll be in terrible pain. They think the cancer's in her brain, and the end is very near, so she's in a private room.

"Rachel, it's just unbelievable how fast it all happened. A week ago she was coherent, playing cards. Suddenly she was spitting blood. Later that night she had a seizure. They rolled a cot in the room for me and I haven't left.

"Carla's living at the Beasleys. Thank God for Dwight and Cathy, they just keep feeding her chocolate chip cookies and telling her Claire's okay. I have to tell her the truth, I know, but it wasn't until this morning that I knew it myself. Shit, Rachel, I just kept waiting for the drugs to take hold. Every hour, studying her face, watching it bloat from chemo, watching her eyes blacken, watching her hair fall away in strands and bits.

"She never complained, y'know? She joked that all there'd

be left after World War III would be her and the cockroaches. I asked why her and she said there had to be someone left to step on them. Isn't that just her?"

He ran a hand through his hair and made a futile attempt at composure. The tears started again, and he wiped his eyes and looked at her. "I'm sorry, Rachel—the minute I saw you it came tumbling out. I didn't want her to know I was crying, y'know? I didn't want her to see that, even when she was delirious.

"I know, Rachel, when I touch her, even if she doesn't seem to respond, or wanders off in a fantasy, that some part of her knows I'm there, some part of her wants me there.

"She looked up last night, about three, and said, clear as a bell: 'Don't worry, George. Everyt'ing's gonna be hokay.' Then she put her arms out and made some kind of whimpering noise, and Rachel, I knew, don't ask me how, that she wanted me to hug her, so I did.

"I have to go back now. I don't want her to be alone, not for a minute." He squeezed Rachel's hand and tried to smile to show how grateful he was that she was there. "Come with me, Honey. Just be ready for a shock, because it is a shock."

They walked into the anteroom and Rachel was struck by all the flowers, cards, and dish gardens crowding each other along the wall. She couldn't believe her mother wouldn't be sitting up, revelling in all this tribute. But then she turned the corner and saw Claire. She stopped dead, staring at her mother, who looked smaller than ever and oddly naked without her hair.

Claire was asleep, her mouth open, and as Rachel approached she could hear a soft, wheezing gurgle. A thin brown line seeped from Claire's lips down the side of her face and onto the collar of her gown. George grabbed a tissue off the tray and dabbed away the drool.

"She'd hate that," he whispered, looking at Rachel who managed to nod, barely. She couldn't equate this ravaged woman with her mother, and suddenly understood why her father hadn't told her or her sister. Somehow he must have hoped that he would walk into the room one morning and Claire would be herself again, sitting up, joking, with all her hair. It just didn't happen, and what her life had come down to was this hourly agony of aspiration.

To accommodate the process Claire was tied by the waist and shoulders to the top half of her mattress. The top of the bed was cranked as high as it would go, and pillows behind Claire's head and back kept her upright to get that last little bit of air into a space at the top of her lungs, a space no bigger than a dime.

Nurses were suctioning the space hourly. Claire tried to fight them off as they forced the tube down her nose, tried to push them away by flailing her arms, while George stood there helpless, hating the nurses for hurting her, and hating himself for not stopping them.

He held her hands after they were gone—gently, because they were so puffed. He told her how sorry he was, and looked at the bruises that seemed to grow on her arms as he watched. Now for twenty minutes she would breathe without that rasping gurgle.

There were moments when she lay absolutely still, and George hoped it was over for her. But then her chest would heave and the rasp would start again, and George was grateful, for all her pain, that she was still with him. He'd wince, turn his face toward the flowers at the end of the bed, and cry.

Rachel looked at the heap of plastic tubing on the tray table over the vacuum bottle. In that bottle was the brackish runoff of her mother's lungs, and it was over half full. The gurgling in Claire's throat was becoming more audible, and above the gurgle came a moan. It came in two parts, like syllables: Fuh mah. She did it again: Fuh mah.

Rachel went to the other side of the bed, gently put her hand on her mother's bruised arm, leaned over and kissed her. As she leaned back her mother's eyes slowly opened and Claire looked directly at her daughter. A tear rolled down Claire's face. She opened her mouth and moaned again. Fuh mah. Fuh mah.

Rachel looked over at George. "Daddy, what's she saying?"

"Rachel, she's been saying that ever since the second seizure. I think she means her throat's on fire, *fumer*, that's what they told me aspiration feels like. Hell, it's the only thing I can think of." He looked at Claire, who looked back at him, reaching up to touch both his face and Rachel's.

Fuh mah, she wheezed.

Rachel felt her scalp contract: she knew what it was. Her eyes filled with tears as she said: "Mommy, I understand. We'll fix it."

She looked over at her father and said: "*Fait mal*, Daddy. That's what she's been trying to say. It *hurts*. Cross my heart, I'd stake my life on it. Please, Daddy, have the doctor double that pain medication."

George didn't move. He had Claire's hand against his face and was afraid to let go.

"Now!" screamed Rachel. "Daddy, go now! If we're only looking at hours here what's the difference?"

The tears poured down George's face. Why hadn't he understood? What the hell could have been more obvious? "Coma my ass!" he snarled. He whispered to Claire that he was sorry, and begged her to forgive him, that he'd make it better now. Slowly he placed her puffed green hand on the pillow and ran for the doctor.

Dr. Merkle knew that nothing could make the dying woman comfortable now, but sent a nurse to the pharmacy for morphine. He knew that it would only slow Claire's respiration and hasten her end, but at least the family's pain would be addressed.

Forty minutes later the nurse came with the morphine. As she walked through the door she heard the wailing of the family, and knew that the little Williams woman was dead. She walked to the foot of the bed to confirm what she already knew and saw the husband, his cheek tight against the dead woman's, holding her in his arms, rocking her and moaning. The young woman on the other side of the bed was face down on the patient's knees. Her long red hair covered the patient's shrivelled calves and she was crying, "Oh Mommy." The little bald woman stared straight over the man's shoulder and the nurse was struck by the marblelike similarity of corpses' eyes: maybe it was the lighting.

Lilacs in November

Because of what happened to his parents, George and Claire had a joint will which specified open caskets if the bodies were intact, and two days' viewing to give people the chance to say goodbye. Afterwards they were to be cremated and the ashes scattered "anywhere they loved."

Then, with Claire's family and her daughters, George placed her ashes under the bare lilacs in the back yard.

A week later he was stunned to discover a small insurance policy in Claire's box of personal letters. She had started it when her sinuses began to bother her. That piddly sixty dollars was about to become ten thousand, more than enough for the hospital costs.

George stared at his name on the beneficiary line, fixing on the large looped capitals of her beautiful script. She never scrawled, not even notes: in her hand even the simplest message was a work of art.

He looked past the letter to the cardigan on the sewing table and wondered if she knew, even then. She seemed to have a sixth sense about so many things. Of course, it didn't always work, as he was fond of pointing out. So why in hell did it have to work this time? George took up the cardigan, buried his face in her smell, and cried.

Rachel was trapped between Carla and her father, feeling she had to be silent to let the others act out their pain. She wrote long letters to Aaron, who called her frequently and advised her against playing the white knight. Armor's more cumbersome in the end, he said.

"What the hell do you know about it!" Rachel screamed: "Who did you ever lose?" and hung up on him. His letter of apology came quickly, but Rachel didn't answer for months.

Carla's reaction to Claire's loss was terrible. It started when she saw her mother in the coffin. She touched the wig and ask why Mommy was wearing a hair hat. Then she touched her face and told her to get up.

Rachel said no, it wasn't possible, that Mommy had gone to Heaven.

Carla said no, Rachel was wrong, Mommy was right there.

Rachel tried to explain that Mommy's body was there, but that God had taken her voice and her soul, and all the things that made her special, up to Heaven to be with the angels, to sing in their choir, rather than leave her all sick and hurting on earth. She was hurting very badly, Carla. It was the only way to stop the hurt. God had to stop it, the doctors couldn't.

Carla held her mother's hand and stared at the still face for several minutes, then turned to her father and said: "Daddy, it's a mistake. Dead people are supposed to be cold. Feel her. She's not cold."

George didn't move so Carla grabbed his hand and pressed it down on her mother's face. A chill went through him, for she did not seem cold at all: in fact there seemed to be a kind of energy emanating from her, like the static aura around a color TV.

"See, Daddy?" said Carla.

George stared, wondering if it wasn't some kind of electrical discharge they were emitting themselves. He said: "It's nothing, Honey, just some kind of static in the air. Believe me, she's dead."

"Why should I believe you?" snapped Carla, looking from her father to her sister and back at her mother. "You said she'd be cold if she was dead. Well, she's not cold so she's not dead, and you tell God He made a mistake, and to give her back. He doesn't need her: He's got plenty of angels to sing for Him. Go on, Daddy, tell Him to give her back so's we can all go home. I know she's hungry." Carla tried to shake her mother's arm, as she had so many mornings. "C'mon, Mommy, get up."

Rachel and George looked at each other, and waited for the truth to sink in on Carla. After twenty minutes of entreating the still figure with promises to be good and clean and make her bed and walk the dog without being asked, she lowered her head on her mother's chest and cried hysterically. An hour later George asked her if she wanted to leave. She screamed no, she didn't want to leave her mother there, couldn't they take her home?

"No, Honey," said Rachel, "this is where she has to stay till the funeral's over and she's cremated."

"NO!" screamed Carla, for they'd explained cremation to her: "NO! You're not gonna burn my mommy!"

"Honey, she's dead, she can't feel anything anymore," said George and Rachel in one voice. "It won't hurt her: we promise."

Carla didn't believe them, and George finally had to carry her screaming out of the building. She was furious with him and Rachel, and refused to sleep in her bedroom. She lay on the couch in the livingroom, staring at the ceiling, wishing she knew a way to rescue Mommy.

Finally she pulled the musty old sleeping bag down from the hall closet and let herself out the back door. She unrolled the bag on the back porch and lay down, holding Murph-Arful-Sultan, who yapped and yowled and gurgle-growled until she let him go.

In the morning she went to her father and said she was
sorry for the way she'd acted: she knew he wouldn't hurt
Mommy. If Mommy was watching from Heaven, she wouldn't
be mad at her, would she?

"No, Carla," said George, "where Mommy is now there's
nothing but love, and she's not mad at anybody."

"Would she be happy if I call Murph Sultan?"

"Honey, she'll be happy with you whatever you call him.
You wanna call him Sultan?"

Carla made a face then looked at the ceiling. Up there,
somewhere, Mommy was listening. "Mommy," she said,
"You win. We'll call him Sultan."

As if in answer, a breeze came through the window,
carrying the scent of lilacs. But there were no blossoms, all the
leaves were gone. Every tree and bush along the back fence
was bare. George and Carla stood transfixed in the sweetness
of the perfume.

Rachel came into the kitchen, smelled the lilacs, and
looked around in amazement. She felt herself being hugged
softly, sweetly, and it didn't stop at her skin: every organ in her
body was being massaged and perfumed by lilacs. She saw the
smiles of the other two and knew they felt the same. George
beckoned Rachel over and wrapped his arms around his
daughters. Then the three of them, hugged by invisible lilacs,
stared out the window till the smell and the sensation passed
away.

A Misplaced Scandal

George thought about that morning often in the months to come. He wished there were more (he hated to use the words) comforting visitations, but if they did turn up they must have come when no one was home.

All of them cried, usually when they were alone, especially Carla. She didn't want to tell them but she was still upset about the cremation. Daddy and Rachel didn't seem to be, but they certainly didn't know everything about pain: they didn't know when Sultan howled because of a burr in his paw how much he was hurting. So how did they know about Mommy, if she couldn't speak? One day, she decided, if I ever meet God, that's the first thing I'm gonna ask him about.

Rachel was also perturbed, less about her mother than her father. He was thin as a rail no matter how much food she tried to force on him, or how much he tried to eat to please her.

She attempted to duplicate her mother's recipes, but the one day she managed to perfect a "Meal a la Mom" it was a terrible mistake: the flavor was identical and they all looked at Claire's chair, wishing she would laugh and sit down.

A month later George exiled the chair to the tool shed. When Carla asked where Mommy's chair had gone, George explained that he simply couldn't eat and look at that chair, he missed Mommy too much.

Actually George felt his whole life was coming apart. The gradual disintegration he expected with age was accelerating in the chaos around him. His job, for one thing, had changed. Five years ago his students acted as though he had something to contribute to their lives and the world. Now, thanks to the computer revolution, discussion was out and grades were in. Those who excelled at rote did well while those who couldn't found ingenious ways to cheat or dropped out.

Teachers as role models were dead: they were old, wrinkled and poor. Old threats like "Bring in this assignment or you fail" fell on deaf ears. Threaten away, fogey. Failure, suspension, expulsion, none of it mattered because school was just a pre-party interval, a place to line up the next score, and make the old dogs think they were raising puppies instead of parasites. The most activity George ever saw in their faces happened the day they were threatened with a strip search of their lockers, following the death of one of their classmates.

Ronnie Argus was found dead in the boys' locker room. How he got in there nobody knew because his mother (who later turned out to be his girlfriend) had said he was at home in bed with a fever. Actually he was on a boat in a marina with his girlfriend and three other 'good buddies' doing some coke, a little weed, and washing it all down with some great Mexican beer. Ronnie was the youngest of the group, and bragged that he had "Injun blood" in his veins, that no drug would ever hurt him because he and the snake were brothers. Of course that story came from Castenada, whose bogus mushroom hallucinations made instant Indians out of every druggie in the country.

Ronnie was ready for something new that morning, peanut butter and jelly. Everybody ate it, but who'd have the guts to inject it? They sat there and watched him and laughed, and when he shuddered and keeled over they realized they'd have to get him off the boat, and dump him somewhere that wouldn't connect them. School was the perfect place.

Everybody else was watching the football game when they carried their friend into the locker room. They dumped him naked in a shower stall, turned on the water and drew the curtain. Then they went out, sat in the bleachers, and lined up their next score.

The Brayton Bucks won that day, their first game against the less-than-mediocre Greystone Wolves. The boys came back jumping, howling and hitting each other. They were oblivious to the steam billowing through the locker room.

It was only when they left to celebrate that the coach yelled, "Hey hey hey, the gang's all here, so who the hell's in the shower?" He walked to the curtain and yelled, "Hey you, get outta there!" When there was no response he pulled back the curtain and said: "Holy shit!"

He yelled at the boys to stay back, but this was too good to miss, and they piled up behind him as he turned off the tap. Through the vapor clouds they saw a face only one of them knew—and wow, it was dead, just like in the movies.

"Jeez," said the team captain. "Ya think one of the Wolves got pissed?"

The shock that went through the school when the story got around was minor compared to the shock of the school board faced with a three million dollar lawsuit. The Argus family suit didn't stop there: they wanted charges brought against the coach, the principal, the janitor, and any teacher who had shirked his duty that day by not running a dead-kid check in the building every ten minutes.

George was absent that day, part of what his friend Al Herndon called "grieve leave," and Al couldn't resist calling to tell him the story. There was a proposal to strip-search the kids' lockers, and suddenly parents who didn't know The

Constitution from reconstituted orange juice were picketing the school. The one thing these instant civil rights activists definitely knew was that their little darlings couldn't be involved in anything so heinous, and only over their dead bodies would those lockers be searched. "For God's sake," laughed Al, "Don't let 'em die on the premises, or kids who can't say masturbate'll all be yelling litigate."

George chuckled and "yupped" (he hoped) in the right places, but he was having trouble paying attention. Images of Claire kept disrupting his train of thought. Al began to catch the drift and as a tack-on before goodbye he gently advised George to get some counselling.

George sat with the phone in his hand and felt the pains starting in his chest. Al was right. The problem was, George didn't want to talk about Claire to anyone who hadn't met her. He could see this dispassionate person with a notepad making judgments about his sanity, and he would not insult Claire by having someone describe her as a vision of grief. Yes, he was grieving, but not for any image: Claire had left a hole in their lives the size of The Grand Canyon, and how do you describe that to someone who's never seen it, when pictures only give a flat rendering?

He found himself looking for her in places she would never be, following women in supermarkets and students in hallways that reminded him of her. He never allowed himself to get close enough for the fantasy to be dashed.

He also found it helped him to sit in his studio and talk to the fish. They were so calm, fat, substantial. A little shake of food and they would last forever.

By the following October George was still grieving, and it was getting worse. He was literally losing his grip. He would pick up objects and watch them fall as though they were an image on a TV in another room. Twice he had cut himself this way and when the glass splinters gored his feet, felt nothing.

He began to experience the same sort of numbness while driving. He'd feel the ends of his fingers on the wheel but was almost too tired to hold or turn it. He just wanted to put his head down on the wheel and go to sleep. Three or four times he pulled off the road and sat there till darkness fell, then drove home to the worried hugs of his daughters.

He was sorry he wasn't more supportive of them but it was all he could do to walk from room to room. Noises bothered him, light bothered his eyes. He drove to work and couldn't remember the trip, taught all day and couldn't remember a class. He was too tired to care about much of anything, and no amount of sleep seemed to help.

He would excuse himself early in the evening and lie down on his bed, hoping that sleep would find him, a deep, quiet sleep, but he'd start to drift off and a muscle spasm would wake him, or the dog would yap at a falling leaf and Carla would yell at him to shut up, Daddy's sleeping!

When he woke up he was miserable, because even when he had bad dreams about Claire, at least he could touch her and tell her that everything would be all right: waking up was the real nightmare.

Eventually George went to grief therapy sessions and found to his relief that his agony was normal, that he was suffering from a depression commensurate with the loss of a treasured spouse. There were even people there who had lost a mate they weren't happy with, it was just too late now to rectify anything. All of them had in common that sense of detachment, like their bodies were operating without them.

After one of these sessions George came home to find a message on the refrigerator from Principal Kelbrough. He dialed the number and Kelbrough answered himself, which surprised George because usually there was a female voice to intercede.

"Hello, Martin," said George. "I got your note. What's up?"

"Uh, how are your counselling sessions going, George?"

"Well as could be expected, I guess. At least I'm not crazy, just massively unhappy, and they say the cure is time and talking it out, so that's what I'm doing. Why?"

"George, we have a problem. I'm not even sure how to tell you this… "

"Look, Martin, not to worry: I can take it, whatever. I

mean, you're aware of my situation. I'm about as numb as you can get short of total paralysis." George felt sorry for Martin. He was a kind man and a hard worker, with degrees in both psychology and education, and had taken the principal's job simply because he was aghast at the paper-pusher mentality of the other candidates. Then he watched his efforts to be fair and efficient disappear in a mounting pile of paperwork, personality conflicts, and political infighting. Then came the Argus lawsuit, which utterly devastated him. Now he spent his days checking papers with his signature to make sure nothing would appear improper. George hoped this cover-your-ass frenzy was only temporary, but with the new school year it had worsened. Whatever was troubling Martin, George could bet it was a paper dilemma.

"George," said Martin slowly, "you know that little dark-haired girl in your chemistry class, Melissa Samuels?"

"Sure. She looks like Claire. I loaned her a book to help her on a science project earlier this year, but it didn't do much good. Why, what's up?"

"Uh, actually," said Martin, reluctant to continue, "the problem is that she thinks you've been hitting on her, and that's what she told her friends, who told their parents, who told her father, and who knows how screwed up the story was by the time it got back to me. I just spent the last hour trying to tell Samuels it's a big misunderstanding, but he's hot to sue you for attempted corruption of a minor. I don't even know if there is such a charge, but whatever he thinks he can hang on you, he's going for it."

"Dammit, Martin, that's preposterous! Talk to Melissa, she'll straighten it out."

"I don't think so, George. Let me give you some background on this kid: she's apparently spent the last two years at Brayton trying to get her parents' attention. Melissa made top grades, went out for cheerleading, joined the orchestra. I remember her toting her violin down the hall, waving and smiling, always friendly and polite.

"One afternoon after band practice I saw her standing by

the side of the building, bawling her eyes out. Turns out her parents never come to see her play, never come to a game, never have anything to say except keep those grades up. She must have got caught with a story she only intended her friends to hear, but when her dad approached her about it she couldn't be caught lying, so she stuck it out and here we are.

"It's a perfect set of strokes for all of them: the parents get to prove to poor Melissa they loved her all along, she gets the attention she hasn't had in years, and you get your balls nailed to a cross because two negligent SOBs who couldn't give their daughter the time of day are suddenly chock full of righteous indignation. Oh yeah, and since the Argus debacle hit the front pages, who's a better target than us? Amazing, isn't it, how you never get away from politics?"

George looked around the kitchen, wondering if he was going to be asked to resign. He asked, and Kelbrough exploded. "Hell no, you're not! We're gonna give 'em a fight! Sacrifice a top-notch teacher so some part-time parent can win social laurels in some sexual witch hunt? No way! Damn 'em to hell, George, we're gonna fight those bastards every step of the way!" Kelbrough was rolling now, practically screaming. "You should have heard how that fucker talked to me! Oh, and you want to hear the capper? 'My daughter and I are very close and she wouldn't have said this if it weren't true'—this from a man who only talks to her when she's making him look good!"

His voice dropped, and his breathing slowed. The reality of what they were facing had started to sink in. Martin sighed. "God help us, George, we're gonna need it. Now, what do you remember of your conversations with her, because that's what you'll need to have very clear when you talk to the lawyer."

George looked out the window and drummed his fingers on the counter. He didn't remember anything apart from the book, and that was just a conversation at the end of a school day. He said he'd call Martin back in an hour or two, when he was able to put more of the pieces together, maybe try to write it down. His memory wasn't the best these days, part of his depression, you understand.

Kelbrough was surprisingly understanding. It was only by a fluke that he himself knew the girl's father was lying, or maybe not so much lying as hooked on his own fantasy of fatherhood. He didn't want the girl to suffer, "But hell, George, better them than us. Think hard, George. I'll be waiting on your call."

George got off the phone and yelled for Rachel, then remembered she had taken Carla to a movie. The quiet of the house was beginning to ambush him. He wrote Rachel a note saying he'd be back at ten, crossed it out and wrote eleven, then called Kelbrough back and said he'd call after eleven if that was good.

Martin said the morning would be better, that he'd speak to George first thing. "Don't take the day off, George, or it'll look like you're running scared."

George agreed, hung up, and checked his jacket for his notepad. He got in the car and drove to Big Ben's, a bar near the Trout River Bridge where he and a few counsellees went to unwind after their sessions.

Driving over the bridge the bar loomed up on the left like a big red brick, its riverside deck covered in picnic tables. George liked to sit there at sunset, watch the traffic race over the bridge, and know he wasn't part of the hassle.

Big Ben's was the local watering hole, a little of every-thing for the down-homers and horny teens. It had a long bar, pool tables, pinball machines, and a jukebox with whiny country songs and hard rock. Red vinyl booths and tables with stubby candles lined the dance floor.

The barmaids all wore Big Ben's T-shirts, and tight black shorts that barely made it over their hineys. They had cotton candy hair and generous smiles, and by now they all knew George's name and he knew theirs: Charlene, Debbie, and Lulabelle—and yes, that really was her name, or so she said. They all seemed very friendly, and George tipped them very well. Best of all they didn't bug him, they just asked if he wanted to be served on the deck and he usually did, so they would bring him his beer and go away.

Right now George wanted to sit on the deck, hear the water lap at the pilings, and get his thoughts in order, which meant writing them down. When the counsellor first encouraged George to keep a diary he balked, afraid that writing Claire's name would make him cry. But he found that he could cry and still write, that it was like talking to the fish, only better, because the thoughts didn't just float away; he could review them, get a handle on their direction.

Gradually Carla and Rachel began to occupy more pages in the notepad. Even goofy old Sultan got a few words (not kind ones). The counsellor was very pleased because it meant the numbness was receding and that George, however slowly, was starting to reach for life again.

George imagined their next session: So, Doctor Blackwell, I'm just thrilled as I can be about my progress, but I can't continue because people in your parking lot are about to fire-bomb my car. What did I do? Oh, I loaned a book to a student of mine, and somewhere inside it had the words chemical affinity. Now, every alert parent knows that's an invitation to sweaty sex after class. What? No, I don't know your son, Dr. Blackwell, not in any sense. Besides, I like girls, especially under the age of consent and a little stupid, y'know? You wouldn't happen to have one of those I could loan a book to, do you?

George made a face and eased the big blue Monterey into the parking lot behind Big Ben's. It was Tuesday night, so there weren't a lot of cars.

There wasn't as much light on the deck as George needed. Sighing, he walked into the bar and was surprised by the time: the red numerals above the glass rack flashed 10:10. A few couples turned slowly on the dance floor, and seeing them made him sad.

He recognized Charlene and asked her for a Molson Golden, then pointed to one of the booths that had more light and walked over to it. On the way he snitched two candles to highlight his notepad.

After twenty minutes of scribbling he was thirsty, and looked for Charlene. They must have been a girl short for she was way down at the other end of the bar, popping bottle caps, emptying ashtrays, and yelling orders. He got up to serve himself and save her the trouble. She saw him and waved, yelling sorreee, then started bitching at the barman because Elaine had gone on a ten-minute break over twenty minutes ago. Damn her anyway, she knew the place was filling up and who the fuck does she think she is even if she can afford a boob job?

The bartender said, "Wooo, don't knock 'em cause ya don't got 'em," that he'd seen her go out back with, you know, Godzilla. Undoubtedly she'd be back as soon as she could get rid of him.

"Oh, there's another prize," snarled Charlene. "But if you ask me they deserve each other. I mean, I wouldn't let anyone knock me around like that. Have you seen those bruises on her? I mean it's sinful!"

George shook his head, took a long gulp of beer, and walked back to his table. He wanted to look at that list again. Bits of conversations were coming back to him now, things said in jest that might have been misconstrued. Of course his ogling her was a problem, because there was no denying that. She looked like Claire, he missed Claire; would a judge understand that he never intended and certainly never invited her to be Claire?

He opened the notepad and something else occurred to him, then something else, so out came the pen, and soon he was scribbling away.

Her Champion

The tables began filling up with groups and couples that looked like his students. The small circle of light above him suddenly went out. Some guy sitting at one of the tables yelled in high falsetto, "Gee, it's dark in here. Did they close the library?"

George pocketed his writing utensils and relinquished the booth to an approaching couple. He glanced around at the Halloween faces above the small red globes and thought of those fish in the blackest ocean depths, with shimmering outlines and faces that were all teeth and eyes.

He walked out and felt the breeze from the river, and decided to sit on the deck for a few minutes before he left. His checked his watch: 10:45. He frowned at himself for acting like a kid on a curfew, but he knew how Rachel worried. She'd seen him drop those bottles, and several times asked about his driving. There was a pay phone in the lobby and George thought he should call her, then: What, am I crazy? All she has to know is that I'm in some juke joint on the Northside and she'll have coronary arrest. A half hour and I'll be home. A half hour won't kill her.

He strode around the corner onto the darkened deck and froze. Some big tattooed bozo was holding one of the waitresses against the far wall, slapping her face bloody.

"I don't have anymore, I swear!" she gasped, trying to bring her arms up to defend herself, but she was half his size.

George turned and ran for the doorman, and the two of them rounded the corner as a jacked-up blue and white Ford screeched out of the parking lot. The tattooed lump screamed, "Fuckwaaadds! I'll break both yer asses!" and waved his fist and middle finger as he passed.

The doorman ran to pick up the girl, who was kneeling down holding her face. George passed him his handkerchief then ran back into the bar to get some ice. The bartender wrapped the ice in the only clean towel he could find and handed it to George. "Helluva thing," he said. "I told her to ditch that psycho months ago. Good thing you were here. Thanks, mister."

George ran back outside and the girl and the doorman were hunched over the farthest table, the doorman saying, "Jesus, Elaine, you gotta get outta here before that demented SOB breaks every bone in your body!"

"Oh yeah?" She spat blood. She sniffed, she coughed, and lines of blood ran from her nose. "An' jest how'm I gonna do that? He's done took all my money, Billy. I got nowhere ta go, an' nobody t' stand up fer me after they seen him in action. An' why should they? Billy, he's got me, right where he wants me." She looked up at George as he handed her the ice pack and said: "Thanks. Who're you?"

"This is the guy you can thank for savin' your butt, Elaine. It's his hanky yer bleedin' into."

Elaine passed him the wadded up handkerchief and said,

"Sorry." Then she said: "You could've saved yerself a trip."
She put the towel against her nose and shrieked, then threw it
down, crying: "Goddamit, Billy, it's broke. Oh shit. Shit shit
shit."

George said: "Look, my car's right here. I can take you to
the hospital. I can spring for any medication you need. Your
nose won't make it without help, Elaine. What do you say?"
Elaine's eyes were puffing up. Slowly she nodded, still
crying, while the two men helped her into George's car.

The drive to the hospital was strange for George because
he suddenly felt in control. He waited while she got her nose
popped back, medicated and bandaged, then offered to drive
her to anywhere she felt safe.

No, she said, she couldn't expose her friends to any more
shit: he'd already brained some poor shnook with a two-by-
four for yelling "How 'bout them Dawgs!" not twenty minutes
after the game, chased somebody else through a bar with a
chainsaw, and almost ran someone else down with a buddy's
tractor.

"Huh, this maniac has friends?" asked George.

"Sure," said Elaine. "You're his friend or his enemy.
Which would you pick?"

"Nuff said," said George. "Now where can I take you?"

Elaine was suddenly animated. "I know where! I got a cousin
in Texas I never tol' nobody about, kinda like my ace in the hole,
y'know? I mean, much as I run my mouth I know nobody listens,
but the one thing I learned a long ways back is the only way t'keep
a secret is don't tell nobody. Well, George, if we kin get me on a
bus tonight, I'll be outta this shit an' he'll never find me. How
about it? Can ya do it? Will ya do it?"

She could see he was hesitant, and she was sharp enough
to figure out why. "Look," she said, "I'm not one of those
morons who'll let some'n knock me around jest so's I kin say
I got a man. He wasn't like that in the beginning. But then," she
sighed, "they're always nice at the start. Nobody'd stick
around for the crap if they didn't think it'd all go back to the
way it was—y'know, the presents an' nice words an' all." She

put her hand on his sleeve and tried to smile, but with her bandages it came out as a wince. "I won't go back to 'im, George. Not if ya can help me."

"Let's go then," said George, and drove her to the bus terminal.

Raggy loiterers with sour blanched faces slumped along the green walls. The terminal stank of urine, cigarettes and bleach. George wouldn't leave her in such unsavory company, though she said she'd seen worse. He waited while the ticketeer mapped out a route for her, paid for her trip with his credit card, and they sat on a bench till her bus arrived. George walked her to the door to see her safely onboard.

Then she held his left hand, looked at his ring, and told him his wife was a lucky woman, she hoped someday she could be as lucky. The doors closed, the bus pulled away, and she waved at him through the darkened window.

George walked back into the terminal, had a coffee in the coffee shop, then called Rachel. He told her he'd had a kind of adventure and would be home in an hour. No problems, not to worry, he'd tell her all about it tomorrow.

Then he hung up and reached in his pocket for the handkerchief to mop his brow. It wasn't there. He felt in all his jacket and pants pockets and didn't find it. He knew Elaine didn't have it. He went back to the car but it wasn't on the seats or the floor. He sat behind the wheel and tried to tell himself Dammit, George, it's just a handkerchief. But no, it wasn't just a handkerchief, it was the one his mother had embroidered for him the year before she died, the one Claire cried into the day he proposed to her, the one he had handed her at christenings and weddings, the one he had cried into for almost a year.

He went back to the emergency room and it wasn't on the floor or any of the seats.

"That leaves Ben's," he said aloud, and climbed back in the car. He cranked open the vent window and it came to him: he'd placed a napkin holder on it to keep it from blowing off the deck while they helped Elaine to the car. Whew, he smiled, and drove back to the bar.

It was a little past closing and bodies were milling and staggering around the parking lot, laughing and cussing, leaping in front of departing cars. George was afraid if he came in the front way he might run over one of them, so he drove in by a back road and parked at the end of the lot. He walked up the steps by the back entrance, onto the deck and over to the table under the visored light. The napkin holder was gone, along with the handkerchief. He looked around and saw that all the holders had been removed from the tables.

Shit, he frowned, here we go again.

He walked in through the front door, and both Billy and Charlene asked how Elaine was doing. He said that her wounds were taken care of, that he'd left her at the hospital with some cabfare and instructions to find a new boyfriend.

The barman said: "Mister, you did a nice thing. Now get yer ass outta here before Cy gets back or you won't need a doctor, just an undertaker."

"Well," said George, "I'll be gone as soon as I can recover my hankerchief. Y'see, it's been in my family a long time and—"

"Yeah yeah," said Billy. "Wait now, that was the one ya give to Elaine, right?"

"Right."

"Charlene," Hank called to her, "when you cleared the stuff off the tables d'you remember that bloodied-up hanky?"

"Jeez, George, I'm sorry. I just threw it in the dumpster. C'mon, let's go get it." She shook her head and shrugged. "I'm awful sorry."

Billy took the large flashlight from behind the bar and followed them out. George apologized for asking them to dig through garbage for him, but Charlene said "Hey, I got a blue rabbit's foot my momma gave me when I was just ten, an' I still got it. Hold that light up there, Billy. Nope, more in the corner. I useta hold onto it at night when I said my prayers, figgered if I held onto it tight enough the Russians wouldn't bomb us all to Kingdom Come. An' I guess I was right, we're still here. Billy, hold it. I think I see the edge of it."

She folded her leg over the rim and slid onto an inverted box, which crumbled under her as she grabbed the shadowed triangle out of the debris. She handed him the handkerchief with a flourish, saying: "Tah-dah!"

Then George and Billy pulled Charlene out of the dumpster, and George insisted on treating them both to dinner in the restaurant of their choice.

"Whooee," said Billy and Charlene in one voice: "George, you got a date."

George handed Charlene two dollars to cover her shredded nylons, and Charlene stuffed the money under her T-shirt, holding down the edge of her bra. George couldn't help watching her and she laughed at him, explaining that on good nights she took the padding out of her bra and stuffed the dollars in.

"Oh," he laughed, "and what do you do with the change?"

"In the pouch," she smiled, pointing to the brown leather bag on her belt. Her face changed as she looked over his shoulder, and George followed the direction of her frown.

Standing about fifty feet away was the brute who had beaten Elaine.

"Clear out, Charlene. Me an' sweet George here's gonna have a little talk."

Charlene whispered: "Don't let him get near you, George. I'm calling the police."

George didn't move. "If you want your girlfriend, I put her in a cab at the hospital. Where she went from there, I don't know."

"So what business is it of yers, huh? Where'n the fuck do you get off tellin' me an' my woman howta run our lives? Or have ya got 'er all snowed thinkin' yer her new sugar daddy? That's it, ain't it? Nothin' ta say, huh? Betcha had plenty t'say to her, all that sweet stuff those little cunts love t' hear. That's what ya did, din'tcha?" He had taken a pair of brass knuckles out of his pocket and slid them over the fingers of his right hand.

George spread his legs in a fighting stance. There was a

coke bottle on a crate by the door, one step away. If he could reach it before the bastard hit him at least he'd have a weapon.

"Whaddaya know," said Cy, and snorted, "A leftover college boxer. Well, gramps, ya been a long time outta the ring. My bookie wouldn't give ya seventy-five to one on this round. Last chance, pops. You take me where she's hid an' I'll letcha go. Otherwise yer dead."

As Cy walked toward him George grabbed the coke bottle. As he was bringing it around he felt the brass fist hit his stomach and he doubled over, dropping the bottle. The next blow shattered his cheek and jaw, the third smashed two of his ribs.

Cy grabbed the collar of George's jacket and yanked it up over his head, dragging him up the stairs to the deck. Billy, Hank the barman, and Charlene, had all run out the door and were yelling at Cy to stop, that the police were on their way.

Cy snarled to them to get back, to mind their own business or they'd be next. He dropped George on the planks by the table under the light, saw the bloody distorted face, and realized George couldn't talk.

"Shit!" he screamed. "You goddam moron, look what ya done to me. I'll never find 'er now!" Screaming: "You fucker!" he cracked George's sides with steel-toed kicks while Billy and Hank tackled him.

Charlene came running with the jack from her car and walloped Cy in the back of the head, hard as she could. He made a noise and fell to the deck.

"Christ, Charlene!" yelled Hank. "Ya didn't hafta do that, we had 'im!"

"Sez you," said Charlene. "Till he gets up, ya mean. Well, I didn't want fer him to get up. Besides, I figger poor ol' George here's had enough excitement fer one night. Y'all wait on the police, an' I'll see he's okay."

It was the first chance they had to look at George's face, and Charlene screamed.

George spat and gurgled, trying to form words. He wanted to thank them and tell them to call Rachel, and he wanted them not to call Rachel. The pain in his head was worse, and the light when he opened his eyes made their faces strange. He heard Charlene say she would go to the bathroom to get some ice while the two men went to flag down a police car. "Don't worry, stay still," they said, and their faces disappeared.

George's head and lungs were on fire. If he could just get closer to that breeze from the river he'd feel better. His hand found the leg of a table and he pulled himself up. If he could just get some water on his handkerchief and hold it against his head.

The water was beyond his reach, so he knelt on the edge of the deck and tried again, holding the rail with a shaking hand. He was almost there. One more swipe.

Suddenly the water was all around him, taking him like the first dive of summer. He decided to float for awhile, then strike out for the surface. The cold felt good, and Claire appeared in her flannel nightgown, turning out the light. He felt her hair against his face, and gently pulled the comforter over their heads. The cold began to fade, along with the pain in his head and lungs.

Winter makes great cuddling weather. Doesn't it, Honey?

Yes, George. Good night, George. I love you, George.

I love you, Claire.

An hour later the search party found him floating face down in the weeds a mile from the bar. Clutched in his right hand was a tiny piece of embroidered linen.

Sore Paws and Limelight

The year after George's death was an agony of details and
countless cruel reminders for Rachel. George's lawyer, Av
Grossman, guided her through all the legal hassles. First there
was the will, which was held up in probate pending the
insurance company's investigation of possible suicide. After
all, this was a man being treated for severe depression, about
to face a scandal. A pillar of the community falling from grace;
perhaps he just took the easy way out.

"Easy!" Rachel screamed, almost punching the investigator. "You call getting beaten up and drowned easy? What, you
think he paid someone to beat him senseless, and then threw
himself in the river?"

The investigator got statements from both Charlene and
Hank, and delivered his report to the insurance company,

which then coughed up the fifty grand.

Av was with Rachel when she picked up the check, and could see the guilt in her face, as if somehow she agreed that her father's life was worth the amount on the paper. "Rachel," he said, "I know how you feel. But your father wanted you to have that money. He'd have made it a million if he could have."

Rachel was sobbing into her sleeve.

"Listen now, Rachel, because I'm gonna tell you what to do with that money. You're head of the household now, and I know that looks like a lotta dough, but it's not. Take whatever's left after the funeral expenses and invest a good chunk of it in something solid, like Sears or Bell or McDonald's.

"Listen, young people always think they can putz around and bail themselves out later, but only the rich can afford that. For the rest of us it's a matter of plugging along and making careful choices. I know. I know you don't want to talk about this now, but I don't want you doing anything stupid just because you're angry. You've every right to be angry, Honey, you just can't afford to be stupid. It's the pits, Rachel, but you're in charge now, and however you make it happen, you and Carla have to eat. I'll help you any way I can." He wondered if he should broach the subject of suing the night-club, but that was too painful right now. Let her anger simmer awhile.

Av was chatting up the wrong girl: Rachel was too stunned to be angry, but Carla was a steaming kettle of rage. She'd already beaten up several kids in her schoolyard for yelling "Nyah nyah, yer daddy screws little girls."

In fairness, it wasn't the kids' fault. They'd seen the interviews with the Samuels family on TV. Rachel considered suing the Samuels family for libel, but all the evidence seemed to be on their side.

Av told Rachel to forget it, that George's friends knew the truth, and piss on the rest of them.

Rachel spent the next year and a half as a "floater" in a large legal firm downtown—running errands, a little typing, relieving the receptionist, and general gofer. It paid very well considering the position and the fact that she only worked six hours a day. This way she could be sure that Carla would be alone only one hour at most.

The problem with that hour was that Carla loved to climb things. Telling her to stay off the roof only worked if Rachel was there to make it stick. Lately Carla was so hyper that she only seemed calm petting Sultan, and what could he do if she fell out of a tree? After all, Sultan was no Lassie.

Sultan, on the other hand, had seen Lassie in action, and concluded she had the brains of a tennis ball. She dragged horses from burning buildings and ran hundreds of miles for a hug. Nobody ever fed her. What a life! Let her have the limelight and sore paws: nobody was going to put him through that torture! Sultan stayed stupid to keep Hollywood away, and it worked.

It bothered Rachel that Carla's closest companion was this barking rug. She resolved to find a better use for Carla's energy, and no solution seemed appropriate till the night she saw Carla on the livingroom floor trying to do splits. As Rachel, amazed, watched Carla bring her torso to the floor, she suddenly had the answer.

"Hey, little sister, how'd ya like some lessons in gymnastics?"

"Would I?" gasped Carla. "Wow, would I!"

Gymnastics turned out to be Carla's salvation: she couldn't do drugs, she couldn't overeat, and she became conscious of her body in terms of mastering it while her friends were fretting about pimples and popularity. Sure, there were a couple of boys she wished would pay attention to her, but she could forget it all trying to mold her inadequacies into a perfect tumbling run. She could feel it getting better, little by little, and sometimes it was absolutely right. The coach didn't have to tell her, she could feel it in the smoothness of the take-off and the moment of contact.

The kids thought her strange and stupid for running off to the gym every night. Why? What made them so great, other than their clothes? And why was that such a big deal? Carla found them all pretty boring.

The truth was she still missed her mother. Only her mother made stories and everything fun, and best of all she could clown without hurting somebody.

Carla saw that TV sitcoms made people look foolish. What was so funny about that? She would leave the room when that happened, and come back when all the faces were smiling.

At night she climbed into Rachel's bed, clutching her stuffed Lambie. Sometimes she would whimper and call for her mother, and Rachel would hug and kiss her till the crying stopped. Carla would stick her thumb in her mouth and drift away, the fingers of her other hand curled around Rachel's arm.

The Perfect Ten

It was the Summer Olympics in Montreal, and Rachel's birthday present to Carla was a day of watching the gymnasts. They were staying in Colette's apartment while she was on her honeymoon. All their relatives were thrilled to see them, commenting on how beautifully Carla was growing up.

On the third morning they joined the throngs marching to the Olympic Village, and were glad they had binoculars when they found their seats.

Carla scanned the floor for Turescheva. The Soviet star was easy to find. Even among perfect postures her carriage was outstanding. The cameras devoured her bosom and pout: Turescheva had brought sex appeal to the Olympics.

Two hours later it happened, the event that confounded the computer and made perfection a reachable ideal. A skinny pigtailed ten-year-old bounced through a robotic display that blew the numbers off the scoreboard. When the giant beaded "ten" appeared minutes later, everyone shrieked in amazement but Nadia. After all, she said to a spot somewhere below the microphone, she'd done it before.

Then Olga Korbut gave a performance on the balance beam that brought down the stadium. She lay on her stomach and brought her legs down over her face like a scorpion curling its tail to strike. She pushed her legs forward till she was eye level with her feet, her arms braced on nothing but air, her face contorted and sweating. The audience held its collective breath, waiting for her spine to snap. When she rolled up for her dismount the shouts, whistles and cheers told her everything she needed to know. Her coach was ecstatic. Everyone waited for the score to appear and they watched, incredulous, as the number came up and it wasn't even a nine. The crowd booed, shook its fists and threw papers.

Carla looked at Rachel and her face mirrored Olga's trauma. "Rachel, that's nuts! If they gave Nadia a ten, this was worth at least an eleven! Who's judging this thing anyway?"

Rachel threw up her hands. She had just lowered her binoculars from Olga's drained, crestfallen face. "I dunno, Carla." She shook her head. "I hope it's contested." The crowd booed louder.

"Never mind, Olga!" Rachel yelled. "We know the truth!"

That night she looked at the *Montreal Star*'s version of the day's events and considered the injustice done to Olga. But then, Olga was yesteryear's sweetheart, and the world wanted a new face.

And what a face! Rachel saw some of the Olympic coverage on TV, and noticed how the cameras tracked Nadia's scowl almost as much as her performances. It was as if she couldn't give them enough: she had three perfect scores, but it wasn't enough, they were going to pester her till she smiled. She didn't give in to them, though. She kept that last piece of herself aloof from their prying, and went home with her teddy and her medals.

Rachel looked at the photo of the little girl on the platform and thought what an unflattering picture it was. Then she thought of all the women in history described as "beautiful" whose pictures looked worse than her driver's license. And if artists were paid to be flattering who's to say what anybody looked like? What if Nefertiti's famous full lips were just a stylization, or the result of being popped in the chops by Pharaoh for fooling around with the lute player? No wonder all this past life regression had gotten so popular: whose eyes could you trust but your own? Shit, she thought. Here I am, captive to centuries of bad judgment, reworked stories and outright lies.

But that wasn't all she did on her summer vacation.

She had a good laugh along with the rest of Montreal when one of the Russian gymnasts disappeared for a few days. While the Soviets and Americans speculated about his defection or kidnapping, Montrealers said don't worry, he'll turn up. He did turn up, grinning from ear to ear, having been "kidnapped" by a beautiful girl, and wasn't the least apologetic about it. Montrealers grinned and said we told you so, eh?

Carla was anxious to be off with kids her own age. There was a dance party that night in a church in Outremont, and two of her cousins had invited her along. Rachel said okay, and watched Carla skip out the door, blowing a kiss as she passed. Wow, thought Rachel, any minute now I'll be asking her for make-up tips.

Carla's life had changed radically in the last few months. Gymnastics had given way to primping, parties, and Mick. Mick was one of the jocks, and his interest in the former weirdo was her instant ticket to popularity. Carla joked with Rachel that her social rise had been so fast it almost gave her the bends. Still, she had been in the 'out' crowd for so long she wasn't wholly comfortable being 'in.' For one thing, there was a lot of pressure to 'have sex.' Everyone did, or said they did, and the standing joke at the time was: Why do they teach sex education in the eighth grade? So you can find out what you've been doing wrong for the last two years.

Carla liked Mick a lot, but maybe not enough to have sex with him. Still, asking Rachel about birth control was a good idea. If anyone knew what worked and how well, Rachel would know. Also, the romance of the city made the topic a natural. Tonight she would ask, after the dance.

After Carla left, Rachel stared at her address book, wondering if she should dial Aaron's number. His last letter had come four months ago. Still, she wanted to see him. Well, here goes nothing. She dialed.

A strong Jewish voice answered "Yallow?" Then the voice yelled for Aaron. Then the voice demanded to know "Who's calling?"

It was Rachel's luck to have a Biblical name, but for mischief she said: "Tell him Yankee Doodle."

The voice delivered the message, twice, and a great clattering could be heard in the distance, then Aaron picked up the extension, gasping: "I got it, Dad. Hang up."

There was a reluctant click and Aaron laughed. "Yankee Doodle. That's terrific. He probably thinks you're a spy or a rock band. So Rachel, how're ya doing? You know, it's amazing you caught me, because I don't live here anymore, and I was just on my way to meet my girlfriend at the Sheraton. Why don't you meet us there? It's a fundraiser for various save-the-earth groups. They've rented the Grand Salle, and there's a dinner included. Afterwards you get to hear all the doom-and-gloomers preach clean air and hawk their books. My treat. How can you resist?"

"How indeed?" She was downcast about the girlfriend, but she still wanted to see him.

"So, an hour from now at the Sheraton, then?" He was dressing while he talked. Same old high-speed Aaron. She wondered how he could sit through three hours of listening to someone else talk. She asked him. He laughed. "Hey, no problem. I am very mellow these days. Hey, I'll still recognize you, won't I? You haven't done anything strange like dye your hair purple or get fat, have you?"

"Nope. Same old boring, predictable person."

"No, Rachel. You were never that." The sincerity and admiration in his voice surprised her. The warmth, too, that seemed to have eroded with the years was suddenly back. She didn't feel awkward anymore. She was ready to meet his girlfriend.

The Weight

The stage of the Sheraton's Grande Salle held five chairs behind the podium and a large scale beside the stairs. Next to the scale with its disk weights was a smaller scale.

On the floor of the salon was a bar, and four long tables set for service of thirty. A table by the door held pamphlets from the host organizations, while another corner table was set for coffee and dessert.

In the middle of the room was a magnificent chandelier.

Rachel followed Aaron and Consuela to the bar and insisted on buying drinks.

"Well in that case," Aaron grinned, "make it Champagne."

"Done," said Rachel, and they clinked their glasses to old friends and new.

Aaron said, "Geez, look at all the press. Must be a really big deal." Then he smirked. "Of course I'm sure the free food and booze was a big draw. God, before I die, let me ask for nothing more than a press pass." Then he recognized a man at the pamphlet table, waved to him and said he'd be right back.

"Hah!" said Rachel and Consuela in one voice as Aaron disappeared into the crowd.

"It's just an excuse," said Consuela. "He wants us to get acquainted. Probably praying we exchange notes. So," she smiled, "who starts?"

Rachel told her the family history and that her little sister, who could hardly be called little anymore, had come up with her to savor some of the Olympic hoopla.

"So," said Consuela, "we are both products of a shrinking world." Her father was a Cagnawagan Indian who died in a construction accident. Her mother, a beautiful Jamaican, was a maid in a Westmount mansion. When Consuela was sixteen a high school photographer suggested she be given modelling lessons. A movie producer saw her portfolio and wanted her to appear in a local movie but when she wouldn't suck him off he had her blacklisted. She then took night courses, supporting herself by typing and waitressing. She was working on a Degree in Environmental Science and her main concern was trees. She spoke as though they were her family, moved to tears to think of them torn from the earth and heartlessly cut to pieces.

One man standing nearby tapped her on the shoulder and asked if she was one of the speakers. Consuela said no, wiping her eyes. He said: "You should be."

Consuela was a devout listener too, squinting when she heard something worthwhile, as if by squinting she could trap it inside those upturned brown eyes. After twenty minutes of squinting at Rachel she said, "Aaron was right about you, Rachel. You're super. Friends?"

"Oh, I've passed the test, have I?" said Rachel, only partly sarcastic.

"Oh yes." Consuela nodded, flipping her black hair behind

her shoulders. "First impressions set the tone for me. I don't have time to dig things out of people, and for some reason they just spill their guts the minute I meet them. You wouldn't believe the stuff people tell me. One night some pig-faced girl chewed my ear off about her boyfriend's premature ejaculation. Sheesh." She rolled her eyes, then giggled. "Later that same night somebody introduced me to him. Jesus, I could barely say hello. I mean really, what else could I see?"

Rachel laughed. "It's your face, Consuela. That scowl. Now where did your true love go?"

Consuela raised her eyebrows. "Don't you mean our true love?"

Rachel looked down, blushing.

Consuela took Rachel's arm. "Look, I didn't say that to be mean. I meant: you loved him, I love him, and y'know, I think he loves us both. Well," she sighed, "I guess he loves, as much as a millionaire's son can love anything outside his inheritance.

"You see, Rachel, I have no illusions. He's a Jew, and he'll marry inside his faith—someone with starched hair who'll spend his money and raise his kids." Her voice was steadily rising and her eyes had narrowed to slits. "He'll have a mistress, of course. Someone like me or you, 'cause we're outside his group, so that makes us sexy.

"Damn it, I hate it. I mean, it's perfect for him: what better deal could possibly exist? A woman completely at his mercy, to use any way he wants, that can't ask for anything back. What a deal: free to feel and not to care. Like rape, y'know?

"The only difference I can see between a rapist and a married man on the make is that one uses brute force and the other tells lies. And the real kicker is, it's all for an illusion: that's all you are. And you know what you can do about it? Nothing, that's what. You can agree to it, or get beaten for it, or get left for it. Those are the choices. Fun, huh? I know, 'cause I've had 'em all."

Throats cleared around her. She spread her hands and said: "Sorry, folks," then put an arm around Rachel's shoulders and guided her toward their seats, saying in a loud voice: "I hate small talk, don't you?"

Rachel looked at Consuela and the two of them burst out laughing.

Consuela went to the washroom, leaving Rachel to absorb the shock. Just what Aaron needs, thought Rachel. I like her, but I wish she'd tone it down a little. Then again, maybe words are all she's got to fight with.

Consuela returned, armed with two more glasses of champagne. "I'm sorry I shot my mouth off," she said. "It just gets too much sometimes, y'know?"

Rachel smiled and told her it was okay. She wanted to tell Consuela that she liked her and the rest didn't matter, but knew that was the last thing to say to someone of passionate convictions.

They sat down and looked around for Aaron.

Consuela was chewing a celery stem. "How many minutes to blast-off?" she asked.

Rachel looked at her watch and said five.

"Good," said Consuela, "time for coffee." She crooked a finger at the busboy who had been staring at her since she arrived, and he scooted over to get a better look at her. "Coffee, please," she smiled, and he charged off to the coffee table.

Rachel was left with her mouth hanging open in the middle of an order. She looked at Consuela and laughed. "Well, he might have waited to find out what I wanted."

Consuela smiled wickedly. "Oh, he'll be back in a minute, if he doesn't trip over his feet trying to get here."

Rachel frowned. "Consuela, that's cruel."

"No it's not, just observant. Besides, I'm not hurting that boy. Have I snapped at him? Have I ordered him around like he's dirt? No. All I'm doing is giving him something to think about besides coffee pots and dirty dishes. Now me, I've carted plenty of coffee pots and dirty dishes, and flirting's about the only thing that makes it bearable—well, that and a good tip. We'll tip him well when we go and give him a double goodie. Aha, here comes the little darling now. Give him your magnolia best smile, Scahlett, and he'll prob'ly get you-all some coffee, too."

The chairs were filling up around them.

Aaron arrived with a sheaf of pamphlets. "Well," he smiled. "Do I get to sit between you?"

"Absolutely not," said Rachel. "You have to pick."

Aaron said no problem and eenie-meenie-miney-moed his way over beside Rachel. He shook his finger at Consuela. "Y'know," he said, "that Dr. Arden with the amulet trick is slated to speak tonight. That's why they have that scale there. And you told me this was a serious ecology seminar. Really, Connie, I'm ashamed of you. Well, Rachel, you'll get to see some hocus-pocus tonight. It'll be interesting to hear what you think of it all."

Rachel looked at Consuela. "What's he talking about?"

Consuela made a face at Aaron, then shuffled through the pamphlets until she found a small blue booklet which she handed to Rachel. Inside were ten pages of cramped type, a drawing of the Great Sphinx, and a grainy photo of the head of a cat. A drawing beside the tiny photo clarified its smudged outlines as the head of a lioness with closed eyes, hence the title: 'The Sleeping Lion.'

Rachel said to Connie, "Tell me what this is about, will ya? They've started bringing out the plates and I don't want this book in my gazpacho."

She dropped the booklet in her handbag as the waiters and waitresses began offering wine from different countries. Fresh-caught salmon from British Columbia was the main course, and oohs and ahs of appreciation followed the arriving plates. The cameraman briefly turned his lens on the happy eaters and everyone winced in the floodlight.

When the dinner plates were cleared away the dessert table was loaded with silver trays of chocolates, fruit and cheese. Coffee was brought to the tables for the many too stuffed to stand, and Aaron went over to the bar for three snifters of Courvoisier. He asked Consuela to tell Rachel the story of the scale, saying that it might sound more believable coming from her.

Rachel wanted to tell Aaron to forget the cognac. She had barely sipped the glass of Bordeaux in front of her, and the sour gingerale taste of the champagne lingered above the salmon. She had her father's inability with booze, and was holding down a burp. God, she thought, how tacky, put her hand over her mouth, and burped anyway.

Consuela apologized for Aaron's cynicism, saying medical science had him snowballed, that if he'd been alive when they were bleeding people he'd be knee-deep in blood.

Then she talked about the televised special on Dr. Michael Arden, the discredited Egyptologist, and his strange discovery in one of the tels near the tomb of Tutankhamen. Arden uncovered seven golden amulets shaped as the head of a lioness with its eyes closed. He found this peculiar because the eyes of animals in Egyptian art are traditionally open. He thought he was either very tired or possibly ill because each of the amulets was the size of a high school ring yet seemed incredibly heavy. With great difficulty he lowered the little heads into a basket, then transferred the basket to a hoist. Once the amulets were out of contact with his hands the basket rolled up easily.

When his assistants gathered to inspect the find, one of the bearers on the edge of the crowd looked in the basket and shrieked. He fell to his knees imploring the heavens for forgiveness, then ran away screaming: "Sek-met! Sek-met!"

"So," said Consuela, wiggling her eyebrows, "he had stumbled upon the remnants of a temple of Sehkmet. Wheeyooh, what a find! And what a dangerous creature. This baby makes The Mummy look like a benign pile of rags. But we'll get to her in a minute; meanwhile back to the amulets."

That night Dr. Arden weighed the amulets by rolling them out of the basket onto the little scale on his desk. Each one weighed eleven ounces.

But when he tried to pick one up he could barely lift it, even using two hands.

Robert, his associate, tried to pick one up and gasped: "This isn't possible! The damn thing must weigh forty pounds!"

He dropped the amulet back in the basket and carried it to the big scale by the office.

Each man weighed himself and then, standing on the scale, took an amulet from the basket. The moment his fingers closed around the cat face, a great heat poured through his arm and chest and the pointer on the scale clanged against the bar.

They added five-, ten-, and one-pound weights until the pointer hung free. With Robert the amulet weighed forty-five pounds; with Dr. Arden, thirty-seven.

They handed the amulet to another assistant and it yielded twenty-five pounds.

Watching them, the son of one of the archaeologists thought they were teasing him. He said he had picked up one of the little cat heads while the grownups were at dinner and it was like a big marble, that's all. "Here," he said, "I'll show you," and grabbed one of the amulets off the table, tossing it in the air. He caught it, grinned, and said, "Funny joke, Daddy. Ha ha." He returned the amulet to the table, stuck out his tongue, and skipped out of the room.

In the weeks to come people of all sizes and ages stood on the scale to be weighed with the amulets. Usually the weights were smaller as the person was younger, but one little girl almost broke her arm trying to hold it. Everyone commented on the heat in their arm. Some said they felt their hearts were on fire.

While the populace gaped and chattered, archaeologists joined forces to denounce poor Dr. Arden and his silly 'parlor trick.' Obviously the desert air had dried out his brains. Such a fine scholar, too. Tsk tsk.

Michael Arden didn't take kindly to being called a crackpot. He was too dedicated a scholar to engage in wild conjecture. He vowed to learn the secret of the amulets and redeem himself in the eyes of his colleagues.

Alas, the journey he had set upon led him further and further from any accepted interpretations, until he was finally forced to conclude that the ancient cosmogony had been read wrong.

According to the accepted version, the Sehkmet legend was millenia old and easily explained by anyone familiar with the living conditions of pre-dynastic Egypt. Villages had sprung up along the banks of the Nile, dependent on the harvests of irrigation. At night when powerful carnivores came out to hunt, the people gathered around fires or lay in their huts and listened to terrifying sounds—even bullfrogs were scary at night.

The moon, however, was their friend. Its wistful round face lit up the blackness even as it changed the world to pearly gray. Now it was possible to venture out: predators could be seen and avoided, fish leaped into their nets, and seeds planted under the gaze of the moon grew best of all. Obviously the lady in the sky must love them very much to bring them all this bounty, and they loved her back. They called her Hathor, meaning "Where The Face Dwells," and thought she must also be a giant cow, for on certain nights only a horn was visible. Hathor was more loved than feared until a night in August during the grape harvest, when a pride of lions ransacked a village.

Lions hunt at night, and the females lead the attack. Undoubtedly some inebriated revelers fell prey to a few lions, and the next morning the villagers found their friends disemboweled.

The villagers then dipped their spears and arrows into poison and crouched by the trees at the edge of the village, waiting for night to fall. Sure enough the lions returned, confident of an easy catch. As they slunk into view they were stung by the arrows, and the poison made them do a wobbly dance of death. Then the triumphant villagers carted them off for skinning.

The story of the villagers' bravery grew through the years to become the legend of Sehkmet, the white lioness that fell from the moon: white, because everything's white by moonlight; one lioness instead of a pride because they all looked the same—five lions with five victims became one lion who was magically everywhere, with ten victims, then hundreds, then thousands. The nerve toxin that felled the lioness to quick rigor mortis became a torrent of wine that drugged her till she turned to stone. The stone left as a reminder of the lion's life became the gravestones, tombs, and pyramids that stand in memory of departed souls the world over.

Dr. Arden saw the story of Sehkmet everywhere, in versions that reflected the falling status of women in a world of widening patriarchal wars. The summer signs of astrology, for example, Cancer and Leo, were merely retreads of Hathor and Sehkmet, with the details altered so as to diminish (in the case of Hathor) and destroy (in the case of Sehkmet) the feminine role.

Consider Hathor, the moon, massive in July. The Mother of Mankind, whose great udder nourished his soul, and lit up the night sky to help him forage and plant. She was reduced to Cancer, a small silvery crab at the mercy of the tides, not their author. Cancerian mammary glands were small and ineffectual, for the new "goddess" of the moon, Diana, had traded motherhood for a quiver of arrows. Arrows over milk became guns before butter as the nurturer became the destroyer.

Thus came Sehkmet, either the daughter of Hathor or her warlike incarnation, to prowl the earth in August. The lioness called by Ra to rip out the hearts of evildoers and thereby heal the sufferings of humanity was now Leo the Lion, the heart and protector of the family. His golden coat reflected the royal rays of the sun, rather than the white eerie glow of the moon.

The healing function of Sehkmet's attack, her whiteness, and Hathor's loving care of the earth, were shuffled over to the month of September as that cosmic figure of reticence, Virgo.

Libra, the balance of justice, was the final resolution of Sehkmet, her clear-sighted wrath against wrongdoing wimped down to blindfolded dependence on lawyers' interpretations. Right and wrong were gone, shades of truth were in.

More than that, the Heavens had acquired a new God so that the noble cosmic functions of Hathor and Sehkmet were stripped away, and something evil was put in their place. The wonderful old moon became the patron saint of werewolves,

who like Sehkmet were furry and fanged and came in August,
as in the old poem:

Many a man who's pure in heart
And says his prayers at night
Can become a wolf when the wolfbane blooms
And the August moon shines bright.

Invincible white shapes called ghosts came to right the
wrongs done to their departed souls, just as Sehkmet had tried
to right the wrongs of humanity.

Witches, those sweet believers in the healing power of
nature and the goodness of the moon, became confused with
devil worshippers and were persecuted for it.

The name Mother Nature was used to describe capricious
attacks on civilization by hurricanes and earthquakes, just as
the Egyptians once believed that Sehkmet had brought these
things as a punishment for evildoing.

The fact that Sehkmet was history's first vigilante made
vigilantism accepted throughout history: if God (or Ra) could
send down a white Angel of Death to destroy the wicked, why
not save Him the trouble and do it ourselves? Vigilantism ran
amok in lynch mobs, and many innocent souls died. But
Sehkmet also ran amok. She was turned to stone by consuming
gargantuan quantities of wine, "And the human race has been
getting stoned ever since," laughed Consuela.

"That's some story," said Rachel.

"Oh, I'm not done," smiled Consuela. "This is where it
starts to get lively. Dr. Arden received a package from a
colleague who was working around some Mayan ruins, and
this guy was maybe the only man in the world who believed
him. Guess why."

"Hmmm. Is this a test to see if I'm paying attention?"
Rachel turned the cognac in her glass. She knew the answer,
but it was slow to surface. "Let's see. It must be that he found
an amulet of his own. How'm I doing?"

"Right on, Rachel. Anyway, this guy had been studying
the disappearance of the Mayans, and came to the conclusion
it had something to do with Sehkmet. He discovered his

amulet somewhere around the Temple of the Jaguar, and recognized the face from the description and the photo in the disputed Arden paper. In this amulet, though, the eyes and the mouth were open, but the weight was identical, eleven ounces, and the strange properties the same."

Rachel waved away the story with her free hand. "You don't think this is some kind of elaborate hoax?" said Rachel.

"I'll say," said Aaron. "Connie, let me tell her the rest so it can be said with the proper tone of sarcasm. You see, in the Mayan and Aztec civilizations, hearts were ripped from living bodies as a gift to the sun to keep the night from swallowing the earth. Now, Arden says that the Olmecs who initiated all these 'hearty' (pardon the pun) sacrifices did so in fear of Sehkmet, they just got it backwards. You see, Sehkmet was The Great Jaguar, who could see into men's eyes and read their hearts. Thus they called all jaguars 'The Lords of The Smokey Mirrors'—referring, I suppose, to how we humans see 'but through a glass darkly.' The jaguars harvested the evil hearts to keep the soul of mankind pure. Women mated with jaguars—so the story goes—to produce a race of beings that could walk amongst people and divine the bad ones by looking into their eyes. Then, at night, the jaguar people—reverting to their divine form, the jaguar—would seek out the bad humans and kill them.

"Apparently the Mayans misread Sehkmet's message, building colossal monuments, carving out hearts, and killing each other in wars, when her message was just the opposite: don't blanket the earth with monuments or harm each other. But they went along, believing they were right, and one night she came back and killed them. The whole civilization: poof. The few that managed to escape were in the outlying villages, away from the bloodthirsty spectacles of the major centers. Those few were the ancestors of the Maya of today, who still avoid cities, and who can blame them?

"Now, here's the part that lost me: Arden identifies Sehkmet as the Passover Angel, the killer of the firstborn of Egypt, who could still a beating heart as easily as carve it out.

Striking the blood of a lamb on the lintels and doorway arches was to distract her, and just in case she came inside they set that glass of wine for her at the table. Boy, just what the Hebrews needed, some cosmic drunk for a mascot.

"Well, I got some questions for the old Herr Professor. If this Sehkmet's a spirit, why drink blood or wine? Why be male or female? Why the image of a lion? Why does it need a body? And mostly, goddamit, if this Sehkmet was there for the Exodus, why didn't she turn up to clobber the Nazis? The world's a million times worse than it ever was, and the fault is all mankind's, so where the hell is she, this white avenger, this Sehkmet?"

"Hey, Honey," whispered Consuela, patting his arm, "Take it easy. It's just an idea, after all. There's microphones around the room. You can quiz him after his demonstration. I know you won't be alone."

Rachel was smiling up at the chandelier, so beautiful, as if all the Milky Way had clustered under this roof, just for tonight. It was funny to think of Consuela calming Aaron. Undoubtedly they took turns with one another.

It occurred to Rachel that the vital question had gotten lost in Aaron's tirade. She looked at Consuela and said: "So what about the amulets? Why do the weights differ according to who holds them?"

"Haul that book out, Rachel," said Consuela, pointing to the handbag, "and I'll read it to you."

Rachel handed the booklet to Consuela, who flipped pages and squinted till her finger landed on the proper paragraph. "Yup, here it is. 'The Sehkmet amulet kept its wearer safe from bad acts and intentions—including his own. It did this by absorbing the evil around it—the more evil it absorbed, the heavier it grew. What the Sehkmet amulets weigh, then, is the amount of harm a person has been subjected to in life. This explains why some children cannot pick up the amulets, and why all the weights differ.' Boy, talk about the weight of the world!" she grimaced. "If that's true, isn't it awful?"

Aaron was rolling his eyes. He pushed himself back from

the table and said: "Poppycock, my dear. Stuff and nonsense. Why any fool can see it's fat electrons."

Rachel and Consuela frowned at him. "Fat electrons?"

"Hey, I'm entitled to my theory," he smiled, stretching and yawning. "It's quite simple, really. If heavy truths have a measurable weight, and electrons are a measure of negative energy, what else can it be but fat electrons? All we need now is for someone to write 'The Electron Diet Book' and the world will smile again. There," he said through a yawn, "I've solved it. Now we can all go home." He grinned at them. "Gullible wenches," he chuckled, then straightened up and yelled at the stage: "All right, enough already. Bring on the dancing girls!"

He sat down and five minutes later the speakers trooped on-stage, their eyes as glazed as their audience's from the mountainous dinner. The five took their appointed chairs and winced as Dr. Arden, white-haired and gulping air, rolled by them in his motorized wheelchair.

"Jesus, what's wrong with him?" Rachel whispered to Consuela.

"Stroke," replied Consuela. "It's taken him two years to get to this point."

"Yeah, well, I can see Sehkmet's done a lot for him," sneered Aaron.

Consuela squinted him to silence.

One by one the speakers devastated their audience with harrowing statistics, while on a screen behind them the chilling facts came to light in stills and on film. By the time Dr. Schaeffer took the podium, the festive air had given over to shock and angry murmurs. The cameras and hot lights only added to the discomfort.

Schaeffer—dubbed by his detractors The Great White Hope of Ecology—was tall, gray-bearded and gray-suited. He dressed like an accountant, he said, to make people accountable. Then he rolled out what he called his Chamber of Horrors to prove that the planet was dying of refuse.

"We have fifty years left," he concluded at the end of his

presentation. "I do not exaggerate. You can pray all you want for your soul, but for your body to survive it needs clean air and water. Lobby, write, contribute every dollar and hour you can spare. Finally, remember this: Think of every tree you see as human, for when the last one goes, so do we. Thank you for coming tonight. I hope you can join me in this effort. And think about this: When God comes for us He'll be lifting up the gardeners, the ones who tried to help His planet, not the ones who killed it. Thank you."

Schaeffer sat down to thunderous applause. His book and television series, 'Fifty Years and Counting,' had mounted the most celebrated attack on automobiles since Ralph Nader took on General Motors. Almost everyone in the room, Consuela included, had brought a copy of his book to be signed.

The wheels beneath Dr. Arden squeaked as an assistant attached the microphone to the tray in front of him. He took a gulp, smiled crookedly and said: "Don't be upset, ladies and gentlemen." He gulped again. "Being babied has its advantages." There was an inaudible sigh of relief. No one had to feel sorry for this man anymore, his handicap wasn't the main event.

Dr. Arden thanked the foregoing speakers and said that his only point of disagreement was the fifty years and that he would tell them why after he finished recounting the tale of Sehkmet and demonstrating the amulets. These amulets were on loan from the Egyptian government—"under tight security," he smiled, indicating the portly security guard by the wall. The audience tittered.

He said that since the demonstration required the subjects' weights to be called out, he would understand if the ladies declined to partake, especially after that humongous meal. Everyone laughed, and goaded one another to go up, but Dr. Arden wanted only five.

Five curious souls climbed on stage, and each one pointed to a different amulet. The amulets were put in separate boxes and carried to the small scale which had been placed on the podium. There the weight of each amulet was verified as eleven ounces. Then, one by one, the five people were weighed on the large scale, their weights and names called out by Arden's assistant.

To pick up the amulets they were admonished to use both hands, bend their knees, and not be afraid to call for help. One by one, the five picked up their selected amulets, gasped and groaned, and were helped back on the scale. The additional weights ran from thirty-seven pounds to a whopping eighty-nine.

At this point Aaron excused himself and walked to the stage in front of Dr. Arden.

With all due respect, he said, he'd like to conduct an experiment on the amulets to prove the scale hadn't been tampered with, and there was no hucksterism involved. Accompanied by the security guard, he'd take one of the amulets and a group of onlookers to various scales outside the hotel. If all the scales yielded the same weight, there could be no doubt of the results, and all of them would sign a testimonial to that effect.

"Young man," gulped Dr. Arden, "you are incredibly naive. Do you know how many testimonials... I have already acquired... in exactly the same way as you have suggested... and still the next group of people... to witness this demonstration... believe that it's a gimmick? That the participants have been... paid off?"

Then he sighed and said: "Very well... but I want the camera to follow you... and I want a print of the film afterwards. Agreed?"

Aaron and the camera crew agreed, and a briefcase was produced to contain the amulet.

Then Aaron with the briefcase, the security guard with his gun, and the camera crew with their equipment trooped out the door with a gaggle of onlookers, yelling the promise to be back in an hour.

Consuela got up to go with them and asked Rachel to stay, to hear the updates on the legend and to fill her in when they got back—especially the part about the abacus, because she had never heard about that. It must be entirely new.

After they left, Dr. Arden told the story of Sehkmet in his

halting fashion. He told them about Anton Gervaise, contemporary of the famous Egyptologist Flinders Petrie. Gervaise's translations provided most of the information about Sehkmet, and he concluded not only that Sehkmet was the Angel of Death, but that the Egyptian image of the cosmos and man's place in it were absolutely accurate, that further scientific study would only prove its authenticity.

He said that the Egyptian vision of the universe was of a giant, beating heart, and its 'expansions' and 'contractions' the proof of that. He said that space was not empty, but that the inter-stellar spaces were filled with non-luminous matter that moved with the pulse of The Creator, call It whatever name you will. He preferred Ra.

The focal point of humanity was therefore its heart. This single organ united all mankind with the universe, and thus the heart of man must be good so as not to disrupt the universal vibration. This is why the Egyptians enshrined all forms of life, for they realized the holiness or 'wholeness' of it all. They knew, too, that man was the most complex creation, the logical and appointed guardian of all the others. Only the children, creatures and fields that were nurtured and protected would bring the bounty consistent with universal harmony. If mankind began to harm the world it would send a discordant vibration through the universal heart, and Ra would not tolerate it. He would then send Sehkmet to cut away the disease as had happened at numerous times throughout history. "I have listed those occurrences in the booklet," said Dr. Arden. "Everyone will recognize Sodom and Gomorrah."

Then two triangular abaci flashed on the screen above him. Both triangles were the same size and held eleven rungs of different stones. One was Egyptian, made of obsidian; the other possibly Olmec, made of turquoise. They represented the prophesied attacks of Sehkmet on succeeding full moons in August sometime around two thousand A.D.—but only if mankind had broken its trust with Ra, and harmed his brothers on earth, and his sister the earth itself. Any questions?

There was a great deal of murmuring at the tables as people

worked out the mathematical formulae of the triangles.

A woman approached the microphone in the middle of the room and said: "Dr. Arden, how do you know this is what the triangles represent? And if you're accurate, by my calculations that means two attacks in the first year, twenty two in the second, two hundred and some in the third, two thousand in the fourth, and by the eleventh year we're up to two billion. What will all that carnage accomplish?"

The doctor said: "I have one last demonstration...to perform, and I will begin it... as soon as the verification crew gets back. This will answer all your questions... and no one here will doubt... the existence of Sehkmet. Now, let's break for a few minutes, please."

Rachel watched as the doctor leaned his head back and breathed hard. Poor man, she thought, and looked absently at the inside front cover of the booklet until the words began to register. The credit read: Anton Gervaise, translation of papyrus fragment, 1927:

> *And the light of the moon fell upon a woman wholly wronged, and raging at the iniquity.*
>
> *She raised her fists, and Hathor saw her anguish, and the moon shed tears.*
>
> *The tears fell in a storm upon the earth, and touched the woman's smouldering heart,*
>
> *And from the fire of her rage and the pureness of her grief a great white she-lion grew.*
>
> *And the beast that grew was tall and terrible, and knew every man by his heart.*
>
> *Those that were pure she left, and those that were evil she slew.*
>
> *And the name of the beast was Sehkmet.*

Rachel shut the book, worn out from all the food and drink and dire predictions. She was on the commode staring dully into space when one of the women from the seminar poked her head in the washroom and yelled: "Hey, anybody from the Grande Salle, the amulet bearers are back. Demonstration time, if anyone wants to see."

Αfτεr-Dinner Drinks

As she entered the room Rachel saw Aaron in front of the stage, talking up at Dr. Arden. Consuela was beside him, smirking. When she saw Rachel she skipped toward her with open arms, and hugged her.

"So what happened?" Rachel looked sideways at Consuela.

"What else?" laughed Consuela. "We went to five different scales, got the identical results, and he still thinks it's a phenomenon science'll crack in a year. I told him if the goddamn lion walked through the goddamn wall and ate me right in front of him he'd still be yelling 'Science'll solve this!' Well, Rach, science might do that one day, but in the meantime I'll side with Dr. Arden, and so will the people who went out with Aaron tonight."

She looked over Rachel's shoulder at the service staff,

who were removing all tables but one, which was shoved to the wall opposite the stage. A huge plastic bowl wadded in cotton was placed in the center of the table, and into that bowl was poured the dregs of the all the wine.

Dr. Arden was conferring with his assistants on stage, and one of them pointed to the chandelier. The doctor attempted a smile, and the microphone picked up: "Well, let's hope she has...nothing against...artificial lighting." A ladder was brought in and the assistant climbed up beside the chandelier to check its moorings. He gave the thumbs up, and Dr. Arden began the demonstration.

"I want to impress on you," he said, "that I don't know how this works... I only discovered it by accident. It is dangerous, however. Any sharp or breakable objects you have on your person...please take them out of this room. That includes cameras. Then arrange yourselves... in groups of any size up to eleven...form circles close to the walls, and hold hands. I know it sounds kindergarten ...but please, believe me... Your safety depends on your... not letting go of each other. Anyone who thinks they cannot do this...please leave the room. The doors will be locked... for the balance of this display...and I don't know what will happen... or how long it will last. Please decide now. We start in five minutes."

Several people left the room, fearful of being smashed by the chandelier.

As the remainder gathered in groups of eleven, Dr. Arden told them to watch the bowl on the table—if they could keep their eyes open.

He took a corked plastic vial from one of the five assistants who were holding hands behind him. The vial held a drop of each one's blood. He said he was going to pour the blood on the amulet with the open eyes and jaws.

He placed the amulet on the desktop attached to his wheelchair and said: "This is it, folks. Hold on tight...and don't let go. Is everyone ready?"

Hesitant grunts of assent came from the audience as they gripped each other's hands more tightly.

Dr. Arden took the cork from the vial and upended it over the amulet. Then his assistants grabbed his hands as the liquid found its target and the vial fell to the floor.

A terrible growl came from the amulet. It grew to a roar, and the roar became a wind that shot around the room, hurling people against the walls or smashing them to the floor.

The wind brought visions of dark men in jaguar skins, their spears and eyes red with firelight; dark men in white tunics casting the amulets; and regal bronze women in white gowns setting wine in silver dishes before the colossal statue of a woman dressed as they were, but with the head of a she-lion. Then came the image of the Great Sphinx, its head returning to its original state, sprouting the ears of a lioness. Its closed gray eyes opened on flames that burned with the greens of a forgotten Eden. Then came visions of personal transgression, and answers to questions they didn't dare ask. They dug their fingers in each other's hands, begging for the visions and the wind to end.

The bowl on the table flew against the wall and clattered to the floor, then rolled into the corner and stopped, inverted and empty.

The wind subsided, the chandelier stopped rocking, and the people could stand straight again. Reluctantly they released each other's hands. Some burst into tears. They pointed at each other's hair, standing out like porcupine quills. Then the doors were unlocked, and slowly the people with their spiky hair and dishevelled clothes filed out.

Aaron went to inspect the bowl. He returned to Consuela and Rachel and said: "I think that lion had the right idea. I need a drink." He looked at Rachel, and she was frowning into space. "I meant coffee, Rach. Whaddaya say? We'll take you back to your cousin's place after."

Rachel said she wanted to talk to Dr. Arden. Aaron offered to wait for her, but she declined and he was stung. "All right," he said, "Be that way."

"See you tomorrow, then?" said Rachel, suddenly aware he was leaving.

"Yeah. Maybe." Aaron smiled with narrowed eyes, and as

he turned away Consuela hugged Rachel and said yes, they would see her tomorrow—or if he wouldn't, she would.

Rachel watched them go, but her eyes were fixed on another vision entirely: when the roaring wind passed through her she was in black, freezing water and saw her father floating before her, with weeds around his happy broken face—and his arms around her mother. The image faded, and left her staring at her hand on the wall. She pulled her arm back, and walked toward the stage.

Dr. Arden was fielding questions from the few people who could talk, who kept touching their hair to remind themselves it wasn't a dream. One of his assistants walked among them with a clipboard, getting them to sign a mailing list. Rachel shook her head when he approached her, feeling she shouldn't have her name on such a list but not sure why. It was almost as if she heard someone say, "Don't." She even looked around to see who was there, but no one was behind her.

Dr. Arden said one last thing before he left the stage, that a group of concerned patrons (he couldn't, after all, organize these "shows" for free) were getting an 800 number to consolidate further findings. He was particularly concerned about the return of Sehkmet, which should happen at some point in the next fifteen years, that is if the prophecies were correct and mankind continued in its gross misconduct. "In about five years," he said, "we'll be able to afford it... and anyone will be able to call...1–800–SEHKMET... Cute, eh? That's all I can manage for now, folks. Thank you for coming... and may Ra bless and keep you... as I hope he does me."

With that he wheeled offstage, surrounded by his assistants. One of them leaned over his shoulder to catch something he said and Rachel saw the outline of a shoulder holster under his jacket. She thought about his assistants, all suited, even the women, and realized they were all armed. Jesus, she sighed, what that man must be up against.

She checked her handbag for the booklet and left the room, then saw that it was 11:27. She dialed Colette's number and after six rings Carla answered.

"Rachel!" Carla exploded. "Guess what? I just saw you on TV! You were with this beautiful Indian girl and this real foxy guy, and they followed him around to different places to weigh this weird little cat head. They said his name was Aaron Meisel. Is that the same Aaron you been writing to?"

"Yes, Carla. That's him."

"Wow, Rachel. He is the prince of foxes. When're ya gonna invite him to Florida? I'd love to see that guy up close."

"Jesus, Carla, enough already! One more squeal and I'm gonna strangle you!" Then she said she was sorry, that she just wasn't up to any teen shriekfests tonight.

"All right," said Carla, in her old-style thoughtful voice, "You wanna talk serious? Let's talk birth control."

Rachel gulped. "Okay." she said, "But not tonight, please. Tomorrow, I promise. Okay?"

Carla agreed.

Rachel said goodbye and watched the receiver dip the bright aluminum tripod. She tried to imagine her baby sister writhing on somebody's couch. God, she thought, what can I tell her? Well, at least she came to me.

She closed her eyes. God, she wished Aaron were free.

She walked past the stores of the underground city to the Metro turnstiles, then into the fluorescent glare of the subway station. She galloped down the escalator past the Olympic posters and the beautiful tiled mosaics to catch the train as the whistle sounded. The doors rolled shut behind her and the blue bullet shot off into the heaving darkness of the tunnel.

Kenny

The city was abuzz next morning with the effects of Dr. Arden's demonstration. Wine stewards in every restaurant and bar near the Sheraton Hotel found corked wine bottles untouched and empty. No explanation could be found for this, and the people from the demonstration weren't talking.

Rachel was talking, though—telling Carla to marry Prince Charming and use condoms in the meantime. Too many diseases out there. While it wasn't the answer Carla was looking for, Rachel must know something—boy, was that Aaron a fox.

Four years later Carla found a fox of her own.

It was a boiling Saturday afternoon in August. Carla and her look-alike best friend Cathy were lying on a sheet at the beach when rain fell on them from an approaching cloud. The rain pumped harder, driving them from the beach. They bundled their belongings in the sheet and ran to Cathy's little Pacer. It was two blocks away, but Cathy couldn't find her keys.

They ran back along the road, looking for a flash of metal, and found the keys a foot from the 'No Dogs' sign. They ran back to the car and threw the sheet in the back, then jumped in the front seat, pointing and squealing at each other's dripping mascara.

The storm got worse, and soon they could see nothing out the windows but rain. They watched the windows fog up and giggled that it was like being at the drive-in. Their giggling fit was interrupted by a knock on the driver's side window, and both of them jumped.

It came again, as the rain magically stopped. Cathy cracked the window to find the most beautiful blue eyes she had ever seen. Her jaw dropped with the window: he was every bit as gorgeous as his eyes promised, and smiling to boot.

"Hey," he said, "my friends and I saw y'all running around in the rain. We were gonna come help, butcha seem to have it under control. We're setting up for a party down here." He pointed down the street to a deck where two tanned boys were waving, "So we thought, hey, why not invite them. So whaddaya say? You wanna come?"

The girls bumped shoulders for a last look in the mirror, then climbed out of the car, rolling their eyes at each other as he put his arms around their waists. He walked them to the huge duplex where three-foot speakers boomed out Glenn Frey and The Rolling Stones.

Carla tried not to stare at him. His name was Kenny Merritt, and he was so laid back and friendly, but she didn't dare hope he could be interested in her. She knew she was pretty, a cute kind of pretty. She knew she had a nice body, the rounded sort—but that didn't make her particularly special, not like him. So when she saw him coming toward her after the first hour she moved aside to let him pass. He stopped, bent his head to look in her eyes, and flashed a smile that made her heart stop.

"So Carla," he said, "what're you afraid of? I'm not gonna bitecha."

True, thought Carla. Too bad. "I think you're gorgeous," she blurted out, and blushed.

"So?" he said, "So are you. Tell me something I haven't heard."

"Well," she said, raising her eyebrows, "I wish the Rolling Stones could finish a song—those damn choruses go on forever."

He grinned. "Not a Stones fan, huh? So what do you like, Miz Carla? Tell me." He took her hand and led her to the couch behind them, sat down, and pulled her onto his lap. He looked in her cup and saw that it was empty. "Wanna refill?" he offered.

"Nope. I'm fine." She smiled, instantly comfortable on his lap, and put an arm around his neck.

As she touched the blond curls that swept his shoulders he grinned: "Look ma, no roots."

They talked about a lot of things, surprising each other with their range of interests and experience. Everything she said pointed to a kind, gentle person, and he liked that. He liked that she had been a gymnast and was willing to learn how to surf. He said he was tired of these lazy bitches who just lay around the beach waiting for someone to drop 'ludes on them.

"You're not afraid out there? Ever?" Carla asked, thinking of the record hammerhead that was hooked off Jax Beach pier last week.

"Hey, you got a lot more to fear from some drunk on the road than a little old shark in the ocean. They don't say to stay out of the water on Labor Day, just off the road. So, girl, when'm I gonna larn ya how ta surf?"

Carla giggled. "Boy, wait'll my sister hears about this."

"Why?"

"Oh, she's deathly afraid of sharks. She was deathly afraid when I got into gymnastics, but she figured better that than drugs."

Kenny rolled his eyes and looked at her sideways. "Now

she sounds like a barrel of laughs. Tell me, does she keep you in a cage? How did you escape?"

Carla told him about her mom and dad, and how Rachel had assumed the mantle of parenthood and over-reacted to everything.

"Hey." said Kenny, "It's nice to know somebody loves you... even if they are a pain in the ass." They finished the sentence together and laughed.

She told him about Montreal. He said he'd like to go there. He talked about surfing in the Bahamas. She said she'd like to go there.

She asked him about his family. He said his parents were gone and he lived with his uncle.

The rain had stopped and widening shafts of sunlight broke through the clouds. He asked if she would like to take a walk on the beach. She said yes and he went to the beer keg to fill their plastic cups for the trek. On the way he was stopped by a beautiful blonde girl who put her arm around Kenny's waist.

Well, thought Carla, that's the end of that. She sighed and sat down, wondering if Cathy would be willing to leave, when she saw him coming back. Nice to the end, she thought, and was surprised to hear him say that the girl was a bitch, that he had to talk to her for a minute but he'd be right back, don't go away.

Dumbfounded, Carla watched him return to the regal beauty with the Farrah Fawcett hair. Her perfect tan was interrupted only by strings of gold and a white knit bikini. Undoubtedly they were lovers, and she had come to fetch him.

Carla was right: Marielle Tannen was after Kenny. She held his hand, flicked her tongue at him and whispered: "C'mon, Ken. Ya gonna join me in the tub? Or is little straggle-puss over there gonna try for second place?"

Kenny looked down at this rich man's toy he'd been back-dooring for months, and said in a low voice: "It's over, cunt. Find yourself another weenie."

Marielle let go of his hand and sneered: "You'll be back, you know. Begging for it."

"Not this time, sweetcheeks. This time I've met someone nice for a change, somebody interesting."

Marielle didn't believe him, and she didn't miss a beat. She cast another withering glance at Carla and said: "Well, I guess when that's all you can afford, nice and interesting is what you get. Meanwhile, I'm gonna get myself a beer."

She bent over the keg as provocatively as possible, pumped the white foam into a plastic cup, and walked back to Kenny. She raised the cup under his nose and whispered, "See, you were wrong. I can do something for myself." Then she announced, "Toodle-oo." Bodies parted before her. At the doorway she turned, blew Kenny a kiss, and was gone.

His good buddy Brian was on top of him instantly. "Hey, man, you let go of that? Are you crazy, man?"

"Nope, feel fine," said Kenny. He looked at Brian's salivating face and said: "Hey, you want her, go get her. Be my guest." Brian shot out of the room and Kenny yelled after him: "Butcha better have a million to spend on her, or a foot-long shlong."

People laughed and Carla winced.

Kenny finished foaming up the cups and walked over to Carla, who was looking at the floor and pulling at her hair. He squatted down beside her and said: "Hey, I got the refreshments here. You ready?"

Carla looked at him and felt like she was going to cry. She said: "Look, if you wanna be with that girl, it's okay. I mean, I can't measure up to her and I don't wanna even try."

Kenny cocked his head at her. "Hey, if I'd wanted her, I'd a left with her. Besides, I think you got that measuring-up stuff backwards. She could take lessons from you." He watched her blush, and grinned. "Ooh," he said, "Cute. Now, c'mon, there, little bit." He took her hand and hauled her to her feet. "C'mon, let's get those buns in gear before they crank up another Stones chorus."

Carla said she had to check with her friend and Kenny said to cut her loose, that he'd drive Carla home later—that is if she didn't mind being seen in a semi-retired VW bug.

"Hey," said Carla, "any set of wheels is fine."

"We'll put your pocket book in my trunk," he said, and they did.

They walked off down the beach as the clouds rolled aside to let the sky breathe.

"How'd you get into surfing?" she asked.

"Well," he said hesitantly, "I had kind of a rotten child-hood, and I needed something where I didn't have to deal with people and their bullshit, y'know? Surfing has it all. It's an art, it's a sport, it's fresh air, it's never the same, and it's always a challenge. Runners talk about their highs, and druggies mess up their bods for it, but nothing beats that moment when you're flying, totally in control. Well," he allowed, "sex comes pretty close."

"So what do your girlfriends do?" she laughed. "Pretend they're surfboards?"

"Hey," he grinned, "with some of the girls I've known that would've been an improvement."

He kept waiting for this gentle girl to turn bitchy. Usually people floored by his looks were either prostrate before him or defensively bitchy. He hadn't known a day since he was fourteen that men and women alike didn't whistle at him from cars, follow him, gawk at him, and generally drive him crazy. Gays thought he was one of their own because so many gays were spectacularly handsome, but he couldn't stand their bitchy caricatures. He heard his father's voice when he was eight calling him 'pretty boy' and 'fagmeat.' His other memories weren't any better.

Kenny was the cause of a forced marriage between two handsome high school dropouts, Bo and Edie. Their parents rented and furnished a trailer for them, but Bo and Edie were furious at having to organize their lives around "the baby." They fought with their parents, making up with them just as the rent came due or the phone was about to be shut off. After a year of bankrolling their bickering, the parents wised up and closed ranks to insist that Bo "do right and get a job."

But Bo already had a job, one that brought in the necessary

dough when Mommy and Daddy couldn't be conned out of theirs. Bo was a small-time drug dealer, and he and his wife gleefully sucked up the proceeds. Every morning Bo would head out on his bicycle with his backpack and revolver, come home at three, shoot up with his wife, and lie around until the kid did something to 'irritate' him, like ask for lunch or breakfast.

Bo would then take off his belt and clobber Kenny till the boy lay in a ball, crying. Bo would call him a coward for not fighting back, and then if Kenny tried, he would really get whipped.

On his ninth birthday Kenny was studying the bruises under his too-small shirt and planning to run away when his father beat him to it. Bo yelled that he was leaving and never coming back, but Kenny had heard that every day for years— it was the way Bo and Edie built themselves up for sex, by picking a fight. That night, however, Bo didn't come back.

Whatever dreams Kenny might have had about his father's leaving, life was no better without him. Now a series of men trooped into the little trailer, and whenever one came in Kenny's mother would send him off to visit his uncle.

Uncle Tyson lived in a bungalow off Timaquana Road, with a brown and white cat named Freckles. Tyson could talk about anything, and his face always lit up when he saw Kenny. Tyson was Kenny's closest friend, but he could only suspect the depravity of his nephew's home life because Kenny was always scrupulously clean, polite and helpful. Kenny was clean because he showered fanatically and filched money from his mother's stash under the rug to get his clothes cleaned.

He also began to steal, a simple task for one so beautiful. Salespeople, dazzled by his face, were gladdened by the helpful boy holding his mother's shopping bag. His 'mother' was always some haughty blonde unaware of the boy a few feet behind her. While the salespeople indulged her he would pick shirts, pants and sweaters, vanish among the racks, and pop them in the bag. Then he'd return to the counter with one of the cellophane-wrapped shirts, make a face and dump it on the pile. He would wait while the woman made her purchase, then follow her out the door. He was never caught, he just got better at it.

By the age of fourteen Kenny knew that his looks could bring him anything he wanted.

Anything but his mother's love. She blamed him for the bills, for the lack of hot water, for roaches in the kitchen, for anything that "irritated" her. Sometimes he'd come home when she was flying and she'd try to come on to him. He'd grab her bony arms, yell and shake her, and the fantasy would evaporate along with her slatternly look. No, it wasn't anybody important, just him, that irritating presence that shared her living space.

God how he wished he could walk in the house one night and see his mother looking like the beautiful woman in the wedding book. She looked so happy—what went wrong? But he knew what went wrong, that he was the thing that was wrong. Somehow, because of him, his father was gone and his mother was a slut.

But as he got older he started to disbelieve it, and the more he disbelieved it, the more he began to hate her. He couldn't hate her totally because he still wanted her love, and his despair at not being loved fueled his hatred all the more.

Only his relationship with his uncle served to diffuse his anger, because he recognized the caring, even if inside he felt empty towards this kind person. There was a fold-out couch in the livingroom of Tyson's little bungalow, and Kenny often spent the night there. His uncle would make him dinner, usually some form of eggs, and he and Kenny would watch TV. Tyson was always conversational and interested in what Kenny was doing, though without much money there wasn't much to tell.

On Kenny's fifteenth birthday Tyson bought him a surfboard, and Kenny found his salvation. The board became his bridge to sanity, paddling and floating and riding the swell, home at last in the womb of the world. Surfing brought him comrades his own age, and as for women—well, if Mama didn't want him she was the only female he knew that didn't.

Women of all ages loved to stare at him, touch him, spend money on him, take him places, dress him, undress him, go down on him, and peer into his eyes after sex with that same searching look, amazed it could be her that he wanted. He would live with one or another until her jealousy started to irritate him, then he would camp at his uncle's for awhile, using Tyson's home as a permanent address.

Once in a while he would go home to visit his mother, smell the stench, and leave with tears in his eyes. The only thing she said on the day he finally moved out was: "Don't be givin' Tyson no trouble now, y'hear?"

Two years later the landlord found her rotting on the floor of the trailer—stabbed, the coroner said, in fifteen places. Surely by one of her tricks, said everyone in the neighborhood who was questioned.

At Edie's funeral, her mother burst into tears when she saw Kenny. Then she screamed at him to go away, that he was responsible for her baby meeting a bad end, that her life would have been different if only he hadn't been born.

Kenny screamed back that he couldn't help being born, that they were responsible for that, that he wouldn't be blamed for the death of that whore. If someone hadn't stabbed her the drugs would have finished her off anyway.

That night he let himself back into the trailer before the new occupants took possession. My, how different it looked and smelled: they must have been cleaning for days. Happily the bedroom rug hadn't been replaced. Kenny dug his hand underneath and dragged out the last of his mother's stash, three hundred and eighty-seven dollars.

"Thanks, Mama," he whispered, pocketing his inheritance.

Then he looked for the wedding book. Damn, it was gone. Someone had taken his one sustaining image, the only thing he wanted to keep.

Three years later he met Marielle Tannen, the image of the girl in the wedding book, but Marielle wanted him. God, how she wanted him. She told him so every time she saw him. She loved to watch them cavort in her mirrored bedroom, and Kenny's hunger to be held led him to endure the yo-yo relationship, dragged inside the door whenever The Creep— as called him—was gone, pushed out whenever The Creep returned. Gradually it dawned on Kenny that he was just a prop for Marielle's magnificence, like The Creep who paid for her penthouse.

Damn, he was tired of it. All to be touched, stroked, held and sucked. God, he thought, what men have to endure for those moments. It wasn't fair. Those fucking bitches.

He wanted to meet a woman who was genuinely kind, instead of bitchy, demanding and jealous. There had to be one, somewhere. This Magic She would break the cycle of need and rejection. She would touch his arm with just the right pressure, and he would know it was her.

Then he met Carla, who touched him in that magic way, and a happily-ever-after bomb went off in his brain.

He spent the afternoon testing her to see if she would turn bitchy: nope, there didn't seem to be a bitchy bone in her body. She even blushed: bitches didn't blush. The more they talked the more she blushed and the more he smiled.

It wasn't just his looks, she said, it was his attentiveness that made her color rise. She rarely met a man willing to listen to her, and she said it was a pleasant change. So, she wasn't stupid either. Kenny began to hang on her every word, the same way he'd hang on his surfboard. Maybe this was the Magic She that would pluck him from the clutches of bitchiness and indifference.

They walked down the beach as the setting sun made the shoreline a ribbon of shimmering pink. They sat in one of the lifeguard's red scaffold chairs, pointing at the faint outline of the moon and the bright dot of Venus in the darkening sky.

Kenny found himself telling her things he had never told anyone, like the time he and a friend thought they had seen a U.F.O. She was so easy to talk to, and he didn't want the night to end.

He took her home and kissed her, and the kiss was like an

electric shock. It was the kiss he had waited for; he couldn't believe it. He wanted another kiss like that, but something told him to wait. Everything always came to him in such a rush, and then it got spoiled. No, this time was going to be different. He let his arms drop and felt instantly empty. He leaned against the door and looked down at her, waiting to see what she would do. She didn't move. "What're ya doing tomorrow?" he ventured.

"Seeing you, I hope," she smiled. The blood was pounding in her ears, it was all she could do not to scream.

"Count on it, Carla," he said, grinning, then climbed in his car and drove off, tooting the horn twice as he rolled out of the driveway.

Carla closed the door behind her and ran into the kitchen where Rachel was extracting cookies from the oven. Rachel looked at her sister's flushed face and knew something incredible had happened.

"God, Rachel!" Carla gasped. "Wait'll you meet him! He is the most gorgeous guy I've ever seen! Yow!"

"Well, congratulations," said Rachel, unimpressed She laid the tray on the counter and smiled. "Have a cookie."

No News is Good

Rachel first saw Kenny when he came to pick Carla up for a rock concert, a month after he and Carla had been dating. Rachel was thrilled that this mysterious stranger was treating her sister like a princess. So far he had given Carla a gold necklace and a beautiful cotton sweater.

And what did he do, this wonderful Kenny? Oh, he worked part time in a surf shop and part time in a local bar, arranging his hours around the surfing conditions.

Must be nice, Rachel grimaced, locked into nine-to-five and often later. Then she saw him.

He looked in her eyes when he shook her hand, and she was so embarrassed by her attraction that she blushed.

"Oho!" laughed Kenny, pointing at her face. "Family trait, huh?"

Rachel laughed and looked down. "Yeah, I guess."

She looked back toward Carla's bedroom, and Carla bounced out on cue.

Carla glowed. She grabbed Kenny's hand, then Rachel's, and told them how happy she was they'd finally met.

Rachel offered to make dinner for them that Sunday. What did he like to drink?

"Oh," smiled Kenny, "you pick. Carla here tells me you're a real connoisseur."

"I think she's overstating it," laughed Rachel, looking away from those eyes lest she blush again. "Now Mom," she continued, "was the real connoisseur. But I'll do my best. I mean, hell, if you're brave enough to swim with sharks you can surely survive my dinner."

They all laughed and Carla put her arm around Rachel and kissed her cheek. Kenny bent down and kissed her other cheek.

"Thanks, Sis," he said, catching her eyes, and he and Carla climbed into the car, grinned and waved, and were gone with two honks of the horn.

Rachel stood in the doorway touching her cheek, stunned by his looks and his easy familiarity. So that's Kenny, she sighed. Wow. Guess I better get used to looking away. Hell, what's to worry. It may all be over by the weekend.

Five months later Carla came shrieking into the house, waving an engagement ring. Rachel hugged her, amazed, and waited for it to evaporate in a few months. After all, Carla was just twenty.

"Well," said Carla, "Mom was twenty when she married Dad."

"True," said Rachel, "but…"

Three months later they had set a date: June twenty-fifth. Rachel was sitting in her father's studio when Carla bounced in with the news.

"Are you sure about this?" Rachel asked. "You're not pregnant, are you?"

Carla shook her head, then put her arms around Rachel and said, "Rachel, stop worrying. I know that's like telling a cat not to scratch, but stop anyway. Do you remember what you said to me that night in Montreal, the night you came back from that big Olympic banquet?"

Rachel shrugged and shook her head.

Carla went on: "You said you hoped I'd marry Prince Charming. Well I am. I'm the luckiest girl in the world, and Rachel, you have to know it's true. You've seen how he treats me. I mean, there isn't anyone handsomer, kinder or more loving than Kenny. How can you doubt him?"

Rachel sighed and rolled her eyes. "Look, Carla, you're right. You're right, he treats you like a queen, he's every woman's dream, and I'm acting like a—a—"

"A parent?" Carla laughed. She squeezed her arms tighter around her sister. "And I love you for it, Rach. You just don't have to do it anymore. You can get on with your life now. Hell, you think I don't know that's what you've been doing all these years, putting off college and turning down dates, all to see me get 'reared proper'?

"You can go after that degree now, Rach, bloom in that career, marry some guy who'll treat you like a queen. I mean hell, why not? Look at Mom. Look at me. Snagging nice men is the family destiny. Hey, if I find a Kenny clone who recites Shakespeare and collects weird little cat heads, I'll send him over."

Rachel laughed. Carla never let her live down the amulet story, for Rachel had told her about it one night when she was drunk and Carla thought she was on something much stronger.

There was a howling at the window, and they turned toward the fish tank where the wavy face of Sultan kept popping up and down, wanting to be part of the action.

"Are you gonna take Sultan?" asked Rachel.

Carla shrugged and twisted her mouth. "No. I wish I could but Kenny's allergic to fur or something, so you get to keep him. Besides, this is his home, and it's not like I won't get to see him a lot."

Rachel sniffed: "Well then, better go tell Sultan he's about to lose his best buddy."

"Oh, Rach, that's silly. Let's see, how does it go, you haven't lost a sister, you've gained a brother-in-law?"

"Oh, goody," said Rachel, reaching for the last tissue from a box she kept for show. She tore it down the middle and handed one of the serrated halves to Carla.

Carla shook her head and smiled. "Just can't stop doing for me, can ya?"

"Nope," said Rachel. "Right to my last Kleenex. Sorry, you'll just *half* to live with it."

Carla's eyes filled with tears. "I am the luckiest girl in the world," she sniffed.

They talked about where to hold the wedding, and Carla suggested the back yard. They could fix up a canopy of lilacs, and Sultan could come if he promised not to eat everything on the tables.

"Muzzle time for Sultan," Rachel said. "Let's get him one to match the decor. What color, then?"

"Blue," said Carla, blushing, "to go with Kenny's eyes."

Carla and Kenny were married in the back yard under a hazy sun, and everyone wore light blue, including Sultan, who sported a giant silk bow. Cathy was the maid of honor and Kenny's uncle Tyson was the best man. The reception was in every room of the house. The guests entered the study to sign the wedding book and ask why there were only three fish in the huge tank.

The three oscars were from the original group, and Rachel had left them as a tribute to her father. Hell, they'd be dead soon enough. Everything you love leaves, she mused, watching Kenny and Carla in the garden, feeling happy and lonely by turns.

As a symbolic send-off to a new life for all of them, Rachel wrote a check for three thousand dollars and slipped the envelope in Kenny's coat pocket when he laid his jacket aside to open the gifts.

Four hours after the party was over Rachel heard a loud knock on the door and went to check the peephole. It was Kenny. She opened the door and he came storming through, waving the check and ranting: "What the hell do you mean by this?" Rachel was stunned. "It's for anything, Kenny. For the honeymoon, for furniture, to celebrate your life. I mean it may seem like a lot, but Carla's my sister, and I—"

"Oh yeah, Carla's your sister all right. Rachel thinks this and Rachel thinks that. Well what you think doesn't mean shit to me, lady. Carla's my wife, now, and I don't wanna be hearing how nice Rachel was to give us that money. No way. You're not gonna control our lives, and you sure as hell aren't gonna buy me."

"Buy you?" Rachel could barely get the words out.

"Yeah, that's what I said. I seen that look in your eyes. I seen it in all kindsa faces, women faces, fag faces, and every one of 'em wanted to buy me. But I'm married now, and all you whining money bitches can take a flying leap." He was tearing up the check as he spoke, and threw the pieces in the air. Then he brushed the fallen pieces off his suit and jabbed his finger in Rachel's face on the way out the door. "From now on, don't interfere in Carla's life, sister dear, or mine. We're nunna yer business anymore."

Rachel looked at the hunks of paper amid the confetti and wondered how she could have been so misjudged, then wondered if he was right.

Two weeks later Carla called with stories of the honeymoon in the Bahamas. She had pictures she wanted to show Rachel. Could she come over tonight?

"Sure," said Rachel, happy for the warmth in Carla's voice. Kenny wasn't coming, he'd gone to play pool at Pete's. Rachel wondered if she should tell Carla about the check and the aftermath, then decided against it when she saw how happy Carla was. I'll just let her do the calling, thought Rachel, and that seemed to work out pretty well. She never saw Kenny and that was a blessing.

Two weeks before Christmas all hell broke loose at the ad agency where Rachel worked. Bigelow and Whitsun were among the top designers in the southeast. Bigelow was the gladhander and country clubber while Whitsun created the campaigns that filled developers' coffers. Rachel was one of the fulltime staff, playing customer service, helping the typesetter or photographer or mechanical artists as necessary. She knew everything about the business but the books, which were kept in the safe in Bigelow's office and transferred once a month to the office of the accountant, Dabny Sims.

On December 11th Lawrence Bigelow rerouted the company profits into a cash disbursement made out to the owners, signed his name and forged Whitsun's, and left the country with a faked passport. It turned out that he had been dribbling cash out of the company for years, with the help of the proper, bespectacled Sims. The question wasn't how could the bastard do it, but how could he do it and leave them nothing?

Bill Whitsun, however, was no fool. He had saved a bundle in his own right, rather than funnel his share back into the company as Bigelow suggested. He told the five employees that none of them would suffer through Christmas and New Year, that they'd have their bonuses, and if they could tough it out another three months he could turn it around.

They all promised to stick with him, and he gratefully shook their hands.

"Rachel!" he barked as she walked out the door, "What do you know about bookkeeping?"

"I know what a debit and a credit is," she said, stopping.

"Good," he said. "You're the new bookkeeper. Write yourself a raise and you're dogmeat."

Rachel laughed and gave him the thumbs up, then walked back to the front desk. There a tall blond man stood with his back to her, perusing the awards on the wall. As she approached he turned around and she said: "Kenny?"

He smiled, and she blushed in confusion. "What's going on?" she blurted out.

"Came to invite you to lunch, Rach. To bury the hatchet. I, uh, decided I was wrong. Shake?" He extended his large hand, and Rachel took it gratefully. "I also came to invite you to dinner." He didn't stop smiling. "At our place. Carla 'n' me's got somethin' to tell you."

Rachel was anxious throughout lunch. She ordered the buffet so that she could escape from the table and plan unmeddlesome sentences.

Kenny was smiling, completely in control. At one point he put his hand on her arm and said: "Hey, take it easy, that other stuff's in the past."

So if it was in the past why didn't she feel comfortable?

Dinner that night consisted of spaghetti and two bottles of beaujolais. When Rachel saw how happy Carla was she began to unwind. After dinner she told them to make their announcement, the suspense was killing her.

Kenny was sitting on the couch by Carla, kissed her on the cheek and said: "She's pregnant. The baby's due in July. That is, if it's on time."

Rachel leaped out of her chair, Carla stood up, and they hugged each other.

"Way to go, little sister." Rachel squeezed her. "Mom always said summer babies are the best." Her eyes were closed while she hugged Carla, but as she smiled they opened a tiny fraction and she saw Kenny glaring at her.

He saw her eyes and settled his face in a smile, and Carla felt Rachel's distress.

"What's wrong, Rachel?" she asked.

"Oh, nothing." Rachel lied. "Just that stuff at work with Christmas coming and all. I feel bad for Bill Whitsun."

"Well, don't worry, Rachel. We're gonna have a great Christmas," Carla beamed, and Rachel forced a hollow smile, knowing Kenny's was even hollower.

And Baby Makes Two

♥

It was a long labor with many false starts, and the baby was already two weeks overdue.

"The first thing I'm gonna teach that kid is punctuality," Carla gasped, as Jessica Claire Marie presented her bloody little bald head to the world. It was ten minutes to midnight, July twenty-seventh, in the birthing room of the local hospital.

Kenny was there in scrubs, as gleeful as Carla was drained. He brought the rinsed bundled baby to her mother, and kissed Carla's dripping face. "Happy birthday, Mom," he grinned.

The nurse took the baby away, and Kenny helped wheel Carla back to her room.

"Hey," he said, "you wanna see Rachel? She's waiting in the holding pen out there."

"Oh, yes," whispered Carla. "Please ask her to come in."

Rachel tip-toed into the room holding a bunch of white lilacs and a little teddy bear. She put them down on the table tray and kissed Carla. "So, I hear I have a niece," she laughed. "Yep," said Carla, "and already she's running the show. You two should get along great."

Kenny laughed at that a little too loudly, and Carla was suddenly aware of his special animosity for Rachel. She looked at Rachel and saw the discomfort, almost fear, then back at Kenny's smiling face, sensing the menacing "niceness." What the hell was going on?

Then a wave of tiredness carried her off and she fell asleep between them, holding their hands.

She wanted to ask Rachel what was wrong but weeks later she was still too busy with the baby while Rachel was too busy at work for any deep discussions. Once in a while Rachel would drop by with doughnuts and little gifts for Jessie, but if Kenny was there she left quickly. Kenny found her "irritating," he said, and when he was irritated he went surfing.

The baby he so adored when it arrived he found especially irritating. It would cry at night and interrupt his sleep, cry when they were making love, and always Carla would get up to check it. "You're spoiling her," he complained.

"She's a little baby, Kenny," Carla huffed, tired of this ongoing battle. "We can get into disciplining her when she's old enough to conform to our schedules."

"Which will be never," Kenny crabbed. His jealousy was tearing him apart. The arms that were his refuge and the pussy that was his comfort were suddenly taken up with this bundle of endless yowls. No wonder women were such demanding bitches, look how they started out.

As for Carla's sweetness, that began to grate on him too. He found himself saying things to hurt her, like why didn't she lose twenty pounds or fix herself up for him like she used to?

Confused, she would cry until he held her and told her he didn't mean it, that he loved the way she looked. She felt it was true, so why did he say these mean things?

He found other things to fight about when she was nursing.

Those were his tits after all. Watching her nurse, he wanted to suck out all her sustenance for himself and fuck her at the same time to show the baby who was boss. He would sit by them feeling the anguish build, then when she put the baby back in the crib he would grab her and fuck her, slamming her against the pillows, begging her to say she loved him: "Say it! Scream it!"

And Carla did, but it wasn't enough.

Worst of all the baby brought back Rachel, Rachel with her gifts and mother-henning suggestions. Kenny felt outnumbered and shut out. He wanted to feed the baby to the sharks. Watch it yowl then, he sneered, strapping his surfboard on the car.

On the morning of Kenny and Carla's second anniversary Rachel phoned to offer herself as babysitter for their night out. Kenny took the call and said that would be nice.

He looked at Carla sleeping naked with the sheet around her, kissed her face, sucked her tits, fondled her pussy, and said good-bye.

He walked into his daughter's room, kissed Jessie's cheek, held her little foot a few moments, then said good-bye.

Carla heard the door slam and Jessie howl. She got up, got herself and Jessie dressed and fed, then headed for the beach.

She came home at four expecting Kenny to be there, but he wasn't.

Rachel called, and Carla said she was waiting on Kenny to find out what was going on.

Hours went by, and Carla called the surf shop and the bar and the few numbers she had for his friends, but no one had seen him. Then she called the hospitals and police stations: surely someone would have seen him, he wasn't the kind to go unnoticed. She whimpered the evening away, afraid to use the phone lest he be trying to reach her.

Rachel came over at eight and both of them fell asleep on the couch with the phone between them.

Carla awoke next morning to Jessie's hollering. She went to tend to Jessie and Rachel followed her, asking what Carla wanted to do.

"Shit if I know," said Carla. "It's too early to file a missing person's report." She burst into tears, fearing the worst.

"Listen," said Rachel, "I'll take the day off. One day won't turn'em belly-up."

Carla squeezed her sister's hand, then asked her to go for groceries. She made up a short list and wrote a check for twenty dollars. Rachel left and Carla slowly sat down beside Jessie's high chair.

"Yelly!" Jessie exclaimed, spreading her arms. Her hands and bib were covered in grape jelly, she had a grape jelly beard. "Yelly," she enthused, reaching out to give her mother some of the good stuff.

Carla went to the sink and returned to wipe off her purple daughter. She picked up the little girl and hugged her while Jessie fought to get to the floor. The child was eying her bright rubber telephone, and the only thing standing between her and a power lunch with the Jelly Cartel was Momma, whose face was wet as a diaper.

The phone rang and Carla ran to it. It was Rachel.

"Carla," she said hesitantly, "I think you better get down here. I'm at your bank. It, uh, seems there aren't enough funds to cover the check. I'll drive you down here to straighten it out. Are you ready to go?"

"Sure," said Carla, and gulped. She didn't want to leave the phone. Why the hell hadn't they gotten that call-forwarding? Well, what would it take to unravel the mistake, a few minutes?

It took a half hour but there was no mistake. The morning before Kenny had come in and cashed a check that cleaned the account down to ten dollars.

"Oh," said the teller, "and he cashed in the money market fund. Pardon me for asking, but have they settled on a time for the operation?"

Carla stared at her blankly.

"The operation," the teller repeated, "the one your father's going to have. Oh, I'm sorry, I guess I shouldn've mentioned it, but Kenny seemed so distressed." Then she said brightly: "I jest know he's gonna git better, Miz Merritt. I mean, how can he lose with The Lord an' his fambly behind him? What's his name? We'll pray for him in Church this Sunday."

"George," said Carla, "George Williams," figuring that no prayers for her father were ever wasted.

Carla went to the safe deposit box, opened it and stared at the topsy-turvy mess inside. Her mother's opal ring was gone. Dumped behind the envelopes was the one marked "Jessie's college fund," empty.

She had been telling herself that Kenny had been kidnapped, forced at gunpoint to take out all their money and tell this crazy story. The missing silver dollar showed her something else. She wanted to scream and beat the walls. How could he do this? They could be evicted, they could starve, and he didn't care. How could he not care? Holding Jessie and crying, Carla left the bank.

Rachel had overheard everything waiting with Jessie in the bank lobby. She drove them home while Carla cried *Why?* over and over.

Rachel could do little but shake her head and shrug. She called her office and said, "Look, I'm in the middle of a family crisis. I'll see you in a couple of days. Sorry," and hung up.

"It's all right, Rachel. I know he's not gonna call," said Carla, her voice rising as the words ended in sobs.

Rachel tried to put her arms around Carla, but Carla leaped up and said : "Look, I need to get out of here. I'm just gonna take a quick walk on the beach to clear my head. Do you mind?"

Rachel shook her head and said Jessie was in capable hands, so go.

"Thanks," said Carla, and bounded out the door.

Two hours later she was back. "I need to get as far away from here as possible. Montreal sound far enough to you?"

"Excellent idea," said Rachel. "Taking Jessie?"

"Yup. Time for ol' Jess to meet the family, maybe start squalling in French, and wear pea soup instead of strained prunes. Whatcha say, Jess?" She scooped up Jessie, who laughed delightedly and stretched her arms toward the kitchen. "Poons?" said Jessie.

Carla laughed. "Uh-oh, now I've done it." She kissed Jessie's fat little face and said: "No, baby. Not prunes, pea soup. We're gonna ride the Metro and sing French songs, and we're gonna be happy again. We are." Carla's eyes clouded up.

Jessie wasn't interested in pea soup or Montreal. She knew what was important, and it was inside one of those heavy square doors she couldn't open. "Poons!" she said again, and Carla carried her into the kitchen.

Saturday morning Carla and Jessie were winging their way to Montreal.

Carla pulled the pocket mirror to study her swollen eyes and pink face. Then she tried to shush her squalling pink daughter. No problem telling who's mother and daughter here, she thought, and ordered a tiny bottle of Tia Maria. She poured a drop in the milk bottle and popped it in Jessie's mouth. Jessie was soon asleep and people walking by stopped to remark what a little angel she was.

Hellnight

It was 8:35 on a Saturday night and Rachel was sitting alone, enraptured, watching "Romeo and Juliet" on the small screen. It was the Zeferelli film and every time she saw it she fell in love again with the beauty and opulence of the production. She used to joke that it was the only horny teen film she cared to see, and every time she saw it she knew why.

She made coffee during the commercial break.

The commercial yelling stopped, and the music of the Capulets' ball drew Rachel back into the livingroom. Romeo had just discovered the dimpled Juliet and she was about to meet the blue-eyed stranger behind the gray cat mask.

Rachel didn't see the shadow at the kitchen window. Why would she, Sultan hadn't barked. Besides, she had learned to ignore him. He would bark fiercely at frogs or chameleons or any hapless squirrel in the yard. People would walk up to the house and he'd wag his tail, waiting to play.

Some nights he got lonely and howled. Then Rachel would take him biscuits and sit with him on the stoop, and he'd slobber and thump his tail in appreciation.

Tonight Rachel was feeling lonely but curled her lip at the picture of people saying: attractive and alone on a Saturday night, what's wrong with that girl? Rachel didn't care. She was holding out for what her mother called "the whole kit"—someone passionate, smart, handsome and kind, who would take her in his arms and say: "Rachel, I need you. The world is a gray place without you." Well, tonight she would see the love she sought, eloquently expressed and dazzlingly displayed.

A boy was singing about women as ice and desire while Romeo in his cat mask stalked the innocent Juliet. Rachel had just gotten settled on the rug, crossing her legs against the big throw pillow when Sultan SCREAMED.

It was a terrible sound, like none he had ever made, and Rachel's hair stood straight up.

She pulled herself up, ran to the kitchen, and grabbed the carving knife off the rack. Damn, she fumed. Why don't I have a gun? What if it's a rattler?

She grabbed the doorknob and flicked the lightswitch but the windows stayed black. My god, not now.

She rifled the utility drawer but the flashlight was gone. Dammit, what did I do with—oh shit, your dog's in trouble, just go.

Streetlight shone over the tall hedge but the yard was all shadows. On the porch Rachel yelled: "Suultaan. Here boy!" She whistled then clapped her hands as if summoning him for dinner: if that didn't bring him, he couldn't come.

Scanning the blackness again, listening for sounds of panting, she noticed the "v" in the shadow of the fence on the shed: someone had opened the gate and left it ajar. My god, what if it's a dognapper?

Maybe some kid had chased him out to be mean.

She decided to go out the front door and leave the back

door open for him, then walked back into the kitchen for his leash.

There was a creak in the livingroom, followed by a clatter of things dropped on the coffee table.

Rachel froze, tightening her grip on the knife, and took a slow step toward the livingroom.

There was a creak as her foot left the linoleum and a voice yelled: "Hey, Rachel!" It was Kenny's voice, but groggy. "Rachel!" he yelled again.

Dammit, how did he—dammit, Carla's key.

"Hey, Rachel, get in here. Yer missin' yer show." The voice trailed off: "Besides, I need ya to explain this limey shit t'me."

Rachel walked to the counter that separated the two rooms and peered around the cabinets.

Kenny had his feet crossed on the coffee table beside a sixpack of Moosehead. One bottle was in his hand, half drunk.

"C'mon, Rachel," he said in that same slurred voice, then: "Nope, take a break. Looks like these two are about to do something I understand."

Rachel shook, holding on to the divider.

Kenny wiped his mouth on his arm and grimaced. "Whyn't ya put that thing down before ya cut yerself?"

"Wh-why are you here?" she stammered.

He looked at her face, then down at the knife. "Put that thing down, will ya? Yer makin' me nervous."

He had a point: if they got in a fight she was no match for him, and if she cut him that would just make him madder.

Well, she thought, stepping back and dropping the knife on the counter. Nothing left but to appeal to his chivalry. She asked if he would help her find Sultan.

"Sure thing," he offered. "In a minute. Have a beer with me first, Rach." He patted the couch next to him. "C'mon, siddown… Make yerself at home." He held up the unopened bottle. "See?" he smiled. "Yer favorite kind. I remembered."

Rachel sat gingerly on the edge of the couch, several feet to his left. She wished he had never seen her drinking.

"Hey, relax." Kenny twisted the cap off the green bottle and handed it to her. He smiled and caught her eyes, then snapped his fingers under her nose. "Hey, Rach, lighten up. I can see those wheels turning and turning. Tell me, doncha ever get tired of it? I mean, why doncha just take a load off, go down to the beach, and kick back? Get some sun on that anemic-lookin' bod. I mean really, what're ya savin' it for? You don't date, you don't go nowhere, so who're ya savin' it for, Rachel?"

His voice was harsher now, clearer. Rachel wondered if he was even drunk. "Drink up, Rach," he commanded. "I went to a lotta trouble to get that for ya."

Rachel upended the bottle and took a short swig. She was so nervous that she breathed while swallowing and choked. She coughed the beer up and Kenny whapped her lightly on the back. He got up, went to the kitchen, and returned with a paper towel. She took it, still coughing, while he walked around the coffee table and sat down next to her so that their legs and sides touched.

His bronze hand spread treelike over her back. He felt the line of her bra under the gauzy white blouse and gritted his teeth. Not yet, he told himself. But it was hard, she was so damned irritating. Everything about her was irritating: the hifalutin' language, the meddling, the whiteness, those owlish eyes that tracked him whenever she thought he wasn't looking—where did she get off anyway, gawking at him one moment, ignoring him the next?

She had stopped coughing.

"Better now?" he said soothingly, sliding his fingers lightly down her back.

She shuffled her buns forward to make a gap between them and Kenny moved up to close the space. It was funny to watch this refined person come apart with a little crowding.

Kenny took his hand off her back and leaned back against the couch. "Relax, Rachel." He smiled. "I ain't gonna bitecha. Hey, wha'd ya think?"

"I didn't know what to think," she whispered, looking straight ahead.

"WHAT?" he barked at her eye, and she blinked. "Did I hear the great Rachel Williams actually admit she didn't know something? Hell, even I know the answer to this one, Rach. It's so simple—too simple, maybe, for the likes of you. Y'see, there's no questions here, no opinions, just plain ol' animal lust. That's it, ain't it?"

He grinned, willing her eyes to turn his way.

"Can't handle it, canya?" He barked. "Can't handle it that yer just a common bitch, panting after yer own sister's husband? Well, join the pack, princess. Tonight it's your turn t' howl!"

He grabbed her arms and yanked her around to face him, tightening his grip till she screamed.

"Look me in the eyes, goddamit!" he yelled. "You never look me in the eyes, you white-ass tight-ass bitch, and I hate it! I hate it!" He dug his fingers in, then relaxed his grip so that she was still hurt but couldn't fight.

"Why are you so angry?" she blurted, tears starting at the pain in her arms.

"Why am I angry?" he screamed. "You don't ask the questions here! This isn't your game anymore, Rachel, it's MINE! I make the rules now, an' if yer not too damn stupid, you follow 'em. UNDERSTOOD?"

He shook her back and forth, fast, so that her head flopped up and down. "Thaaat's right. Verrry good. Now you're getting the idea." He grimaced and flung her against the back of the couch, releasing her arms. She crossed them immediately to rub the sore spots.

"Take yer hands down, Rachel," he instructed. "Yer gonna need 'em fer this next number."

He told her to take her clothes off and Rachel winced.

"Start with your shoes," he said, pointing to her feet. She was confused; her feet were bare.

He grinned: "See how easy that was?"

Rachel gulped. She didn't know what to do with her hands, she was afraid to run, she couldn't bear to think what might come next. Don't fight, she told herself: Do exactly what he wants and you might get out of this with just a couple of slaps. Oh God, what about Sultan?

"Still thinkin', huh, Rachel? Still thinkin' yer smarter'n me, doncha... Well yer NOT, see?"

He stood up, and screamed at her to do likewise.

Slowly she got to her feet and he watched her with narrowed eyes.

There was less than two feet between them, and he placed his hand on her breast. Rachel started to shrink away.

"DON'T MOVE!" he yelled, and she froze. "Don't you dare move," he warned, as his fingers fanned out over her chest and continued their slow progression up her collar till the fine lace was eaten by his fist. He repeated the process with his other hand, until he had both fists clenched under her chin, and the stretched rim of her collar bit the back of her neck.

"Aooww," she whined, and he told her to shut up.

"You broads think ya can cry an' get anything, doncha?" he fumed. "Well it don't work with everybody. It don't work with me."

He dug his fingers in her arms, spitting the words: "Tell me you WANT me! Tell me how you've WAITED for me—go on, SAY IT!"

He shook her, yelling: "You think I dunno ya been waitin' fer mê, ya think I dunno whatcha do here every night—well, ferget it, cause I been watchin' you a LONG time, see?"

He put his mouth to her ear and whispered: "I seen ya stroke yer tits in the shower with that pink soap an' cut yer cooter hair 'n' spray it down the drain. Oh yeah, I saw all that. You knew I was watchin', dincha?" he whispered, nuzzling her cheek, tightening his grip. "Ya did it fer me, dincha? Left that bathroom window cracked just enough so's I could see. Weeelllll SAY IT! Go on, tell me. I've waited a long time fer this."

Rachel opened her mouth slightly and out came a little moan.

Kenny released her arms and grabbed her hair, pulling her head from side to side as his hands climbed toward her face.

He pulled her head back and rammed his tongue down her throat.

Rachel tried to pull away and he tightened his grip. Every move she made brought pain, and there was no blocking it—or him—out. Would this be the last she knew of the world—just him and his sour tongue, his painful grip and stinking closeness? All he'd have to do was transfer that grip to her throat—she could barely breathe as it was.

Whatever he wants just do it—oh God, just keep me alive. She barely had time to form the thought; he threw her down on the floor beside the coffee table and kicked the table over.

He unzipped his shorts, grabbed her hair with one hand and pulled her head toward his crotch, stuffing his half-erect cock between her lips. Then he held her head in his hands, working her mouth back and forth along his shaft, slamming his groin against her face, filling her nose and mouth with hair, revelling in the bite of the zipper on his skin while it raked her jaw. He slammed her head faster and faster, pumping his cock against the back of her throat while she struggled to keep from choking and biting. He held her head still while he ejaculated, cutting off her air, making her heave and gag.

She gave one tremendous push when he was done and he let her go, leaning back against the couch.

Rachel gagged up dinner and semen in a bubbly gruel on the rug.

Kenny winced and curled his lip. "Jeez Rach," he sighed, "hate to think you tossed yer cookies fer me. Weelll, let's see what we can do about scroungin' you up another course."

Rachel, curled over her knees, shrank away as he got up. She wiped her nose and mouth with the back of her hand, raising the other above her head.

Kenny thought about kicking her but changed his mind, grabbed her hair, and yanked her owwing to her feet. He pulled her into the kitchen, holding her by the back of the head so that her face was hip level with him and all she could see was his lower half. She tried to keep pace so he wouldn't pull her hair out, but he walked erratically so she was forced to trip up against him.

He slammed open the drawers till he found what he was looking for and pulled out a roll of duct tape.

He pulled her back to where the elongated counter ended in curved shelves over the livingroom rug. Two painted steel posts two feet apart ran up through the shelves to the ceiling. Kenny taped Rachel's wrists and forearms to the posts, yelling at her to "stop yer damn whimpering—I can't STAND that noise. STOP IT! I'll feed ya, y'ugly bitch, jest gimme a minute here."

He marched back to the cupboard above the sink, ripped one of the doors off, then pulled the top plate from her mother's china and dumped the rest in the sink. Rachel cried when they crashed.

"SHADDUP!" screamed Kenny. "I told ya I'd feed ya. Here!" he snapped, shooting the plate down the counter; it stopped a foot from her blouse.

He picked up the carving knife and jammed it under her chin; she could feel the tip of the blade digging a hole. "I told you t' stop cryin', you want me t' cut yer tongue out? Come t' think of it, that'd solve alotta problems. NOBODY'd hafta listen to yer shit then…"

Rachel tried to back away and he yelled at her not to move. He held the knife under her ear while his other hand moved over her body, squeezing hard where it was soft.

"Ya know yer body's not as nice as Carla's. Ya know that, dontcha?" he sneered, standing behind her. Suddenly his face was in front of her and the knife cut deeper. "You know I think yer ugly, dontcha? Huh? Specially those eyes, I HATE those eyes. Maybe a little surgery might do you right. Hell, you can't get any worse.

"Y'know, maybe we could make you look like those fish in the tank… Yeah," he nodded, smiling, "then everybody'd see what's REALLY there, what I been seein' all along. Whaddaya think, Rachel, wouldja like that? Huh? Huh?" he prodded her with the knife.

"ANSWER ME, GODDAMNIT!" he yelled. "STOP WHININ' OR I'LL CUTCHER TONGUE OUT, HEAR ME?"

Rachel gulped, trying to make the moans inaudible. Kenny took the knife from her chin and said that he, the great white hunter, was going out to bag some dinner. Then he grabbed her jaw and snarled: "NO NOISE! One sound and you'll never talk again!"

He hiked his shorts back on and told her not to worry, that she'd get to taste that scrumptious shlong again, that he'd leave her tongue in there at least long enough for that. Then again, maybe not: she had other holes to explore, "though prob'ly not near so wet or warm as Carla's—she drenches me, y'know," he sneered, and walked out the front door whistling.

Rachel collapsed against the counter crying, fearing for her tongue and her eyes.

She watched the clock above the sink. Four minutes passed and Kenny came back with a small green garbage bag. Rachel shuddered. Oh God, he's gonna make me eat garbage...

Her shudder turned to screams when he upended the bag on the plate and out fell Sultan's ear. The tail came next, bouncing off the counter onto the floor. Kenny kicked it across the linoleum and it landed in front of the refrigerator.

"Eat up, Rach," smiled Kenny. "Gee, I'm glad yer so thrilled. Hell, you oughta be: no red dye, no preservatives, ya even grew it yerself. Oh dear, no knife and fork. What a low class joint. Tell ya what, I'll jest cut it up for you, all neat 'n' bite size like that chink shit you love so much. I'll even hand feed it to you, whiny li'l baby that you are—FUCK, FOR CRYIN' OUT LOUD STOP WHININ'!"

Rachel wasn't conscious of her own sounds anymore. She wept as he carved the hairy mass into small chunks, pressing each one against her mouth and returning it to the plate. "Ummm, yummy. Don't you agree, Rach. SAY IT!"

Rachel said yes and he rammed the last carved piece between her lips. She tasted the dirt, the blood and the fur, and started to gag.

"YOU BITCH!" he screamed, and hit her across the jaw, knocking the hairy lump down her throat.

Rachel choked, sputtered and struggled. With her arms held up she couldn't bend to disgorge the lump, she couldn't inhale, and it was too far down to cough it up.

Kenny grinned: he could leave her like this and watch her die—but no, he hadn't heard her beg yet, and he wanted to hear her thank him for saving her life. He got behind her, pressed her chest cavity into forcing up the obstruction, then slapped her back when she coughed.

The furred chunk fell from her mouth and made an amoebic splat on the plate, followed by frothy red drool from her tongue—she had bitten it hard when he hit her. Her whole face ached. She heard him tell her to thank him but could barely get the words past her swelling tongue. He screamed it again and she got out "hank hoo."

"That's not what I asked for," he screamed, "Say it RIGHT!"

Rachel tried twice, and on the third round she got it.

"Very good," he commended her. "Now eat cher dinner. I went to a lotta trouble t' get that for ya."

Rachel winced, wept, and chewed. It was either bite those filthy chunks down to swallowable pieces or choke. While she chewed, trying not to gag, Kenny was tearing off her clothes, making disparaging comments:

"You need that bra, yer tits are saggin'. You should get one fer yer ass, it's hangin' too. But I got somethin' good fer yer ass, jest wait—KEEP EATIN', DAMN YA, AN' KEEP YER FACE WHERE I CAN'T SEE IT. I DON'T WANNA SEE IT TILL I'M READY T' CHANGE IT, GOT THAT?"

Rachel could barely chew, fearing for her face. Oh God will HE be the last thing I ever see? Please God save me, send somebody, oh please please…

Kenny walked across the kitchen yelling: "DON'T LOOKIT ME DAMN YOU!" and picked up Sultan's tail. He walked back behind Rachel and ran the tail up and down her sides, between her legs, jabbing her anus and vagina, calling her a dog, less than a dog—a useless piece of tail, just like what he was holding.

Watching her shudder and seeing her buttocks constrict as he reviled her excited him: he wanted to grab them and tear them off. After all, he could do it: he could have anything he wanted, right now, and what he wanted right now was to climb inside her ass and shoot come so high it'd spew out her nose.

He shut his eyes and tossed the furred bone on the floor, slamming the knife down in front of her. "You'd like t' have that, wouldn't cha? Like to cut me t' pieces, wouldn't cha? Well it's MY show here, honey, not yers, an' I'LL do the cuttin', you just wait. An' just watch that thing while you can." He loved the sound of his voice, threatening and in control.

He spat in his hand and worked the drool over the end of his crank, pulling fast, then slow, shutting his eyes and parting her buttocks with his other hand, wetting the wrinkles around the opening and jabbing his finger through the clamped sphincter into the slick soft chamber above.

Rachel gasped, coughed, and shivered.

"KEEP EATING!" he snapped, rolling his finger around then pulling it out. He pushed his cock through the protesting muscle, grabbed her cheeks and pumped, slamming her so hard she came off the floor. Her legs banged against the lower shelves and the top shelf cleaved her midriff, making her vomit, making Kenny ejaculate. He screamed and clawed and tore her flesh, digging his fingers in the scratches and yanking up whatever he could.

Rachel shrieked as the pieces left her: "AAAHHH! NOOHH! GOD! GOD!"

Kenny slumped over her, loving the shrieks, then stepped back dazed and grinning. Her backside was like bloody tire treads, bits of fatty muscle poking through the oozing red, some he had in his hands. He wiped his fingers on her back and warned: "SHADDUP!"

He reached around her and picked up the knife, laying the flat side on her cheek, the blade tip level with her eye.

"Don't worry, Princess, I'll be right back," he smiled, and walked out of the kitchen, knife in hand.

He wanted to kill her but he wanted her money too and he

knew she didn't keep cash or checks in the house. But he could have that money: in a few more minutes she'd be begging him to take it. Hell, she owed him—they all did, those twats, for all the aggravation they'd caused him.

Kenny walked back into the room with the fish tank and started knocking over furniture.

He picked up the heavy oak chair by the writing desk and shattered the tank.

Water and fish plunged over the fragments. One of the fish got impaled on the glass. One flopped on the rug until Kenny stomped it. The last one circled amid the glass shards on the bottom of the tank till Kenny reached in and stuck the carving knife through its sides.

He upended the knife and carried the still-flopping fish into the kitchen, setting it down in front of Rachel. She could hear the water pouring in the other room, and watched in agony as he held the fish by the tail, picked out its eyes, and threw it over the sink. It backboarded on the window, left a bloody oval, and slid down among the dishes.

"Your turn, Honey," he grinned, grabbing a handful of hair and sawing off a hunk of her scalp. Rachel screamed as blood spurted down her face, pulled and screamed, shutting her eyes, and heard Kenny say: "If ya dohwanna be like that fish then you'll do exactly what I say. That goes fer Carla an' yer precious li'l niece too. HEAR ME? Right Rachel? Well SAY IT!"

Rachel managed a yes, though she didn't hear it.

She heard him say, "Good, now here's whatcher gonna do. Yer gonna go t' the bank when yer outta the hospital, take out five thou in small bills, put 'em in a brown bag an' leave it in yer garbage. I'll be by fer it later an' I'll be callin' you from time t' time, GOT THAT? Say YES, Rachel. Very good. Now yer not gonna say nothin' ta nobody, arya Rachel? ARYA RACHEL? ANSWER ME WHEN I TALK T' YA, GODDAMNIT!"

Rachel choked out a no.

"Gooood, goood." Kenny smiled, walking into the living

room and pulling the picture from its frame. He zipped up his shorts, stuck the hair with her scalp in his pocket, then walked to the kitchen phone and dialed the operator, affecting an hysterical female voice which just managed to blurt out the address. Yes yes, I'll be here, he gushed, and hung up.

He walked to the back door, picking the fish out of the sink and shaking it at Rachel. "You just remember that, Rachel," he advised, "cause if I call an' ask fer fish face yer in DEEP SHIT, you 'n' my wife 'n' the little twat, allayas."

He tossed the fish back in the sink and walked out, waving and smiling as he closed the door.

Rachel tried not to cry, it made the pain worse.

She tried to figure out how crazy he was, how much he would remember. He was sane enough to demand money instead of killing her, to lay out instructions. Now, would she be able to follow them?

Blood trickled steadily from the gash in her scalp, dripping down her face. Rachel began to cry.

The paramedics found her twenty minutes later trying to chew through the tape her fingers couldn't reach. She screamed: "Don't touch my head! Don't touch my head!" and when she saw the scissors they brought out to cut her down she fainted.

The Gift

Colette and Carla spent the day on Mount Royal pushing Jessie in a stroller and chasing after Colette's boys, Guy and Jean-Luc. The temperature was in the nineties and all the trees were haloed in vapor.

It was 9 P.M. when they filed through the door of the apartment, covered in sweat, ice cream and grass stains.

Colette shooed the boys into the bathtub, and both were so sticky they were actually glad to go: it was a three-minute battle instead of the usual twenty.

Carla laughed. "Why the fight, if that's what they want to do?"

Colette shrugged. "Well, we don't want dem to get out of practice, eh? God forbid anyt'ing should be done just because it makes sense—whoof, where's da fun in dat?"

Over the rushing water the boys were yelling at each other—one had drowned the other's transformer.

"Carla, please make up some wine coolers," said Colette. She sighed, pointing to the bathroom. "I'll be right back, an' den we can run away togeder, okay?"

"Agreed," said Carla. They had given up telling the boys to be quiet because of the baby, and Jessie had finally dozed off in spite of them.

Colette looked down at Jessie on her way to the bathroom and made a face at Carla. "You know," she said, "she's smarter dan us."

Marcel would be home soon so Carla filled up a pitcher with rose, lemon, and watermelon. The melon changed the tang of the citrus and both women said hmm, different, nice.

Jessie, sponged and powdered, was rocked back to sleep.

Carla watched Jessie settle in the crib, then a wave of nausea rolled up her throat. Too much heat, too much food. Then images of Kenny flashed in front of her—Kenny smiling, Kenny frowning, Kenny yelling at someone. Kenny holding a rose to give her, the rose turning into a knife. Blood splashed across the blade and over a pattern like the linoleum in her parents' kitchen. The image faded.

Carla fell back against the bed, the left side of her head pounding. So much for wine coolers with watermelon. She was sweating so much her skin prickled. Little licks of fire ran along her butt.

She stood up, walked to the bedroom door, and asked Colette if there was enough hot water left for her to shower now.

Colette came and put her hand on Carla's face. "You 'ave your shower an' hit da bed," said Colette. "An' no more wine coolers for you, my girl!"

Carla showered and crawled into bed. My girl, she mused. She hadn't heard that since her mother passed away. Between the echoes of her mother and the warm soft sheets she felt very loved. If only Kenny...

The moment his face came back her head began to pound

and her butt was so sore she had to lie on her side. Damn that's weird, she frowned, trying to rub her temples the way Rachel used to. The headache did not subside until well past 2 a.m. It surfaced the following day at sporadic intervals, and every time she thought about Kenny or Rachel it came back. Kenny she could understand, but Rachel? Maybe because she and Kenny didn't get along.

She talked it out with Colette and Marcel, who took turns giving her neck massages. Both of them said Carla's headaches were the natural expression of her trauma—plus she was English, thus by definition "uptight," they teased. They tried everything to relax her—herb teas, good food, long walks, time to talk, time alone, but Carla's headaches would not go away.

Part of it was that promise she made herself not to call Rachel, but by the second Monday she gave it up and dialed Rachel's office.

A woman's voice said: "Good morning, you have reached the offices of The Whitsun Group."

"Is this the answering service?" Carla asked. Maybe she was early.

"No," said the voice, "this is the office."

"May I speak to Rachel Williams? This is her sister, Carla, and I'm calling long distance from Canada." That should light a fire under her.

"Just a minute," said the voice. The receiver clattered and footsteps katumped away.

There was a click and a man's voice could be heard above the returning footsteps. "Hello, Carla? This is Bill Whitsun. I'm so glad you called. Everyone's been looking for you."

Carla's head began to pound. "Where's Rachel?"

"She's all right, Carla." He paused. He cleared his throat, and then another pause. "Carla, Rachel was attacked last Saturday. She was raped and—"

Carla cut him off and dialed the Eastern ticket office. Two hours later she and Jessie were flying to Jacksonville.

Rachel was heavily sedated in the intensive care unit.

Sometimes she would gag before she regained consciousness and they were afraid she would choke on the swill. Her clenched jaws tore open the scab on her head, and the violent contractions in her abdomen ripped open the stitches on her butt. Any pressure on her arms made her scream and fight. She floated in and out. When the pain came back the visions came with it—the face, the knife, the bloody pieces of ear lying in vomit. Then she would cry NOOOHH! and lurch forward, barfing on the plastic cover.

The nurses would tell her she was safe, he was gone.

"Did I say anything?" she would ask, tears rolling down her face. "Any name? Anything?"

No, nothing, they assured her. Then she would cry in pain and one of the nurses would inject the Demerol. Rachel would lay sideways on the pillows and their faces would fade away. In four hours the hurt would start again and the nurses would return to reassure her.

When Rachel woke this particular afternoon Dr. Kittrick was standing at the end of the bed with Dr. Phillips, the rape counsellor, whose aqua eyes matched her dress.

"Hello, Rachel," said Dr. Phillips. "Listen, if you don't want to talk you don't have to. We'll get to it when you're ready."

"I'm ready," said Rachel. She resented being prone and bandaged while the others were dressed and standing. She sat forward and her head ached.

"So," she said. "Tell me what happens when we catch this guy."

"Well," said Dr. Phillips, "There'll be a trial—"

"Look!" Rachel interrupted. "All I want to know is if they catch him how long it'll be before he gets out and comes after my family again. He threatened to kill us, you know, and I believe him—I've already seen what he can do! Anyway I don't want him locked up, I want him DEAD!"

She pointed at Dr. Phillips. "You're here to rehabilitate me, but I don't need adjusting—it's that maniac out there, and he's too far gone. Boy, if I'd had a gun it sure as hell wouldn't be me in this bed—or him: he'd be six feet under! And dammit, the police know that—why else would they allow people to own guns? It's our only chance against crazies like that. Trust me, I'm gonna buy a gun the minute I get outta here, an' if that bastard tries to hurt me again, I'll blow so many holes in him there won't be anything left to try or bury!"

Bloody dots zigzagged over her bandage, and she put her hands up to it, crying.

A figure appeared at the window, and Rachel focused on her sister.

Rachel spread her arms and smiled—not a whole smile, a smile that came from seeing Carla safe. As Carla came into the room Rachel asked, "Where's Jessie?"

"Jessie's fine, Rachel. I dropped her off at Cathy's."

Rachel looked up at Carla, then at the IV line running from her leg, and frowned. She asked Dr. Kittrick: "How soon can I leave?"

Kittrick stood a little straighter, glad to be back in charge. He hadn't expected her to rise from burbling unconscious to shrieking harpy and said, "You can go when you can hold down solid food, wake up without vomiting, and have a few sessions with Dr. Phillips here. Your employer's picking up the tab for your stay so you can concentrate on getting well."

"Yeah," sneered Rachel. "Very nice. Meanwhile, who's picking up the tab for my water and electric? And who's gonna feed my—" Rachel stopped. She shut her eyes tight to keep the image from forming, but it was too late. She screamed. "NOOOH!" and sobbed, "Oooohhh, Sultan, why did he do that to you? Why? Why?"

The gagging started. Rachel waved her arms and kacked green drool onto the plastic sheet.

Carla pushed past the doctors and wrapped her arms around Rachel, who cried against her shoulder.

A nurse came in with a sedative injection while Carla held Rachel and wept with her.

After the nurse replaced the plastic sheet Rachel fell back, moaning, and lost consciousness.

Carla released her and left the room in search of Dr. Kittrick.

He was with another doctor in front of the dayroom. He looked at Carla and saw her mother—taller, paler, but still Claire. It was the set of her jaw and the molten green of her eyes.

Dr. Kittrick took Carla into his office and showed her pictures of Rachel's lacerations. He described the process they went through to replace the missing flesh on Rachel's head. Plastic surgery could, in time, replace the scar tissue on her head with plugs of hair. As for her rear, it would always be scarred and ripply—no amount of surgery could totally correct that. Then there was the trauma about the dog and the fish.

"What about the dog?" Carla asked, afraid of the answer.

As gently as he could Dr. Kittrick told her what the paramedics had found, about Rachel trussed up and the mess on the plate and the carcasses of the dog and the fish.

Carla gripped the arms of the chair, seeing it all. "Oh, Sultan!" she sobbed. "Why? Why? And why Rachel? If anyone doesn't invite that kind of attention it's Rachel."

Suddenly Carla leaped up. She wiped her eyes and declared: "I'm going to the house. Maybe there's some kind of clue that'll help us track that bastard down."

Dr. Kittrick stood up, commanding, "Carla, don't go there! It's not safe!"

"Excuse me, Doctor, but isn't that kinda obvious?" snapped Carla. "Besides, I'm gonna take my friend's boyfriend and he'll have his rifle, so don't worry about me. Now excuse me, I hafta go." She shimmied past him and ran to the stairs, mentally checking off: Leave Jessie with Cathy. Get Mark. Scour every inch of that fucking house.

It was still light when they arrived at the house. The door was locked, but Mark had a door-opener prong and moved it around till the deadbolt rolled back. The door opened on a foul odor that made them cough. They stepped through the doorway and water squished up around their shoes. The wet circle on the carpet came from a puddle on the kitchen floor that seeped from the hall. Empty bottles lay by the upended coffee table and flies buzzed between the bloody sink and a plate of stinking lumps on the counter. Carla screamed when she saw fur in the lumps. Then, in a puddle a foot from the refrigerator she saw Sultan's tail.

Carla put out her hands to stop the images and cried.

Mark put his arm around her, and said: "C'mon, we're leavin'. You don't need t' be lookin' at this. C'mon."

He helped her into the truck, almost as shocked as she was. Some sicko out there hated women and fish and dogs. He could see how Rachel's highfalutin' ways might get under somebody's skin, but enough to carve her up? No, surely she didn't deserve that. "Carla," he said, "if I can help her any way, I will."

"I know that, Mark," said Carla, and thanked him. She stared out the window at the reddening sky, crying at the images of Rachel and Sultan. "I want that man dead for what he did. I'd kill him myself if I could!" she cried.

Rachel awoke an hour after Carla left and was trying to stay calm, formulating a plan. Her eyes were closed. How to be methodical without an actual written list. Mustn't leave any clues. On TV murderers got felled by a detail, whereas in reality that detail was often a stoolie. So no one must know the target of her hate.

Secondly, he would have to be killed some way that couldn't be traced. Sharks? Now, that was feasible: knock him out, slash his foot, and dump him. She could rent a boat for a day and chum the waters with the contents of a special cooler. Well, whatever I do, I gotta get a gun. And a silencer. How long does it take to perfect your aim? Her eyes opened on a sudden inspiration: Hey, I could dump the body in a landfill. The county landfills are overflowing and they're gonna hafta shut a couple down soon. Perfect ending for that piece of filth.

Her head oozed and fiery lines raked her backside. "Owwh!" she cried, and rang for the nurse.

She asked the nurse if she could leave a message for Dr. Phillips. And maybe tomorrow they could start her on solid food? The nurse said she would ask the doctor.

Rachel said thanks and reclined, waiting for the Demerol to kick in.

It would take two weeks to discharge her, even if she acted the model patient. Well, she sighed. Better start practicing. Didn't help anything with that outburst today. But Dad said bureaucrats were easy to fool. Just be boring like them: they call that 'adjusted.'

She was starting to relax. She made a list, tracing the numbers in the air, her lips forming the words but making no sound: One, a gun. Two, surgeons' gloves. Three, plastic bags. Four: drive to Atlanta and Ocala to check possible dump sites. Five: do something to protect Carla and Jessie. Help me, God. Help me find a way. ❧

She was almost asleep when she thought she heard someone say her name. Then she heard a clunk beside the bed and opened her eyes. No one was there but Rachel was sure someone had been there. She called the nurse and asked if she had had a visitor.

The nurse said no, other than her sister a few hours ago. Then the nurse noticed something behind the aspiration tubes next to the monitor. "I don't remember that," she said. "Did your sister leave that?"

Rachel sat up and reached over the tubes. Her hand closed around a small dented ball that she could not lift. Damn, I mus' be more drug than I thought. She reached out and swept away the tubes to reveal a small gold object that made her gasp: "Who was here? Who left this?"

The nurse said it must have been her sister and asked if Rachel wanted the object transferred to the safe deposit box downstairs. No, said Rachel, it was clearly costume jewelry, not to worry, and the nurse left the room.

Rachel sighed, glad the nurse hadn't tried to pick it up. She smiled at the cat with its closed eyes. "Thank you, God," she whispered. "I'll never wunner if You exist anymore."

She placed her hand over the amulet and a great warmth spread through her, bringing her the first calm sleep since she entered the hospital.

The next morning she woke to see Carla at the end of the bed, rolling the amulet in her hands.

"Hi, Rach," said Carla. "Welcome back. Who broughtcha the gift? I thought only relatives were allowed in here. Damn, this thing is heavy."

Rachel pointed at Carla. "It was brought for you, Carla. I want you to wear it."

Carla drew back and frowned. "You must be joking," she said. "The damn thing has got to weigh five pounds at least. What am I supposed to do, make a ring out of it and use it for brass knuckles. What's it made of, anyway? Lead?"

"No," said Rachel. "It's solid gold. It's a Sehkmet amulet, Carla. The real thing. I can't pick it up, that's how I know. I don't know how it got here, but I want you to wear it, to keep you and Jessie safe."

Carla stared at the cat face. "I will not," she said firmly. "Dammit, Rachel, this is like crosses and vampires, and if you talk about this they'll put you away. And God, please don't tell that counsellor about this—or about that night in Montreal. It may count against you when you go to court against that guy."

Rachel shut her eyes. There it was, the Voice of Reason, telling her she was hysterical, that they would find this man, that justice would be done. Brainwashed, the lot of them. Nothing to do but play along. "Okay, Carla," she sighed, "But do me a favor. Put the amulet in the safe deposit box, okay?"

"Sure thing," Carla smiled, and squeezed Rachel's hand. "Right after I leave. First stop," she promised, and that seemed to mollify Rachel. The amulet would lie next to her mother's cross. Surely it could wish for no finer company.

Carla was saying something about the rapist.

"What?" said Rachel. "I'm sorry, my mind wanders in and out."

"D'you think I should talk to that counsellor?"

"Sure, Carla." Rachel reached for Carla's hand and said, "Look, this didn't just happen to me. You're gonna hafta deal with the aftermath, so you should probably get some guidelines to go by."

Carla smiled, relieved to hear Rachel sounding sane. She talked about Jessie and Cathy and Mark, and left after Rachel's next injection. She resolved to get the house cleaned before Rachel got home, and that night Mark and Cathy helped her with a rented steam cleaner.

Two weeks later Rachel was out of the hospital, putting the money as instructed in the shed. She stayed in the Whitsuns' guest room and waited for the bag to disappear, checking every morning. The day it disappeared she planted a FOR SALE sign on the front lawn and went looking for a place she couldn't be ambushed.

A month later she found a bungalow in Neptune Beach that answered her needs. It had no shrubbery or shed and sat on a corner hundreds of feet from its neighbors. Windows formed a line around the house so that the rooms were flooded with light, day or night. Because of its gray stucco walls and triangular roof it the neighbors called it The Gingerbread House.

Two months later the ink was drying on the deed to The Gingerbread House, sold to "one Rachel Marie Williams, a single woman," and she had an alarm system installed that day.

The next stop was to trade in the car. She bought a Volaré which seemed like a plastic toy next to the old Monterey, but parking it was a breeze compared to the old upholstered tank.

Rachel drove the car off the lot and over to the gun store. She was sweating as the salesman showed her different guns. Comfort didn't concern her, but range did. He advised her on three different models. She ignored him and bought something that made Mark's eyes pop.

"Rachel, what in hell are you doin' with this?" he said. "This ain't no gun, it's a cannon."

"Yup," Rachel agreed, looking up at him with a flat-lipped smile. "If it's good enough for Clint Eastwood, it's good enough for me. Besides, I've been taking lessons. I can handle this baby real good now."

Mark shook his head, checked the safety, and handed her

the gun. "Just make sure you point it in the right direction, okay?"

"Hey, no prob." She squinted up at him, and as he walked back into the livingroom she lined up the barrel with his back. She gritted her teeth and slowly brought the gun down to her side.

Cathy and Carla stared at her openmouthed, frozen in the act of sitting.

"'Samatter, girls?" Mark grinned: they were always over-reacting to something.

The girls chirped "nothing" and sank onto the couch, exchanging glances.

Carla called Dr. Phillips next day and was told to keep an eye on Rachel, and to call with anything she found 'troubling.' Carla said yes, but it was the gun she found troubling. She couldn't live with Rachel armed and jumping at everything, and reluctantly told her so.

Carla went inland, found a crackerbox apartment, and a job waitressing six blocks away.

Rachel gave her the money to move but hated the apartment complex. Its pink stucco and black metal staircases reminded her of cheap underwear. Dirty kids yelled and engines revved under every window, but Carla didn't care, it was hers. Soon she'd have the money to pay Rachel back. Besides, Rachel had enough on her mind. It was Carla's turn to be brave.

One Good Man

Carla met Paul on the worst possible day, the anniversary of her desertion.

Rachel had taken Jessie to some Disney classic while Carla walked along the beach, wondering if she was still attractive. The sun was high, the breeze was nil, and the humidity was so dense she could taste it.

I could go for a beer about now, she thought.

She put on her sandals and walked up Atlantic Boulevard. The Right Set were crowding into Ragtime, and people with money were drifting in and out of the boutiques, but Carla had on a long shirt, tank top and shorts—a far cry from the Yuppie dress code.

She walked up the boulevard and saw a new bar, Marguerita's, next to the laundromat. She wondered if she could get in; she didn't feel like walking any further. There was no one to stop her at the door so in she went. There wasn't much to it, just the bar, a line of tables, and a jukebox at the far end. The back door opened onto a wood-covered patio lined with plants. Other people sat out there sipping drinks, but no, Carla decided, she was tired of light, light that demanded she smile and keep up a good front.

Nope, she'd had enough. She was going to sit at one of those candlelit tables and feel sorry for herself. Hell, she thought, I've been brave all year, I deserve it. She stuck out her chin, sashayed up to the bar, and ordered a Moosehead.

The barman raised an eyebrow and asked to see her driver's license. Carla pulled it out of the big flowing shirt and the man studied it by the light of the register. He handed it back to her, commenting that it didn't look much like her and he could get in a lot of trouble for this. Now what did she want again?

Carla smiled and took the beer over to the farthest table. She had lifted some matches out of the bowl by the register and sat down at the table, shivering. She wrapped her hands around the red half-globe that held the candle and it seemed to warm her.

Then she lit matches over the candle and watched them burn down to her fingers. She'd sniff, whisper "Sonofabitch," and blow out the matches. A match pyramid was growing in the ashtray and Carla got up to order another beer. She wanted to be woozy—woozy would be better than empty.

A hundred feet away in a car by the laundromat Paul Seavers had his nose in yesterday's news. He looked up at the klieg-lit aisles to see if any dryers were done, and the clothes had fallen in one. He checked his watch: oh God, his washer was five minutes from finished.

Sure enough, old eagle-eye at the card table—that big-legged broad with the stringy hair and the tits down around her navel—had planted her moosy self over by the dryer. Undoubtedly that was her kid with the filthy feet jumping up and down on the folding counter.

Jeez, thought Paul, what is it about laundromats that makes everyone look so ugly? I'll bet even Catherine Deneuve would look ugly in here. Nahh, who'm I kidding? He closed his eyes. Ah, Catherine. Soft skin—touchable, inviting, not bony, beefy, or sweaty. Could you picture her huffing and puffing in one of those spandex aerobic jobs? No way. And style: no bangles or jangles or phony glitz. And those eyes, eyes that weren't just color: discerning eyes. Money alone couldn't turn her on, not muscles or thick hair. If she wanted you, it was because she looked at you and found you special. "Ah, Catherine," he murmured, rolling his eyes, "marry me and take me away from all this. On a lighter note, what's at the movies?"

Uh-huh. Last year's best-ever Vietnam movie was playing across the street from this year's best-ever Vietnam movie. He'd already seen them, and both had managed to find the redeeming feature in carnage—slow-motion dying. He wanted to write an angry letter but decided against it. If people wanted to think the officers and lowly grunts cussed their way through the war arm in arm, that's what the movies would show. All he remembered was taking orders: you went where they told you to go, and if they made a mistake it was your ass. You were just a pit-bull in fatigues, and Vietnam was the pen they dumped you into.

A car pulled up on his left and four German sailors piled out, hauling their duffel bags from the trunk. They were handsome and rowdy, joking about the depressing starkness of the laundromat. One of them observed that laundromats were the landships of the navy—noisy, boring, lonely, and cramped. The others looked at each other and raised their middle fingers at him.

Poor squids, thought Paul, and turned his attention to the lower half of the movie page. Nothing there either. Over the top of the paper he could see the sailors dumping pieces of color into raised-lid washers.

He picked up the sports section and checked his watch again: one minute to go.

When he looked up the Germans had reconverged on the sidewalk, bitching and laughing in their native tongue, certain they could not be understood—though they wouldn't have cared if they were. What a boring place, they griped: the land was flat, the greenery gray, the roadsides had more litter than trees; the people were stupid, sloppy and flabby; the food was tasteless—and they call that craftsmanship? No wonder they buy everything from somewhere else. And the women -- what they wouldn't give for some German pussy—some sparkle, some wit, some joy, some legs.

"Hell," said the philosopher, "who needs a Mercedes when you're only driving one block?"

The other three punched him in the shoulder. "We warned you about that thinking stuff," said the blondest one. Then he pointed at the sign on the wall above the fence and out came his only attempt at English: "Tit Bar."

"Let's go," they agreed, and strode across the parking lot, grinning and yukking about getting laid. The last thing Paul heard as they disappeared around the corner of the building was: "I just wish I could find one that wasn't stupid."

"Yeah, but then why would she fuck you?"

Paul shook his head and smiled, glad that his years abroad had given him some French and German. At least there was something to be said for being a military brat.

He rarely thought about his folks anymore, except to wonder if there was a Heaven and if so, he was sure they were there. Their picture-postcard world ended in a boating accident three months after he was shipped to Vietnam. There were days when he told himself they were better off gone. The world was too violent and strange now.

He climbed out of the car and went to his washer, on its last spin shudder. He waited for it to stop, then hauled out and dropped the wrinkled mess into one of those rolling baskets. He wheeled the basket to a dryer that someone was emptying and stood quietly while the woman transferred her load of towels to the folding counter.

He would have offered to help her but she was scrupulously avoiding eye contact with him.

Afraid I'll try to pick her up, I guess, thought Paul, and winced that someone so homely would think that of him. Shit, must be one of my bad days.

He walked over to the head to check himself out after he had filled the dryer. He rubbed a clear circle in the dirty mirror and studied the face that looked back at him. Naahh, not that bad. Those curly lashes were still killer. The eyes were hot. The nose was nice. All in all, an attractive face. Of course, the hair could be a little thicker on top, but at least he didn't have to comb strands up from midway down the side of his head. Hopefully that day would never come. Hard to tell, though: his dad wasn't bald, but his granddad was. God, I hope this isn't one of those skip-the-generation afflictions. Things are tough enough as is.

He held up his palms to inspect the scars. Hey, some people have lifelines, I have scars. Put that in your bag of openers, he winced. He was sick of warning people before he shook their hands, but the alternative was that frozen smile and glazed look, like he was part tree masquerading as human, and they'd felt the roots.

They couldn't possibly understand, these smooth-skinned snobs with their fancy cars. Vietnam was just film footage to them, upgraded from documentaries to Art Films worthy of Academy Awards. There was no room for people like him anymore; he was stuck in the documentary phase.

Paul opened the door and looked down the aisle. Some woman with a scrunched-up face was tossing an expensive sweater in one of the trash cans. The way it fell he could see a large brown stain on the front. She was pretty pissed off. Paul muttered: "Huh, that's me: a stain on the shirt of America. Can't wash me out, so they wanna throw me away. Well," his eyes narrowed, "not in this lifetime, lady. No fuckin' way!"

He looked up quickly to see if she had heard him. This talkin' to myself has gotta stop. He knew it was a result of being alone so much. Hell, what was he supposed to do, build a business and have a social life too?

His last attempts at a relationship were doomed from day one, but he didn't know that going in. Both Betsy and Karen were attractive, sweet, supportive women whose ex-husbands would turn up at peculiar hours. According to Betsy and Karen these bastards had totally devastated them, and every unscheduled visit from the "hated" Bruce or Andy resulted in money passing from Karen's or Betsy's purse into Bruce's or Andy's pocket. There were so many of these midnight visits Paul lost track. Eventually he just lost interest and hit the door.

"Nope," he said to himself, "I'm tired of bein' the nice guy left in the cold. Next woman I meet, I'm the one she'll make the exceptions for. "

He checked his watch: fifteen minutes to dryer shutdown—time enough for a beer at Marguerita's. He walked in the bar and saw the German sailors laughing around a pitcher on a table out back.

Oh, no, thought Paul. No more snotty comments, please. I'll just stay in here.

As he approached the bar the barkeep looked up and waved. "Dry cycle again?" He popped open a Heineken and placed a napkin under it in front of Paul.

Paul was impressed: he hadn't been there in three months. They started chatting, and Paul watched the man shuttle back and forth between his customers. His name was Gary. He had blond hair, a dark mustache, and leathery skin. He wore a California-style spatter shirt that his wife designed, and never forgot a face, an order, or a conversation. He crooked his finger at Paul and Paul leaned forward.

"Can you do me a favor?" Gary whispered, "It's just a little favor. See that girl at the table down by the jukebox? She came in here about an hour ago. Uh, at first I didn't wanna serve her, y'know, she's got the kinda face that should be home watching Smurfs. But her ID was legit, so I served her. Well, after one beer she starts blowin' out matches 'n' talkin' to 'em, so natcherly I start watchin' her, wonderin' if she hadn't been let out of some institution—they've started doing that, y'know—but then I decided naahh, too clean."

He popped a celery stalk in a bloody Mary and handed it to a man three seats down. Then he said: "Now, since I been lookin' at her she hasn't been to the washroom and I haven't seen her sneak any pills. I'm afraid she's either on some medication or she did somethin' before she got here, y'know?

"So, what I would like you to do, Paul, is go over there and coax her outta here before she barfs or ODs or somethin.' I mean this is my bar, an' I could lose it over somethin' like this, y'know? Just cart her across the street and get her some coffee. I'll pay. Oh, and the beer is on the house."

"Sure," said Paul. "I'll get her outta here. But I think another freebie next time I come in is only fair, right?"

"Good enough," said Gary. He watched Paul walk to the back of the room and say something to the girl, who yelled: "FUCK OFF!"

"Look, lady!" Paul yelled back, "You can set yerself on fire for all I care. The bartender was worried aboutcha, that's all, and I was just tryin' to help out. What a mouth! Didn't your family ever teach you any manners?"

Carla started to cry. "I'm sorry," she blubbered, "It's not you. I was just mad 'n' you were here. The person I wanna yell at isn't."

She got up and told the bartender she was sorry for the trouble, that she was leaving—and by the way what was the time? Gary pointed to the red digits above the jukebox and the girl thanked him. She took a wad of rolled-up toilet paper out of her shirt pocket, tore off a foot and daubed her eyes.

Then she looked over at Paul, who had returned to his beer. "Look," she said, "I'm sorry for the yelling. Can I buy you a beer before I go?"

"Well," sighed Paul, staring straight ahead, "maybe my feelings are worth more than a beer." He heard a rustling sound as she dug through her pockets, then he heard her say oh, oh dear.

She said, "Look, I'm sorry, but no matter what your feelings are worth, I've only got two bucks. And a quarter— but that's to call my sister."

"Two bucks. That's it?" said Paul, as he swivelled the stool slowly to face her.

"Yup," she smiled. "Best I can do."

"Well," he sighed, "if that's the best you can do." He dug his fingers in the peanut bowl and gathered up a handful.

"Hey," she laughed, "feel special. How many girls you know give almost everything on the first date?"

"This is how you treat your dates?" Paul rolled his eyes.

"Well," she sniffed, "it's the only one we'll ever have, so—"

"And why is that?" He tossed a peanut in the air and caught it in his mouth. "What am I, a one-beer fling?" He caught another peanut.

Carla laughed. "Gee, Is that your best trick?"

"Gee, I sure hope not." He popped in another nut. "Actually, my best trick is next door. I fold laundry into the neatest, tightest piles. They look like stacks of books when I'm finished. Wanna see?"

He tossed another peanut into his mouth, but his eyes never left hers. She certainly was cute. What in hell could he say to keep her attention? Oh, fuck it, just tell the truth. She's probably a loadie, anyway. "Next show starts in five minutes, and I can get you a front row seat, free. How 'bout it?"

"Why not?" she shrugged. "I was thinking of going to the David Bowie movie up the street but I'm out of money. 'Course I never thought of myself as a laundry groupie, but then I never met Merlin the Folder before. What's your name, anyway?"

"Paul Seavers," he said. "And yours?"

"Carla," she said, wiping her brow.

"Are you okay? Really?" said Paul, holding himself off from reaching for her.

"No," she said, tossing some stray hair over her shoulder, "I'm sorta depressed. Today is not a good day for me."

"You wanna talk about it?" He offered. His offer surprised her. Indeed, it surprised him. He liked her soft directness.

She saw and liked the same thing in him.

They walked out of the bar firing peanuts into each other's mouths and were out of peanuts by the time they reached the laundromat.

Now that he could see her in the light he was glad she wasn't put off by laundry. All that wavy chestnut hair and sweet freckled face. Hell, she looked like she was barely out of grade school. Still, there was something sensual about her pallor, perhaps the porcelain contours, perhaps those large eyes looking out under her bangs, eyes that were—what? Hazel? Green? He couldn't see her body under that floppy shirt, but she had nice ankles, nice calves, nice knees, nice thighs.

They talked while he folded and she rolled socks. She found four with no mates and he said: "They're all gray, just tie 'em together. Who's gonna see 'em under jackboots anyway?"

"You a construction worker or something?" she asked.

"Well, sorta," he smiled. "I own my own business."

She raised an eyebrow and he raised his eyebrows. "I know, it's not every day you meet a business tycoon in a laundromat, but don't you know, Miz Carla, that any fool with twenty dollars can get a business card printed up? Beware of men carrying cards," he intoned, and handed her one of his.

Carla dropped the card in her shirt pocket and dug out a quarter. "I hafta go phone my sister," she said, "and find out about my little girl."

"Why, is she sick?" asked Paul.

"No," smiled Carla, "Wanna see her?" she asked, and whipped out a wallet stuffed with pictures. Oh yes, cute kid. There was even a picture of—wouldn't you know it—her husband.

Oh God, not another one. Let me outta here.

She caught his disgruntled look and said, "Hey, I understand. Why would you want to get involved with a near divorcee, complete with ankle biter? But you might want to go to a movie with a nice woman sometimes. I mean, if you're not involved with anyone. And," she said softly, blushing as she said it, "I'm nice. Or, I think so." She laughed. "That is, unless I'm trapped in a bar with matches."

Paul laughed, then asked the vital question: "This ex of yours. How ex is he?"

Carla sighed and looked at the floor. "Hey, he's history. A year ago today, our anniversary, he walked out and I haven't seen him since. I don't know why, I've stopped asking myself. He emptied our joint account and it was bon voyage. Hell, maybe he couldn't find a suitable anniversary gift for a lousy five thou and he's still out looking. Whaddaya think?" She flashed a quick smile, stretched, and yawned. As she did the blouse fell open, revealing the line of her torso.

Well, whaddaya know, thought Paul. There is somethin' up there besides pockets.

He offered to take them to the Bowie film up the street, and she said great. Then she warned him it was supposed to be a little weird, about modern day vampires and premature aging, but it had Catherine Deneuve and—"Hey," he grinned, "say no more. Just call me Siskel or Ebert. What did they say about it?"

Carla snickered and shrugged. "Look," she said, "if I went to every film critics recommended I'd have died of boredom long ago. All I want is a good plot, good acting, some laughs, and a minimum of bloodshed. If it gets bloody can I hide my face in your sleeve?"

"Sure." He smiled. Then: "Is that the only reason you asked me along?"

She shook her head. "Not a chance. I don't waste my time with people I don't like."

They loaded the laundry into his duffel bags and walked to his truck. He laid the bags on the floor and put one of the towels across the seat for her to sit on. He apologized for the greasy condition of the cab.

"Hey," she laughed, "it can't be any worse than jelly on everything after a morning with Jessie."

Two hours later they were out of the theater, agreeing that the movie was amazingly erotic. They liked the idea of the

head vampire being the one with the strongest will, not
someone who lay in a coffin in mouldy earth. They agreed that
Catherine Deneuve was the most beautiful woman in the
world. They agreed to see each other again.

"When?" asked Paul.

"How about tomorrow?" said Carla.

He was thinking how about tonight but didn't want to
seem pushy. "How's eight o'clock sound? I have a restaurant
I'd love to take you to. Have you ever been to The Bistro? It's
kinda cosmopolitan, sorta the right atmosphere for two well-
rounded world travellers like us."

"Gosh, I wish," smiled Carla. "You're on. See you at eight."
She climbed out of the truck and walked toward the beach,
leaving her phone number, address, and a crude map drawn on the
back of one of his invoices. She told him to tell Rachel they had
met in the restaurant, otherwise Rachel would worry.

The next night over dinner he asked why.

"Oh," said Carla, "she was attacked last year and carved
up by some maniac in a mask, so now she's real nervous about
men."

"I guess so," said Paul. "I'm sorry."

"I'm just telling you," said Carla, "so that when you meet
her, if she seems a little weird you'll know why."

You take a lot for granted, Miz Carla, thought Paul. I
mean, we're only having dinner.

But there were many dinners to follow and by November
most of them were in Carla's apartment, with Jessie in the high
chair drinking grape juice by candlelight.

Paul adored Jessie and felt sorry for Rachel. He told Carla
that Rachel acted shell-shocked, and from what he'd seen it
would be a long time before she was out of it. "Damn," he said,
"I wish I could help her."

"You are," said Carla.

"How's that?" asked Paul.

"You're a nice man, Paul. She needs to know they're out
there."

"Hell," said Paul, "I need to know they're out there." The

week before he hired two helpers who helped themselves to a truckload of tools and the contents of three houses a mile down the road from the job site.

Paul remembered how Bubba had set him up in business—hell, if it wasn't for that maneater Bubba married, there wouldn't be a business.

Charlie Krantz—"Bubba" to his friends—was a contractor who hired Paul to landscape his home on the St. John's River. Bubba's wife, Doris, watched the tiers of cochina dip down from the house to the water, glowing like a necklace in the afternoon sun. It was her idea and it cost a bundle, but Bubba believed money must be spent to be enjoyed. He was too busy earning it, he said, so spending it was her job.

What he didn't know was that her complex projects required hundreds of man hours and gave her her pick of the workmen. All that saved Paul from having his pants torn off was a quick lie: "Look, Doris, I'd love to, I been eyin' you for days, butcha see, I got this herpes lesion between my cock and my balls."

"Ooh!" she yipped. "You are gross! Get out of here!"

My pleasure, you piece of shit. God, if Bubba only knew.

But Bubba never suspected. He was ecstatic with the job Paul had done and offered to launch Paul in his own business, using Bubba's house as the centerpiece for a brochure. Paul just stared while Bubba laughed and pumped his hand. Doris was on the phone, talking in that sultry voice, eying Paul over her husband's shoulder.

Paul agreed to go into business but couldn't think of a company name. He finally decided to use his own name, expanded to sound upscale: The Seavers Group. TSG, as he fondly called it, had been in business four months when he met Carla.

In November Paul showed his business card to Rachel, who gently suggested it could use some reworking. Perhaps he would allow The Whitsun Group to redesign it? Paul said he doubted there was enough scratch in the TSG coffers for such an enterprise.

Rachel then offered to do the logo and stationery as a Christmas present.

Paul almost choked on his beer. "Rachel, dammit," he sputtered, "I can't let you do that, that's expensive!"

"I know," she smiled, "but I feel like you're family, kinda. So you can forget it, I won't take no for an answer."

Carla hugged Paul after they left Rachel's, squealing: "You know what that means, Paul? It means she trusts you—hell, she likes you! Dammit, Paul, Rachel's getting better!"

The Proposal

"Rachel's getting better." Once a week Carla would make this gleeful announcement.

Though he wanted to scream horseshit Paul never contradicted her. He knew it was Carla's way of coping, this prayerful chant.

By Christmas Paul was spending his nights at Carla's. It was pleasant to wake up in the morning with some part of Carla touching him and Jessie bringing them orange juice, trying her hardest not to spill it.

On March 31st Paul came over with a huge purple rabbit in a plastic bag, then offered to treat Jessie and Carla to the Care Bear movie and dinner at McDonald's. Jessie was ecstatic. She asked if the bunny could come too or would he cost extra in the movie?

"Oh hey," said Paul, "let the bunny have his day. So whatcha gonna call him, Jess?"

Jessie stood toe-to-fur with her gift and cocked an eyebrow at Carla. She said, "Mommy, when you were a little girl you had a bunny. What did you call him?"

"I called him Andre."

"I like that," said Jessie, "Andre. Can I call him Andre, Mommy?"

"Sure can, Honey. Anything you like."

"Okay, Andre," said Jessie, hugging her new buddy. "You came on a good day, 'cause we're all goin' to McDonald's!" Then she looked up at Paul and said, "After he shaves, acourse."

Carla stared at her and Paul said, "Not my kid."

"Mine neither," said Carla. "Band of gypsies dropped her 'n' ran."

On April 3rd Paul woke up with morning stubble and dry eyes. He'd forgotten to buy blades, and he was sure that last razor was waiting to nick him. His eyedrops were down to a dribble. Maybe he could extract one last bubbly squish. Shit, the things you go through to avoid waiting in line. Sure enough, the razor blade had passed from dull to lethal. "Ahoww," said Paul, and set it down. He swore at himself for being lazy, at his beard for being thick, and at Bubba for deciding to move and pushing him to move.

"Shit, why move?" Paul asked. "In a coupla years Jax'll spread south to Orlando and we'll probably merge into Disneyberg or something." Paul was grinning, but Bubba wasn't, and his Humpty Dumpty head looked strange without its smile.

Bubba placed a hand on Paul's shoulder and said: "Hell, I'd think you'd be jumpin' up and down over an opportunity like this. Whatsa matter, can't leave the mother-daughter team? What are ya, pussy whipped?" He looked away, smiling slightly, and took a swig of beer.

Paul stiffened, fighting the curl of his fingers and the desire to thump Bubba. It was all he could do not to shout look who's talking! Even so he didn't want Bubba to think he was right. "Uh, well," said Paul, turning it around, "I am thinking of marrying the girl—the older one, anyway."

Bubba blinked. "Geez, Paul, I'm sorry. I didn't know y'all had gotten that serious. Hey," he threw up his hands, "I didn't mean anything by—"

"S'okay, Bubba," said Paul, smiling over his beer. "It won't happen for awhile. Her divorce hasta come through first, which means they hafta advertise or something to locate the bum't deserted her. If he don't answer the ads then she's free to start divorce proceedings without him. I just hope to God he don't come back." Paul's voice trailed off. He offered Bubba another beer, knowing he wouldn't refuse, and strode off to the kitchen.

He was thinking while he pulled the bottles off the fridge door: just what were his objections to moving anyway? Apart from the general hassle it really came down to Rachel. Could she withstand the shock of Carla's leaving? Worse, what if after they left the bastard came back and carved on Rachel again. Hell, that could happen no matter where we were. And what's to stop him now—except of course that dirty big gun of hers.

He grinned and uncapped the beers while Bubba said: "What?"

Paul pushed a beer over the counter and took a long swallow of his own. He looked at Bubba and said: "Nothin'. Just thinkin' aloud—plannin' my life, or tryin' to." He looked around his apartment at what was there: ledgers, receipts and bills scattered across the front room, take-out boxes by an empty refrigerator, an empty bedroom closet. Who was he kidding? His bachelorhood was history long before he hung the mistletoe on Carla's headboard.

He picked up the phone and dialed the restaurant.

"What's up?" asked Bubba.

"Nothin'," Paul replied. "Just doin' what I shoulda done months ago. Oh, and the answer is yes, I'll move to Orlando with you. I just need a couple of months to straighten out some personal stuff here—Oh, hey, Linda? Can I speak to Carla a minute? Just for a minute, I promise."

"Wow," said Bubba. He upended his beer, drained the bottle, then blew a "phooh" sound in the neck. "Am I gonna hear a proposal?"

"Nope," said Paul, "just setting the scene. Hello, Carla? Yeah, it's me. No, no, nothing's wrong, I just called to see if you'd like to go to dinner tonight, someplace special. You know, one of those four-star places. Make a night of it. Huh? Look, Honey, anything you wanna wear is fine, really. Uh, listen. What say I drop by and dump some loot on you, and you go pick out something. Yes I'm serious. I'll be there in an hour. Love ya, Car," he concluded, and hung up. He looked over at Bubba, whose smile-button face was leering at him.

"So," said Bubba, "do I get to be best man, or are you gonna run off to Georgia?"

"Please," groaned Paul, "like I told you, it's gonna be awhile. But I want her to know I'm serious."

"Yeah, well you sound pretty serious to me," said Bubba.

Paul picked Carla up at eight that night and they drove to their favorite Italian restaurant, Puccini's. Carla declared the chicken cacciatore to be the best she'd eaten anywhere, Montreal included. She and Paul said that Jacksonville's cuisine was badly underrated: the food was often excellent, the service and atmosphere a treat. But Puccini's was special for there they first declared their love on a cold November night.

Tonight Carla was radiant in lilac tinted petals that parted over her knees and elbows. Her hair was drawn back in a satin bow and all those freckles he loved to tease her about were blending into the beginnings of a tan. Her eyes, greener than ever against wisps of mauve eyeshadow, followed his every move.

By the end of the meal the sky outside had passed from blue to black. The lights in the restaurant were subtly dimmed to complement the candles. Two waitresses passed their table carrying a large cake covered in sparklers.

"Wow." said Carla, "Must be for that private party." Then she laughed: "I guess somebody's either leaving or pregnant."

"Uh, I think you're wrong," said Paul, as the waitresses walked up behind her then set the cake down between them. Curls of pink icing spelled out: "Carla, will you marry me?" Carla gasped, squealed, and covered her face. She drew her hands away and tears were in her eyes. "Oh, Paul," she whispered, "thank you. Thank you thank you thank you."

"You're welcome," said Paul. "Does that mean yes?"

"Yes!" squealed Carla, her face bright pink. "Of course it means yes!"

The ladies carried off the cake, and Paul and Carla rose up to kiss over the spot where the cake had been. When they left, people around them applauded their love, and the waitress applauded her tip.

Jessie was spending the night at Rachel's so the two of them would get the good news tomorrow. Meanwhile Paul could sound Carla out about Orlando.

They were sitting on the couch, and after her initial smile Carla looked down and said hesitantly: "I can't leave Rachel yet, Paul. She's not strong enough. And you know she isn't, so how can you ask me that?"

Paul said: "I've already thought of that, Carla. We'll just bring her along, that's all. Rent an apartment together. Maybe a change of scene'll help her, start her lookin' out instead of in. Whaddaya say?"

"Um, okay. I'll talk to her. But if the answer's no, what next?"

"So, you stay here till you're comfortable about leaving, that's all." He smiled and shook her arm. "Hey, I'm not tryin' to leave Rachel high 'n' dry, it's just I know there's a future for us down there. Hell, to hear Bubba tell it even the traffic jams sound good. Anyway, I'm goin' down there with him for a coupla days next week, after I wrap up the job in Jax Beach. If you'd like, I could drop you 'n' the Twink off at Disney World—if you could get the time off. We could watch the parade at night, and snuggle in a real hotel room. Otherwise I

figure two days of Donald and Goofy'll send you outta there
screamin.' Whaddaya say?"

"Well, if Linda can work out the scheduling, the answer's
yes. Meanwhile, what say we hold off telling Rachel and
Jessie till we get back from Orlando, and you've had a chance
to really study your prospects—and I mean yours, not Bubba's.
I mean, Bubba's gonna do fine no matter what happens, he's
rich. You know, I mean we're just little minnows, Paul, and
Bubba—he's one big whale." She spread her arms and puffed
out her cheeks.

Paul laughingly agreed. Then he kissed her and called her
Mrs. Seavers. "Thought I'd try it out," he said, "to see how it
sounds."

"Sounds good to me," said Carla, as Paul gathered up his
bundle of shiny petals and carried them off to bed.

They took Rachel's car to Disney World that weekend and
saw the American Dream unfolding before their eyes: clean,
wholesome families loaded up with balloons and souvenirs,
lining up or waving in a clump at some crouched person with a
camera. Everyone wanted to be photographed with Cinderella's
Castle behind them—all except for Jessie, who wanted a picture
of herself with one of the ghosts in "the ghost house."

"Think she's normal?" laughed Paul.

"Sure," said Rachel. "All little kids are into ghost stories.
They like to see the bad guys get whupped in the end. And why
not? We're no different. I mean, for all the complaints about
violence on television, at least there the bad guys don't get
away with it."

Carla couldn't bring herself to talk about leaving with
Rachel, but several days later when she brought it up Rachel
was surprisingly agreeable. She even had a plan to save them
money.

Carla called Paul with the good news and Rachel's plan.
"Rachel's offered to put us up when our leases expire, so that
we—that's you 'n' me—can look for a place in Orlando,
rather than get stuck with a lease here. We can move into her
guest room in the back, and she'll clear out the Florida room

for Jessie. She said we can paint or wallpaper Jessie's room, and it can be hers whenever she visits. Hey, we could even move in one trip. I mean whadda we have for furniture?"

"Jeez, Car," he laughed, "this is too good. I mean, who'd have thought owning nothing'd be a plus?"

Then he heard her sigh and said: "All right, what's the bad news. Hit me."

"Well," said Carla, "Rachel won't come. Oh Paul, I really think it's because she wants to kill that man. I'm sure that's it."

"So, who can blame her?"

"That's not the point! What if she misses, or he grabs the gun out of her hand?"

"Whoa, whoa," said Paul. "Carla, Rachel's not gonna let him get that close this time. I think she's protecting you 'n' Jessie by sending us off to Orlando and I'm damn flattered by her faith in me. I wanna thank her for that. As a matter of fact, I'm gonna call her right now."

Paul dialed the number he knew by heart and heard Rachel's hesitant hello. "Rachel, hi, it's Paul," he said quickly. "Carla told me your generous offer and I thought we better jump on it before you do the sane thing and weasel out. So are we on or what?"

"Absolutely," said Rachel. Then slowly: "Uh, Paul, the day before you move to Orlando I need to tell you something. It's something I don't want Carla to know—nothing big, really. It won't change anything between you two, it's just something about me I'd like you to know. Okay?"

"Yeah. Sure thing, Rachel. And thanks again." When he hung up the phone Paul wondered if she was going to tell him the identity of the rapist. Hell, maybe she'd already killed him. Maybe that's the reason she's so skittish. Maybe—hell, Rachel would tell him when the time was right.

That evening he found Carla leafing through the phone book in search of daycare centers at the beach. One of the most highly recommended was The Tot Spot. Carla called and asked if she could come by for a visit. The little-old-lady voice said, "Sure, dear. C'mon ahead."

It was a cloudless sky and a perfect seventy-eight degrees next morning when they pulled up at the mint-green house on Oceanview Drive. A dozen happy kids were under the magnolia in the yard, some around a lady, trying to sing "Jesus Loves Me."

Paul and Carla climbed out of the cab and walked across the pine-covered driveway to the white fence, where skewed green letters spelled out The Tot Spot. The old lady who belonged to the voice on the phone greeted them at the door and invited them in for tea and cookies. It would be a month before they had a vacancy, said Granny Blair, handing them a list of references and copies of testimonial letters.

Carla pocketed the paperwork but she'd already found what she'd come for: smiling faces. She wanted Jessie's to be one of them.

When they arrived at Rachel's Jessie asked excitedly: "Is Uncle Paul gonna be my new daddy?"

"Sure am, Sugar," said Paul, plunking Jessie on his shoulder. "Not right away though, eh?"

He looked over at Carla, who laughed and said, "No, eh?"

Paul laughed and shook his head. "Jeez, I gotta get away from here," he said. "I'm startin' to talk funny."

Then he noticed Carla was no longer smiling. Her face was white. "Honey, are you all right?" he asked, reaching for her hand.

"No," said Carla, trying to smile. "I think I have a headache. I—I think I better sit down."

Rachel went into the kitchen and returned with aspirin and water. Carla said she felt better and they talked about the move and Jessie's new daycare arrangements.

Carla looked out the livingroom window. The sky was a dazzling blue. It was a perfect day, and here she was surrounded by the people she loved most. So where did they come from, these horrible visions? They came so fast, but the images were so clear, and the colors—first Jessie's big Easter bunny, only it wasn't a bunny anymore, just pieces of purple fur and stuffing blowing along the edge of a ditch. Then oaks

and magnolias, so densely packed they blotted out the sky—
only what sky she could see wasn't blue, but black. And
something else, there in the blackness, twinkling like stars, on
and on, as far as the eye could see. Maybe thousands, maybe
millions. Of what?

I need more sleep, Carla decided. Either that or Martians
are sending me messages.

She went to sleep early that night, woke up early next
morning and made love to Paul.

Afterwards she lay there sweating, thinking how nice it
was to be normal.

Sins of the Father

It was Saturday, May 1st, and the sun was shimmering directly above them when Paul backed the truck up to Rachel's front door and started carrying in the boxes.

"That's all?" asked Rachel, looking at the little pile of cardboard in the flatbed.

"We travel light," said Paul.

Jessie, following behind him, yelled: "Don't step on Calliope!"

Paul halted in mid-stride, apologized to an empty section of carpet, and tip-toed a broad circle around it.

"C'mon, Calliope." Jessie motioned to the nothing on the rug. "Let's go play in the yard." She picked up the box Carla had just emptied, dropped it on the lawn and climbed in, inviting Calliope to join her.

Calliope was the hero of Jessie's favorite story: an invisible unicorn hatched from an Easter egg and befriended by a little girl named Evie, the only person who could see him. Calliope found another friend in Jessie, who took him everywhere she couldn't take Andre, and sometimes took them together. In the story Calliope ate daisies and peanut butter on rye, but once off the pages he developed a taste for all kinds of goodies—chips, popcorn, little powdered doughnuts—and left a trail of crumbs wherever he went. His favorite treat was also Jessie's: chocolate honey grahams. Jessie tried to stop him, but he'd jump up on the chair, push the pantry door open, and stick his face in the package. He'd take four at a time, five sometimes.

"I guess we're lucky he don't eat the whole thing, eh?" said Jessie.

"Really, eh?" said Carla. "Then you just have him finish off those Brussels sprouts, or you're gonna hafta eat 'em all yourself."

Jessie made a face and said, "Naah, Calliope's too smart for that."

"Too dumb ya mean," said Carla. "Those little green guys are good for him. He's just gonna get fat on honey grahams and peanut butter. Then we'll have holes in the carpet where he tried to walk and fell through."

Rocking back and forth in her box, Jessie yelled: "Mommy! Can I take Calliope to new daycare?"

Carla yelled back: "I dunno if they're ready for Calliope yet, Jess. But you can take anybody else you want."

"Andre? Can I take Andre?"

"Sure thing, Honey, but you'll hafta keep an eye on him so's he doesn't hop off and get lost."

"Okay, Mommy, I promise." Then silence. Two minutes later a whisper drifted up to the front window: "Iss okay, Calliope. I'll sneak ya in next time."

Then Jessie yelled: "When does it start, Mommy?"

"Monday, Honey. Day after tomorrow."

"When's tomorrow?"

"Day after today."

"When's today?" Jessie was laughing behind her hand.

"All right, Jess, cut it out!'" yelled Carla. "You're being silly."

"I know." Jessie giggled. Then she whispered to Calliope: "Big people get mad so easy."

Monday came before any of them were ready.

Paul, finally able to ignore the revving motors around Carla's apartment, now had to ignore the whizz of cars at all hours. When the alarm went off he staggered into the kitchen for his morning orange juice and nearly collided with Rachel coming out of the bathroom.

Her hair was wet spikes around her face, and he saw for the first time the great pink zigzag on her head. He stared at it, too bleary to do otherwise, and Rachel quickly covered it with her towel.

"Hey, Rachel," he said as she tried to brush past him, "Y'aint the only one with scars, y'know."

Rachel apologized, flustered. Just his closeness was too much—as if all the safe space she'd built around herself these past two years had vanished, and she and her house were at the mercy of this invader.

Paul sensed her fear and said: "Look, Rachel. You and I, we both been through some kinda hell. I mean, please, you don't hafta get defensive around me. Hell, I'm here to protect you, Rachel—you and all the ladies of this house. Nothing's gonna hurtcha if I can help it."

Rachel looked in his eyes and said thanks, then apologized for overreacting.

He said, "Hey, who can blame you, I look pretty scary when I first wake up."

"Me too," she agreed, attempting a smile.

"See," he laughed, "we got a lot in common." So the tension was broken—for now, thought Paul. He raised the shower head to drench his face and remembered that they were out of toilet paper. God, women go through more damn toilet paper.

Paul dropped Carla and Jessie at The Tot Spot, waiting by the truck while Jessie went through the introductions. He heard her cry, then Carla emerged and walked toward the truck.

"Let's just drive around the block and watch from one of the side streets for a few minutes. Do ya mind?" Carla asked.

Paul shook his head and they got in the truck, then drove to a driveway where they could see the daycare center. Five little ones were with a tall blonde woman in the yard. Then Jessie appeared with Granny Blair, talking excitedly up at her.

"Looks like business as usual to me," said Paul, while Carla nodded and stuck her fingers in her ears.

They laughed and drove over the Intercoastal Waterway into the morning fog of Atlantic Boulevard. Two seconds later they realized it wasn't fog but smoke. Brush fires were common of late, and firemen worked round the clock to contain sporadic blazes. On Atlantic Boulevard particularly there seemed to be evidence of arson.

"What kind of crazy would do that?" Carla wanted to know, her head pounding from fumes.

Who cares, thought Paul. Torch the bastard.

They talked about her finding a job at the beach, then he dropped her at the restaurant.

That night at Rachel's Jessie ran to meet Paul at the door, talking mile-a-minute about all her "new boyfriends."

"New boyfriends!" cried Paul, pretending to whimper behind his arm. "Well whaddabout me? I thought I was your only boyfriend —"

"Yeah, but you can't be my boyfriend anymore, you're gonna be my daddy."

"You rather have me as a daddy, huh?"

"Yup," said Jess, then she put on her mother's smile and asked: "And how was your day?"

Paul laughed and carried her into the kitchen where Rachel was making something tomatoey and garlicy near some rice in a clear pot. The table was set with white placemats, small bowls, and jewelled Japanese chopsticks. Fortunately there was a pile of knives, forks, and spoons "for the faint of heart," as Rachel put it.

"Faint of heart, nothin'," said Paul. "Faint from hunger, you mean."

Paul could never wait on food. He passed directly from disinterested to starving, and now he was barely able to keep his fingers out of the boiling pots.

He watched Rachel drain the rice and spoon it into the bowls beside the placemats. She set the wok on the table, pulled the cover off, and told them to dig in. Scallops, shrimp, and halibut chunks floated in a savory broth along with snow pea pods, broccoli, and fan-like purply mushrooms.

"Wow," they all said, except for Jessie, who said "yuck."

When they were all seated at the table Carla had them join hands and asked Jessie to say the blessing. Jessie agreed, figuring that strange stuff in the bowl needed all the help it could get.

Paul looked around at the faces while Jessie stumbled through grace. For all his worries about being outnumbered and adrift in a sea of femininity, he loved it. He watched Rachel dip the sparkling chopsticks into the fish on her plate. She rolled a scallop in the rice and lifted it to her mouth, saw him smiling at her and smiled back.

Jessie watched her mother pour a little broth on the rice, then ate her way to the soggy spot. She asked: "Do I really hafta eat it?"

Carla said, "Honey, you know the rule: you don't hafta eat it but you hafta try it."

Jessie stuck her spoon in the pinkish rice and complained that she did so hafta eat it to try it.

"Yup," said Rachel. "Big people are sneaky, huh?"

"Yup," said Jessie, closing her eyes tight and clamping her mouth around the spoon.

There was ice cream for dessert, chocolate ripple, and of course all natural, said Rachel.

"Of course," mimicked Paul and Carla.

Jessie, between bites of ice cream, told them Granny Blair had a creepy claw.

"Honey," said Carla, "that's her hand, and it got all shrunk up from a bad sickness called polio. You—you mustn't call it a creepy claw, Honey. You'll hurt Granny Blair."

"Okay," said Jessie, and a moment later Paul said uh-oh as Jessie's face swelled up and she burst into tears. Carla got up and put her arms around her daughter, telling her that Granny Blair knew Jessie didn't mean to hurt her.

Jessie loved Granny Blair. All the kids did. She'd put her good arm around them and sing funny songs, and tell amazing stories from the Bible, like the one where Jesus fed all these people with bread and fish and didn't use a power ring or a money card or even go to the store.

Jessie saw pictures of people in Granny Blair's house that were her "when she was younger" but it was hard for Jessie to connect the pictures with the old lady. She'd point at all the faces in the photos and say, "Is that you?" Then Granny Blair would smile and point to the right face—but gosh, it looked so strange and brown, and the creepy claw was always covered somehow.

Granny Blair's son had "gone off somewhere," she told Jessie: she looked so sad when she said it. Jessie would hug the old lady whenever she saw her smile fading. She got the five other four-year-olds into the act by yelling: "It's hug Granny Blair time!" They'd race over to where the old lady was sitting and take turns putting their arms around her. When Granny Blair saw that Jessie initiated these hugathons she told Carla she had "a very blessed little girl."

Carla picked Jessie up, spun her around and laughed: "Too bad there aren't any job openings for huggers, 'cause I got the chief hugger right here."

"Yeay!" yelled Jessie, as the ground whirled under her. "Faster, Mommy! Make me dizzy!" Two more turns and it was over. Uncle Paul would have to crank up the merry-go-round when they got home, gasped Carla, setting her down.

"Aw boo," said Jessie, as the world turned right side up. She kissed Granny Blair good-bye, and Miz Selena, and Miz Lizzie, then climbed in the stroller, waving as she rolled away.

She sang "Jesus loves me" all the way home.

When they got there Rachel was in the kitchen trying to understand how a refrigerator full of food could have become a collection of empty cartons in just three days.

"Kids," said Carla. "Kids and men."

"Oh, well," sighed Rachel. She jotted some things on a list and headed out the door, yelling to Jessie: "I'm going to the store. Wanna come, Punkin?"

Jessie shook her head. She was waiting for Uncle Paul to spin her around the floor, and boring old dinner could hardly compete with that. It was clearly divided to Jessie: Mommy and AnRachel did the boring stuff while Uncle Paul was in charge of the fun things—spinning her around, tickling her till she couldn't breathe, telling scary stories, stuff like that. Not that Mommy and AnRachel didn't try, they just didn't have as much stamina (whatever that was—it was Uncle Paul's word).

So on the May morning Cally arrived at the daycare center Jessie was thrilled to meet him. He was Granny Blair's son, old and big like Uncle Paul, but with hair that stood up like a chewed toothbrush. There were drawings on his arms, and stories that went with every drawing. He spun the kids around and brought them ice cream. He took pictures of them, too, and handed the polaroids to the happy mothers. Soon he was taking 'real' pictures' with a 'real' camera that he developed in his bedroom closet, which he called his 'darkroom.'

Jessie asked if he would tell them a ghost story but he said no, that Granny Blair didn't like ghost stories. Later he whispered to her that he'd tell her, but only her, and only if she promised not to tell.

"Like a secret, you mean," said Jessie.

"Uh-huh," he nodded, studying her reaction. "So can you keep a secret?"

"Oh yes," said Jessie proudly. "My AnRachel says I'm a good secret keeper. I din't tell Mommy that Uncle Paul was gonna ask her to marry him. It was a surprise."

"That's good," said Cally. "Let's shake on it." He smiled and his huge hand swallowed hers. One of his fingers tickled her palm and she laughed and pulled away. He released her and she skipped off to join some other kids in the sandbox.

He watched his mother on the back porch calling the children to lunch and thought: That's what ya got to look forward to, kids—ugly, old 'n' rottin' away, like fuckin' boards. All yer Bible readin' ain't changed that, Mama. 'Sides, only young 'uns git to Heaven. Don't it say that somewhere? So why try t' be good once't yer old? Hell, Mama, ya think all whatcher doin' here's gonna save ya? Yer wrong, Mama. Yer too late. Hell, God don't want no wrinkled ol' farts. He jest leaves 'em to Satan. That's why Satan's so pissed alla time: he just gits the leftovers.

He looked at the empty swings and thought about how great they looked to him as a kid, how they were nothing but rope and planks and still they were magic.

Nothing was magic now. The adult world had nothing to offer but do's and don'ts. Graded every day, every way, by some jerk or other.

He thought about his mother's expression when she saw him: the shock, the sorrow, the joy. God help me, Mama, I never meant to hurtcha. But it wa'nt me, Mama. Ya cain't blame me. It was Daddy—an' it was you, dammit. You coulda stopped it. If'n it was that bad, you coulda stopped it...

He had walked to the swings unaware, and sat down as he had that day when he was six, but couldn't sit because his sit-upon was burning and sore, and there was blood on the paper when he wiped off in the bathroom. He fell in the grass and cried, and begged God to strike his daddy dead for hurting him.

But God didn't hear him, and Daddy drove away, and Mama sat in the livingroom reading her Bible. Maybe God didn't love him 'cause he'd got too old. Daddy didn't love Mama because she was old. Daddy loved him 'cause he was young and handsome. He was lucky to have a daddy that loved him so much. That's what Daddy said. But it hurts, Daddy. It hurts. Please stop...

He held his arm up to his eyes and felt the tears plop amidst the hair. He had no idea why he'd come back to this house, but that was nothing new: nothing in his life made sense. He didn't trust men and he didn't like women, and his discomfort was so readable it scared people off. At last, beaten by his own inabilities, he'd come back to the house of his birth and betrayal. He didn't know the house had become a daycare center, didn't know his mother still lived there. He simply couldn't go any further: he'd rather dissolve in the pinestraw than face another fruitless journey.

He was shocked when the little girl with the purple rabbit came running over to show it to him. "You look like my Uncle Paul," she said, smiling up at him, and introduced her purple pal as Andre, squeezing it and laying her head on its furry 'shoulder.' "Uncle Paul gave me him," she said, grinning and squeezing. "I love Uncle Paul, an' I love Andre. My name's Jessie. What's yours?"

"Cal," he said, grateful that this tiny person was so comfortable talking to him. In fact, she seemed to like him.

"Okay, Mister Cal," smiled Jessie, granting him the status of a Big Person. Then she walked off to the children seated around Miz Lizzie, singing hymns. She waved and smiled at him when she sat down, and afterwards tried to follow the song.

He wanted to scream, and sucked in a breath behind his arm. He smelled the roses by the fence: funny, he'd forgotten how good they smelled. Maybe it wasn't too late. Maybe God had sent him someone he could connect with, someone who didn't start judging and damning him, someone who liked him—no, more than that. She had sparkly eyes that flashed when she looked at him. No question, she was flirting with him.

He picked some roses for her, put them in a vase and handed them to his mother. His mother wouldn't know it, but Jessie would know the flowers were for her.

ൡary ᴊo

Mary Jo—she wasn't always Granny Blair; she wasn't as old as she looked—had a lump in her throat when Cal handed her the vase. For years she had waited for word from him, waited and prayed, but nothing happened. Then suddenly there he was, and the cloud of bitterness that blackened the air around him seemed to be lifting.

She took the roses as a sign of forgiveness from him, and felt so full she had to leave the room to cry. "Lord," she whispered, "Ya laid a lotta tests on me, an' I never never felt worthy. Butcha brought home my son anyway. Thank ya fer bringin' him home, an' thank ya fer healin' him."

She looked around the room and thought how different it seemed, how happy she felt, that this was going to be a home, instead of rooms full of old furniture and fading photos, and little strangers consoling her with their little loves.

She looked at the roses, small and pink, wondering if he'd pricked himself on the thorns. The tears had started and she had to slam her bedroom door so no one could see the loneliness spilling down her front.

Willy, her little brown dog, popped out from under the bed to comfort her. She kept him in her room while the children were in the house: it kept them from molesting him and him from fighting back. She told Willy everything—leastways everything she could remember, and a lot of it was gone. She didn't know why, she just figgered it was God's gift to save her from those nasty visions. "Count yer blessings, Willy." That's what she'd tell him every day, and Willy'd wag his tail and wait for a biscuit.

But the visions came anyway, bits and pieces of a story linked obscurely in her dreams. Someone was carrying her, folded over like a book, down a long bright corridor. People in white were coming at her from all directions, yelling, and there was a rifle—she could see the barrel over the pants of the person who was running and bouncing her. She saw her mother, her face all bruised, her arms reaching out, and BANG!

Her eyes would fly open, and she'd be lying in bed, her sheets and nightgown drenched in sweat, her body aching all over, even the arm that felt nothing. Frightened by the dark, afraid to turn on the light, she'd stumble to the rocking chair by the window, and Willy would hop up on her lap and lick away the tears.

She had so many bad dreams. So many. They started years ago in the wake of the fever that killed her brothers Jake and Willy. The boys were almost teenagers, Mary Jo almost eight. All were healthy farm kids so when the boys took the fever their father paid no mind because kids was like weather, he said: fevers shot through 'em like twisters, and afterwards they was fine.

Willie Jean and Mary Jo tended on the boys, swabbing them with wet cloths, bringing them broth, and praying fiercely by their sides, but none of it worked. As the sun fell

among the trees Willie Jean begged her husband to go for a
doctor, crying: "Me 'n' God's done all we kin do. They's
burnin' up, Travis."

Travis touched his sons' red faces and she was right. He
hated doctors, who cut folks up 'n' charged 'em for it, even if
they died. It happened to his mother twenty years back, and he
vowed when he had his own fambly that nunna them butchers'd
touch 'em. Besides, doctors didn't care: they went to some
kinda school what taught 'em folks wasn't folks, jest
compleecated monkeys.

The devil was behind it—him't brought the blight, the
hail, the twisters, and every form o' pestilence since the world
began; him't tol' Eve t'deceive Adam. Women 'n' nature,
both slaves t' the devil, an' man'd been fightin' 'em both ever
since he left the garden.

He looked at his wife, distraught from hours of nursing.
Pore thing. Sure she thinks she's doin' right. But the Biblical
warning was clear: women was weak, an' the devil could fool
'em, an' they'd deliver their children into his hands.

"Ah'll be damned!" he screamed, "Afore ah put mah boys
in th' hands've them heathens! Get on yer knees, woman, an'
pray. If'n The Lord sees fit t' take 'em, they's better off with
Him."

Willie Jean watched her sons expire that night within
hours of each other, and as she put her arms around her
daughter she felt that pernicious heat rising from the little
girl's neck.

"No Ya don't," she vowed to herself, "Ya took m'boys.
Y'ain't agonna git mah baby."

She waited till her husband left in the truck to fetch the
preacher. Then she put on her Sunday shoes and dress, soaked
a sheet in water and wrapped it around her daughter. She took
old Jewel out of the barn and rode bareback, holding Mary Jo
in front of her, to the southernmost field by the new highway.
She dismounted, shooed the horse back to the barn, and
stepped out on the asphalt, waving her arm at the first pair of
headlights she saw.

It was a huge truck with two men inside, and it stopped for her. She didn't know either of the men, but they asked what was wrong and she told them her little girl needed a doctor, please please could they take her to one. They put Willie Jean up on the seat beside them and she held her daughter on her lap while the truck raced to the hospital down by the Florida border. Willie Jean began to feel hopeful.

When she got there her troubles had just begun: she couldn't sign any of the forms because she couldn't read and they didn't want to treat the child without her husband's signature. Mary Jo was like hot pudding, and Willie Jean was so desperate she lied: she told them her husband was dead.

"Are you the child's nearest living relative?" asked the lady behind the desk

"Ah am," said Willie Jean, standing as tall as she could.

"Can this man vouch for your identity?" asked the admissions clerk, indicating the worried trucker who hadn't left Willie Jean's side.

"I can," he lied.

"Then make your mark," the lady said to Willie Jean, "and we'll fill out the forms for you."

Willie Jean took the pen and the lady turned it right side up for her. She knew how to write a "W" from the initials she'd seen Travis carve in the tree. She pulled the nib across the paper, and it made a dent but no line. She burst into tears.

The admissions lady took the pen back, held it up and shook it, then tapped it on some fuzzy pink paper and a dark spot appeared. "Here you go," she smiled, passing the pen back to a shaking Willie Jean, who drew four intersecting sticks in the space above the dotted line. She turned her head slightly and squinted: it was exactly the way it looked on the tree. She nodded and passed the paper back to the lady.

Willie Jean told the trucker she could never thank him enough and hugged him hard, looking down. Then she ran to where two women in white were laying Mary Jo on a gurney. Willie Jean walked alongside as they wheeled the child into a room down the hall.

She fretted while the doctor stuck sticks of different sizes down Mary Jo's throat, shone lights in her eyes and ears, poked and tapped and questioned. Finally he asked Mary Jo's mother to wait outside the room a few minutes while they drew some blood and ran some tests.

Willie Jean walked down to the waiting room and collapsed in one of the wide-armed couches under the big clock. Her stomach was hurting, her head ached, and her eyes kept closing. She felt hot, and that scared her: her children had complained of all those symptoms. Lord, she prayed, if'n ah got it, take me, but please please spare mah baby. She had no choice 'bout comin' here. Let 'er live. A moment later her head fell forward and she was sound asleep.

Five hours later she was still asleep, despite the noise around her. The round mirror in the corner of the room showed the glass doors sliding open for her husband, who charged up to the admissions desk, photo in one hand, rifle in the other.

The clerk examined the photo, gulped and turned red. She said something to him, then pulled a file folder out of a stack, and showed him the papers with Willie Jean's mark.

She was about to tell him what was written on the paper when he yelled: "Dagnabit woman, I kin read! Whar's m'wife? An' whar's m'daughter? Y'all ain't gone acuttin' on her, havya? Ah'll blow apart th' first man as touches her."

Uneasily she pointed to the waiting room where Willie Jean was waking up, frightened at the anger in her husband's voice. She saw his image walking away in the corner mirror, but then he came into the room, following his rifle. He yanked her off the couch, yelling: "Woman, what 'as ya done, whar's Mary Jo?"

Willie Jean led him to the room she remembered, but Mary Jo wasn't there. Confused, she shook her head while Travis shook her arm and screamed: "Dagnabit woman, don't lie t'me now!"

The attending physician came into the room and told them their daughter had been moved, that they'd started pumping fluids into her to bring the fever down. Now all they could do was wait.

"Djou cut on her?" Travis growled, and the doctor hastily said no sir.

"We wanna see her," said Travis, and the doctor led them down the hall to a room full of sleeping children with tubes coming out of their arms beside bags on metal poles.

"Doctor, what's wrong wif 'em?" Mary Jo whispered, and the doctor said polio. You're lucky you got your little girl here in time. He then suggested to Travis that they have a look at his wife, too.

Travis wasn't listening, he was looking for his daughter. He spotted her in the fourth bed. Then he asked what seemed to him an obvious question: "If all 'ese here children's sick, and all't kin be done is wait, then why wait here?"

They need the fluid in the bags, said the doctor, and told him not to go into the room, as it was under quarantine. Travis's frown hardened. He knew all about quarantine: every time some farm had that sign posted, the animals behind it—and many times the people—ended up dead.

He looked through the small square glass at his child and thought: Shor 'nuff, they's leavin' her here t' die. Ah'm agonna git her outta here afore it's too late.

"Willie Jean," he whispered, "we's gonna break her outta here, an' yer gonna hep me, hear?"

Willie Jean barely nodded. It was all she could do to stand upright. She followed him into the room as the nurse walked out. He walked to Mary Jo's bed, pulled the Bowie knife off his belt, and cut the tube leading to her arm. Then, as gently as he could, he peeled the tape off the needle and pulled it out. "Thet's it," he said, stripping down the sheet and gathering up his daughter.

The nurse saw him through the window and ran for a doctor. He summoned some orderlies and they converged on the room just as Travis was coming out. His right hand was on the trigger of his rifle, and his daughter was dangling like laundry from his other arm.

"Git outta mah way," he threatened, swinging the gun in a wide arc to include them all, and they stopped. "Git aheada me, Willie Jean. Th' truck's raght out th' door."

Willie Jean stumbled through the sliding doors, saw the truck's flatbed opened toward her, and climbed in. She collapsed on the blanket as Travis placed Mary Jo beside her. Travis shut the back flap then backed into the cab and drove off, pointing the rifle out the window toward the hospital doors. No one came after them, but distraught faces were collecting on the other side of the glass.

"This is terrible," said the doctor as the truck pulled away. "That little girl and her mother'll probably die."

Mary Jo didn't die. After four days of sweaty delirium she began to rally, and by the end of the week the fever was gone. Her face sagged a little on the left side, giving her a crooked smile, and her left arm was without feeling, but other than that she was on the mend.

Willie Jean didn't make it, though. Two days into the burn, like her boys, she died. Travis buried them all in the hill behind the house, bought headstones for them, and surrounded the spot with white rocks. They had no death certificates because that would have meant a doctor telling him what any fool could see, just as there were no birth certificates. The only record of their passage on earth other than those stone slabs was a notation in the family bible and Willie Jean's lone "W" stuffed somewhere in a file in Jacksonville.

Travis watched his daughter struggle to do things with and without her limp arm, and looked at his hands in amazement. Two was the perfect number—anything less made life difficult indeed. He saw her using her toes to compensate and smiled. She ain't much t' look at, he thought, but by damn she's smart. Travis had promised his neighbors that he would pound th' livin' daylights outta any chile as made fun of his daughter.

Soon they were busy at all the church socials, for the neighbor women couldn't wait to marry off this newly widowed man. While he was flattered by the attention, Travis's main concern was Mary Jo. He'd heard that new wives and old children made for bad blood, so he promised himself to hold off marrying till Mary Jo was at least thirteen, and only if the woman really liked her.

Five years later, right on schedule, Travis met an older lady in church who charmed him into visiting and then into bed. Three months later they were married, and Mary Jo was very happy for them. She liked Bettina and Bettina's son, Earl, who was three years older than Mary Jo. And Earl was friends with Orry Blair, the catch of the county.

Orry drove a long red car and came to visit sometimes. He and Earl would drive down the road, buy some shine, then guffaw themselves into a stupor by the garbage dump near the lake.

Mary Jo, like all the girls, had a terrible crush on Orry, and was tongue-tied around him. Orry smiled and teased her about being shy. None of the other boys talked to her at all, barely even looked at her. She reckoned she must be awful homely.

The day Orry asked her to go to the fair with him was the proudest moment of her young life. She came back holding a little pink bear and a purple wicker cane with feathers and bells on the crook. All the girls tried to snuggle up to Orry but he didn't pay them no mind. He held Mary Jo's good hand and kissed her on the cheek, and her heart was pounding so hard she thought it'd leap right out there on the porch and start dancing.

Mary Jo went to bed that night wondering how she got so lucky. He had everything, Orry did—dark good looks, a car, a part-time job at the gas station, and, to top it all off, the perfect gentleman.

Two months later he told her he was going to Jacksonville because there was 'lotsa money in construction there,' and as she burst into tears he put his arms around her and said: "Marry me, Mary Jo? Come with me? Ya won't be sorry."

Mary Jo said yes and her dad said yes and she said it again in front of the preacher. Within the month she and Orry were living in Jacksonville, him working construction and her at a doughnut shop.

She never thought it odd that Orry rarely touched her—on the contrary, she was thrilled. He was nothing like the husband of her foul-mouthed supervisor: why, every day that poor woman was powdering a new bruise or hickey. There was more powder on her than on the doughnuts.

Seven years later Mary Jo got pregnant, and once she had her son it seemed that Orry was never home. He was a Scoutmaster now, getting those bratty city boys on the road to manhood.

"Our son'll be in it soon," he'd smile, and off he'd go to take the boys fishing, or playing baseball, or camping. Mary Jo counted her blessings, happy to have a responsible husband who loved children so.

Orry spent hours with their son, always teaching him something—from the manly art of lacing his shoes to holding a fishing pole, and Cally would toddle after his daddy every chance he got.

Three days after his sixth birthday Cally caught some kind of bad intestinal virus, and after that he wasn't the same child. He had terrible nightmares. He fought his mother when she tried to hold him. Then his father would go in to quiet him, and say things in a soothing voice that Mary Jo couldn't quite hear, and after a half hour or so Cally would quit crying.

Three years later Orry left one morning and mailed them a note that said good bye, that he loved them, and nothing else.

After days of asking his mother why, Cally finally shrieked at her: "If you wasn't so old 'n' ugly he'd nevera gone!"

He ran out the door and Mary Jo, crushed by the possible truth of what he said, sat down at the kitchen table and cried.

Happy Birthday, Rachel

"That's it! I've had it!" yelled Bill Whitsun as the lights went out for the third time that afternoon. He beamed his flashlight through the glimmer of auxiliary lamps and yelled: "Everybody out! I want you all back here EARLY tomorrow, and I want that artwork ready by ELEVEN, is that clear?"

Groans all around.

The parking lot was two blocks away and as the escapees hurried downhill a cloud over the city muttered and boomed, sending white flashes into the green sky below.

Rachel switched on the radio and heard through the crackle that a tornado watch was in effect for Jacksonville. That's nuts, thought Rachel, the air's so wet you could swim in it but we haven't had rain in weeks.

"Oh shit, not again!" The car in front of her skidded to a halt at the top of the bridge and she could finally see what was holding up the line. Two cars had merged their front fenders and the drivers were outside, waving their arms and screaming obscenities. Police cars had pulled up to disperse traffic as it moved in inchworm segments along the expressway. Lights were out and cops were driving on the medians to get to the intersections.

Rachel, her arm out the window, slapped the door in frustration. Damn. At this rate it would be hours before she got home. She looked at the huge stuffed Scottie she bought for Jessie, and patted its plush stumpy face.

Rachel frowned, remembering the afternoon Jessie's bunny was stolen. After lunch Jessie had gone to collect Andre for their nap but the bunny was gone. She knew she'd left him on the bench by the swings. She and Miz Lizzie hunted high and low, looking in all the yards along the street. When it finally dawned on Jessie that whoever took Andre wasn't going to bring him back, not ever never, she exploded in sobs. She didn't stop crying till her mother arrived, and then only long enough to sniffle out the story.

After much hugging Carla tried to put Jessie in the stroller but the little girl shrieked and fought: "No, Mommy! No! We can't leave Andre. He'll be lonely wiffout me, Mommy!"

"I know, Honey. We'll just hafta look for him tomorrow."

Tomorrow came and went without Andre, and Jessie's anguish over his loss surfaced in bouts of possessiveness. She wedged herself between Paul and Carla whenever they were sitting together, saying "my mommy" over a thumb that was spending more and more time in her mouth. She never took her stuffed animals outside anymore, and regularly checked to see that they were all on her bed where she left them.

Rachel hoped the Scottie would distract the little girl. She smiled and shook her head. Sorry, Jess, but I'm the paranoid one in this family. You'll just hafta find your own disorder.

Rachel's car was on its last drop of gas when it pulled up on the lawn beside Paul's truck. People sat on their doorsteps in darkness or roamed behind windows with candles or flashlights.

Rachel left the Scottie in the car—not much point in handing the kid a black dog she couldn't see.

Jessie was on Carla's lap, and Paul and Carla were side by side on the front stoop. "Hey, Rach," said the Paul silhouette, "Glad ya made it. We was gettin' worried."

"Me too," said Rachel.

"Well we knew that," said Carla.

Then Jessie's voice piped up from the middle of Carla's shadow: "AnRachel's got boogies!"

"Uh-oh," said Paul, "here we go again. Can you put a lid on it, Jess? Better yet, can you put a lid on it, Car?"

"Yep," said Carla. "Soon as I can think of a way how."

"What's she saying," asked Rachel, "that I have fleas?"

"Nope, she's referring to your b-r-e-a-s-t-s," said Carla.

"Well, at least it's not fleas," smiled Rachel. "So how'd all this boogies stuff get started anyway?"

"Boogies!" yelled Jessie, and Carla gave her a warning bounce and told her to be quiet, that they'd heard enough about boogies to last a lifetime.

"Don't bet on it," Rachel giggled.

The lights suddenly came back on, flooding the porch from the street as well as the house. They flickered off momentarily, flickered on, flickered off, then in long blocks the neighbourhood came to light.

Later when Jessie was asleep, Paul and Carla sat with Rachel in the kitchen and laughingly recounted the "Boogies" saga.

Paul thought he had the house to himself that afternoon and climbed in the shower without closing the bathroom door. He forgot to activate the burglar alarm and the rushing water blocked the sound of Carla's arrival, so when he pulled the curtain aside and saw Jessie on the toilet he yanked at the curtain and yelled for Carla.

Carla came in and saw Jessie staring open-mouthed at the curtain. She looked up at her mother, pointed at the curtain and squealed: "Uncle Paul's got a thumb in his hoo-hoo. An' lotsa hair. An' it's black!"

Carla asked Jessie if she was finished, that if she was, to

wipe off because they were going to have a little talk. Jessie said okay, hopped off the toilet, and giggled as she passed the shower curtain. She trooped into the livingroom behind Carla, who sat her down on the couch, then planted herself cross-legged on the carpet so that she was eye-to-eye with her daughter.

"Honey," Carla said slowly, trying for a voice that fell somewhere between intent and stern, "You're gonna hafta listen to me real good 'cause this is real important, okay?"

"Okay," Jessie agreed.

"Now, Honey, you mustn't talk to anybody about hoo-hoos or they'll think you're a nasty little girl. Big people don't like to hear that kinda stuff. So if you ever wanna know something about hoo-hoos, or any of those parts people keep covered up all the time you ask me, and only me. Okay?"

"Yeah," said Jessie slowly, wondering what was wrong.

"So," Carla exhaled, hoping she was on the right track, "any questions, Honey?"

"Uh-huh. Do all big people got thumbs?"

"No, Honey, just the men. Lady big people have hair down there. And those thumbs the men have are called something else, but it's a big people word and we'll save it till you're a little bit older, okay?"

"Uh-huh," Jessie sighed. Older again: that place had to be better than Disney World. In Older games like Scrabble and chess made sense, and big people didn't look shocked when you said the same things they did.

Jessie sighed again, raised her arms and looked down at her chest, then at her mother's chest. She looked in her mother's eyes and asked: "Do men get boogies?"

"Well they have them but on men they stay flat."

"Why?"

"Well, boogies have milk for little babies. They don't always have milk inside, only when the babies come."

"Why d'they stick out?"

"Well, they're soft. Makes 'em comfortable for the baby to lean on, like a pillow."

"Well I don't like 'em stickin' out. Do they hafta stick out when you grow up?"

"Well, Honey, not everyone's do, but they will get a little bigger as you get bigger. And who knows? Maybe by then you'll like them."

"Ech, no," said Jessie, curling her lip. Uncle Paul appeared beside her mother, his bottom half covered in a towel. "Uncle Paul, do you like boogies?"

"Uh, well," said Paul, raising his eyebrows, "you know Jess, when I was your age, boogies looked like big ugly bumps to me, but now I think they're just fine. Some ideas you just hafta grow into, I think. Remember how you learned to eat with a spoon?" Jessie nodded. "And I'll bet at the beginning it looked like a whole lotta trouble for nothing, right? But it wasn't—it keeps your hands clean, keeps you from sloppin' up your clothes. Well, boogies are kinda like that: you'll find they're great once you grow some."

Jessie stared at her mother's chest and said, "Mommy, you gots sticky-out boogies."

"I'll say," Paul grinned, "and they're real nice. Yours'll be just as nice, Jess."

Jessie's face puckered and she burst into tears. An ear-splitting "WAAHHH!" wasn't far behind. She sobbed till her nose and mouth were streaming.

Carla sat down and hauled Jessie on her lap, trying to soothe her. Jessie rubbed her face on her mother's chest, then jerked it away and announced between sobs: "I doh want sticky-out boogies!"

"Oh Honey," Carla soothed, "you don't hafta have sticky-out boogies if you don't want them. Why the way medical science is today, you can have boogies any size you want. Okay?"

Jessie sniffled, looked at her mother and spat out: "Promise?"

"Uh-huh," said Carla. "Uncle Paul here's gonna pay for it. Wontcha, Uncle Paul?"

"Yep. Guaranteed. Look, Jess—cross my heart 'n' point

to Heaven. Any size boogies you want. Okay?"

"God," said Paul. "You'd think tits were a death sentence the way she carried on."

The lights flickered again, the refrigerator shooshed and gurgled, and Paul said, "Welcome to summer, folks. This is the day, isn't it?"

"Yep," said Rachel, "June twenty-first." The lights expired at the end of her sentence.

"I think that's our cue to pack it in," said Paul. He found the flashlight and led the ladies down the hall. He said good night to Rachel and shut the door to his and Carla's room, then nuzzled Carla's neck and suggested some horizontal aerobics.

Rachel heard them laughing as she undressed, trying not to listen to the squeak of bed springs. A wave of nausea rolled up her throat and she ran for the bathroom. She grabbed the toilet seat as pieces of stew shot through her nose and mouth. "Damn you, Kenny!" she whimpered, "Damn you to hell!"

She climbed in the shower, her legs shaking, then shivered as the water beat the vomit off her skin. Then the lights flashed on, making reddish arcs of her eyelids. She heard the refrigerator crank to life. She left the shower and lay down on her bed, with the wet towel on top of her. Hot air spiralled down from the fan but the wet towel and her wet hair cooled her.

Sleep found her as Carla and Paul walked into the bathroom, whispering. They soaked two towels, wrung them out, and went back to the bedroom to swab each other down.

Paul expressed his worry about leaving "you three girls" alone. After all, he'd be gone for most of July and August, and maybe the maniac that hurt Rachel was still somewhere close by.

Carla said that between the burglar alarm and Rachel's firearm nothing could get to them—except maybe a hurricane. "And," she giggled, "as paranoid as Rachel is, she'll have the whole beach evacuated before the first wave hits."

"Laugh if you want, I like her attitude," said Paul. "And I feel a lot safer about you because of her."

Carla sat up, frowning. "Well gee, Paul, thanks for the vote of confidence. I mean what am I, Helpless Helen? And what's she, the resident pit bull?"

"Hey whoa, I didn't mean—oh hell, Carla, let's be straight: you're a lovely girl, and part of that's Rachel's doing. Listen, I know what we're doing here. She's just her making her last-ditch equipment check before she boots us out the door, making sure the chute'll open when you jump. And I love her for it. Hey, y'know, I just might end up the only man in the world who wants his in-laws to come for Christmas."

Carla was furious. "I can't believe you're talking like I'm helpless. You and Rachel both. I'm not, dammit."

"Honey, I know you're not. I'm sorry I made it sound that way. Listen, I always figured every woman's Scarlett O'Hara under the greasepaint. It's just a matter of situation: grease-paint in peacetime, axle grease in war. I know you can do whatever you have to, I just like that genteel side—like you like mine, y'know. So please, let's don't fight over what I like aboutcha, okay?"

Carla grinned. "You mean there's something you don't like?"

"Yeah, " he smiled, whapping her thighs with the towel. "All this yacking when we could be—"

"Sleeping, right?"

"Shit, no. I got lotsa time to sleep in Orlando. C'mere, Babe." His eyes widened and he leaned over her so that his cock was within striking distance of her mouth. "C'mon, Car," he whispered, rolling his fingers over her nipples, then walking them slowly up behind her head, drawing her face toward him. "Show me," he urged. "Lemme feel it every way I'm gonna miss you…"

The next morning was Rachel's birthday and she awoke while it was still dark to the hammer of fists on her door.

"AnRachel, geddup!" yelled Jessie. "You gotta open your presents before Uncle Paul goes to Disney World—"

"That's Orlando, Honey, not Disney World," said Carla, and Jessie, not understanding, said yeah, there.

Rachel yelled back: "I'll be up in a moment. Meetcha all in the kitchen," then threw her towel-cum-blanket over her face and whined. Slowly she pulled the towel down her body and saw the luminous haze on the clock harden into numbers. She groaned, pulled her robe around her shoulders and headed for the bathroom. Her mouth was dry and sour from last night. She rinsed it out and gargled with toothpaste—it wasn't mouthwash but it tasted better.

She had pulled her hair over the scar and began pinning it down so there would be no big pink worm for Jessie to gawk at. She heard Jessie's voice at the door telling her to hurry, and her hands were shaking as she yelled: "Hang on, Punkin. Us old ladies look like Frankenstein in the morning. You don't wanna see that, do you?"

"Yeah!" yelled Jessie. "Kin I c'min?"

"No, Honey. You just hang on one minute more and I'll be there, okay?"

"Okay," said Jessie, then raced to the kitchen yelling, "AnRachel looks like Frankastein!"

"Honey, that's a terrible thing to say," said Carla. "Besides, it isn't true. Your aunt's really pretty."

"It is so true!" yelled Jessie. "She told me!"

"Well, she was just kidding," said Paul. "All the ladies in this house are knockouts."

Well, two of them are, thought Rachel, feeling shabby and dented. She stood between the two mirrors for a back-to-front check. Good. Rachel had a story in case Jessie girl burst in on her in an uncovered moment. That story kept the truth from spilling out and washing away Carla and Jessie's love.

She walked into the kitchen and Paul put the paper crown on her head and pulled out her chair. Carla set a candle-studded waffle in the middle of the table and Jessie said: "She's seven?"

"No, Honey," said Carla, "You just can't fit anymore candles on there."

"Lucky thing," giggled Rachel.

"Jessie, you go and bring Aunt Rachel her presents now,"

said Carla, and Jessie ran off to the livingroom, returning with three packages.

One was crumpled and hot-doggish, and contained one of Rachel's chopsticks. "It's fum me, AnRachel," said Jessie excitedly, and Rachel hugged and kissed her and told her how beautiful it was, that no one could have given her a better gift.

The card on the next package held a gift subscription to *The Warrior*, Rachel's favorite environmental publication. And the package contained a book on Egyptian mythology, with a gold crook inserted by the picture of Sehkmet.

Rachel hugged Carla, then tore the paper off a small blue velvet box. Inside on a silk platform was a gold cartouche with hieroglyphics. "It says your name, Rach, and the ankh wishes you a long and happy life—not that I need to tell you that," said Paul.

He raised the Polaroid and the flash went off, catching Rachel between a smile and a tear, with her mouth half open. He set the picture face down on the coffee table and walked to the door, swinging it wide on the summer heat. He took two more shots of the family and one of Jessie with Mugs, the big plush Scottie.

"You gonna be back for my birthday?" Jessie demanded, as the four of them walked to the car.

"Sure am," said Paul, picking her up and giving her a light squeeze. "Yours, too," he said to Carla, wrapping his free arm around her and kissing her several times. He saw Rachel standing in front of him and laughed. "Rachel, Honey, you're too late. I'm outta arms." Then he leaned over to kiss her forehead.

"Thank you, Paul," she said, opening her palm to show the cartouche. "I never expected—"

"Hey, if I could've afforded it, it would've been a ticket to Egypt to meet your friend the moon-lion up close and personal. Maybe next year, huh?" He smiled, and Rachel, not knowing what to do, piled on the three of them and kissed Paul on the cheek.

She walked indoors, waiting for the nausea to start, but it

didn't. She thanked God she was in the livingroom and not the bathroom.

She heard the truck starting up and Jessie came through the door, followed by Carla. Carla sat down beside Rachel as Jessie tromped away with Mugs, and whispered: "We hafta talk tonight. About your friend the moon lion."

"Really?" said Rachel, astounded. "Why the about-face?"

"Well, it's your birthday, and I think you should do what you want on your birthday. Another thing, I read that section in the mythology book, and it's given me some questions of my own. Since you're the only Sehkmet expert I know, uh." She smiled and shrugged.

"Then, too, a certain mademoiselle will be asking any day now who the lady is on her aunt's wall who wears a nightie, a big lion mask, has long gray feet and sticky-out boogies. So, how're we gonna handle that one?"

"Why not talk about it tonight?" Rachel raised her brows mischieviously. "Over scrabble?"

Carla grimaced. "Boy, you really know how to hurt a guy." Then she grumped, "Well, okay, since it's your birthday." She raised her hand. "Butcha gotta promise me no ibex. You clobbered me with that the last time…"

Apocalypse has Seven Letters

Carla could have saved her breath. The game commenced with Rachel lifting all seven tiles off her trough and laying out the word XANTHAN. It was a fluke, said Rachel, unable to stop grinning as she tacked on the extra fifty points for using all seven letters.

"Right," said Carla. Unless BAIYEEEE or BAIYEEEX was a word she was ninety-two points behind. Wait a minute, now, I can make IBEX, and that'll give me ... nothing, thirteen lousy little points with that X on the center square. Jesus, that Rachel. By fluke or genius she'd formed an adjective so Carla couldn't add S and get a triple word score. Jesus, that Rachel. I could have looked at those letters all night and come up with AX. Or TAX. Or THANX. Well, shit.

"You want some time to think about it?" Rachel offered.

"You bet I do," Carla growled. As she studied the board and shuffled her letters she said: "Go ahead, Rachel. Talk about your buddy Sehkmet. You've got all of," she glanced up at the kitchen clock, "two hours before your birthday's over."

"She's not my buddy," Rachel said, her eyebrows high in disbelief as one by one the highest scoring letters on the board, Q, J, and Z, turned up in her palm. "Sehkmet is no one's buddy!" she snapped, angered at the heckling, no matter how gentle.

"Look, Carla," she began, "I'm no expert on this, all right? All I can give you is based on two, uh, visitations—one when I was very drunk, and the other when I was nearly comatose on Demerol. But you know what's funny about it? My memories of those times are crystal clear. Now you'd think if I was that drugged the impressions would be foggy, but no: I can call up those visions and feelings whenever I want, just by saying her name. But," she sighed, "what it all means, that's something else.

"For one thing, I think this prophecy stuff is way off base. Seems to me it's too convenient—like all those millennial forecasts of planetary upheaval, the return of Christ, and so on. The numbers bother me, too. Why would a loving god want two billion and some people dead? How can there be that much evil in the world? More to the point, how could he have allowed so much evil to flourish? I mean, if you believe in Him, you hafta believe He controls everything, so why?

"Then there's that stuff about the moon, which I think was just coincidence, or how could Sehkmet turn up in a locked room with only artificial lighting? As for the wine—well, maybe Sehkmet's outgrown that. No, don't look at me like that. You see, I don't think she's just some empty vessel for God's wrath.

"I think there are degrees of choice open to her, just as there are to us. I mean we've chosen our destiny: we've fucked up the world and built the bombs and killed or poisoned everything we couldn't understand. Obviously we've blown it as rulers of this planet. Time for God to send his hatchet-man—or woman or lion, whatever—to seriously kick some ass.

"Maybe something's supposed to trigger it off, the hole in the ozone maybe. Maybe it'll grow to a certain size and BANG! He'll send her down. I mean, hey, let's face it, it's His moment to pick, not ours. We made piss-poor choices, and they're comin' back to haunt us now. Something else I've been thinking about…" She hesitated.

"Go on," said Carla, frowning at her letters, "I mean if I can get up the guts to play scrabble with you, surely you can do a little thing like figure out God's plan for the world. By the way, you always refer to God as 'Him.' You believe God's a he?"

Rachel rolled her eyes and said: "Really, Carla. It's obvious God isn't a he or a she—God is everything. As for why I call God 'Him,'" she shrugged, "that's the name I grew up with and I'm comfortable with it. Surely God won't mind us assigning him a sex—he," she made quote marks with her fingers, "knows how limited we are.

"Oh, and what'll happen when God puts the kibosh on this earthly run of evil in his maybe otherwise perfect universe? You think he might have this problem in other places, too?" She laughed and shook her head. "Damn, it's hell bein' the boss." She put her hand over her mouth, then tapped her bottom lip with her finger.

"And if he sends Sehkmet, how will she come? As a vision, like that night in Montreal? As a lion? What if she needs to absorb a human body to understand degrees of evil, like Christ became Jesus in order to feel and pity human pain. What if that's the only way the evil can leave the earth? Whoa!

"And what happens after the evil people are dead? How will we fix this mess they've left? Will other angels come to help with the cleanup or will that be the time for Christ to return—not to remove souls but to save the race and the planet too? Or does Sehkmet have other gifts to give us? She was supposed to protect us, you know. Will that be when her protective side is allowed to surface? Or is she just a killing machine?"

Rachel blew out a long breath. "There is one more thing. You know our amulet? Well, I touched it the other day and I swear it's getting warm."

"Big deal," Carla waved her off, "so's the whole city."

"Not like this, Car. It's in an air-conditioned room, stable temperature, and Mom's cross is right beside it. I left them touching for a few days to see if the metal would pick up the heat, but no. It's totally self-contained, this heat. Something's happening, Carla," Rachel sighed, "I dunno what, but it scares me. And it scares me because—"

"Why should you be scared?" Carla frowned. "It's not as if you've done something to fear her, have you?" She wiggled her eyebrows at Rachel. "C'mon, now, fess up, what're you doing? Dumping toxic wastes out your office window?"

"Carla, goddamit, this is serious. You go and look in that safe deposit box and see if I'm not right. Because if I am, then we've been chosen as part of this retribution scheme, and I'm not sure I'm up to the job."

"God, Rach, Sehkmet choosing us." Carla grinned. "I should think you'd be thrilled."

"Dammit, Carla, this isn't funny. You think Moses was happy to find the burning bush? You don't think his life got a little disrupted after that? Well," she shrugged, looking up at the ceiling—no doubt wondering if God's ear was pressed to the roof, "that's why I'm scared. I mean, you hear these predictions of apocalypse all the time now that the year two thousand's just a few years off. I just didn't want it to start so soon. I wanted to have a few more years."

Carla tried to lighten things up. "Rach, listen, I'm sure Noah felt the same way. Besides," she snickered, "I'm sure if Moses had known he was gonna be Charleton Heston he'd have bailed out at the first opportunity."

"Gee, thanks, Carla," Rachel snapped. "Happy birthday to me. Anyway, since we're on my last few minutes, let me ask a final favor. Go check out the amulet sometime this week so you can be right, and I can stop thinking 'plague' every time they say drought or I see a washed-up dolphin on the tube.

Sehkmet was in charge of plagues, you know. And droughts and earthquakes."

Carla stood up to stretch. She felt bad about hurting Rachel, but she was tired of Rachel's thin skin. Besides, Rachel was creaming her at Scrabble, how much more did she want? Carla opened her mouth to yawn and as she closed her eyes an image appeared through her lids, like the ghost image on a photo, but with colors, and she screamed.

"Carla, what's wrong?" Rachel's voice came from far away, from somewhere outside the image, and Carla quickly opened her eyes. She was shocked to see Rachel a few inches away, and blurted out that she was fine, she was all right, it was nothing.

"Nothing?" Rachel echoed. "Is this the same nothing you had before? You're white as a sheet. Sure you don't want to go to the clinic?"

"No, no, I'm fine," Carla whispered. "Just let me get some water."

"I'll get the water. You sit," Rachel commanded. "And if it happens again, you're going to the doctor."

"Yeah, sure," said Carla. She collapsed in the chair and stared into space, listening to the wrib-wrib-wrib of the kitchen fan and the sound of rushing water.

The vision looked as real as Rachel standing by the sink. How could she tell Rachel about the bloody hands holding dripping scalps? It had to be Rachel's rapist. Would she have another vision, this time with a face? Oh God.

Carla lay awake that night, waiting for the vision.

Jessie crawled in beside her when the thunder started.

But no rain came.

Christ, it's hot, thought Carla, licking sweat off her lips, waiting. She rolled away from Jessie's hot body, waiting. Sleep found her, but no face. It was there, though, Carla was sure. Out there, somewhere, waiting.

Problems, Problems

Rachel came home late on June 25th. She had asked Adam Karoly to come to her office because she had something to tell him, and Karoly jumped on it. Since he'd set up the task force to catch the Seaboard Slasher he had gory scenes but no witnesses, and the Williams woman was the Slasher's only living victim. Rachel met him at the office door and he smiled at her, wondering again how she had escaped the fate of the other nine.

"So Ms. Williams ," he began, "what made you change your mind? Two years is a long time to hang on to a lie."

Rachel flushed. Her position had always been that unless the police could guarantee the monster would go straight to the electric chair she wouldn't help them. What would happen to her and her family if he escaped? Ted Bundy escaped, more than once. Was he so smart or were they just stuped? Either way she wasn't prepared to chance it.

"So, Ms. Williams," said Rachel, "but the risks have changed slightly. My sister and niece will be moving to Orlando soon, and the chances of meeting him in a town with no seacoast are nil. You see, he's a surfer." She paused. "Just think of him as a land shark."

"I do," said Karoly, pointing to the envelope she was holding. "Is that for me?"

"Yes," said Rachel, sticking her nose behind the flap. "Let me explain what I've done. There are two head shots. One full face, one profile. They were taken two years ago but this guy's not going to change his looks, they're his stock in trade. I had an artist trace the photos so they'll show up better in *The Public Servant*. Now you've got a face for the question mark. Oh, and I'll bet he's also that Pretty Boy Floyd. All I ask, to protect my family, is that you run the picture under the Floyd name. That'll protect any woman who sees it." She turned to the desk and dumped out the envelope. Two color eight-by-tens slid out, followed by sketches.

"Damn!" said Karoly, staring at the face of the killer and realizing why they could never find any witnesses. The answer was in the face: such beauty was above such acts. No one would ever connect him.

The question Karoly had now he didn't dare ask. All the murdered girls were blonde, in their early twenties, real beauties. This woman was good looking, but not the smasher kind, and she was older. Perhaps this guy had been a model for the agency. She wouldn't venture a name and Karoly didn't press her. It was probably an alias anyway. Right now he was just grateful for the photos. He scooped them in the envelope and thanked her. Then he said, "No, really, I mean it. I know this was tough for you."

"Yes," she agreed. "I'm still scared." She asked him to walk her to her car and he was glad to accompany her.

He got in his car, thinking: Good, there just might be enough time to get that face in the next run of *The Public Servant*.

The Public Servant was an insert that first appeared on June 13th in the popular Sunday edition of the paper. It was twenty pages of photos, composite sketches and fact sheets on criminals and missing persons. "Necessary and long overdue," said its originator, retired police captain William Downey, who had hounded it into nationwide syndication. "What people need is something to read that's eye-level, portable, and keepable. If everybody's armed with photos and fact sheets to examine at leisure, someone might remember something that would save a life—maybe their own." Downey's ambition was to turn the whole country into a neighborhood watch network.

As of June 21st *The Public Servant* had eight pages of criminals, and on page six was a blank face with a mark across it titled "The Seaboard Slasher." On the opposite page was a sketch of the thieving gigolo called "Pretty Boy Floyd." For a long time Karoly had suspected that Floyd was The Slasher because the dates and locations of the attacks were too close to be coincidence, unless the two were a tag team fleecing and mutilating unsuspecting women. But there was a profound difference: The Slasher left blood smeared walls and busted furniture, whereas Floyd left nothing. Everything he touched he either kept or wiped clean.

Now Karoly had the photo that confirmed his suspicions. Before he had only the composite sketch of "Floyd" gleaned from starstruck women who initially called in to report the poor dear missing. Alas poor Jeff, Bob, Bruce, Kyle, Bill, or Eric, he was just so hurt by that bitch of a wife who'd left him penniless and run off with their kid, who was a diabetic, or in need of a liver transplant—or whatever else they'd buy. And buy they did: dinner, clothes, jewlwry, trips to the Bahamas, anything to restore his faith in women. Did they mention he was handsome? Ah, yes, unusually so: blue-eyed, tall, blond, and tanned to perfection—but not hung on himself, y'know? And so attentive. Every woman's dream, really.

The women were called and verified the photo of their darling man.

Then on July 27th *The Public Servant* ran Rachel's drawing in place of the Floyd drawing, opposite The Slasher's question mark face. maybe the heads would be linked by proximity. As Karoly tacked the photos and sketches beside the victims' faces he thought: *This is it. We're gonna nail you now, you bastard.*

Given his usual pattern Floyd should now be plying his trade somewhere around Savannah. If they didn't catch him in the next four weeks he'd be on his way to Florida—unless, God forbid, he headed west. Karoly faxed the photos, drawings, and rap sheet to every coastal precinct on the continent.

When Rachel entered the house that night she found Carla beerily tearily "burning Kenny at the stake," and offered to join in.

Carla said she'd like to kill him, and if he wasn't Jessie's father she'd love to try. "At the very least slap his face till it falls off," she laughed, then looked at the match pile and said softly, "You think any of that shit's genetic? I mean, I look at her and she seems so normal, but what if that stuff kicks in at some age or something?"

Rachel put her arms around her sister and said, "Look, what your almost-ex did isn't so strange. Men have been running out on women for centuries, ever since they evolved into travelling salesmen. I don't think you need to worry about Jessie till you see her stuffing Mugs in a briefcase and she tells you she's dropping out of kindergarten to study with Dale Carnegie—*then* you got a problem."

Carla laughed through her sniffles and Rachel laughed too, wondering again how to broach the subject of Kenny the rapist. Hopefully when Carla saw the drawing in *The Public Servant* it would start the ball rolling. It had to be a better segue than: "Oh, by the way..."

"Look," said Rachel, "I think it's fairly safe to assume there isn't any irresponsible gene, or a lying gene, or a robbing gene. That's all learned behaviour, and look who she's got for her prime role model. So I wouldn't worry, Sis. Okay?"

"Yeah," sniffed Carla, honking into a pile of napkins. "Doesn't leave me much room to screw up, does it?" She laughed, then wiped under her eyes and said, "Jeez, why did God ever invent sinuses?"

They went to the bank on Saturday to let Carla study the amulet while Rachel sat in the lobby with Jessie, scanning the paper. She was going to give Jessie the comics when Jessie got off the couch, put her hand on her crotch, and informed her aunt and everyone else that *her tinkle hurt.*

"Okay, honey," Sighed Rachel, "We'll getcha to the toidy."

Maybe the kid had gas, the way she was bent over. Maybe it was all for attention: Jessie was always asking to be lifted up at water fountains, then five minutes later saying she had to go. Rachel was weary of the routine. Why didn't the geniuses who designed child-high fountains make them six inches shorter?

Rachel stood by the stall listening to Jessie grunt: It was going to be a long siege.

She unfolded the paper and turned to the metro section for an update on Mayor Trask's now public fued with "those greedy yuppie guppie unprintables." He's singled out two developers as "unscrupulous," building malls and condos that stood empty while police and firemen couldn't get money to increase their numbers or upgrade their facilities. "Course, now," said Trask, "these people're slick. You talk to 'em and they're all buildin' for the future. Well there's people here that needs pertection now."

The backlash wasn't long in coming. Trask was fairly foaming ar the mouth when he heard one of the developers had called him "a ripple-haired good ole boy with the brains and profile of a diosaur."

He fired back that he was "proud to be part of any group that didn't have pee in its name," but right now he was, as he loved to say, up to his suspenders in alligators. The July 4th weekend was here and the city was a tinder box.

Messages like "have a safe and happy fourth" would never

reach the kids. Televised images of burning plastic dummies
didn't help: they enjoyed them. Hell, it was summer, and they
were out for fun, and fun had nothing to do with dull old
chickenshit advice, fun was rappin', jammin', dealin', four-
wheelin'—and stockpiling Roman candles.

Oh lordy, thought Mayor Trask, *What'm I gonna do?
Somebody's gonna git hurt, I kin see it comin'. Same ol' same
ol'—everybody's yellin' pertect me, nobody's willin' to pay
for it.* His opponents would decry his tax and spend mentality,
and the same fools that wouldn't fix their car brakes would be
on overpasses waving signs that said "Keep America Free: No
More Taxes."

Trak scrutinized the readings and projections about falling
aquifer levels: already in some places wells were dry and
toilets had to be flushed by bucket. Even in the lusher areas
lawn watering was down to every fourth night. With minimal
numbers of firemen, a really big blaze in a low pressure area
might become uncontainable. *Oh lordy.*

At seven-thirty on the night of June 28th Mayor Trask was
down to the last bullet in his public service arsenal. There
wasn't enough money, and there wasn't enough time, not
through any conventional channels—but that didn't mean
there wasn't a way. Mayor Trask unlocked his private file of
big name sources, pulled out the rap sheet on Marcus Strange,
and dialed the number.

Marcus Strange (alias The Jax Master, The Voice of
Choice, First with the Worst, If Ya Wanna Know the Scam
then Listen to the Man) was Jax radio's superstar, the biggest
thing to hit the airwaves since The Greaseman left town. Mark
swept away the watered-down shock jocks with his "Circus of
Designated Dipsticks" and an endless tirade of reggae-rap
put-downs. From the sands of Neptune Beach to the Westside
naval base, on the ramshackle porches of Beaver Street and at
poolside parties in San Jose, People of all ages were calling in
and listening to The Jax Master, even the mayor.

One morning Trask heard one of the Jax Master personas,
High Mark, the coked-out executive, snearing, "Puh-leeeze,

cocaine is a blessing. I mean I, personally, find nosehairs so unattractive." Other regulars included Higher Mark the greedy evangelist, Highest Mark the perpetual student, Easy Mark the ever giving and forgiving, Mark-Up the designer label worshipper, and Mark-Down the shoplifter. No question, this was the man Trask needed to get his message to the streets. Now, would he do it?

"No problem-o, Yer Honor," said Mark, tapping out a poem on the processor while His Honor talked. "Rest easy, Emmet," Mark assured him, "We got it under control." Mark rubbed his hands together: he loved to blast developers, hated any plan or person injurious to life or limb, especially tree limbs.

So on June 29th, right after Mark's admonishment to read *The Public Servant*—"Scope out those rude dudes and family fueds"—radios across the city boomed out the mayor's message in a reggae-rap ballad of surprising intelligibility over the syncopated whine of fingered disks came the words:

They's cuttin' down the trees so we can't ger any breeze
An' the buildins they's buildin' fall down if ya sneeze
An' those people 'at make fireworks is greedy jerks
They know they don' work, an' still they sell 'em
They be no way t'tell, ya can't see or smell 'em,
But they's bad, dad, an' me mad
Cause you light 'em today an' they blow you away
So don't let 'em scam ya, don't light their fire,
Don't lose yer handles on them Roman Candles
That ain't no Fourtha July...

Carla heard it standing in the safe deposit room that saturday. She rolled her eyes.

Jessie had been singing the line "Bad, dad, an' it makes me mad" which sounded like her *favortist* singer, Michael Jackson. Michael was the great mystery of Jessie's life: how could he turn so quick without falling over his feet? How could he slide backwards and walk forwards at the same time? Carla grinned, thinking of the morning Jessie handed her a quarter to help Michael Jackson get his air conditioner fixed: "His face is allus wet, Mommy. He must be awful hot."

Carla was hot, too. Sweat was on her forehead in spite of the air conditioning—but part of it, she reasoned, was nerves: the moment of truth was approaching. Either there was a hot amulet next to a cool cross or Rachel's obsession was now tactile as well. She didn't want to think Rachel was delusional, that would be like finding out there was no gravity. She opened the metal box, touching its sides and running her fingers over all the envelopes, papers, and jewelry. No heat there.

She snapped open the case with the cross and the amulet. The cross glinted in the shadowed light, warm to the touch, but warm, not hot. There was a dark ring under the amulet, as though the lining was stained. The amulet lay face up, brighter. Tiny beads of water had formed around its miniscule mouth. Carla placed her fingertips on the tiny gold head and there was a sizzling sound as they connected.

"Yowtch!" She cried, jumping back and banging into the wall of boxes behind her.

A concerned face appeared at the rails. "Are you all right?" it asked.

"Sure, fine," said Carla. "Sorry to scare you, I just got my fingers caught when the lid fell down."

The face smiled and went away.

Carla dug her hand in the box and reached for the amulet, which had rolled to the edge of the case. It was hot—not white charcoal, but close. She jammed her sore fingers in her mouth and snapped the case shut with her other hand. She closed the box and then the wall door, thinking: *Jeez, Rachel's gotta come see this.*

She walked back into the bank lobby and saw Rachel coming out of the elevator with Jessie in her arms. Jessie's pants and the front of Rachel's dress were bright red. Carla ran to hold her child as Rachel ran to the car.

They arrived at the emergency room with Jessie crying:

"No, I doh wanna gedda needle!"

"Honey, maybe you won't hafto," said Carla hopefully.

As it turned out Jessie didn't need a shot, only pills and watered-down cranberry juice. It was a bladder infection, painful but not life threatening. She was in bed for two days beside her own private potty chair, and everything she asked for she got: coloring books, paints, paper, TV, macaroni. Wow. By the second afternoon she was out of bed, determined to prolong her gimme game by ending every request with the sad faced announcement: "I have *uhfecshin*."

The following evening Rachel came home to find Carla and Jessie in the livingroom in front of the TV. Carla was watching the news, Jessie was coloring.

The crayons had rolled across the carpet as far away from Jessie as possible. Their lives, short and brutal, were now mishappen as well, melted by hundred-degree heat into a taffy-pull strings and shiny lumps. Jessie loved the slick feel of the waxy globs, loved the way the color poured out behind them as she ground them into the paper. The harder she pressed, the shinier the color, and she'd tilt the paper up, down and sideways after every line or swirl to watch it glisten. When her mother suggested she try staying inside the lines Jessie studied the cramped white spaces and asked what for? She could still see the picture, she knew what it was, why bother? This way she got the picture and the shine, see?

Rachel asked if Jessie would show her the picture, and Jessie proudly passed her the coloring book. Rachel's eyes widened on a set of thick pink and purple lines between the super hero's legs. She knelt down beside Jessie, pointed to the pink and purple lines and asked if they were mountains. Jessie put her hands over her mouth, shook her head, and giggled. "So what is it?" Rachel prodded.

Jessie motioned for Rachel to come closer, amd when she did Jessie hopped up and whispered in her ear: "Issa thumb, AnRachel!" Then she exploded in giggles behind her hands.

Rachel shook her head. "Honey," she said, "You can't draw thumbs on super heros. For one thing, they wear special super hero underwear so's you can't see their thumbs, and for another thing, there are no thumbs in coloring books. I mean, everybody knows they're there, they just don't show them, so you don't have to draw them, okay?"

"Okay," said Jessie. She looked over at her mother and asked what's for dinner.

"How's macaroni sound?" Carla offered.

"Yeay!" yelled Jessie, racing to the bathroom to wash her hands.

Just then the phone rang and Carla picked it up in the kitchen. It was Paul, he was on his way. *Get ready, Babe, I been missin' ya somethin' fierce. So oh, put The Twink on the line, and lemme tell her what Uncle Paul's bringin' her.* Jessie didn't want to talk to him. "Still mad at me for leavin', huh?" said Paul. "Guess I should be flattered."

"Well," said Carla, "she's had a tough couple of days here," and told him about the bladder infection. Paul hung up, and arrived an hour ahead of the fireworks.

Jessie didn't run to meet him, though. She said she was tired and asked to sleep in her mother's room

"Not tonight, Honey," said Carla.

"Why not?" Jessie wanted to know.

"'Cause Uncle Paul's gonna be in there, and there's no room for all of us."

"He kin have my room," Jessie proposed.

"Honey," said Carla, "he can't fit in your little bed. And he's too long for the couch. He's just gonna hafta stay with me."

"NO!" screamed Jessie, clapping her hands over her ears. "NO! NO! NO!" And she ran into her room, sobbing and shrieking.

"What the hell's going on here?" asked Paul, puzzled and hurt.

Carla shrugged and spread her hands. "Look, just give me some time alone with her. If things aren't any clearer in an hour, you and Rachel head down to the boardwalk for the fireworks." She found her daughter curled up against the pillow, sobbing hysterically.

"Honey, listen," Carla said, "Uncle Paul's really sorry he hasn't been here, but he can't help it. Listen, we're all gonna be living together real soon—"

"NO!" shrieked Jessie, banging her head on the pillow and kicking her legs "NO! NO! NO! Tell him to GO AWAY! I DON'T WANT HIM HERE!"

Carla was bowled over: "Honey?" she pleaded, "What's the matter? What is it, Jessie? Talk to Mommy." Jessie just kept screaming. Carla finally said: "Honey, you've gotta stop this. Uncle Paul's awful hurt listening to you out there. He loves you, Jessie. C'mon out and see the big giraffe he brought you."

The words were wasted: Jessie screamed until she choked. Carla scooped her up and slapped her back until she started to cough. The coughing ended in a spasm of drool on her mother's shoulder, then Jessie stuck her thumb in her wet face and placed her cheek against her mother's. She extracted the thumb long enough to whimper: "Can I sleep wif you, Mommy?"

"Honey, you can sleep with me tonight, but Uncle Paul's gonna be there too. And you're just gonna hafta accept it, Punkin. And tomorrow you sleep in your own bed. Now, honey," she soothed, pulling the little T-shirt over Jessie's head, "you try to get some sleep, and Uncle Paul and I'll be in here real soon, okay?"

Jessie sniffed over her thumb: no agreement, just a stand-off.

When Paul and Carla got into bed later Paul reached across Jessie to hug Carla, and Jessie's little hand crept up his arm and pushed it down. He saw her glaring at him over her thumb, tried to kiss her cheek, but she buried it in Carla's nightie. Paul sighed and turned his back on her, thinking: *All right, you little shit.*

The next day was more of the same. Jessie cast covetous glances at the giraffe in the cellophane bag but wouldn't approach it. She wouldn't talk to Paul except to periodically shriek "GO AWAY!" Otherwise she hid behind her thumb and followed her mother and Paul around, frowning fiercely whenever they touched, screaming if they hugged or kissed.

"This is ridiculous," said Paul.

"I agree," said Carla.

Rachel said perhaps she could get to the bottom of it if she had some time alone with Jessie, but Jessie refused to be out of her mother's sight.

When Paul left on the seventh of July, Rachel asked Jessie if Uncle Paul had done something to her. Had he touched her anywhere she didn't want? No, said Jessie with a frown, and it came out too fast and clear to be a lie. Whew, thought Rachel. Well then, what can it be?

It was well over a month before Paul came back, and during that time Jessie came down with another bladder infection. Carla wanted a complete series of tests done on Jessie to be sure there weren't any cysts or tumors. The doctor made an alternate proposal. He said if it didn't clear up on the current medication or it happened a third time, then they'd start looking for cysts or tumors or pinched nerves or allergies. in the meantime don't get distressed, the child seemed very healthy otherwise. However, she did seem to be going through a shy phase, and that too would probably pass, just one of the million ways kids find to get attention.

Carla felt better after that conversation but wasn't wholly convinced. Jessie spent too much time with her thumb in her mouth, too much time on Carla's lap. Was she afraid of something or was it really just a phase, one that was taking a little too long for Carla's liking? There were so many characters inside that little head, why get stuck on this one?

Whe Paul came back on August the tenth Jessie flew into a rage and ran between him and her mother, punching his thighs, screaming at him to go away. This was too much for Carla, who smacked Jessie's fanny and ordered her into her room. Jessie stood her ground, screaming at her mother to tell him to go away.

Carla picked up Jessie and carried her, shrieking and flailing, into the child's room, dumped her on the bed and slammed the door. She yelled that Jessie could stay there until she was ready to apologize.

Jessie would not. She sat behind her thumb and said nothing. Rachel brought her dinner in on a tray, accompanied her to the toidy and tried to draw her out, but Jessie remained mute and mad. She asked from behind the door if she could watch TV, and her mother said only if she was ready to apologize, which brought on another round of howling.

"I am through indulging her," said Carla grimly. She passed a box of cotton batton around the table to Rachel and Paul, and all three stuck some in their ears.

"Ah," said Paul, "much better."

"Listen," said Rachel to Paul, "you're leaving the morning of the twelfth, right? Well, if Jessie hasn't canned this stupid shriekfest by then I'll take her to the zoo and try to talk to her there. How's that sound?

"What?" grinned Paul, cupping his cotton batten ears.

Jessie's strike or tantrum or whatever it was continued unabated through Friday. On Saturday morning Paul had to leave, and part of him was glad to go. He said to Rachel on the way out the door, "It's all up to you, now."

"Gee thanks, Coach," said Rachel.

She told Jessie it was time for breakfast and Jessie shook her head. "I'm not asking you if you want it, Jess. I'm telling you you're gonna eat it!" snapped Rachel, who was sick of her nonsense. She carried Jessie into the kitchen and forced her onto a chair, pouring cornflakes into the bowl with Jessie's name on it. Jessie asked if she could have some bananas too. Rachel said okay and started slicing one up.

"Bye, girls," Paul grinned, and waved as he walked past the kitchen and out the door arm-in-arm with Carla. He loaded his nylon carry-all in the back of the truck and kissed Carla some more. She had that sleepy, sexy look on her face that drove him nuts: he had half a mind to lay her across the seat. "Well, Babe this is it. Take care. Remember, it's all uphill from here." He kissed her again, running his tongue over her tongue stroking her hair, closing his eyes to hold the feel of her. He watched her in the rear view mirror as the truck rolled out of the driveway, thinking, *That's my wife. All we gotta do is get the kid straightened out and it'll be paradise.*

Carla stood in the doorway, one arm raised in the aftermath of a wave. She felt Jessie against her thigh as the little girl asked: "Mommy, what're we gonna do today?"

Carla looked down and said sternly: "Are you ready to appologize?"

Jessie put her thumb in her mouth and nodded. "All right then, let's hear it," said Carla.

Jessie pulled her thumb out and said: "I sorry, Mommy."

Carla said: "Not bad, but it's I'm sorry Uncle Paul. Can we have one of those?"

"Uh-huh," said Jessie, and out came, "I sorry Uncle Paul."

Carla hugged Jessie and Jessie asked if she could draw something special on her mother;s knee because it had this neat white space in the center.

"Sure," said Carla

Jessie ran off and returned with a red marker pilfered from Rachel. She carefully made two opposing curls, joined them at the top and the bottom, then filled them in. She stood back and exclaimed: "Wow, Mommy, awesome!"

Carla laughed and bent over to check out the artwork. "Oh my," she said, and called Rachel over. She bent her leg and pulled it up against her chest so that Rachel could admire the handiwork.

"Gee," said Rachel, "A heart. That's neat. What the well dressed knee is wearing this summer. Can I have one?"

"Yep!" grinned Jessie, and began complaining that Rachel's knee was pillowy and made the marker slide: this was gonna be tough.

"Well," said Rachel, "you just do the best you can. I want an original Jessica Merritt before people start ordering prints."

"Okay," said Jessie, uncomprehending. AnRachel was always saying stuff that didn't make sense.

When she finished filling in the heart she heard Rachel say, "So, Jess, how about the zoo? Wanna go?"

Jessie's eyes glowed. "Really, AnRachel?" The zoo was good for days of chatter: Jessie came back wanting everything, even the water mocassins.

"Word of honor, Honey. You gather up your little raincoat and we're on our way."

"Yeayayay!" Jessie yelled all the way to her bedroom.

"Wow," smiled Carla, "To think that's still the magic word."

"Yeah. Funny isn't it?" laughed Rachel. "Kids and animals. Some things never change. Y'know, I still like it."

"I know you do," Carla grinned.

"Hey, AnRachel," Jessie yelled, "Can you come help me find it? Please!"

"Sure thing, Honey. Be right there." Rachel shook her head. "What's the betting she left it at daycare?"

"Like everything else." Carla yawned. "Rach, can you excuse me while I crash out on the couch? these g'byes, y'know, they're awful exhausting." She grinned and blushed.

Rachel nodded. She was about to get up and help Jessie when she heard: "I got it, AnRachel! Yippee!"

Jessie ran to the door fairly tripping over the yellow sliker, then bounced back into the livingroom to kiss her curled-up mother. To the tune of "Jesus Loves Me" she chirped: "We are going to the zoo, to the zoo-oo, to the zoo." She stood by the car door waiting for Rachel to open it, then climbed on the seat and said: "I know—belt up."

They had driven some distant in silence, then Jessie piped up: "AnRachel, you think he'll rember me?"

"Who? Dumbo?"

"Yeah. Willee?" Jessie called the African elephant Dumbo. She'd point at his big fan ears and yell at him to fly.

"I dunno, Jess. It's been a long time. He sees a lotta people. But that big nose has a pretty good sense of smell, and that's how animals re-mem-ber things. That's how people sometimes re-mem-ber things, too.

"They do? Really? Numbers?"

"No, Honey, sorry. Just faces and places, not numbers and

messages. Those things you got to mem-or-ize."

"Rats," said Jessie, then made a face and said "Sorry, rats."

They climbed out of the car and paid their way into the zoo, and Jessie hauled Rachel along the cobbled walk to the elephant house. The elephant had just been washed and was standing quietly, slick, and dark gray against the white rocks of his home.

"Hi, Dumbo!" yelled Jessie, waving over the iron railing. The elephant spread his ears and looked toward them. "See, see!" cried Jessie, "He re-mem-bers me, AnRachel!"

"Well, so he does," laughed Rachel. "Where to now?"

"Birds!" cried Jessie, grabbing Rachel's hand and yanking her forward. "Let's skip!" They skipped over to the bird house and pointed at all the brightly colored spindles on their perches. Jessie said they looked like wind-up toys and Rachel had to agree: nothing so beautifully alive looked more cheaply mechanical than a bird. Even sandpipers on the beach with their funny sticklike legs and mile-a-minute trot looked like toys running amok.

"Look, AnRachel, the moussed his hair!" cried Jessie, pointing at a clownlike cockatiel with red cheeks and a gray topknot.

Rachel suggested ic cream and Jessie yelled *yeay*, pulling her toward the concession stand. Suddenly she stopped, out of giggles, and said: "Let's go home, AnRachel."

"Honey, what are you talking about? We just got here!"

"I know," said Jessie, pulling as hard as she could in the other direction. "I'm tired, AnRachel. I wanna go home."

Rachel frowned, peered at the concession stand and saw a man in an orange T-shirt coming toward them, carrying hot dogs. It was Granny Blair's son, What's-his-name.

"Honey," Rachel said to Jessie, "you don't hafta go to daycare, today's Saturday."

"Please AnRachel, I wanna go home!" cried Jessie, pulling with all of her might on Rachel's swelling fingers.

Rachel said, "Okay, Honey, but we hafta say hi to Granny Blair's son here."

Cal recognized the woman with Jessie. He was annoyed that Jessie appeared to be running away from him, but he would settle that matter on Monday. He smiled at the woman and raised his arm in greeting. "I see our favorite girl's gotcha comin' and goin'. I saw her draggin' you to the bird house." He smiled again and squatted down to talk to Jessie. "So what's up, Jessie?" he grinned. "Gonna get some ice cream?"

Rachel wished she could remember his name. She kept wanting to say Paul, because he resembled Paul—a scruffy, plainer version. *Damn*, thought Rachel, *I'm not leaving till I get his name right.*

He shielded his eyes with his hand, smiled up at Rachel and said: "You must be the famous AnRachel. Jessie here talks aboutcha all the time."

"Oh yeah?" Rachel smiled. "Well, she's a pretty big fan of yours too," she lied, realizing as she said it *that's why I can't remember his name: Jessie never talks about him. It used to be Mister Cal this and Mister Cal that—come to think of it she never talks about Granny Blair anymore either.*

Jessie was holding tight to Rachel, her body pressed against Rachel's leg. She had put her thumb in her mouth when the Big People started talking, and now she extracted it to inform Mister Cal that she and AnRachel had to go home because Mommy said.

"Oh, hey," Cal Grinned, "If Mommy said then that's the way it is." He stood up, shook his pant legs out and said: "See ya Monday, Jess. Nice talkin' to ya, Miz Rachel." He walked off to join some T-shirted men at the picnic tables.

Rachel looked down at Jessie, waiting for her to look up, but Jessie was watching the retreating figure of Mister Cal. When he reached the picnic tables and sat down with his back to her, Jessie looked up at her aunt.

Rachel cocked an eyebrow at her niece: "Mommy said, huh?"

Jessie shook her head, then shrugged.

"Jessie," said Rachel, "That was a lie. And you know I know it, so why'd you say it?'

Jessie just shrugged and looked down. "Kin we go home now, AnRachel?" asked Jessie, pulling on her hand.

"We can go home as soon as you tell me why you lied to me and Mister Cal."

Jessie said nothing. Minutes went by, then two men got up from the picnic tables and started walking in the general direction of Jessie and Rachel. Cal was one of them. Jessie looked up sharply at Rachel, yanked the thumb out of her mouth and said: "I'll tell. Kin we go now?"

"Nope," said Rachel, "You gotta tell first."

Jessie clamped her mouth down on her thumb and turned her head from side to side.

"Okay," said Rachel, figuring compromise beat frying in the midday sun. "We'll get in the car and you'll tell me on the way home, okay?"

Jessie shut her eyes and nodded vigorously.

"Good," said Rachel, walking hand-in-hand with Jessie to the car. Jessie kept looking over her shoulder, squeezing Rachel's fingers tightly because the heat made their hands so slick. Rachel was relieved to snap the seat belt on her niece and be out of that clammy clutch.

"All right now, Jessie," said Rachel, "We're here. Start talking."

"Kin we go first?"

"Okay," sighed Rachel. She was anxious to turn on the air conditioning anyway. She turned the key in the ignition and several minutes later they were rolling down the highway, Jessie straining to see out the window.

"What are you looking for, Jess?" asked Rachel.

Jessie shook her head, sat back against the car seat and said: "Nuffing."

"Nuffing, huh? Is that the same kinda story as Mommy said?" Jessie looked at her aunt over the finger curled over her nose, and Rachel read the message loud and clear. All that separated them was that the child wasn't old enough to have a plausible lie to cover her pain.

There was an exit ramp a mile ahead.

Rachel patted Jessie's arm and assured her: "It's okay, Jess. We're gonna solve this thing. You 'n' me. You'll see."

Jessie, uncomprehending, knitted her brows as Rachel slowed the car to make the turn.

The Eleventh Hour

Rachel saw a dirt path that veered off the service road into a clump of trees. The car bumped along a trail of rocks and sand, shielded from the blazing sun by a canopy of sycamore leaves. The trail ended in a sandy clearing piled with treadless tires, rusting refrigerators, and other refuse of an outlaw landfill.

Rachel backed the car under the trees, stopped and rolled down the windows. The sycamores buzzed with crickets, and Jessie asked where they were. Rachel watched her struggling under the seatbelt and said: "We're someplace no one can hear us, Jessie. And now we're gonna talk."

Jessie's eyes got big and Rachel patted her arm. "Honey, it's okay. Don't get scared, 'cause you're not gonna hafta say anything, okay? I'm just gonna ask you questions, and you're just gonna do what you've been doing all morning—nod your head for yes, like this," Rachel nodded "or shake your head for no, like that," she demonstrated. "That way he can't hear you, see? And he sure can't hear me.

"Jessie, I promise you won't ever see that man again. Cross my heart and point to Heaven," said Rachel, crossing her heart and pointing up. Jessie's eyes followed the finger. "Okay, Honey? Can we start? Can you nod your head if it's okay?"

Jessie sucked hard on her thumb and looked at her aunt. She squirmed under the seat belt, then looked out the window at the trees. There was nowhere to go, she was trapped. She heard AnRachel ask again if it was okay and she looked down at the floor. Slowly she moved her head up and down and AnRachel hugged her and said good girl. AnRachel asked if Granny Blair knew anything about this and Jessie blurted: "NO!"

AnRachel said, "Okay, Jessie. That's good."

Then she asked if Mister Cal had touched her somewhere she didn't want, like under her clothes. Jessie's eyes filled with tears and she squirmed under the seat belt.

"He did, didn't he," said Rachel, putting her arm around Jessie and unsnapping the belt. Jessie took her thumb out of her reddening face and started to howl. She couldn't look at her aunt, and Rachel said: "Honey, it's okay, you didn't do anything wrong. He's a big person and you're a little person and he forced you. I know that, and God knows that, and Jesus knows it too. That man's never gonna touch you again. I won't let him.

"Now, I just got a couple of more questions to ask, and then we're outta here, okay? Home to Mommy." The word Mommy brought a vigorous nod. Rachel pulled a few tissues from the seat caddy to sop up Jessie's face. As she wiped away the wet she said: "Honey, did he touch your hoo-hoo?"

Jessie started to cry again.

Rachel had her answer. She felt sick. She didn't want to ask the next question. "Honey...did you see his thumb?"

Jessie nodded between wails. "Did he touch you with his thumb? On your mouth or your hoo-hoo?"

Jessie screamed and covered her eyes. She banged her head back against the car seat, pointed at her crotch and screamed: "Got stuck! Got stuck!"

"What—his thumb got stuck there?"

Jessie let out a horrible howl, followed by "Mommy! Mommy!" She dug her little fingers into Rachel's arm and screamed: "I told! I told! An' if I told he's gonna kill Mommy, jes' like Andre!" She curled her fingers into stubby claws, twisting them as if opening the lid of an invisible jar.

Oh my god, thought Rachel, so that's what happened to the bunny.

"Jessie," said Rachel, starting the car, "don't worry about Mommy. I'm not gonna let that man do anything to Mommy. We're going home now, and you'll see, Mommy'll be there and she'll be fine." She snapped the seat belt across Jessie then fixed her own, backed the car slowly along the winding path and stopped when she reached the service road.

This was the final hurdle, and she wanted Jessie to know they were on their way so she'd feel less trapped and scared.

"About Uncle Paul, Honey. Jessie, he's not hurting Mommy, no matter what Mister Cal said, 'cause he lied to you, understand? He said you liked it when he put his thumb there, didn't he? But it hurt, didn't it?"

Jessie nodded and slammed her back against the car seat, tears rolling from the sides of her eyes. Rachel put her arms around Jessie and waited for the crying to subside, then she continued: "Listen, Honey, it's not the same with big people. When big people love each other, it doesn't hurt when a man puts his thumb in a lady's hoo-hoo. They're the same size, see, so they don't get stuck. And it doesn't hurt, it feels good to them."

Jessie winced and Rachel said: "Really. Even if you hear them make funny noises that sound like they're hurting, they're not. It's kinda like you screaming when somebody gives you a present. If somebody heard you yell they'd think you were hurt, but you're not, are you? You're really happy. See what I mean, Jessie? Jessie? Do you understand?"

Rachel waited for a long time while Jessie looked straight ahead.

Again she asked if Jessie understood. Jessie slowly turned to face Rachel and slowly she nodded.

Rachel hugged her and didn't let go. Then she said: "Honey, you don't need to worry about Mommy. Uncle Paul isn't hurting her, and he would never hurt you. He would never do to you what Mister Cal did. Never. And if that horrible Mister Cal said that he loved you when he was hurting you, that love feels like that, that it hurts, he was lying. Do you understand that, Honey? He lied to you, Jessie. Love doesn't hurt, and it wasn't your fault, no matter what he said."

Jessie was crying, looking down.

Rachel repeated her assurance: "Honey, it was not your fault, so you don't hafta feel bad about it, okay?" Rachel waited for Jessie to nod, and after she did (again slowly) Rachel started the car.

"Good girl, Jess," said Rachel, hugging her and swabbing her face before they started down the road.

"Are we going home now, AnRachel?" Jessie whimpered.

"Yes, Honey," Rachel assured her. "Home to Mommy. She's gonna be fine, you'll see."

Jessie cried and sucked her thumb all the way home. AnRachel said Mommy would be fine, but Jessie remembered Mister Cal's words and Andre's bits and pieces. He'd tear off Mommy's head, then her arms, then her legs, then throw her stuffing in the ditch—only it'd be all bloody, like that uhfection.

As the landscape grew familiar Jessie began hollering: "Mommy! Mommy!" and by the time they reached the driveway she was screaming hysterically. Rachel let her out of the car and she ran to the door, jumping up to bang on the doorbell, pounding on the painted wood with all her might, screaming: "Mommy! Mommy! Lemme in! Lemme in!"

When the door opened and Carla emerged from the shadows Jessie gave a joyful shriek and flew into her mother's

arms. Tears of relief rolled down her little face: AnRachel had
told the truth.

"Jessie, Honey, what's going on?" asked Carla, picking
the little girl up and listening to her coo "Mommy, Mommy,"
while she nestled her gooey face on Carla's neck.

Carla raised her brows at Rachel, who was standing at the
bottom of the steps, and said: "Well, can you tell me what's
going on?"

"Nope," said Rachel, nodding at Carla over the back of
Jessie's head, "I promised Jessie it's our secret. Meanwhile, I
think you 'n' the Twink should go across the street for some
ice cream."

"Well, whaddaya say, Twink?" Carla whispered to Jessie.
"Gonna mope all afternoon with your nose in my hair, or are
we gonna get some chocolat-ee ice cream?" Jessie turned
slowly to look at her mother. "Well," smiled Carla, "let's wipe
off that sloppy mug and go get some more goo to put in it."

Jessie nodded slowly, still whimpering, and Carla carried
her off to the bathroom.

When they came out of the bathroom Jessie was clutching
her mother's hand and wouldn't let go.

"Tonight, huh?" said Carla to Rachel in passing, and
Rachel nodded. She sighed as the mother and daughter went
out the door.

By the time the six o'clock news came on Rachel knew
what she was going to say.

They were eating on trays in front of the TV when the man
appeared who'd caught that nut case Robert Gadsen bare
handed—and boy, said Jessie, is he ever mad.

"Yes," said Carla, "he has every right to be. I really can't
get into that coddling scenario—I mean, it doesn't make any
sense. These people have no remorse for what they do—not
before, during or after the fact—as if that could possibly atone
for what they've done anyway. Nope, Rachel, I've had two
years under my own roof to see what kind of damage those
lunatics leave behind, and I say kill 'em."

Jessie went to sleep a little after ten, with her head on her mother's chest and her thumb in her mouth. Carla carried her off to her bedroom and closed the door. Almost an hour passed before she reemerged.

"Gosh," she said when she walked back, yawning, "You almost lost me there. I lay down beside her and it was so peaceful I started to doze off myself. So," she yawned again, "what was the problem?"

Rachel told her to sit down, and Carla crossed her legs in front of her. "So?" she repeated, pulling the hair behind her ears, and Rachel, unable to look at her face, repeated what Jessie had told her.

Carla didn't interrupt. She didn't scream. She sat there, absolutely white, tugging at strings of carpet fiber, moaning slightly and wincing at the breaks in Rachel's discourse. Before Rachel was finished Carla raised her hands to cover her eyes and shut away the image. She turned her head back and forth but there was no escape. Finally she sobbed, not to Rachel but to her own eyes: "STOP! NO! I CAN'T TAKE ANYMORE!" and fell forward, her eyes shut tight, pounding her fists on the carpet.

"That sonofabitch!" she moaned, "That sonofabitch. How could I have been so blind? Oh, Jessie. Oh Jessie baby, please forgive me." She wanted to grab her daughter and never let her out of sight again. "That little girl," she wept. "How could he? Oh God, Rachel, how long has it been going on?"

Rachel shook her head and shrugged, then said falteringly: "We—we have to—"

"What!" snapped Carla. "What do you recommend, Rachel? You who sat here all fucking afternoon when that monster could be in jail by now!"

"I don't think it works quite that fast, Carla. I think we hafta talk to one of the HRS child abuse investigators first. Jessie will hafta repeat her story so they can get it on tape—and there's one other snag. They're working to make it a law in Florida that the child must face the molester in a court of law, something to do with the accused facing his accuser. The theory is that it'll keep kids from wrongfully accusing adults of sexual abuse—"

"But isn't that just in custody cases, where spouses train their kids to lie about sexual abuse to get back at their mates?" Carla was on her feet, striding around the livingroom, waving her arms. She stopped and growled at Rachel: "Hell, this isn't any custody case!" She flung herself down on the couch and immediately bounced to her feet. She strode around the room, holding her temples so that her eyes slanted up, then barked: "Rachel! Do you remember Emily Whitehead?"

"Yeah, vaguely. She went to Atlanta, didn't she, with her two kids?"

"Yeah, and do you know why?"

"No."

"Well, what happened to Emily should never have happened. She suspected that one of her little boy's playmates had been abused, because the little girl said stuff like lick my weenie all the time. So she called the child abuse people to investigate, and somehow the little girl's father got the woman's name off a police report —"

"Wait a minute, I thought all that was supposed to be anonymous —"

"Yeah, well so did she, but the police have the name of the complainant on file, and apparently it's not too hard to get that information because one day later this bastard was calling Emily at home, at work, threatening her life, threatening to cut up her kids. She put a tap on her line, but tapes aren't admissable in court. Her kids were both in different schools and he followed them there. When that happened she left town. I know because me, Cathy and Mark. helped her move."

Rachel scrunched up her eyes, her head cocked to the side. "Why didn't I hear any of this?"

"You had your own problems at the time," said Carla, looking away. "All I know is a maniac's a maniac, and if you're gonna take one on, you better go prepared, and I'm ready. With my bare hands I'm more than a match for that sonofabitch!" She snarled, heading for the door.

Rachel, still sitting, grabbed her leg. "Whoa, Carla! Hold it right there! If this guy's got a gun or a knife and he's the crazy we know he is, then you might get carved up or killed. And if you get him first then you're in the slammer for murder. You wanna do that to Jessie, either way?"

She got up and Carla threw her arms around Rachel's neck, sobbing, "Oh Rachel, what're we gonna do? What're we gonna do?"

"Hold on, Button." (The 'Button' popped in from nowhere.) "We'll figure it out as soon as I get back from the can." She guided Carla over to the couch and sat her down, saying, "Hold on now, I'll be right back. Then we'll figure out who we call to get the ball rolling."

Rachel released Carla and walked with difficulty to the bathroom. Her intestines were wheezing, which meant she'd have to sit quietly to unloose their cargo. Relax. Relax. Soon it'll be over and you can get back. Oh, Carla, PLEASE stop crying.

Outside the house the frenzied whistling of crickets and cicadas seemed to saw through the walls. There were all kinds of noises at night, and every one made Rachel jumpy. She heard the creak of Carla rising from the couch. Then the TV got louder. Then there were clatters and clunks which she took to be Carla making coffee in the kitchen. Well, it didn't exactly sound like that but Rachel had long since learned not to trust her hearing at night: sounds and their whereabouts seemed to go in different directions after dark.

At that point the weatherman's voice overrode her concerns. Seismic disturbances in the Nile Valley made massive reddish clouds billow up, bringing terrible storms wherever they appeared. There was, also, a large cloud system settling over Jacksonville and with any luck it meant rain at last.

Rachel heard a car start and tires screech somewhere close by—close enough to be in the yard.

Then she heard a reporter on the national news say: "Tonight our story comes to you from Cairo. There is great excitement here in the museum because of some religious artifacts thousands of years old that suddenly appear to be sweating. There is apparently no scientific basis for this, and of course many here are calling it a hoax, but I have seen these amulets, and they certainly do appear to be sweating. Let me introduce" (there was a loud noise outside) "Director of Antiquities Preservation and Procurement for the museum."

By now Rachel was back in the livingroom. On the screen a heavy-faced man with black hair and moustache was explaining the significance of the amulets and the almost forgotten deity they represented, a giant white lioness sent by God to stop the wrongdoing of mankind. "To you," he said to the camera, "it is what you call a myth. But there is an American who came here many years ago that knows this is not a myth. You smile, yes? Look at these amulets. You cannot look on the face of the sleeping lion and not be afraid. For she knows your soul, the good and the bad. All of it."

The reporter's face came back into view. Something about the contents of the case behind him had profoundly affected him and he couldn't disguise it. The camera moved over the glass case and inside was a line of tiny gold cat heads on red velvet, the heads and the velvet drenched and glistening. As the camera zoomed in for a close-up the lens got progressively fogged. The last image before the lens cracked was of tiny gold cat faces with dots of water around their mouths. Then the picture went black and the anchorman reappeared, apologizing for temporary technical difficulties and promising an update tomorrow.

Rachel noticed that Carla wasn't in the kitchen or the livingroom and assumed she'd gone back to the bedroom.

She flicked off the TV and walked down the darkened hall into her bedroom, then tripped over something on the floor. She pressed the light switch and there was the metal box that held the gun, open and empty.

She ran to the front door, threw it wide, and the car was gone.

Frantically she dialed the fire-rescue number on the wall phone. Busy. Shit. She dialed 9-1-1 but it was busy too. She alternated the numbers, over and over, to no avail. Jesus Christ, c'mon people. She flipped through the phone book and tried the downtown police, the St. John's police, and the Clay County number: all were busy. My god, what's the matter? Rachel kept dialing. SHIT, C'MON SOMEBODY. ANSWER ME GODDAMN YOU!

After ten tries she dialed Carla's friend Mark.

He and Cathy were soon-to-be parents so there was no way they'd be out carousing tonight. On the ninth ring Mark picked up. "Hello?" he said groggily.

"Mark!" she sobbed, "it's Rachel. Oh, Mark, please come over right away. Carla drove off with my gun a few minutes ago and I can't reach the police. She's gonna try to kill somebody and I think he's got a rifle. Oh, Mark, she's no match for this guy. She's never fired a gun, nothing. Please, please, come quick! I'll keep trying to get the police. PLEASE HURRY!"

"Rachel, don't worry, we're on our way," said Mark, but he was cut off in mid-sentence.

"Mark, what is it?" said Cathy, yawning.

Mark flicked on the overhead light, buttoned up his jeans and tossed Cathy her robe. He pulled the rifle out from under the bed and said: "Carla's in some kinda trouble. You're gonna hafta babysit while Rachel 'n' I go after her. Damn, it's gonna take twenty minutes to get there: the cops're everywhere tonight."

The Eyes of God

Mark was right. Once upon a time the cops had only three nights to worry about: Friday, Saturday and Wednesday—Wednesday because half the town was at church and the other half was getting tanked on twofers at Happy Hour.

Now a more insidious evil had taken hold of the city, the demon crack. North and Westside Jacksonville had become war zones. Eleven-year-olds carried beepers and Uzis, and random killings began to erupt in apartment complexes on the Southside. Jax Beach, with its revamped Boardwalk, was getting rowdier by the minute.

So on Saturday night when two Neptune Beach cops saw a beige Volaré doing eighty up Third Street, they spun their car around and gave chase.

But Carla didn't see the blue lights or the street lights or even the road: she saw Jessie, gasping and struggling under this huge man whose voice rose and fell as he moved on top of her: Don't fight it, Jessie. I know ya love me. Jessie's face was puckered and red. Her mouth made quivery figure eights. She had cried so hard she was drooling.

"YOU BASTARD!" screamed Carla, pounding the wheel, "You'll NEVER NEVER hurt my daughter again!"

She was three blocks past Florida Boulevard when she heard the faraway siren. She saw the blue lights, looked at the speedometer, and spun off the main road, almost crashing into a church. The alley by the beach was two blocks away, and Sid's beachfront house with its huge patio driveway would soon cover her in bushes. Tonight he and Sally were out of town, but they always left a spare key for friends in distress, and tonight Carla would be that friend.

She killed the lights and swung the car onto the darkened drive. It was pitch black between the hedges, but Carla had walked that driveway a hundred times. She knew every twist, turn, and leaf.

Alas, she did not know that Sid had installed a large metal barbeque in the middle of the patio. She thought it was a shadow, and cut the motor.

The car slammed into the lagged-down grill, throwing her against the windshield. The car bounced back and she fell against the seat, blood pouring down her face. But she was unaware, suspended in cooling dark.

Gradually noises began to intrude: repeating, rolling kabooms—and voices, between the booms, getting closer: Damn, he's gotta be hidin' in one of these driveways. Let's wait a bit, and listen.

Carla heard it through a fog. Her head throbbed, her eyes hurt. Her lids parted on a confusion of shadow and light—light streaking over the fence, slanting through the stairs, threading a gossamer web from the bloody whorl on the windshield.

She shoved her shoulder against the door, pushing down on the handle, and picked up the gun.

She heard voices near the front of the house, interspersed

with thunder. So it's a Volaré, not a Nova. Yeah, we got it. She what? Oh great. Let's find the dumb bitch before she shoots herself.

Carla put the gun in Sid's tackle box by the door, glad the thunder masked the sound. Now what? The pain in her head was swallowing her thoughts. She fell against the patio stairs, thinking: Please, God, take the pain away. Please do something to hide me.

Suddenly the neighborhood went black.

Cold dots stung Carla's arms, then a blast of wind covered her in dust and rain. The rain hit her face and AOWW. Something sticky was dribbling down her face.

Dear God, she thought. Just keep me conscious, keep me movin'. Two more miles, that's all I ask. And gimme something to hit him with when I get there.

The building was swaying, along with the stairs and the fence. She tried to right herself by grabbing the banister but it was slippery with rain, and more rain splashed across her hands, drubbing her fingers off the wood. Her eyes were closing in spite of herself.

"No!" she heard herself scream. "Don't let this happen! Don't let him get away! Please God, help me! " Her scream was swallowed in shaking air, hurled back to earth by cymbalic clouds. She saw the concrete coming up to meet her and lay there, face down, blood pumping from the hole in her forehead, her mind floating free in the dark.

After awhile she felt her arms stretching before her, parting the darkness as though it were a substance. A light up ahead showed the darkness swirling around her like soft cotton. Suddenly it dissolved into yellow-white light and brilliant blue, and Carla soared like a glider over a landscape she knew but had never seen.

It was a beach, but not like Jacksonville Beach, not gray with clay and flat after the tide. Here rocks and sand sloped down to a green expanse unlike the murky ocean. Tall reeds shadowed round-leafed rafts of spicy-sweet blossoms. Crocodiles with red eyes floated loglike through the reeds.

Above the water beyond the rocks were terraces of stone, and rising above them almost to the sky were obelisks and colossal buildings. Here massive beasts encased in stone guarded the souls of their makers. Carla felt herself dropping. She was gently deposited feet first and barefoot on one of the walkways leading to a flat-roofed open temple. She walked under the great stone lintel, warmed by shafts of sunlight that reached around the columns to find her. There was only herself and a statue under the canopy at the heart of the temple. Even so the ghosts of centuries flitted before her. Women in white with silver bowls of wine and armloads of grapes. They deposited these gifts at the feet of the gray-white statue, begging forgiveness as they backed away.

Carla was mesmerized by the statue, by eyes that seemed to see and were but stone, by the teeth inside those powerful jaws, though the mouth was closed and no teeth were visible. Those huge crescent ears seemed to be listening. To what?

Then Carla heard it, that tiny cry lost in the clouds over Jacksonville, carried up and up beyond the whirling meridian and down through the corridors of time—to this very spot by the River of Life. And her voice was not alone: the cries of the world came with it—the cries of the murdered, oppressed, and violated, screaming through the centuries.

And behind them, hard and hideous and shaking the earth, the Voice of Ra. It commanded Sehkmet to shake off that gray mask.

Carla fell to her knees in terror. Slowly she looked up at the statue, drawn to its eyes.

Those dull gray almonds with their greenish glow sprang open on all the greens that mankind was destroying.

The she-lion's head bent forward and her mouth stretched into a snarl. The huge crescent ears that had listened for centuries flattened down in fury, then came the roar that shook the temple.

Carla's mouth opened in concert with the lion's and the next roar came from Carla's heart, louder than thunder, loud enough to shatter time—and it shattered her. She exploded like a star and the atoms showered out to a new dimension, then shrank back to form another being.

This one saw what humans could never see, though the vision was as yet embryonic—a red mass pulsing and shimmering in all directions, separating into thick clusters of twinkling lights, like stars. Each star then beat to generate its own universe, a human body, for each star was indeed a heart, and each heart shone with colors beyond but equivalent to the visible human spectrum, ranging from white to black. Each color came from a different quality and the dark brackish shades were sins: the different colors around each heart formed a spectral signature.

There were many good hearts in this endless parade but none were pure, for purity has no color, just as it has no drive— it is wholly realized, without need. Human life, however, can never be pure or perfect for its needs are many, and so many needs complicate the choices.

Alas, the most prevalent choices were greed and the violence that sprang from greed. Ra had waited for humanity to grow beyond rapacity but every turn of the earth brought more people and new horrors. They would not stop. They claimed they couldn't. There was only one thing left to do, and He took a woman—complex, kind, and riven with doubt—to house and temper Sehkmet's rage.

Sehkmet rose up, a blinding white light born of moonglow and anger, crossing the meridian in less than a moment.

Her light shimmered over the body on the patio tiles, absorbing and transforming it, giving Ra's anger bone and flesh, teeth and claws. Carla's soul was already conscripted; now her every molecule was smashed, stretched and reshaped to fill the magic proportions of Sehkmet. A series of gleaming crescents grew under the light, reflecting her mission and the eleventh-hour status of man. From tail to incisor she was eleven feet long; incisors and eyes eleven inches. The eyes were pupilless, burning green—no pupils because what her eyes sought no earthly light could show. Last to grow were the claws, at the edge of the circle of light. The freckled hands thickened and furred, the nails curved and glowed: eleven-inch daggers harder than diamonds, bright as crescent moons. She stood there, glistening white in the darkness, scanning the dark procession of souls, and furious at the concrete underfoot. This was not the bricks of Egypt nor the stones of Maya—no, this pernicious coating choked the ground underneath: she could hear it gasping. The horrid smell of gasoline assaulted her nostrils: for this man gutted the earth. She saw the plastic creature next to her and billions like it—strewn across the continent, weighing down the ground, useless, insensible, and designed for just this function: to lie discarded while more were made.

She reared back and roared, a sound that dwarfed the thunder in the sky.

She roared again and two hearts on the far side of the building stopped dead. They resumed beating—thudding, fluttering—and one of the men gasped: "My god, what in hell was that! Felt like—"

"Felt like it came through the wall, right?"

"Hell, I say we call in an' say we got an escaped somethin' out here –"

"Yeah, let's figger out where it is first –"

They stood back to back, trying to listen over the thudding in their chests and heard cars on the streets but no movement behind the house.

"This is weird," gulped the taller man, "I feel like we're bein' watched."

"Maybe it's sizin' us up fer dinner," whispered the shorter man. "One thing for sure —"

"What?"

"It ain't no damn Volaré."

The Cat saw the two fluttering hearts pinned against the wall. Another roar would hold them while she crossed the street.

Two other hearts inside the next house, thumping strong in the aftermath of love, now quaked as the third roar shook the building. The lovers dug their fingers in each other's shoulders as their hearts shrank, then stopped. When they felt The Presence had passed, the first one whispered: "Damn, I've heard of the earth moving, but never the floor –"

"I'm that good huh?" laughed the smaller man.

"No, I am," sniped the first.

The Cat had moved out from the shadow of the house. There was nothing on the street except a car that made crackling noises. The Cat crossed the street in a single leap, snarling as she landed on the asphalt: she saw ghosts of sweaty brown men dumping buckets of tar on dusty gravel and along the roofs of these manmade caves.

She marched over a line of cars into the back yard, then stood for a moment on the grass as white light shot round the roaring clouds and a volley of Hathor's tears warmed her back. The tears washed away the extraneous visions and allowed The Cat full view of her chosen targets.

There were two hearts that night, liars and violators both, each different colors, dark beyond redemption. The closest was orangy-black, the heart of a tiger that eats its young. The other was purply black with dark jets of red, a murderer.

Other hearts glowed darkly around these two, but their night of reckoning was not now. Soon, very soon: The Cat snarled and her mouth curled in anticipation.

She gazed up at the branches of scrub oak and sycamore twining over the back fences; they made a perfect path to the house of the first heart. She leaped up on a low-hanging limb then felt her way along twisting branches that sagged and swooned under her weight—but the trees knew why she had come, and were proud to hold her. At the end of the trail the waxy leaves of a magnolia waited to stroke her back.

Between cracks of thunder cats were mewing all over the beach, and dogs were howling and whining to warn their owners. The owners believed their pets were afraid of the storm and tried to shush them. They had never seen their animals so frantic, never seen lightning that made no streaks or flashes, just a steady white glow around the clouds. Perhaps a hurricane was gearing up: with triple-digit temperatures conditions were ripe. The owners looked out their windows, yelled at their dogs to shut up, and attempted to call the weather hotlines, which were jammed. The lights came back on, but the thunder got louder, and more dogs' voices were heard.

In one yard along The Cat's path the foghorn woof of a brindle mastiff warned owners that weren't home. Unfortunately for the dog the yard's two spindly trees broke The Cat's aerial bridge and she jumped down, snarling at the smell of pesticide.

The mastiff, true to its last breath, launched itself off the orange-lit patio to stop the intruder. A tap of that giant paw sent it sailing over backwards, its gashed intestines sticking out like coxcombs. It landed with a thud on its side, neck broken and eyes staring. Those unseeing orange disks held the image of The Cat as it crossed the yard and soared into the trees.

She strode on through the branches as thunder shook the sky. In every other house a dog whined and scratched at the sliding glass doors. The owners would slide the doors open but the dogs wouldn't go. They yelped, danced, and ran around in circles, but were terrified to cross the threshold.

The Cat meanwhile was crouched along the lower limbs of the last tree. When the tall magnolia held her its blossoms rustled over her, drenching her in perfume. Birds that never sang at night were singing now, and people in the neighborhood remarked that they had never heard so damn much noise in all their days.

The Cat prepared to spring, drawing her feet under her. She saw the tiger heart, tilted and unaware. Her green eyes widened, the great lips curled back—and the dog in the house of the tiger heart went crazy.

Granny Blair awoke with a start, almost pitching out of the rocker. She had fallen asleep there as she often did, wrapped in her old yellow bathrobe, staring at the light from Cally's window and wondering if he was happy: she desperately didn't want him to leave.

But Willy had her full attention now, jumping up and down in front of the door, growling and barking and scratching. "Willy, Willy, what's wrong?" she asked, reaching for the cord on the table lamp. She knew every note, mood, and message of his querulous little bark, and he had never sounded like this: this time he was really afraid.

When the light came on she saw him scratching at the bottom of the door—ears, tail and belly down, hind end and hair standing straight up. "Awright, Willy, thassa good boy, we'll go see what it is."

Granny Blair wasn't about to face whatever it was alone. Her father had taught her never to walk strange paths without a rifle, and he gave her one before she went to Jacksonville, saying that the city was about the strangest path a body could choose to walk. All those years in that house the rifle stayed under her bed, except once a month when she drug it out to clean, reload and practice aiming it one-armed. She had thought of leaving it with Cally, but what if he left one day unannounced and took it with him?

She had hoped and prayed they would grow closer, but after the children left at night Cally would lock himself in his so-called darkroom, come out for dinner, then go back again. Alas, not much passed between them but food. She had no idea what he did all alone in his room. If she asked to see some of his pictures he'd tell her he wasn't ready yet, they weren't good enough. She worried about his being so shy. He barely had any friends. He did have a lot of pen pals, though: large hard envelopes were constantly arriving from all over the country, particularly California. These must be the people with whom he shared his talent. She wouldn't be nosy, though, and drive him away.

She hauled the rifle out and opened the door. Willy charged down the hall to Cally's bedroom, barking as loud as his lungs would allow, and Cally screamed from behind the closed door: "Momma, shut that damn dog up afore I kick his ass clear through to the next county."

"Cally, that's no way to talk. He's tryin' to pertect ya."

"Yeah, from what? Frogs? Thunder? Hell, Momma, he's jest afraida the storm. Go to bed, Momma. There's nuthin' here but a li'l rain on the window."

Cal was afraid that he hadn't locked the door and she might walk in. Her eyes were old, but she wasn't blind. He said anything he could think of to keep her out, frantically gathering up the photos on the bedspread and stuffing them under the pillows, trying not to bend them. The prints he had tossed on the floor he shoved under the bed. Oh shit, the dog—what if he crawls under an' grabs one? Fer sure thet's all she'd need to see, her precious li'l tots all nekkid with their hands all over each other. Sure thing.

One photo was especially dear to him and he held onto it while he buried the others. He gave it a last look, savoring the green eyes of the little girl, so haunted, the seal-like roundness of her body, the half moon nails fanned across her shoulders. He kissed the spot below her belly, laid the pillow across the picture, and stretched out on the bed, crossing his legs and arms.

"Momma," he said, puffing the pillows behind him, "You can come in if you want but the dog stays out."

The dog was getting crazier by the second—now it was howling and whimpering, and Cal could see his mother's slippers at the bottom of the door while she tried to push the dog away, to no avail. It would dance around behind her, then crawl back to the door. Cal could see its nose and the ends of its paws. Damn dog, what's wrong with him anyway?

"Cally, you come open this door an' I'll tie Willy up in the kitchen. C'mon, now, Willy," she called to the dog, "C'mon, now, we'll git us a biscuit." Normally the word biscuit would have sent Willy flying into the kitchen, but not this time. He continued to stand there, growling and whining.

Granny Blair didn't want to put the rifle down, but she couldn't grab Willy any other way. She walked into the kitchen and set the rifle on the table, figuring she'd need both her glasses and a flashlight—as it was she couldn't see the pattern of the rain on the window. She pulled out the drawer beside the sink and extracted a roll of string: there wasn't much but then Willy didn't need much. She walked back to Cally's door, tucked her fingers under Willy's collar, and dragged the choking dog over to the table. She knotted one end of the string around the table leg and half knotted the other end around Willy's collar: that way he could escape if something really was happening. She didn't like the sound of him, that's for sure.

"Cally, open the door now, the dog's tied up—poor li'l thing." She patted Willy to show she didn't like this any better than he did, but Willy went on barking.

Cal came to the door. The deadbolt made a slucking sound, and the door opened.

"C'mon in, Momma," he said, and Granny Blair said just a minute, she was going to get her glasses. He sighed, listening to her slippers slap-m slap-m down the hall.

He sat on the corner of the bed facing the door and caught his reflection in the mirror—big, handsome, tired. On the heels of that observation he yelled: "Shaddup, Willy!"

The dog gave a last whimper, crawled as far back as it could under the table and lay there, shaking.

Well, that fixed him, Cal grinned, slapping his hands together, and went back to his reflection. He flexed his arm to study the tattoo, thought about getting another, and yawned. So where was Momma? Had she lost her glasses? Nope, never happen, that'd be too good. He yawned again, curled his fists and stretched, and opened his eyes. He went back to his reflection, and behind his face he saw something huge and gray fill up the window. What?

He half turned for a better look and the window came crashing down, glass splinters tearing at him as he raised his arms over his eyes. "MOMMAAA!" he screamed. He saw The Cat's glowing eyes, those scimitar hooks reaching for his face and—WHAP! The blow smashed his skull and tore it from his body. The Cat pulled the body to the center of the bed, its giant claws furrowing the breastbone, cracking the heart's armor and extracting the bloody muscle. She swallowed the dripping organ with its orange and black aura, and the moment her jaws closed it turned white—seared by the fires of Ra, bathed in the tears of Hathor.

Sehkmet roared, licked the blood from her face, and looked out over that glimmering procession of hearts for her next target. Ah yes, there it was, beating faster now, very close.

Then she heard Ra's voice commanding her to give up the woman's body—that there were others waiting, thousands more. But Sehkmet had fused with the woman and had come to love her, to pity her fate. Ra was adamant that she leave; she was equally adamant that she stay. She had absorbed all those human frailties again—doubt, reason and obstinacy—but Ra had anticipated this. He promised her the woman would be at peace, that she would be exalted and live among the angels. And her family would be Sehkmet's special friends, on earth and after. The next heart's end would help them, too.

Sehkmet agreed. The light of her being showered into the room, became a blazing ball above the body of the woman, and shot through the window into the night—leaving Carla, her head still pounding, her face, hands, and arms a mass of blood.

She screamed at the bleeding carcass on the bed. She tried to wipe the fleshy strips off her hands but couldn't get her balance, kept falling forward. She tried not to touch the red sheets or the man's legs, but the mattress was soft and she kept sinking, falling against him.

She made a grab for the headboard but her hand fell short and pulled away the pillow. There was something strange under the pillow, an upsidedown picture of a child, a full body shot, naked, and—Oh my god, my baby!

"NO!" screamed Carla, clenching her fist through the flesh on her palms. She picked up the edge of the photo thinking: gotta get help and staggered toward the door. She heard noises in the hall: maybe it was the police. Good. She dropped the picture on the dresser and pulled herself upright, holding both sides of the door molding.

Then she saw the tearful old lady with the rifle under her

shaking arm. The barrel wobbled upward and Carla put her hands out screaming: "NO! DON'T! STOP!

Granny Blair didn't listen: she'd already heard and seen more than her old heart could take—first her son's head on the floor, then a white monster gutting his innards, then a blast of light that froze her as she ran for the rifle, now this red-faced demon with a woman's naked body stretching its bloody arms, imploring her to stop—No, by God, no bloody demon was gonna flimflam her!

She shut her eyes, pressed the trigger twice—and the rifle bucked out of her hand. It clattered across the floor as the demon fell down in front of her, spraying her slippers and gown with blood.

She gasped and staggered back, her hand over her heart. A burning weight crushed her chest, pushing out the air—then suddenly there was no air. She felt herself falling on the kitchen floor, and lay there looking up at the light, silently begging God to bring back the air.

After a while the air didn't matter, only the light—and Willy, her last friend, who had crept to her side as he saw her fall and stood over her, licking her face.

Unfinished Business

At midnight Cathy was sweating by the kitchen phone, waiting for word from Mark or Rachel. She wanted to call Paul but was afraid she'd end up spilling the story and tying up the line—and what if Jessie woke up and overheard? Drat that Rachel: why doesn't she have Call Waiting—smart as she's sposeta be and scared as she always is?

Cathy walked into Carla's bedroom and found the flowered address book. There were three numbers for Paul and she had no luck with the first two. The clock on the nightstand read 12:05 when she dialed the number marked 'Bubba.' She wished that infernal howling outside would stop. Holy Mary, listen to 'em. What IS with those dogs?

While Cathy peeked through the living room blinds to see why the dogs were barking Paul was sitting on the edge of

Bubba's couch, wishing he'd called Carla before Bubba conned him into this lifeless party. Now it would be at least an hour before he could slide out.

Bubba was holding court with the wealthy and arty in the kitchen, while the manly and bored, like Paul, were stretched out in the sunken livingroom in front of the giant TV. A grade Z horror flick was in progress and footwide mouths either closed in the middle of sentences or kept moving after the sentences ended. The werewolf was scheduled to arrive any minute by way of Rome or Tokyo.

"My God, who turned this shit on?" groaned one of the watchers.

"Yeah," said another.

"Well, we can't watch Saturday Night," whispered a third, "cause of the Sunday School crowd in the kitchen. Wouldn't want Bubba to lose that fat contract now."

"Nooohh," they mooed in unison, and laughed.

"Shouldn't be long now," grinned the third one, "they've about wore out all them postcards 'n' baby pictures. Hell, what's left to do but go home 'n' hang 'em up? Say Paul ol' buddy, whatsa 'matter? Can't get comfy? Miss yer snatch? Awww."

"What I miss is nunna yer business," Paul grinned, "but what I need's a beer. I mean who can sit through this shit sober?" He didn't want to pass Doris in the kitchen so he offered to make a beer run.

"Good idea," echoed the loungers, and reached for their wallets. Paul collected the waving dollars and vowed to be back before the towering shag rug chomped his first moon-light maiden. He left as the old gypsy woman was imploring the slick-haired man not to go into the woods, not tonight!

He was almost at the truck when he decided to walk. The convenience store was only two blocks and besides, he was tired of sitting. It was hot outside and he was clammy by the time he reached the store.

He winced as he walked to the phone, which stood by the dumpster at the darkened end of the sidewalk, butts and candy wrappers strewn around the base. A half-empty cup with a wilted straw leaked a puddle onto the shelf below the phone. No phone book, just a dangling chain. Roaches tapped their way up and down the casing. Two minutes and I'm outta here. He stood with his back to the wall so he could see who was coming, dropped the coin in the slot and hallelujah, it chimed. He told the operator it was a collect call to Rachel's number, but the line was busy. Now that didn't seem right. At 12:15 who'd be calling them but him? Maybe he'd transposed the numbers. He tried again and got the same answer, busy. Nope, that wasn't right.

He bought two six-packs, popcorn and chips, and trotted back to Bubba's.

He dropped the groceries in front of the TV, then asked Bubba if he could use the phone to call Carla. Bubba said sure, go ahead, something wrong?

"I dunno," said Paul. "I just tried to call and the line's busy—"

"Hey," said Bubba, "maybe the kid knocked the phone off the hook, or maybe it's trouble on the line."

"No, it's none of those," said Paul, and walked into Bubba's office. He switched on the light and was struck by the bareness of the room: obviously Doris hadn't gotten to it yet. But then, bookshelves and a desk weren't as aah-inspiring as a hot tub—or so he hoped, and locked the door behind him just in case.

Too bad about that bitch. It was inevitable they would come to blows over Doris. He could even see the way she'd set it up. He'd turn her down once too often, she'd tell Bubba she had been attacked by that brutal lowlife, and Bubba would come after him with a shotgun. Well, maybe he could hold on a little longer—hell, that money was hard to turn down.

Dammit, why couldn't this work? He banged his fist on the desk pad, the receiver bounced up and the phone rang. Paul sat back on the chair, thinking he'd jarred the bell when it rang again. He picked it up and said: "Hello, Krantz residence."

The voice on the other end said, "Hello, this is an emergency. Is Paul Seavers there?"

"This is he," said Paul, feeling his stomach quiver.

"Oh God. Thank God." The voice dropped to a whisper. "Paul, can you hear me? It's Cathy, Carla's friend. I got this number out of her book. Listen, you need t'get up here right away—"

"What's wrong?"

"I can't explain," she whispered, "I'm here at Rachel's with Jessie. I don't want her to hear nothin.' I'm gonna hang up now, okay? You just come, hear? Put yer fuzzbuster on an' burn rubber, huh?" Her voice got louder. "Jessie, Honey, what're you doin' up? And where's your sleepshirt? Yeah, I know it's hot—but see, I'm dressed... No, Honey, Mommy and Aunt Rachel are out lookin' for a ring Mommy tried on that was too big and fell off. I'd be out lookin' too only I can't bend over. Sides, somebody's gotta stay here with you, Baby... Who's this? I'm talkin' to Uncle Paul, Honey. He jest called cause he misses you. You wanna talk to him?"

There was shuffling, then Jessie's voice said: "Uncle Paul?"

"Yeah, Honey, I'm here."

There was a long silence, followed by short breaths, then Jessie said slowly, "I sorry, Uncle Paul. See, I din't know it was okay. AnRachel told me."

"That's okay, Honey," said Paul, wondering what she meant. "Are we friends again?"

"Uh-huh," said Jessie, then Paul said he'd see her in the morning, to go back to bed, and that he loved her. Would she take the giraffe now? Jessie said uh-huh, then asked Cathy if it was a 'spensive ring Mommy lost, cause they're always smaller an' harder to see. Cathy told her to say good bye and hang up so Mommy could call in if she found the ring.

"Okay," said Jessie, "G' bye Uncle Paul. Mommy lost a ring, a 'SPENSIVE ring." Cathy told her to hang up and the phone clicked in Paul's ear.

Ring my ass, thought Paul. He hit the door so fast he forgot to turn the handle and slammed his shoulder. He swore, grabbed his shoulder, ran for his truck and screeched out of the driveway. The flesh above his collar bone jumped, and his stomach was shaking like it had in the war. Instinct or luck had kept him alive then, and all his instincts were telling him this was bad. Hang in there, Carla, I'll fix it. You'll see. The truck sprang onto the expressway and the needle zoomed to ninety.

Rachel and Mark were driving between the daycare center and Atlantic Boulevard, looking in the lanes for Rachel's car. They left her house as a burst of thunder killed the lights in Neptune Beach, but minutes later the area was bathed in a strange white glow. Atlantic Beach was bright too, and dogs howled everywhere they turned.

"I don't understand. Where can she be?" Rachel whimpered. "Why haven't we seen the car?"

"Look, Rachel, y' know how she is when she's mad: she takes off runnin', beats her feet on the beach awhile and comes home. I'd lay money she's sittin' on some bench, windin' down. I bet if we cruise the public access lots we'll find the car, and her not fifty feet off."

"No, Mark." Rachel shook her head. "She didn't take that gun to blow off steam, she took it to blow that bastard's head off. Look, let's just go back to The Tot Spot and wait—shit, we shoulda just stayed there."

"Okay, Rach," said Mark, and they drove back to Ocean Drive. They stopped for a red light and when it turned green they heard sirens behind them. Two police cars came screaming into view, followed by the fire-rescue truck. The cars sped down Plaza and left on Ocean in the direction of the daycare center, Mark's truck right behind them.

Twenty miles inland another person had cause to curse a pay phone. He listened to his coin bingbong down to the return slot and growled, "Damn thing gets more strokes 'n' I do." It was the fifth trip down for that quarter. "Damn people, where are they all anyway?" Out, gone, or unlisted. Kenny pocketed the quarter in disgust: nowhere to party, nowhere to sleep— nowhere free, anyway. Friends. Fuck 'em.

He looked at the wan face watching from the car window. The parking lot light made her ghoulish, yellowing her skin and making purple holes of her eyes and mouth. He hated that purple-eyed punk stuff: it was too much like his mother's eyes, shadowed and swimming. Maybe she was a jinx, too—hell, nothing had gone right since she approached him at that truck stop.

On her way to Fort Lauderdale, she said, and offered to pay for the gas. Hop in, said Kenny, figuring anyone headed for Fort Lauderdale had to be carrying plenty, but she would only pay for gas.

He decided to take a positive view, to wear her down with his eyes and cautious flattery, but acting enthralled was tough when she was so ugly and wouldn't shut up. She said she was from New York and Kenny could see it for New York to him was Liza Minelli, cap-haired and lashy. Her name was Ariadne—or maybe it wasn't, maybe she made it up for the trip. Couldn't be more unreal than that hair, which looked like a chopped up fire engine. She wore holey jeans and clumpy shoes and a black sweatshirt with CATS over the nipples. How could anyone wear so much in summer? Was it some New York thing, fashion by the yard? He asked her about the shirt so he could stare at her nipples and ignore her fingers, which were bleeding stumps—yet still she sat, nibbling the ends like carrots.

"Willya cut that out!" he finally yelled. "Your damn fingers are like raw meat!"

"Well excu-oose me!" She stuck out her tongue. "And you're perfect, I'm sure."

Maybe not, he thought, but I'm way aheada you.

They drove to St. Augustine Beach that morning so he could "show her the sights," and she thanked him for being a wonderful guide but wouldn't spring for lunch. In her small pouch was a constant twenty dollars, so she must be keeping a stash somewhere on her body, maybe in her shoes. Not that Kenny was hurting for money, he had cash and jewels rolled in a blanket in the trunk. He just wanted hers.

Worse, her indifference was driving him crazy. He had never before met someone impervious to his eyes. Even dykish women warmed to his smile. So what was wrong with this one?

It had something to do with New York, as if New York was the world and anywhere outside was dead space, including him. No wonder she chattered endlessly and didn't care how he responded: it wasn't a real conversation because it wasn't happening in Manhattan, and he wasn't a real New Yorker, so he was nobody—less than nobody, a chauffeur. No wonder she thought she could just trot into Fort Lauderdale and find her friend: probably thought the bitch would be carrying a sign that read 'Earth to anyone—get me home to Manhattan.'

Dammit, he wasn't gonna stand for this, he thought, getting back in the car. By God no, he was gonna get back in the human race, and she was gonna cough up some dough.

"So what happened to all your friends?" she smirked, and he shrugged as she chewed the side of her pinky. He frowned to show he disapproved and she ignored it.

"So what now?" she asked, and he said they could rent a motel room. There was one on the corner of Atlantic and University, about two miles away. "Is that near the beach?" she asked, and he said hell no, the beach ones are expensive. She sighed and asked how expensive.

"Dunno," he said. "Guess we'll hafta call."

"Guess so," she said, and dug a quarter out of her bag. "My turn," she smiled, arching her barely-there brows. "Maybe I'll have better luck."

Kenny winced at the sarcasm. He hated her face and her sickening fingers. Even so he wanted her to want him, to stroke him, to beg him. He wanted to stop seeing that picture of her and her ugly friends laughing about the dumb surfer who drove her to Fort Lauderdale. What, he never herda Julie yard? Ha ha ha. He gritted his teeth and banged his fist on the dash as Miss Phony Name opened the door.

She said, "Well, that's out, too much money." Then: "God, what's wrong? You look awful!"

"Nuthin'," he snapped. "Nuthin' that'd mean shit to you."

She stood at the door, bent over and frowning, and he growled at her to get in the car.

"The hell I will!" she yelled, slammed the door and ran.

She was headed for the back lot of the strip mall, which—
if memory served him—was totally enclosed by a high chain
link fence. With almost no tread on those rabbit foot shoes, her
chances of getting over that fence before he got there were nil.

All right, bitch, he grinned, starting the engine. This time
I win.

He drove the car slowly through the parking lot so as not to
arouse any passing suspicions, and followed the asphalt lane that
divided the corner buildings. He turned the corner onto the back
lot and damn if some kids hadn't cut a hole through the fence and
she'd vanished into the woods behind it.

Well, she couldn't get far. That stretch of trees ended in the
deep ditch by Merrill Road. In the dark of the woods she could
only go for the light by the road, and slogging through the
underbrush would take her at least three minutes. Then there
was the ditch, and he'd already whitened her face with stories
of cottonmouths, so she could take her choice—him or the
snakes.

He cruised along the road, saw her scrambling and sliding
up the embankment, and yelled out the window, "Hey, Ariadne,
ya wanna cut the crap, there's snakes in that water. So do ya
want some help or wouldja rather die?"

He stopped the car, walked to the edge of the ditch, and
offered his hand.

She looked up and frowned, holding two branches amid
the slime and bracing herself to jump away.

Reach for me an' ya live. Try ta run yer dead, he thought,
and stood there smiling with his hand out while she looked
down into the blackness, scrambling to keep her feet out of the
water.

"Cottonmouths'll strike above the water, you know," he
guffawed. "Yas'm, they love that Yankee meat. Now really,
if I was you, and y'all were as smart as you think you are, I'd
come with me. Whoa, you hear that? When thunder gets that
loud around here it means we're in for a downpour. That'll
slide you right down in wunna their nests if ya don't get out
now."

She looked down and up and down again, sure he wasn't lying about the snakes, afraid to take his hand. Maybe she could lull him with thanks and praise long enough to disappear through a washroom or back kitchen. At least on dry land she could run and her hands would be free to pull the razor out. Oh god, was it even there anymore, or had she lost it slogging through the brush? She couldn't reach for it now anyway, not with that smirking face hovering over her.

"Okay," she tried to smile. "You win. Get me outta here." She forgot the dweeb special please but it was too late to get fancy. She reached up her left hand, thanking him as their fingers touched, and she smiled as he smiled, thinking he wasn't such a bad guy after all, that maybe she'd blown it all out of proportion, maybe made too much of their differences, maybe—she felt his fingers close around her wrist with garotting force.

"Ow!" she yelled, "That hurts!"

"I know," he grinned, and dragged her up by that one wrist, keeping it bent so all her weight was on the joint.

"Owww!" she screamed again, louder, as he slammed her on her knees in the gravel by the ditch. She tried to scramble to her feet and he kicked her in the stomach. He laughed as she tried to roll away, and aimed another kick at her butt, which was softer than he thought it would be. He waited while she staggered up and ran behind the car. He saw the comb in her hand and laughed. His laugh changed to a whoohoo of fake admiration as she ripped the comb sheath off the blade.

"That's it for you, bitch, you're shish-kabob!" he yelled, striding toward the flashing Zs of the knife. He made a fast grab for her wrist but she was quicker, slashing his fingers and forearm and leaping out of range.

There was a terrible crash as the storm burst overhead. The rain burned his cuts but he grinned because with the rain and her hopping backwards she was bound to miscalculate. Sure enough on their fifth circle of the car her sneakers stuck on some gravel and she stumbled.

Kenny leaped. He grabbed her arms and slammed her

against the side of the car, twisting and squeezing her wrists till they cracked and the blade fell away. He held her by one off those broken joints, digging his fingers in the swelling flesh while she screamed and tried to pull back, but she couldn't brace against the breaks, couldn't wriggle out of his grasp.

He stooped to pick up the knife, and slashed her torso in shuddering streaks to match her screams, to match the rain. He smiled at his choreography—hell, this was better than any video. She flopped and screamed till he drew the blade across her neck, and a fountain of blood gushed over his hand and her eyes rolled up. He threw her down beside the car, suddenly smarting with the pain of his cuts. Damn bitch.

He seized her ankles and looked down at her face, turned toward the wheel of the car, the blood spilling brightly down her neck. Brightly? How could that be? The body was in darkness, barely a silhouette. Kenny shook his head and pulled the body off the pavement onto the gravel: two more feet and she'd be history. First, though, he'd carve off a hunk of that fire engine hair to add to his collection.

Suddenly a blast of light came with a crash so loud it stunned the air, as if God had ripped the sky in two and banged the halves together. Kenny covered his face with his arm, wondering if it was lightning and how close it had hit. When he took his arm down there was brightness all around the dead girl. He blinked but the light was still there, forming spirals above and through her body.

Gradually the light began to fuse with the form on the ground until there was nothing but brightness. The brightness swirled up from the ground in eleven thousand spirals, which slowed to form the outline of a cat bigger than any lion. The image began to fill out: the glossy coat, the tail, the head, the mouth opened on great incisors. The last of the light fused into shining claws, and the eyes of The Cat opened.

Kenny shook his head, sure it was a nightmare till he saw those eyes, green as Eden before the snake, saw clearly what he'd done, felt the pain of his victims, and knew what was to come.

"NOOO!" he screamed, sprinting down the road, looking for the house that matched the light in the distance.

The light was moving: a car was coming his way. Dear God don't let there be a driveway! he gasped. Don't let it turn off! He waved his arms and kept running; he didn't dare look back.

The car rolled over a little hump and the driver, who had just cut his wipers, saw the open-mouthed man running straight toward him and a glowing white something hundreds of feet behind. He swerved to avoid the man, then back to keep from crashing in the ditch.

Then he saw The Cat dead ahead, galloping straight for him. He braced for the impact and saw The Cat's glowing belly as it soared up over the hood, then he slowed the car to watch the glowing beast disappear in the rear view mirror.

He heard the man scream—and then came a terrible, unearthly roar that stunned him like a shockwave. He hunched over the wheel, stepped on the gas, and charged down the road.

As the lights of the strip mall came into view he looked in the mirror and saw only road. Good, he was safe. Now, what to do about that poor man and that thing. Who could he call? The police? The zoo? Ghostbusters? He dialed 911: whatever this was, it was definitely an emergency.

The line was busy. What? Are they kidding? He tried the operator and she was finally able to connect him with the local police station. He told them what he'd seen but wouldn't give his name because they might decide he was drunk and arrest him—and they could, because he was.

"Listen," he pleaded, "just go down Merrill Road near St. John's Bluff and look for a body, but for God's sake bring all the weapons ya got, 'cause this thing ain't no kitty cat. And hurry, 'cause that poor dude was on foot, and anyone else on foot's got diddly for chances… Hell I dunno lady, maybe it got loose from a circus and that guy was its trainer—I say *was* 'cause he ain't no more, that's for sure. I heard him scream and I heard that thing roar, and I ain't goin' back there for nothin', hear? It's your problem now, get busy… Hell, ya can't miss it.

They painted it so it glows white, and it's about the size of a horse, except it's a lion. No, really. Get out there or somebody's gonna die!"

He hung up the phone and the woman laughed. "Guess what, there's a giant glowing lion running loose on Merrill Road."

"Sure," said the other operator, "probably started out as the worm at the bottom of the bottle. Maybe it's that guy from Wickham Terrace—y'know, the one who was attacked by the giant spider. Oh, you weren't here? Well, it's almost funny, unless you like cats. When they got there, see, he'd shot the spider—emptied the whole damn cartridge—and it was his cat. Somma these people, boy, I dunno—hello? Hello? Speak up, please, I can't hear you..."

Idenτifying CDaRκs

When Mark and Rachel arrived at the daycare center it was like a lit hive, with people scurrying through the front door and carefully stepping around the back yard by the exposed room. A yellow ribbon was strung along the fence, and people gathered outside it were asked to stand back and be quiet.

This was possible for everyone but Rachel, who knew Carla was there and was determined to get in. She grabbed every uniform and cried in every ear. The answer was constant: wait until they bring out the bodies, someone may yet be alive in there, we're still checking it out.

Check they did, and the only living soul was a little howling dog who they carried out the front door and handed to a neighbor.

The photographer was having trouble because of the body

in the bedroom doorway and had to perform some peculiar calisthenics to get all the shots and stay off the evidence.

When the forensics team arrived they filled bag after bag: the man in charge didn't want to miss anything. There was a puzzle here, but alas some of the pieces were sadly visible. The blood-smeared picture of the naked child on the dresser confirmed the motive and probably the identity of the woman in the doorway. But why was she nude?

The locked closet yielded stacks of kiddie porn magazines and a shelf with pans of developer fluid. Pinned above the shelf were large glossies of smiling children with their hands on each other's genitals. One of the men in the closet swore: one of those kids was his nephew. He emerged from the closet snarling, "Damn, she had the right idea—though how she managed it I'll never know."

And that was the piece that didn't fit. The woman's fury might have given her the strength to attack the man, but how did she take down that big window and not show any cuts? Small bits of glass stuck to the soles of her feet, but the hands under all that curled flesh were pink and perfect.

Also the house was up on blocks. The bottom of the window was five feet to the ground. So how did she get in, pole vault?

And where were her clothes?

One of the men in the back yard called the man in charge to show him something by the picnic table forty feet from the window. Garbage cans had fallen on this curious depression and shielded it from the rain. It looked like four gigantic paw prints, as though something had landed and taken off again in the direction of the window.

"Take a casting," said the man in charge, and wondered about that bloody blotch on the sheets by the pillow. It did look like a pawprint, bigger than any he'd ever seen.

He went back to the bedroom for another look as the young woman's corpse was lifted on a stretcher. As they were about to pull the cover up the man saw the heart on the woman's knee and asked if the crying woman was still by the front gate.

"Yes, and she hasn't stopped crying," said the officer. "Well," said the man in charge, "ask her if her sister had anything on one of her knees." The officer returned saying that there were matching hearts on both women's knees. The man in charge had the stretcher loaded in the ambulance and called Rachel over.

Mark came with her, his arm around her waist, and the cover was drawn back on what was left of Carla. "NOOOH!" cried Rachel. "Oh God, no. Oh Carla, Carla." She wrapped her arms around Carla's legs, as she had with her mother all those years ago, and cried and begged to go with them. She didn't want Carla in some cold drawer, she just wanted to keep her warm. She couldn't let go, she just couldn't.

An hour later she was still holding Carla's legs, rocking and moaning.

Mark, who had been holding off the ambulance driver, took her by the wrists and pulled her away. "Rachel," he said slowly, tears in his eyes, "we gotta go, Honey."

Rachel couldn't. As the ambulance doors closed she screamed, "NOOO!" and fought Mark to get back.

"Rachel, stop!" he yelled, holding her arms and wrestling her toward the truck as the ambulance left the curb. "Stop it, Rachel! Stop it now! Ya gotta think of Jessie! We gotta think of what to tell Jessie."

Rachel couldn't see for tears, and Mark said, "C'mon, Honey, we'll go get some coffee an' try to work this out," but it didn't register.

Nothing registered till she was sitting in the restaurant and the waitress came to get their order. When asked what they wanted Rachel burst into tears and said: "My sister. I want my sister back."

The Heaven Plane

Mark winced as he glanced out the restaurant window. The sun would soon be up and Jessie with it.

Rachel honked into another soggy napkin and dumped it on the pile. Mark said they'd have to leave soon and Rachel nodded. She pointed to the washroom and said she'd be right back.

She walked into the washroom and splashed water on her face, then became aware of the smell on her hands and clothes, that sweet floral scent in the ambulance. It was everywhere she had touched Carla. She took another splash at her face but the pink globe refused to shrink.

They walked out of the restaurant and Mark helped her to the truck. She cried when she saw the house and they sat in the cab as the sky went from gray to pink.

Suddenly Jessie appeared with Paul and Cathy in the front yard, and Jessie saw the truck. She waved and ran toward it, with Paul and Cathy close behind.

"Didja find it, AnRachel?" Jessie asked as her aunt climbed down from the truck. Then she saw Rachel's swollen face and knew the answer was no. She hugged Rachel's thighs and said, "Thass okay, AnRachel. You'll find it. I'm sure." Then, to make her feel better, Jessie told her how nice she smelled, all flowery. She looked in the cab and asked, "Where's Mommy? At the store?"

Rachel took Jessie's hands and squatted down in front of her. Poor AnRachel, her face looked awful. "Don't cry, AnRachel," said Jessie sadly, "we'll find it." She knew however that didn't always work. Sometimes you could say it back and sometimes you couldn't.

Rachel asked Jessie if she knew where Heaven was. Jessie said sure, and pointed to the sky. Rachel then said that Mommy had gone to Heaven and Jessie said: "Oh? When will she be back? Tomorrow?" Jessie knew Heaven was far away, farther even than Disney World, but straight up. Mommy must be in one of those planes that go to Heaven. Jessie saw them sometimes flying high above the clouds, leaving their white chalk marks on the sky. Then God, who liked a tidy sky, would come by and dust off the marks.

"Will Mommy see Gramma and Grampa?" asked Jessie, knowing the answer but wanting to hear it anyway. Jessie was an expert on Heaven. Heaven was a huge green lawn in the clouds where God, who looked like Santa in a nightie, ate lunch with Jesus in front of a special TV where they could watch people pray. They decided who deserved to get things while angels cleared off the table trays. All the grammas and grampas lived in a house next to God's and were kept from falling through the clouds by a huge fence made of pearls.

"Honey," Rachel said slowly, "Mommy isn't coming back. Mommy's gone to Heaven to stay."

"No she's not, AnRachel. She'll be back. You'll see. It just takes the plane awhile."

Rachel was lost. She couldn't bring herself to say dead or killed.

Paul asked Jessie to go get the giraffe to show Aunt Rachel. When he thought Jessie was out of earshot he asked what had happened.

Rachel was still squatting. He held her arms to help her up and she whimpered out the story, ending with the words: "The daycare lady shot her after she killed the guy, and all of them are dead. God help me, I had no idea she would—"

"You couldn't have called me before you told her?" yelled Paul, shaking her in spite of himself. "Hell, I could've stopped that pervert in his tracks. Instead she's been killed, all because you didn't have the sense to pick up the phone before shooting your fat mouth off!"

"Hey, now," said Mark, his arms around his sobbing wife, "Rachel didn't—"

He was interrupted by Jessie's scream. Her face appeared at the window, then she ran screaming into the back yard. She had heard the words told, killed, and Carla, and knew her worst fears had come true: Mommy wasn't coming back from Heaven because Mister Cal had killed her, and all because Jessie told.

Jessie waved her arms above her head and leaped around, hoping that the Heaven plane would see her. It wasn't there. Maybe Mommy had taken a taken a later flight. Tears streamed down her face as she reached for the sky, screaming: "MOMMY, COME BACK! I DIN'T MEAN T' TELL. HONEST, I DIN'T. AN RACHEL MADE ME. PLEASE MOMMY, DOH LEAVE ME, I WANNA GO WIF YOU! DOH LEAVE ME, MOMMY! DOH LEAVE ME!"

She hopped up and down, flailing her arms, and as the adults came toward her she screamed at them to go away, they would block the plane's view of her. They watched from the sidewalk as she screamed, hopped and reached—but there was no plane, no chalk marks, just gray morning haze changing to blue sky.

All day Jessie waved and cried. Hunger didn't budge her.

Finally as darkness came Paul carried her shrieking into the house, saying that she and her Aunt Rachel had to talk. Jessie yelled no, that AnRachel told, so Mommy was killed. She fought her way out of Paul's grasp and ran for her mother's room, trying to slam the door on him, but Paul pushed it open.

She leaped up on the bed, hauling the pillow across her and tucking it around her, then stuck her thumb in her mouth and faced away from the adults.

Rachel had to speak. "Jessie, Honey, I'm sorry—"

Jessie cried: "Go way! You told!"

"Jessie," Rachel said, "you have to know Mommy's happy in Heaven—"

"But I doh wanna be here," Jessie cried, "I wanna go wif her!" Rachel approached the bed and Jessie screamed: "NO, GO WAY! I WANT MY MOMMY!"

"Honey," Paul said, "we all want her. We just can't have her anymore, she's in Heaven. She'll come to visit you at night, though—"

"How?" Jessie stared at him, wiping her face on the pillow. "Will she come in the Heaven plane?"

"Well, sort of," said Paul. "After the sleep fairy comes she'll come and stay all night with you till you wake up."

Jessie whimpered, "But I wan her naaow," and sobbed into the pillow.

Paul nodded. Watching her cry was making him cry.

Rachel was crying too.

Paul saw the suffering in her face and knew he had to do something. "Listen, Jessie, " he said, "I got something to tell you about your Aunt Rachel."

Jessie screamed "NOOO!" and covered her ears. Paul pulled her hands away and Jessie screamed louder. He waited for her to stop and said, "It's about Mommy, too. You wanna hear it or you just wanna keep screaming?"

"Tell," said Jessie, and put her thumb in her mouth.

"Awright," said Paul, "but no screaming. You scream and I stop. Okay?"

Jessie nodded and watched him over her thumb.

"It happened when you were just a baby, no bigger 'n my hand. A very bad man was gonna hurt you and Mommy, and he would have but your Aunt Rachel stopped him. He had this big knife," he spread his arms to demonstrate, "and he cut your Aunt Rachel up real bad, cut a whole hunk off her head—"

"No he din't," Jessie said, pointing at Rachel. "Lookit her."

"Now you see, Jess, things aren't always the way they look. You know what a scar is?"

"Like on your hands, Uncle Paul?"

"Yeah, Jessie, like my hands. If you get a big cut, it leaves a big scar. It takes a long time to heal, and it hurts real bad."

"Do your hands still hurt?"

"Yeah, sometimes, but nowhere near as much as your Aunt Rachel's scar hurts her."

"She doesn't got any scar, Uncle Paul," Jessie announced, and Paul said: "That's where you're wrong, Jess. C'mon, I'm gonna show you."

Rachel had been listening in a daze, and came to as Jessie stood up.

Paul put his arm around her and said softly, "It's the only way, Rach. I'm sorry. I'll help you if you want," he offered.

Rachel shook her head, watching Jessie totter down the mattress toward her. She raised her hands and extracted the combs and barrettes, then pulled out the bobby pins and bent her head to let Jessie see the scar.

Jessie said, "Ooh, kin I touch it?" and Rachel fell to her knees, sobbing.

Jessie's hands were around her face. "I sorry, AnRachel. It must hurt awful bad. Here, I kiss 'n' make it better."

Rachel felt the sloppy little pecks along her scar and folded her arms around her niece, gritting her teeth so as not to crush the child in her hug.

It was a long night full of tears, and all three slept on Rachel's bed, with Jessie in the middle.

The next morning Jessie tugged at Paul's shirt and said,

"Uncle Paul, Uncle Paul—didja see Mommy?" Paul was too groggy to respond and Rachel, barely awake, heard Jessie say: "I saw Mommy, Uncle Paul, just like you said. She's got a white nightie and we were in this big park with all 'ese diffint trees. An' you should see her kitty! It's big as a horse, big 'n' white, an' it's got big big green eyes wif no black in 'em..."

Later that morning Rachel called Bill Whitsun and after her first few words he said, "I'm so sorry, Rachel. If I can do anything let me know. Take all the time you need."

Paul had the same conversation with Bubba, but he had no intention of going back. He would stay with Rachel and Jessie so they could help each other adjust to Carla's loss, and do some construction work when he was up to it.

Later that afternoon Rachel was visited by the Neptune Beach police. Her car had been found in the back yard of a Mr. Sid Jarvis, and they drove her there.

Rachel held her hand over her mouth while she walked around the car. She saw the shattered windshield and the blood on the seat. The gun had been found in the tackle box by the door, and was now part of the investigatory evidence. She asked the officers how a small woman could lose all that blood, run twenty blocks, then jump through a window and tear a healthy man to pieces, a man twice her size.

The officers said that many people were asking the same questions, but the strangest questions concerned a circus cat of incredible size that appeared on the beach that night and drove the dogs nuts. Someone also reported seeing one on Merrill Road— of course that guy was a little wasted and said that it glowed.

On Tuesday Rachel went to the bank to get Carla's will. It was in the safe deposit box, a notarized document that left everything to Jessie and made Rachel her legal guardian. It was in Carla's envelope of private papers, but when Rachel tried to extract the envelope it wouldn't come. She wriggled and tugged to no avail. Maybe it was caught on an edge of the box. Damn. Rachel dragged the rolling footstool from behind the wall, climbed the rubber steps to the second tier and looked down into the box.

What? The envelopes were stuck in a red-black coating that ran the length of the box. The guck had also seeped into the jewelry case, and Rachel opened it to check on the cross and the amulet.

There they lay in what looked like dried blood, and the amulet was lying face down, still warm. Rachel turned it over to wipe off its face and gasped—the eyes and mouth were open. The eyeholes had a greenish glow, and as she watched the newly opened mouth—that hole behind those pinprick teeth—reddened. There was a sound like a low growl and a red droplet formed in the hole, dribbled through the teeth and onto Rachel's finger.

Rachel wanted to scream, to point, to bring the whole world in to see it. Alas, she couldn't. The hard-nosed would say hoax, the religious would yell demons, then some judge would declare her unfit and make Jessie a ward of the state.

Rachel put the jewelry case down, took Carla's will from the envelope and closed the box. She climbed off the footstool as the attendant came in with another boxholder, and both women remarked on the new air freshener.

"Yes," said the attendant, "we've had it since Monday."

Rachel coughed to cover her surprise. It was *her* smell they were talking about, the one from the ambulance, and it was all over the room.

"Y'know," said the boxholder, an older lady, "that aroma reminds me of my honeymoon—too many years ago. We took a cruise down the Nile and the flowers in our stateroom were lotuses. That's what the smell reminds me of. Y'know," she chuckled, "I might just spend the rest of the day right here."

HeaRts and FlouieRs

The weekend of August thirteenth produced a record number of "suspicious deaths" and the medical examiner's office was backed up with bodies. Since Carla was now part of a police investigation no one could tell Rachel when she would get custody of Carla's body—or if there would even be one after the autopsy.

Paul agreed with Rachel about going ahead with a memorial service. Both of them hated closed-casket funerals. Why say good-bye to a box? It was the face you came to say good-bye to. Without that face it didn't seem final, didn't seem real.

On August twentieth Rachel sent Jessie off to a movie with Cathy, and held a memorial service for Carla. She wanted Jessie away from the tears and tributes, from anything that might harm the image of her mother's nightly "visits."

Jessie didn't believe the dreams anyway: she wanted her
"real Mommy" to touch and hold her, and cried often that she
wanted to see Mommy. Sometimes she'd see the jet tracks in
the sky, and yell for Mommy to "come on down!"

Three nights after the memorial service the moon was full,
its fat face staring through the curtains in Jessie's window.
"Wow, AnRachel, come look!" yelled Jessie, and Rachel
scurried into the room. It was her third trip in twenty minutes
because Jessie didn't want to go to bed. She didn't want to be
read to, she wanted to talk about Mommy.

"Will Mommy ever come back?" she wanted to know,
again.

Rachel pursed her lips and sighed. "No, Honey," she said
slowly, again. "Mommy's in Heaven now."

Jessie's face reddened and she cried, drooling. Paul appeared at the doorway and Rachel shook her head at him and
shrugged. Jessie buried her head in the pillow, then suddenly
turned over and looked at the window. She wiped her face on
the bedsheet and said, "Mommy?"

Rachel followed her gaze, catching the aroma from the
ambulance as it came through the window.

Paul walked in and cried: "Look!" pointing through the
billowing curtains.

The three of them looked over the moonlit lawn at the
birdbath thirty feet away. Floating in the little pool was a
colossal white blossom with red-tipped petals that opened on
a yellow center. The blossom whirled, showering its perfume
on the sad dry yard and the people in the window. It stopped,
then turned on its side, its bright yellow center beaming
toward them like a mini sun. Then it floated skyward, shed-
ding its petals till nothing was left but the radiant center, which
faded as it rose and left them looking at the round bright face
of the moon. They all felt the hug as they watched it go, the
tender kiss that travelled over them, inside and out.

Jessie, smiling, said: "Bye bye, Mommy!" She looked up
at Rachel and explained: "Mommy's gone ta Heaven," and
stuck her thumb in her mouth. She didn't seem upset, or want

to go with Mommy, she just hugged Rachel's thigh while Rachel hugged her and Paul.

The three of them slept that night wrapped in the sweetness of unearthly love, and all of them felt stronger the next day. That was especially good for Rachel, because at ten o'clock next morning Lieutenant Karoly called, ostensibly with good news. Her rapist was dead—killed by some enormous jungle cat while her sister was locked in mortal combat with that sicko from the daycare center. The autopsies revealed identical marks on the sicko and the rapist and in both cases a prominent organ was missing. Would Miss Williams care to guess which one?

Miss Williams declined to guess, and Karoly said, "You wouldn't have any idea?"

Rachel responded, "No, fuck, and I don't care, I'm just glad they're dead! I just wish my sister hadn't gotten hurt." Her voice trailed off as she realized he was measuring her answers. "Look!" she snapped, "you wanna tell me what's goin' on here?"

"Now I have some questions for you, and I suggest you have some damn good answers. First, why were you crying so much before you even saw your sister? How did you know she was in that house? Second, where were you and your friend before you showed up there? 'Driving around, looking for the car,' is what you told Detective Grimes. So if you didn't see the car, how did you know your sister was in the house?"

"I didn't, really," said Rachel. "We saw the police and fire-rescue heading for the daycare center so we followed them, and when they stopped there I knew, that's all, I knew."

"Fair enough," said Karoly. "However, you think about this and call your lawyer: two men you have good reason to hate were killed the same way at the time you say you were out looking for your sister. You say you tried to call the police earlier and couldn't get through, but our records indicate it wasn't you who called but someone else, calling from your house. We want to question her, too. You see, Miss Williams, so far our only links to these murders are that cat, and you."

"So am I being charged with something?" she faltered.

"No," said Karoly. "We're just doin' this by the book. It's for your own protection—and ours. A lot of other people will have to be questioned. So you call me when you're ready to talk, Miss Williams, and don't you go anywhere without telling me first."

Rachel was shaking. All this, she knew, was Sehkmet's doing. How could she tell him that?

Karoly had her tailed for awhile, but finally decided it was hopeless. Her friend in the pick-up vouched for her alibi, and no cat anywhere matched the size the zoologist picked for this one. A Manchurian tiger, maybe, but there were none of those at the zoo. Even drug dealers who kept dangerous beasts on leashes had nothing this size.

He tried another tack and called S. G. Horvath in Orlando. Horvath was Florida's leading expert on sacrificial cults, one of the men responsible for nailing the connection between the Manson and Berkowitz atrocities.

Karoly asked if there was something Satanic about the missing hearts of the victims, and Horvath said that's possible till he heard the details and said no, I think it's something else.

Then he said: "Wait a minute. You said it was a huge cat? There is something about that. Olmec, I think. Egyptian, too. Maybe it's Natassia Kinski." He laughed, and explained to Karoly about the people that turned into cats. Then, sensing Karoly's impatience, he said: "Look, I'm going to do some research on this. Dangerous people are always taking honorable old symbols and making them stand for something murderous—like the swastika, or the seven-headed serpent. Whoever did this, the cat's their trademark, and they'll be back. Let's just hope they continue to concentrate on scum till we catch 'em."

A week later Karoly got a call from Horvath, who said: "I've got it. I've found the source." Horvath told him about the ancient deity Sehkmet, and how there was a Sehkmet Society in The United States, with worldwide affiliations. It was a small band of harmless doomsayers periodically monitored by the FBI. Their "bible" was a little pamphlet called The Sleeping Lion, and most libraries and occult bookstores didn't have it. Their leader was a discredited archeologist, and none of them would do something like this, so strong was their faith in the return of this mythical lioness.

"How do you know it's a lion-ess ?" asked Karoly, and Horvath said, "Simple, it's in the name. Sehkmet is a title meaning 'She Who Prevails.'"

"You don't think it could be some nuts using the cat as a cover?"

"Sure," said Horvath, "anything's possible. Get the Society's mailing list, then go ask your chief suspect if she's ever heard of Sehkmet. And search the house. You're looking for a blue booklet seven by eight, stapled down the middle, and anything you can find on ancient Egypt."

Karoly thanked Horvath, then called the FBI, which FAXed him copies of the mailing list, and Rachel Williams wasn't on it.

He then called Rachel at work, who covered her surprise with: "No, who's that? Am I supposed to know this person? Did he say he knew me?"

Rachel's heart was pounding: she'd have to go home, ditch everything, and swear Paul to secrecy. She was glad now that she hadn't signed the Society's mailing list, and that Carla had forced her to keep silent about Sehkmet.

Rachel charged across the hall to a friend's office and called Paul. He was on a construction site, and it was a fluke that he was anywhere near a phone. She told him that if anyone asked him about Sehkmet he knew nothing, that her guardianship of Jessie might be at stake.

"No problem, Rach," said Paul, adding: "I knew them weird ways'd catch up with ya one day."

"Let's hope not," said Rachel. "Let's hope I'm still a step ahead."

With her heart racing ahead of the car, Rachel sped home. She knew Karoly was getting a search warrant.

She didn't know he was kicking himself for calling her

first. He just figured the whole thing was preposterous till he heard that unnatural chirp in her voice. When he called back ten minutes later and was told she had gone to lunch he knew he had to move fast.

Rachel drove up on the lawn by the door, leaped out of the car and up the stairs. She opened the door, shut the alarm, and raced to her bedroom. She tore down the poster, gathered up the books on Egypt and the pamphlets on Sehkmet and ran to the back door.

She saw a police car pulling up beside her car and burst into tears. Tears poured down her face as she thought about Jessie and about going to jail. They would subpoena the contents of her safe deposit box, and find the amulet. Then what? She clutched the books so tightly her nails dug into her arms. She heard the two men mount the steps, opened her eyes as the doorbell rang, and looked down at the books.

Oh my God.

The doorbell sounded again.

She walked to the door stiff-legged, opened it and invited them in. They saw her standing with her arms full of flowers, showed her the warrant, and she said go ahead, glassy-eyed and tearful, hugging the flowers.

While they searched, Rachel put the flowers in a bowl on the kitchen table and sat by them, staring at them. They were white with sunlike centers, the petals tipped blood-red, and their perfume filled the house.

Karoly's partner felt sorry for her. Obviously she'd had a fight with the boyfriend and this was his way of making up. He made a mental note to pick some of those flowers up later for his wife, but couldn't bring himself to ask the woman what they were—after all, they'd just torn her house apart.

And all for nothing, apparently. There was nothing about this Sehkmet character, no books on Egypt, and the only book on myth was a general studies kind of thing from college. There was no basement, no cat in the basement, and nothing in the surrounding area outside. She even invited them to search her car, which they did.

Karoly apologized to Rachel when it was all over and Rachel said it was okay, he had a job to do, and walked them to their car. She could see in his face he felt cheated, but perhaps with her special ally she had nothing to fear.

She walked back into the kitchen, sat by the flowers and talked to them. "Thank you," she whispered. "Thank you, Whoever. Just don't let 'em take Jessie."

Karoly's partner was fascinated by the flowers and their heady perfume. He called a florist later and described the blooms, and the woman said it sounded like lotus, but she knew of no variety that was bright white with red-tipped petals. They must be some new kind of hybrid, privately grown.

Karoly sat in a bar that night with one of his cohorts, venting his frustrations. He had a drink in hand, water on the rocks with a twist—the twist being no alcohol. He was handsome once, before the job and the booze wore him down. Now he wanted some of it back.

"The way I see it," said Peters, "Without the cat, ya got no case."

"Yeah," said Karoly, "but there is one somewhere, and that bitch knows where, and if I leave her alone for awhile, she'll get careless. Oh, she's clever all right, in a sick kinda way, settin' up her sister and all. My guess is she blamed her sister for the husband's actions—transference, it's called—saw her shot and took it."

"You don't think she had help?"

"Sure I do. I'll bet that guy with the pregnant wife's got something goin' with her and she talked him into it. And maybe all of it wasn't her doing. It's complicated, that's for sure. We'll get her though," he vowed, taking another swig of water. "Something'll break. We'll just keep sifting till we get it."

Eleven Times Two

Jessie came home that night and found an empty bowl of water on the kitchen table. "Oh boy!" she chirped, "Are we gonna have fish?"

"No, Honey," said Rachel, "but I've made an appointment for you tomorrow with a lady called a counselor, and you two are gonna be great friends."

Jessie knew all about "appointments." She asked if she was going to get a needle.

"No, Honey," said Rachel, "This is just a lady you can talk to."

"About what?" Jessie wanted to know.

"Anything you like," Rachel said.

"No needles?"

Rachel said no, no needles. She was anxious to get Jessie

on some track to normalcy, though she wondered about normal in a world where books became flowers that melted into air. Nonetheless, for Jessie's sake, she decided to ignore the supernatural and concentrate on the so-called "manageable" elements in their lives.

She went to the bank to clean up the safe deposit box and in case she was being followed carried a sponge and paper towels in a vase of silk flowers. It was a Friday morning in the middle of the month, so everyone was waiting on paychecks, and the bank would be deserted.

In the safe deposit room the floral scent had faded everywhere but in the box.

Rachel dumped the contents of the box into a large envelope, then stuffed the bloody envelopes in the vase.

She picked up the jewelry case, still open and wet—but the little head no longer glowed, and it didn't growl. She tapped the amulet, expecting it to burn, but it was merely warm. She planned to put it in a velvet pouch wrapped in plastic—the plastic alone seemed too crude. She wondered if she should keep the cross with it. Why not, they're like stablemates now.

She took the jewelry case out and swabbed down the box, lining it with paper towels, then put the large envelope inside. She wiped off the amulet and the cross, then rolled them on a cardboard square. She was going to curl up the cardboard and upend them into the pouch when she saw that the amulet was still wet.

She daubed its little face but a moment later it was wet again. Miniscule droplets at the bottom of the cat's "eyes" were spilling down its face.

Rachel, watching, started to cry too: she saw starving black children, naked and crawling with flies, men shooting elephants and hacking off their faces, seals fighting for air as they slipped beneath the waves, whales screaming and rolling in blood, and money of all denominations changing hands under multi-colored grins. She grabbed the stairstep railing, blinking to chase away the visions—but they were so strong, so wrong, she couldn't stop crying.

She apologized to the little crying face, curled up the cardboard, and rolled the head and the cross into the pouch. Still crying, she put the pouch untied in the box, closed the box and left the bank, then walked up to the fourth floor of the building.

She entered the ladies' room, checked the stalls, pulled the flowers out of the vase, and burned the envelopes. Then she dumped the reeking ashes in the trash. She wiped out the vase, put the flowers back in, and drove to work. She put the sponge back in the darkroom, put the vase on her desk, and sat down.

Bill Whitsun told her to go home. He was very worried about her: the last few days she seemed to be cracking up. "Just another day, Rachel," he said, putting his arm around her shoulder. "The place'll still be here when you get back."

The next few months were rough without Carla, especially Christmas. Paul moved out in February and came to visit, but his visits began to taper off in April.

Drought was predicted for the country that summer along with an upsurge in crime, and by June twenty-first both predictions had come horribly true. Jacksonville neighborhoods were at the mercy of neighbor hoods, and there was no mercy. The police were outgunned, outrun, and outnumbered.

On July 9th a policeman found a delinquent named Leroy Stanton hot-wiring a car. He raised his gun to fire a warning shot as Leroy spun around and blew him away. The only witness was the parking lot attendant who claimed that Leroy shot in self-defense; that the officer, being white, was out to "get" Leroy. Cries of racism erupted in the papers, and that was Leroy's defense -- never mind that Officer Pettinger wasn't a racist, that he was married to a black girl more chocolate than honey—the focus had shifted from right and wrong to black and white, and there was no turning back.

Karoly went to Pettinger's funeral the following week and all the cops were commiserating. It was the fifth funeral in three months, and all of them saw their own names on the tombstone. Oh for the days of bad guys getting their just desserts—speaking of which, are you any closer to solving those cat murders? Karoly shook his head. The file was still open on the mysterious Miss Williams, and for his money underage hitmen like Stanton were a whole lot worse than his Ninja pussycat.

Three days later Paul invited Rachel to dinner to celebrate his going back to Orlando to work with Bubba. It seems that Bubba had come home early from a seminar and found Doris in bed with something other than a cold. Bubba was divorcing Doris, charging adultery so she wouldn't have half of everything he'd sweated for, and Paul couldn't be happier.

"So you two'll be batchin' it, huh?" laughed Rachel.

"Yup," said Paul. "Two wild and crazy guys on the loose. Don't worry, though, Rach," he added, "I won't give him your number."

The statement surprised Rachel. She didn't think of herself as "dating material" anymore, she was too busy raising Jessie. She said so and Paul laughed.

"Rachel, honey," he advised her, "maybe it's time you took a real look in the mirror."

Rachel hung up and thought maybe it was. She began to wonder if the one man she found attractive might be calling her for reasons other than business—maybe their business was so pressing he never had time to get personal. Maybe it was up to her. Go on, Rach, throw something subtle out. Maybe he'll bite. Go on, girl, what's the worst that can happen? She called and the worst didn't happen because Karoly was on vacation.

"So who's minding the streets?" she asked, and the man who answered laughed. Rachel wanted to say something intriguing, but realized it was all in vain: she could never share her life with him anyway. He'd never believe the truth. How could he? She could barely believe it herself. Ah well, she sighed. Maybe in another life.

Paul and Rachel didn't get to their farewell dinner till August. Jessie wanted to come along and Paul said sure. They went to a sumptuous restaurant on the St. John's River and were seated by a window overlooking the water.

Paul ordered champagne for the tall people and a Shirley Temple for the short person, and Jessie pestered them to try the champagne.

"I won't swallow it," she promised. "I'll just taste it." She took a slurp, scrunched up her face, said the stuff was gross and yuck! and spat it into a napkin.

Later they made toasts, Jessie proudly raising her Big People glass, and after that they threaded their way down to the buffet line. Paul lifted Jessie up to examine the spread and make her selection. She was dazzled by the ice sculpture, by the strawberries swathed in chocolate, by salads in the shape of animals and crab legs the size of her arm.

She asked if Paul would tell her a scary story about the giant crab and Paul said sure but later, okay? Jessie nodded vigorously. She got to keep a crab leg, which she kept touching, wishing it was morning so she could show it to her friends.

The three sat down with their plates, the adults comparing choices and encouraging Jessie to try different things—without spitting. She solved the problem by stabbing the new food with her fork, raising it to her mouth, and touching it quick with the end of her tongue. She looks like she's catching flies, Paul joked, and Jessie almost cried. Paul apologized and promised to get her another crab leg to give to her boyfriend, and Jessie felt better. After that she stuck to the things she knew she could swallow, devilled eggs and salmon patties.

They made a few more toasts and watched the river turn to silver lines under the fat-faced moon.

They were standing by the dessert table, loading up their bowls, when a terrible roaring shook the room, as though an airplane had crashed into the building.

Paul grabbed Jessie and Rachel, yelled "HIT THE FLOOR!" and dived under the dessert table. The lights flickered off and on as they curled down against the baseboard, Jessie in the hollow of Paul's crouch. He had one arm over his head, the other over Rachel's. He kept them huddled even after the roar and the shaking stopped, afraid to move lest it be just the first attack.

Twenty minutes later they crawled out from under the table. Smashed glass, food and china lay all over the floor while befuddled people stepped gingerly through the mess, asking what happened. A woman's voice came from the foyer, screaming for a doctor.

Paul told Rachel to keep Jessie by the table and be ready to dive at the first sound. He went to the foyer. The woman was screaming up and down the lobby, and a group had gathered around her husband. He was lying on the carpet, bejeweled and dead, his hands clutched over his chest, his eyes filled with that shock and fear Paul knew only too well. He didn't want Jessie to see this, and decided to find another way out. Maybe they could leave through the kitchen.

Paul tracked down his waiter and was taking out his wallet when he saw the sommelier collar the maitre d' to say that all the bottles of Bordeaux and beaujolais in the cellar were smashed, to come quickly: someone must verify that the wine was there before, that it wasn't his fault.

The maitre d' told him to calm down, that breakage was expected in an earthquake, but the sommelier snapped that it wasn't the breakage: "It is the wine, Mon Dieu, it is GONE!" There was nothing in the burst bottles and nothing on the floor. Worse, he picked up several unsmashed bottles and they were too light, both in color and weight, to contain any liquid. He uncorked four of the bottles and they were empty—but there were so many more, Mon Dieu, come look!

Rachel, who had come up beside Paul, heard the sommelier's tirade and watched the two men run through the kitchen. She and Jessie followed Paul out through the kitchen door and one of the chefs was complaining that his wine had disappeared, the whole damn bottle.

"You mean somebody stole your bottle?" asked the sous-chef, and the chef cried: "No, you idiot, they DRAINED the bottle AND the glass! If I EVER get my hands on the sonofa—"

He saw Jessie and clammed shut, tipped his white mushroom hat to Rachel, and offered Jessie one of the pastries he saved when the cart tipped over.

The next morning Jacksonville headlines screamed: QUAKE ROCKS FLORIDA COAST. The roar had shaken buildings from Jacksonville to Miami, and the toll in human life was still being counted.

The medical examiners' offices were loaded up with bodies of all descriptions, most diagnosed as heart attacks. It wasn't until the third one was opened that one coroner insisted on surrounding himself with police and cameras before he touched another body. He said that no one would believe it and they almost didn't, except that there were ten people in the room, all ostensibly of sound mind, who saw the same thing.

Three cameras recorded the event from different angles, and this is what they saw: The body had suffered cuts and bruises from the quake prior to expiration, but there was nothing to indicate the trauma inside—nothing but the look of terror etched on the corpse's face. The skin over the chest was unbroken, and cuts were made to allow the skin to be peeled up, revealing the breastbone. A huge uneven hole in the middle of the breastbone extended into the chest cavity where the heart should have been. The lungs were there, wholly intact, but the heart was gone: plucked, scooped or torn out— but by what, and how did it get in there?

Three other corpses of different ages were examined, chosen for their expressions of terror and apparent lack of outward physical damage—at least, nothing that could match or explain the carnage inside. All the witnesses in the room felt queasy as they watched, and it wasn't the corpses' smell, for this particular bunch smelled delightful—spicy sweet, like flowers or incense. Several of the witnesses remarked on this, but the coroner was as mystified by the scent as he was by the lack of hearts. There was nothing in or on the bodies to produce that smell, but it was there just as surely as the hearts were not.

After the third body the coroner said he'd had enough, packed up the instruments for cleaning and told everybody to hit the road, show starts again in eight hours—or sixteen, if they cared to wait for him. The police swore all the witnesses to silence and the coroner laughed. His best assistant was on vacation and he was punchy from hours on his feet, double-checking everything.

"C'mon," he guffawed, "Even the tabloids won't touch this one. Women giving birth to frogs and Martians landing in Vegas, but this—this nobody'd believe."

Five days later the body count of the mysterious deaths had been tallied: twenty-two in all, many of them familiar faces in The Public Servant. Besides drug kingpins, murderers, and porn runners were three men whose companies were charged with toxic dumping. They were at dinner that night planning to pay someone handsomely to dispose of some EPA reps. The man they were planning to pay was dead too. Their cause of death was listed as "Heart Attack," an absolutely correct diagnosis. How they died nobody knew.

But Rachel knew the minute she read the numbers. She knew the night of the quake when she heard about the missing wine. She knew the day after the quake when she went to the safe deposit box to check on her "friend" and the room was sweet with perfume. The bag that held the amulet glowed and light triangled out from the top of the bag, brighter than a high powered flashlight.

This is it, she thought. Dr. Arden has to be told.

But Rachel didn't act immediately. She argued with herself for weeks whether or not to call—what might that call set in motion? Ultimately she didn't want to be branded a nutcase and lose Jessie. And after all that, what difference would it make? It was going to happen anyhow, and nobody could stop it.

But Dr. Arden deserved to know he was right. Maybe he already knew, but what if he didn't?

There must be some way she could tell him without getting it traced back to her. Writing it, she knew, would be a mistake. Then it came to her, almost like a voice in her ear.

Since Karoly had her statements on tape she made a tape of her own, replaying the conversation in as much detail as she could remember. She spent the next two weeks studying her speech for distinctive words or phrases, then practiced different voices, pacing and inflection. One week later she had a voice with no giveaway speech patterns, and the following Saturday she sent Jessie to the beach with Cathy and little Carla.

Jessie was slathered in sunscreen, wore her cartoon hero sunglasses, and carried a hat which she promised to wear, though Rachel knew better.

Rachel then drove to Gainesville, a college town where all things weird and wonderful were blamed on youthful excess. She had on jeans and tennies, a floppy hat, and a floppy shirt. The sun was high so sunglasses were mandatory. No one would notice her, she looked like a student.

She headed for a pay phone in a hotel she remembered: calling from home could still be dangerous. She smiled at Karoly for giving the game away. His blunder was her safety net.

Now rehearsing what she was going to say, she wished the amulet was…what? If only it didn't keep changing she could describe it better. And what was it doing now? Shining, crying, sweating, bleeding, showering the air with perfume?

Were there maybe other people with amulets, shaking and scared, like her?

And was this the call that would bring them all together?

She drove to the hotel, and there was still a pay phone in the ladies' room. She dragged a chair from the vanity over to the phone and sat down. She was shaking. She put her hand on the phone and practiced her new voice.

She shut her eyes and felt a surge of strength. Maybe it was the decision to tell the truth, to unburden herself. Or maybe, with her eyes closed, she could ignore the mundane and concentrate on the miraculous. Maybe it was something more, maybe Sehkmet wanted her to tell.

The shaking stopped.

This is it, she vowed, and opened her eyes.

The world didn't look any different but she was stronger. She was ready.

She took a deep breath, lifted the receiver from the cradle, and the fate of the world chimed beneath her fingers:

1– 8-0-0 – S-E-H-K-M-E-T